Lloyd Shepherd is a former journalist and digital producer who has worked for the *Guardian*, Channel 4, the BBC and Yahoo. He lives in South London with his family. He is the author of *The English Monster* and *The Poisoned Island*.

Also by Lloyd Shepherd

The English Monster
The Poisoned Island

SAVAGE MAGIC

LLOYD SHEPHERD

**SIMON &
SCHUSTER**

London · New York · Sydney · Toronto · New Delhi

A CBS COMPANY

First published in Great Britain by Simon & Schuster UK Ltd, 2014
A CBS COMPANY

1 3 5 7 9 10 8 6 4 2

Simon & Schuster UK Ltd
1st Floor
222 Gray's Inn Road
London WC1X 8HB

www.simonandschuster.co.uk

Simon & Schuster Australia, Sydney
Simon & Schuster India, New Delhi

A CIP catalogue record for this book
is available from the British Library

Hardback ISBN: 978-1-47113-606-1
Trade Paperback ISBN: 978-1-47113-607-8
eBook ISBN: 978-1-47113-609-2

Typeset by M Rules
Printed and bound by CPI Group (UK) Ltd, Croydon, CR0 4YY

For Mum, with love and thanks

I wander thro' each charter'd street,
Near where the charter'd Thames does flow,
And mark in every face I meet
Marks of weakness, marks of woe.

In every cry of every Man,
In every Infant's cry of fear,
In every voice, in every ban,
The mind-forg'd manacles I hear.

How the Chimney-sweeper's cry
Every black'ning Church appalls;
And the hapless Soldier's sigh
Runs in blood down Palace walls.

But most thro' midnight streets I hear
How the youthful Harlot's curse
Blasts the new-born Infant's tear
And blights with plagues the Marriage hearse.

William Blake, *London*

DEAL

The ship is resting at anchor out on the Downs. She is easy to spot, having none of the splendour of the dozen naval vessels that surround her. She is fat and ungainly, her plain lines evidence of her ugly purpose. A convict ship, just returned from the southern seas, her cargo of abandoned humanity swapped for sacks of tea and a handful of passengers.

In his room at the top of the tallest hotel in Deal, Henry Lodge watches her through an eyeglass stolen from an inebriated officer of the Rum Corps more than a decade ago. There is no doubt. She is the *Indefatigable*. But is she carrying the cargo he has been watching for these past years?

The April air is clean, just washed by spring rain, and there is no sea mist. The vessels clustered between the Goodwin Sands and Deal beach look calm and settled. Local boatmen row from beach to ship to beach again, busy water ants with oars and strong arms.

Henry supposes he will have to go out into one of those boats, and as always the thought fills him with fearful memories. He hates these boats, for they remind him of the worst weeks of his life, shivering inside the sinking wreck of a listing frigate, icebergs hidden in the mist, ice spurs slicing through the cold depths, including the one which had torn into the hull of the ship and removed its rudder with apparently diabolic intent. He was not yet twenty, a convict-gardener, sent to New South Wales to try and scratch a harvest from the thin, rocky soil. Between him and Cape Town, unknown hundreds or thousands of miles of empty, ice-cold sea.

Since his own return from New South Wales, Henry Lodge has performed his little pilgrimage to Deal a dozen times. He pays a man a retaining fee to watch the ships coming and going to the Downs, and to alert him when one of those new arrivals is a returning convict transport. The money required for this undertaking is not insubstantial, but it is also afford-able. He is, after all, by now a man of some means, grown rich on hops and natural cunning. But when it comes to boats, he is still a scared convict-gardener clutching on to life in a little pinnace suspended above freezing canyons.

He had survived that disaster, the rescue coming from, of all things, a whaler. With war billowing out from Paris and Europe shivering, it had seemed another petty miracle, as ordi-nary and as wonderful as an ice mountain trying to snatch away a rudder.

The operation runs like this: his fellow in Deal learns of a new arrival. He then despatches a messenger, post-haste, to the hop gardens owned by Henry Lodge around Canterbury. The system has become so efficient that Henry can be in Deal within a day-and-a-half of a new transport arriving. This is fast enough; the vessels out on the water are still moving to oceanic rhythms at this point, where a day is an hour and a hurried tack into the wind would look to the landlocked observer like a massive animal changing direction.

On this occasion, however, the system has not run quite so

smoothly. His man in Deal was away on business in Ramsgate when the *Indefatigable* arrived, such that Henry did not learn of the ship's arrival until three days after she dropped anchor. He is not particularly worried by this. For these vessels, three days is still barely a heartbeat after so many months at sea.

All the transports he has seen at Deal have looked like the *Indefatigable* looks now. An exhausted woman, is what she is. A silent, disregarded female approaching the end of her disappointed road.

He closes his eyeglass and takes it with him downstairs and onto the beach, where a boatman is waiting to take him over to the convict ship. The man is unpleasant and crude, and shouts at Henry as he struggles to get into the boat, reluctance biting into his bones like the gout which has, in recent months, slowly been making its jagged presence felt.

How many more times will I do this? he asks himself as they make their way across the glassy water of the Downs. *How much longer will I care to watch for this woman?* It is an old question; one to which he has no answer.

He keeps an eye on the *Indefatigable* as they row towards her. Slowly the other vessels move away from his perspective, as the transport rises from the water, becoming bigger and altogether more impressive the closer they get to her. He imagines the three decks within, the bulwarks between male, female and sailor quarters, the tiny cots in which the convicts are chained. He imagines furtive wanderings beneath tropical skies, as female prisoners are called to the hammocks of sailors and marines, pressed into service as journeying whores, each sailor given individual permission by God and the King to take his pick of the women on board.

These are childish pictures. The decks of the *Indefatigable* will have been cleared of bulwarks and chains while she was in New South Wales. The instruments of imprisonment take up valuable space which will have been cleared for cargo on the return voyage; tea instead of desperate girls. He pictures the piles of unwanted ironware on the quays of Sydney Cove growing higher with the visit of every transport that discards its chains just as it discards its human freight.

He asks himself, as he has done times beyond counting, how a man with such a runaway fancy can possibly have become rich. He remembers why he makes these pilgrimages. To see the woman again, to speak to her. This nonsensical compulsion which he cannot deny.

Now they are alongside the *Indefatigable*. The boatman calls up to the deck, and a head pops over the gunwale.

'Visitor from town!' the boatman calls in his oaky Kentish accent.

'What kind of visitor?' replies the seaman, in a West Country voice.

'One who visits all the transports.'

'What's his business?'

The boatman looks at him. It is a well-worn routine, this. Henry shouts up to the gunwale himself.

'I am a representative of James Atty and Company, the firm which built this vessel. I am to come aboard to ascertain her seaworthiness, and the expected period before she will be ready to voyage once more.'

It is a practised lie, and one day it will fail. One day, another seaman's face will stare down at him and inform him that the owner's agent has already been aboard.

Not today, though. The sailor disappears for a moment, and reappears with instructions that they may climb aboard. With goutish difficulty and no small amount of self-disgust, the man of means makes his way up onto the deck.

He is introduced to the master, who has as much common humanity as a bleached piece of driftwood on Deal beach, but he listens to Henry's second story, which he produces only once he is on board and only in the hearing of the master. He is a representative of the Home Department in London, charged with keeping an eye out for ex-convicts returning from the penal colonies of New South Wales, tracking their arrival back in England for purposes related to the mainte-nance of the peace. The master half-believes it, and agrees to provide some additional information (for a small fee, as always with such men) about his passengers. Five men returned to England, two of whom were former convicts. The master gives the names, and Henry pretends to note them down.

'Any women?'

The master frowns. Why would he be interested in women? But yes, there were three women among the passengers. Two were wives, and one is abroad.

'Their names?'

'Simpson, Gardener, Broad.'

The Gardener woman is still on the ship, with her sick hus-band and her three children. But Henry barely hears this. The name *Broad* clatters like an anchor dropped on a quayside.

'The Broad woman. She is no longer on the ship?'

'It's Broad who is abroad,' smirks the master. 'She was in a great hurry to leave.'

'Did she converse with any of the other passengers?'

The master frowns. Something about the Broad woman has discomfited him, and seeing this only excites Henry Lodge further. She'd been a quiet passenger, says the master, though she'd spent as much time on deck as she could. She'd had little to do with the crew or with the other passengers. The crew avoided her. She'd taken a bit of a shine to two children trav-elling with their parents.

'Did she bring anything with her?'

She'd had some goods shipped with her from New South

Wales, at considerable expense. The goods had already been unloaded, onto a vessel bound for the Thames.

'What was the nature of these goods?'

The master has no idea. They were boxed. He suspected something botanical or herbal.

'You did not investigate further?'

Again, that uncomfortable frown. No, the master had not investigated the goods. The woman had made it quite clear that they were not to be touched, and she had a way of making sure people obeyed her wishes.

'What do you mean by that?'

The master did not mean anything by that. Mrs Broad was just very forceful, is all. Henry asks if he can speak to the children who'd conversed with this mysterious passenger. The master, who appears relieved at the focus of the interrogation turning away from him, shows him below-decks.

The small number of passengers who have returned from New South Wales are accommodated alongside the officers' quarters below the quarterdeck, but the family to which he is directed have moved away from these rooms and taken up their own space between the cargo and the cabins. Henry sees why, instantly. There are two boys and a girl, watched over by a haunted-looking mother. The father lies in a hammock, the stench of illness coming off him. A doomed family, shunned by the crew lest the father's disease carry beyond his own body.

Seeing the family accommodated like this, in a space which a year before would have been filled with chained convicts, men or women or perhaps both, revolts him. It is as if the ship will not let them go.

He asks them about the woman, and the mother says yes, such a woman was on board, her name had been Maggie Broad, and the boys said something of her: how she worried the crew, who thought her a witch. And so the master's discomfort is explained.

And now Henry Lodge must sit down, for his heart is racing. He collapses onto a sack of Canton tea. The children look at him, curious but patient. The mother looks at her sick husband. Henry tries to imagine the woman he seeks waiting here below-decks, gazing at her cargo, cursing anyone who came near it, alarming the crew with her hostile presence.

His waiting is over. Maggie Broad has returned to England. After all these years, his watching is done, and yet he has missed her. That damned three-day delay.

He has failed in his task, and feels suddenly afraid. She was here, and now she is gone.

PART ONE

Madhouses

*For you shall understand, that the force which
melancholie hath, and the effects that it worketh in the
bodie of a man, or rather of a woman, are almost
incredible. For as some of these melancholike persons
imagine, they are witches and by witchcraft
can worke wonders, and do what they list: so do others,
troubled with this disease, imagine manie strange,
incredible and impossible things.*

Reginald Scot, *The Discoverie of Witchcraft*

WAPPING

She feels a prodigious and fearful sorrow when she closes the door on the little apartment in Lower Gun Alley, though Abigail Horton has of late become so suspicious of her own feelings that she is wary of this clenching sadness. For much of this past year she has been aware of two Abigails in attendance behind her eyes: one acting, the other watching and judging. She feels, and another part of her observes her feeling, and draws its conclusions, as if a mad-doctor were in residence between her temples. Increasingly, the conclusions of this watching Abigail are ominous.

She barely sleeps, and when she does her dreams are so terrible that most nights she wakes with a cry of fear which startles her husband Charles awake, and she must once again face that morbid expression of guilt which descends on him. The one she has come to loathe.

She walks down the stairs and out into the street, peeking round the corner of the door like some cowardly lurking footpad. Her husband must not see her leave, for he will stop her and she will not be able to resist the weight of his crushing obligation. She knows that he has a veritable invisible army of small boys watching the streets of Wapping, reporting back anything interesting or odd. He is a constable, after all – one with responsibilities for the peace. Perhaps the peace of this street has been bought with the peace of her own marriage bed. She wonders if Charles pays the boys for watching the comings-and-goings so assiduously, or if they feel they are taking part in some kind of game.

The street is clear, at least of any faces she recognises. She closes the outside door and locks it, little remembered activities for the hands as her mind scurries through its two-headed dance of dismay and observation. With her heavy canvas bag she walks down Lower Gun Alley, for all the world like some seaman headed down to the London Dock to catch a ship to Leghorn or Guinea or Arabia.

Lower Gun Alley gives out onto Wapping Street, and if she were to turn right here she would find herself at the River Police Office, her husband's place of work. The street is crowded with people this morning, and the thick early morning fog has lifted. She looks left and right again, but the gesture is futile. She would not notice Charles, or one of his small boys or even the other constables of the Police Office, out here on this crowded street. She must hope that she blends into the crowd as easily as they would. She turns left and walks away from the Police Office, away from Lower Gun Alley. Away from Charles Horton.

There is a good deal of panic in her head as she goes. She has barely left their rooms for six weeks now, ever since her anxiety had suddenly deepened, like dark-blue seawater off a reef. Charles has taken to buying the food and drink necessary for their meals. When necessity has forced her out into the street she has found the crowds oppressive. The brick walls which lace their way through Wapping, holding in the spaces of the London Dock, have become to her like the walls of a prison, holding her and all those on the streets in a state of isolation from the metropolis, squeezed in against the river, unable to flee. A madhouse on the water, with its own streets, its own watching eyes, its own stenches and mysteries.

This feeling of imprisonment has been acute, because it is flight she dreams of. Not flight from Wapping, or even from Charles, but from the woman in the forest, the one who pursues her and fills her head with unclean thoughts as she comes. A savage woman promising violence and revenge and despair for those who oppose her.

She catches the glance of a small boy who is staring at her. He is standing in the door of a shop, chewing on something indescribable, wearing a man's hat which looks like an upturned bucket, his clothes scruffy and dirty as his face. But his eyes are sharp and watchful, and she sees in them that something about her – her scurrying walk, her bag of clothes, maybe even her frantic expression – has caught his attention.

She hurries on, the urgency in her as great as it is in the dreams. If the boy finds Charles and tells him what he has seen, Charles will know, immediately, what she has decided to do, for she has spoken of it before. He will chase after her, perhaps with a carriage. He may even guess at her destination; Charles is mystifyingly good at such guesses.

Things start to change as she nears the top of Old Gravel Lane, the Ratcliffe Highway in front of her. She turns around to look back down the hill towards the river, to look for attentive small boys or even pursuing constables, and the flow of people running up and down the lane seems to blur into a single stream, with only one person left distinct and clear, standing down by the wall of the Dock, staring at Abigail with those dark Pacific eyes.

The woman from her dreams is standing on Old Gravel Lane.

Abigail does not quite scream, but the noise she makes in her vice-tight throat is loud enough to draw the attention of several bystanders. She turns, and the chase begins.

The two Abigails behind her eyes squabble over this new development. The woman has never appeared to her while awake before. But what if, asks that calm doctoring voice, what if she isn't awake at all? What if this is all just another dream? Abigail has enough of herself left to vanquish this thought, to push it back into the mists for future consideration. But it doesn't quite disappear.

The woman is not real, says her mind.

The woman is chasing me through London, her mind replies.

Her body takes no view on the question. It just propels her, half-running, half-walking, across the Highway and north towards her destination. She has no money for a carriage, and it is perhaps four miles from Wapping to Hackney. The only currency she possesses is a letter, and that can only be used for admission when she reaches the end of her journey. It cannot help her fly from whatever it is that pursues her.

There is nothing pursuing me, says her mind.

She will destroy me if she catches me, her mind replies.

She looks back every few minutes, and every time she does the woman is there, standing out clear and prominent in the blurry street scenes, always still and staring, never apparently moving. But always there.

North of the Commercial Road, open fields and wasteland present themselves as options for flight, but she avoids them, not wishing to be caught out on open ground by her pursuer. So she follows a more zigzag route than she would otherwise have chosen, keeping to the streets, to the blurry crowds, which slow her down and shout angrily at her as she barges her way north, her heavy bag knocking into stomachs and shoulders, her own body tiring with every hurried step.

But as she nears Bethnal Green, the roads begin to open out on both sides, as the metropolis starts to loosen its grip on the landscape. Rope walks and tenter grounds give way to open fields and farms. The Hackney turnpike stands at a crossroads, facing three or four clusters of houses which developers have built in anticipation of the inevitable encroachment of London.

She looks back as she passes the turnpike. The woman is closer now, and she is running, her arms rising up in front of her. Twigs and branches and leaves poke out from her clothes and her hair and even her skin, as if she were part-woman and part-tree, an echo of the most awful flavour of her nightly dreams.

Despite her exhaustion, Abigail runs now, her husband forgotten. Luckily for her, the building she seeks is obvious, the largest building in the neighbourhood, its crowded lines rising up above the fields to her left, its elegant front facing eastwards across the road. She bangs on the porter's gate and screams for entry, desperately waving the letter she has carried from Wapping, the one which guarantees her security.

A huge man with a simple face opens the gate and with a final desperate lunge Abigail Horton enters Brooke House, a private madhouse for the deranged.

A Treatise on *Moral Projection* and its
Manifestation among Certain Women at Brooke
House Asylum, Hackney, in the Year of Our
Lord 1814

By Thomas Bryson, Dr, of St Luke's Hospital,
Old Street, London 1845

PREAMBLE: TO WHOM IT MAY CONCERN

It is an unavoidable certainty, which must be obvious to
any knowledgeable observer, that mankind knows more
of his world, and the Prime Causes that guide it, with
every year that passes. The past hundred years have
seen a galloping chain of discoveries and revelations by
which the world – nay, even the Cosmos – has become
an open book to the eyes of men.

It is Britain, of all the Great Powers, that has led this
march towards knowledge. It is in Britain that science
has been yoked to technology and to progress. It is here
that engines powered by steam first clattered down iron
tracks. It is here that the earliest adventurers in
understanding – heroes like Priestley and Davy and
Faraday and Brown – first divined the operations of the
air, of gases and, perhaps most of all, of Electrical
Forces which, I do believe, will affect a bigger change

16

on this Planet than any preceding innovation. And of course all these great Divinations were set down upon the early edifice built by the mightiest genius of us all, Sir Isaac Newton.

But there is a baleful paradox behind all our discoveries. We know what causes the plants to grow and multiply, so to feed the planet and ourselves. We know how to harness the hidden forces of the world to pump water from mines, to send engines down tracks, to speed our massive ships to the far ends of the Earth. We know what fixes the stars in their heavens.

But the engine which powers all these transitions, the mighty organ that is the Mind of man, remains an essential mystery to us. I speak as one who has laboured for decades within institutions which we once called Madhouses, but are now known as Lunatic Asylums. I have lived through a period of great change in the matter of mad-doctoring, and I have been one of its key innovators.

What is the mind, and how does it conceive? It is a question that has haunted our finest doctors and our most brilliant philosophers. We have argued about the mysteries of the understanding, the relationship of the mind and the body, and the matter of consciousness. We have treated the head *somatically*, as a part of the body, and *philosophically*, as the seat of the soul. To hold a brain in your hands, as I have done on dozens of occasions, is to wonder at how something can be at once a slab of meat and the throne of Reason.

I do not seek to answer such questions in this paper. I seek instead to broaden our understanding of the mind's capacities. For the past four decades I have made the matter of mental disturbance my ground for research. I have investigated melancholy and hysteria, fury and mania, and I have long held that the mind is a stronger instrument than we have ever credited, though I should perhaps say the Brain. I wish to emphasise the, as it were, muscular capacities of this extraordinary organ.

The present paper is not a complete treatise on this matter. I have been forced to commit these thoughts to ink because of the publications of another doctor, who has published his own theories of a concept he calls *hypnotism*. I speak of Dr James Braid of Manchester, in whose book *Neurypnology* this concept is introduced. Dr Braid's book has been greeted with some derision among my colleagues, but I will not stoop to mockery. Although Braid's concepts are misguided, and his conclusions wilful and positively dangerous, there can be no doubt that some of the theories which he has published have affinities with thoughts of my own.

I have been at this particular work for thirty years now. My interest began with events I witnessed at Brooke House, the private asylum (or madhouse, as we then called such places) in Hackney, in the year 1814. The things I saw were so extraordinary, and so out of the range of human experience and theory, that I have made it my life's work to try and place them within a theoretical whole which can at least accommodate them. Now that Dr Braid's ideas are, as it were, out in the public sphere, it may be that a more receptive audience will be available for my own theories.

I believe the events described herein – and the medical conclusions I have drawn from them – will be seen by future generations as a great leap forward in human understanding. My depiction of those terrible nights at Brooke House may attract derision and disbelief, but I speak as a doctor of forty years standing when I say they are real, they happened precisely as I describe them here, and they point to a theory of the mind which will shake our current notions of human ability to its foundations.

And the most remarkable aspect of this saga is this: the capacities I shall describe within this treatise were all exhibited by females, and exclusively females. Is this not miraculous? For if Women are capable of the feats described herein, how much more incredible might be the feats of Men?

WAPPING

A carriage stands outside the River Police Office in Wapping Street, its two black horses flicking their tails through the damp September air, its driver sitting hunched inside dark oilcloth, unmoving, possibly asleep. The seamen and shopkeepers and street-hawkers who trudge and trot up and down the street have to squeeze their way past the coach, and many of them complain about this to the dark figure of the driver, who has as much to say in reply as would a statue.

A man emerges from the Police Office and shouts up to the driver, telling him to wait a little longer, not noticing or not caring about the disruption his carriage is causing. This man is something of a sight to see on this grey late-summer morning. He is dressed fashionably and brightly, in the high style of a man off to the gaming tables of St James's: white silk stockings, dark heeled shoes, duck-egg blue breeches, a grey coat edged with gold brocade, an elegant top hat on his head. In coal-dark, shit-brown Wapping, he looks like a parakeet visiting a murder of crows.

He turns to look back at the Police Office, in a measuring

way. The building is an elegant suburban villa adopted for other uses, now housing two dozen water constables and related clerical staff under the eye of its chief magistrate, John Harriott. Yet today it seems quiet and at rest. In an odd gesture, the gentleman removes his hat and looks at the ground, his lips moving as if in a prayer. He replaces his hat and turns, walking downstream along Wapping Street and left into Lower Gun Alley.

If it is possible he looks even more out of place down this alley, which is surrounded by poor housing. Dirty-faced boys watch from doorways and the gaps between buildings where they play their games of high adventure and moderate violence. The braver ones may be contemplating approaching this man, tapping him up for some change or perhaps even inserting a questing finger into those no doubt well-stocked pockets. But then the gentleman walks up to a door they all know, and as one they back away into the urban shadows of their play.

The gentleman raises his silver-topped cane and knocks on the door, firmly and without embarrassment. He is of course aware of being watched by the street boys. He is not a naive man, and as ever he is watchful and intelligent. Wapping may be rougher at the edges than the Covent Garden theatres and coffee houses he knows so well as a magistrate at Bow Street, but it is, he is well aware, a good deal less lethal.

There is no reply. He knocks again, and this time he steps back and shouts up to the first-floor windows.

'Horton! The door, if you please!'

After a moment, one of the windows opens, and a face appears. Even though he had been led to expect it, the gentleman is still surprised by its appearance: gaunt yet bearded, the hair in disarray, the expression dumb and tired.

'What do you want?' says the face at the window.

'I wish to talk to you, Horton. Now, if you would be so kind.'

The gentleman's voice carries an expectation of obedience. For a moment the bearded face at the window says nothing, perhaps contemplating refusal. Then it looks behind, into the room beyond the window, before turning back to the gentleman below.

'Wait. I shall be a minute or two.'

The window is slammed shut with some asperity. The gentleman, forgetting himself for a moment, sighs mournfully. He turns to the street, his back to the door, using the time to make an inspection of his surroundings. The street makes its own inspection in return.

After some minutes, the door opens, and the man from the upstairs window appears. The gentleman turns to face him.

'What do you want?'

'Horton, I am not about to discuss sensitive matters in the open air, however bracing Wapping's odour may be. Will you not invite me up to your rooms?'

'They are . . . not clean.'

'Neither is the street, particularly. And I would prefer to be warm.'

With a scowl the bearded man relents, and the two of them go inside.

The rooms within are filthy, as advertised. But the gentleman has been in them before, and makes himself comfortable in a chair he recognises. The bearded man says nothing.

The fire is dead in the grate. It has been dead for some time, by the looks of it.

'I have just visited the Police Office,' the gentleman says. 'Harriott is still unwell.'

The bearded man says nothing to this. After a moment, he sits down in the only other chair in the room, his hands on its arms, ready to endure whatever is to come.

'He is in his office, but he should not be,' the smart gentleman continues. 'I have advised him to retire to his bed. We can find others to manage his daily duties. My fellow magistrates at Bow Street could help, if need be.'

The bearded man seems uninterested in any of this. He looks at the dead fire as if it were reading him a tragic story.

'Horton, I wanted to ask Harriott for your help in a more personal matter.'

The bearded man looks at him. The gentleman sees the change in his expression; sullen acceptance has given way to a brow-quickening irritation.

'Help? Whenever you ask for my help, Mr Graham, it ends badly for me.'

The Bow Street magistrate twirls his cane for a moment in one hand, and purses his lips. He is carefully choosing his words.

'Horton, you do not trust me. This much I know. But if you knew how I had shielded you . . .'

'Shielded me? Are you now my benefactor, Mr Graham?'

'Yes, Horton. In ways you will never know, I am your bene-factor. And your wife's, too.'

Horton leans forward in his chair, and his yellow teeth show clearly through his beard. His fists are clenched, and for a moment Graham fears he may rise and strike him.

'Not my wife, Graham. You do not dare . . .'

'Abigail is a patient at Brooke House in Hackney, is she not?'

'Graham, I—'

'Brooke House is a private hospital, used only by the wealthy families of those poor wretches whose sense has flown. Its fees are considerable. And Abigail has been a patient there for a month now, her fees met by the same benefactor who gained her admission to Brooke House. They will continue to be met by him. By me, Horton.'

Graham is met by a stupefied stare. He remembers the last time he was in this room, almost three years before. Then, he'd defeated the man in front of him with revelations of Horton's own past. Now, he has done the same with information on the present. It brings him no pleasure. He needs Horton's help.

'She came to you,' says Horton. 'She came to you when she could not come to me.' He says it more to himself than to Graham.

'She did, Horton. She knew she needed professional assistance to tame her unquiet mind. She knew that assistance would be expensive. And she knew how I had used you in the past, and how much I owed you, and her. She is an extraordinary woman, fearless and charming and clever. And she knew you would refuse my help.'

Horton looks at him, and Graham sees a sadly familiar look of desperate unhappiness in the man's eyes.

'She was wrong about that, Graham. I would have done anything to help her.'

'Really, Horton? Would you really have turned to the man who blackmailed you?'

'Anything. *Anything.*'

Horton stands and turns away from him, hiding his face. Graham finds himself believing him, and wonders at the intensity of the constable's feelings for his wife.

'How does she do?' asks Horton, his face still hidden. 'She is not permitted to write to me, nor I to visit her.'

'Yes, that is my understanding of Brooke House's methods. I know no more than you, Horton. But I do know that, under the supervision of Dr Monro and his assistants, she is receiving the best care possible. The great majority of Brooke House's patients recover their . . .'

He stops, feeling indelicate. He has lied about knowing no

more than Horton. But a hidden lie is less upsetting than a poorly chosen description.

'Their wits?' says Horton. 'Their senses? Their sanity? Abigail is not insane, Graham. She is merely disturbed. And her disturbance begins and ends with me.'

The man's guilt infects the filthy room like the smell from a drain. Aaron Graham, who is a more sensitive man than those who know him realise, begins to understand why Abigail Horton decided to flee from her husband's guilt. The dreams Abigail described to him when she visited his dwelling in Covent Garden clearly had their roots in Horton's investigations of the previous year. Abigail even believed that she had somehow been poisoned by the man Horton had been pursuing. Now Graham can see that Horton believes the same thing, and the knowledge is suffocating.

'Sit down, Horton. Please. I do not bring up my assistance of Mrs Horton to earn your admiration. I only speak of it to make clear that I respect you, and your wife, and am a friend to you both. And, as friends tend to become, I am now a man in need of your help.'

Horton breathes out, once, through his nose, like a horse coming to a decision. He turns and sits down in the chair, leaning back this time, looking directly at Graham, as if seeing him for the first time. Graham, for his part, sees the lights come back on in Horton's eyes, and feels himself watched in that peculiarly intensive way which Charles Horton can bring to the matter. Normally it unnerves him. Today, it brings relief.

Graham twirls his cane again. What he has come to say is unpleasant to him, and bitterly odd.

'My wife, Horton, does not live with me any longer.'

Horton frowns. He looks confused.

'It is one of those things which is little spoken of. Some of my oldest acquaintances, such as John Harriott, know nothing of it. It is a matter of great personal pain to me that Sarah has decided her future lies with another man. But now she has asked for my help in the oddest matter imaginable.'

There. It is out. He takes in a very uncharacteristic breath, and blunders on, natural wit departed, elegance of expression forgotten.

'Sarah now lives with a baronet named Sir Henry Tempest. He is her cousin. Our daughter Ellen lives with them. Am I to assume you know nothing of this man?'

Horton, astonished into silence, shakes his head.

'Then all I will say, Horton, is that Tempest is one of the worst men in England. A rogue. A scoundrel. His fortune comes from an heiress he has abandoned to an unknown fate. His title is inherited, though he has no issue of his own. Now he acts as father to my daughter and as husband to my wife. Ellen has taken his name as well as mine. Ellen Tempest Graham. An infamous name, but nonetheless . . .'

He drops the cane then, the mention of this purloined daughter with his own name almost more than can be borne. He forces himself to regain some self-control.

'They live – Sir Henry, my wife, Ellen – in a place called Thorpe in Surrey. Tempest has some money left from his abandoned spouse, and I continue to supply Sarah – Mrs Graham – with an allowance of her own. She remains my beneficiary. She remains my wife.

'So, now. You know of my domestic arrangements. You are as informed as any West End gossip. But know this, Horton. I still have bottomless wells of affection and feeling for my wife. Her behaviour . . . well, her behaviour has been poor. But I still want her to be happy, and healthy. And Ellen – well, Ellen is my child. I cannot help my feelings for her. That is why I am here today.

'Sarah came to see me yesterday, at Bow Street. We had not

spoken face-to-face for some months. She was, and I do not exaggerate, beside herself. She said Thorpe Lee House, the estate of Sir Henry, is bewitched.'

'Bewitched?' Graham sees that even through the beard and the mental exhaustion Horton is capable of sudden bemusement.

'Yes, bewitched. Under the spell of a witch.'

Graham waits to see what Horton will say. He watches him as carefully as he has watched anyone, and he is a noted watcher. He knows that what he has said is extraordinary. In most places in London, it would be received with derision. *Bewitched? But witches don't exist! We even passed an Act of Parliament in the last century to say so!*

But Horton, Graham knows, has seen things. Bizarre things which are beyond contemporary explanation. Things which Aaron Graham, in his role as Bow Street magistrate but also as Horton's secret supporter, knows break through the polite veneer of respectable natural philosophy. For himself, he knows a good deal more about these dark matters than even Horton. And he rather suspects that Horton knows that.

He thinks of Abigail Horton and her visions, and wonders if they too are of a piece with the dark histories that have been revealed to him in recent years.

These thoughts go through his head as he watches their analogue go through Horton's. He knows that Horton cannot believe this to be a practical joke or an ill-considered piece of gullibility on Graham's part. He has told Horton of his domestic arrangements – matters he has discussed only with those closest to him – and this is evidence of his good faith. And Horton's next question is perceptive enough to convince him that the story has already burrowed its way beneath the constable's skin.

'Is Mrs Graham prone to such beliefs?'

Even in his disturbed state, Graham must smile at that.

'*Prone*? No, Horton, she is not *prone* to superstition or credulity. She is a sensible, ambitious, clever woman. She is not some hysterical young girl who has flown off with a charming ne'er-do-well in imitation of an empty-headed romantic novel. If she believes Thorpe Lee House is bewitched, something very odd indeed must be happening in that place.'

'She has described such episodes?'

'Some of them. Anyone who knows of the old tales of witchcraft would recognise them. Milk curdling. Strange inscriptions. The sudden appearance of a fairy circle, of all things. An horrific episode – two of Tempest's dogs were found dead on the lawn of the house. Most of these things happened, and were worrisome, but they did not initiate Sarah's approach to me. That has been occasioned by a much worse thing. Ellen has become ill, suddenly and precipitously. If one were to write a story of bewitchment, I cannot imagine a more complete set of symptoms than the ones Sarah has described to me. It is like the script for a play about *maleficium*.'

'I meant perhaps something pettier than that. A village grudge, a resentment from Sir Henry's past . . .'

'Resentments must have piled up in Sir Henry's closets like snow on the Lakeland fells, Horton. He is a terrible fellow. And yes, this was the first thing I thought of. And if this is the case, and if Ellen is really ill . . .'

'Then perhaps she was poisoned.'

'Precisely.'

'And others may be in danger. Including—'

'Sarah. Yes.'

'Have these events been investigated locally?'

'Sarah says she has spoken to the local justice. But these matters are notoriously hard to investigate. As soon as *witchcraft* is invoked, the village constable is likely to veer away in fear. Even today. These superstitions adhere stubbornly in country villages, however sophisticated we seem to be. And besides, Horton, no one in Thorpe – perhaps no one in England – possesses the same skills of detection as you. I have watched you work these past three years, and like your own magistrate have been astonished by your approach. Harriott tells me you have not done any work for him in Wapping since Abigail's commitment. You cannot write to her or visit her. You can do nothing for her while she is in that place. But you can help me, and perhaps yourself. Get out of Wapping, Horton. Go to Thorpe. Investigate what is happening to that damned household. Help my wife, just as I have helped yours.'

A Treatise on Moral Projection

The stage for the dramatic events I will describe herein was the old private madhouse of Brooke House, which still operates in Hackney, just to the north of London. At the time of which I write – the late summer of 1814 – Hackney was still a village, though one through which all sorts of miscreants and ne'er-do-wells made their way to and from the metropolis to the south. Gypsies were common visitors, camping out on the road into London, and causing all manner of problems.

Like many older buildings in this great country, Brooke House is a confusing mixture of styles and periods. Imagine a structure built around two internal courtyards, its longer sides running north to south on either side of these internal spaces, the whole building facing east across the main road into London. The long side facing the road has an elegant frontage built during the reigns of the early Georges, and a wall enclosing the northernmost courtyard. Behind this front are the older original buildings.

Inside, the original rooms have, almost without exception, been subdivided into cells, dormitories, servant quarters and suchlike. Female patients occupied the rooms on the first floor, with the men on the ground.

Being something of a student of the history of these isles, Brooke House was a repository of some fascination to me. The oldest parts harked back to the fifteenth century, but the house's most fascinating years were during the reign of Henry VIII, who (it is said) gave a hundred oaks to his wily courtier Thomas Cromwell to fashion part of Brooke House. In my idle moments in the madhouse I would sometimes look at a piece of protruding timber and imagine Cromwell's wicked hands running down its grain, as he planned the destruction of some courtier, bishop or even Queen. I had even arranged for some investigatory work to be carried out in one particular part of the house, the south-eastern corner where, local stories had it, a chapel had originally been situated. Peeling back some of the plasterwork I was pleased to discover a painting on the wall of an ecclesiastical fellow in splendid raiment standing above a kneeling monkish man. I wished to discover more of this strange space but the events I shall come to interrupted my investigations.

At the time of these events and, as far as I know, perhaps even still, Brooke House was operated by the Monro family, whose name has been somewhat discredited these past thirty years but who, in 1814, were considered the foremost mad-doctors in England. Thomas Monro, my employer and the chief physician of Brooke House, was the third Monro to be chief physician at Bethlem Hospital, and had been one of several mad-doctors who had tried, and failed, to cure King George of his final (did we but know it then) episode of insanity. Brooke House was the family's main source of financial independence, and was run alongside Dr Monro's duties at Bethlem. Like all private asylums in England at that time, it was a lucrative business. The patients were typically of the finer sort, not quite lords and ladies, but certainly not paupers. The cost was too great for the poor, and in any case Bethlem and the recently established St Luke's accommodated the poor who became mad.

I came there as a young man of two-and-twenty. I had been born and raised in the village of Chevening in Kent. I was apprenticed to Dr Monro at Bethlem in 1802, aged eighteen, via a family connection of my father's. Four years later, I was transferred by Dr Monro to Brooke House, following a paper I wrote for him on the therapeutic regime at Bethlem and how it might be improved. Monro, seeing a good deal of sense and intelligence in what I suggested, stated that my innovations might first be tried at Brooke House before being introduced into the larger, more public realm of Bethlem.

My own quarters in Brooke House were in the part of the building called 'the Cottage', on that same south-east corner of the main building where I later discovered the chapel. The house is easy to get lost within, and during my early weeks as a physician there I was forced to seek guidance from one of the matrons on several occasions. Imagine if a manor house and two or three cottages had, over time, become conjoined, their roofs combining, external walls becoming internal ones, and you will have some sense of the internal confusions of Brooke House.

I must now turn to the two main protagonists of my strange tale, both of whom arrived at Brooke House within a day of each other in August 1814.

The circumstances of Maria Cranfield's arrival

appeared to be exceptional, at least by the standards of
Brooke House which, as I have said, had a rather
genteel clientele. Miss Cranfield arrived in a very bad
state indeed. She would not speak and was violent in her
responses, exhibiting a frenzied mania which was not
entirely unfamiliar to my then-practised eye.

This would puzzle me, because the gentleman who
accompanied her to Brooke House was, on the face of
it, an honourable man of some means. He gave his
name as Henry Lodge, and said he was a Kentish
farmer acting on behalf of the young woman's family.
When I enquired as to the identity of Miss Cranfield's
parents, I was told, politely but firmly, that no identity
would be forthcoming, and that all matters pertaining to
Miss Cranfield's treatment were to be directed to him.
He would visit weekly, he said, and could be contacted
either at his home, near Canterbury, or at the Prospect
of Whitby in Wapping, where he was wont to stay.

Mr Lodge assured me that there were more than
enough financial resources to pay for Miss Cranfield's
treatment, and that he was able to pay a good deal of
them in advance. I felt a deep reluctance to accept this
patient on these terms; it was irregular indeed to take on
a case where the family history was not only unknown
but actively hidden. Nonetheless, I took Miss Cranfield
in, for two reasons.

The first was her case, which promised to be
interesting to a young physician seeking to advance
human understanding of mental infacility.

The second reason was less high-minded. Dr Monro
had made it clear to me that, in the matter of Brooke
House, financial matters needed always to be kept in
mind. We could not let our own personal qualms get in

the way of maintaining a successful business. 'This is not, Bryson, a charitable institution,' Dr Monro had said, and he constantly pressed me on how many patients were being treated, what the costs of this treatment were and how extensive were the means of the patients' families.

The simple fact of the matter was this: Mr Lodge's offer to pay the fees for the first three months of care for Miss Cranfield would make a substantial contribution to Brooke House's running costs. I was under some pressure to turn a profit within each month. The equation was impossible to be ignored. Such was how things were in private madhouses at the start of the present century.

So Maria Cranfield was admitted and locked into one of the strong-rooms on the first floor, secured with a strait waistcoat. This last was with some reluctance, for it was one of my beliefs that securing patients in this way was primitive and not productive, but such was Miss Cranfield's manic state that I had no other option at that time. In the next-door cell to Miss Cranfield, in the southern end of Brooke House, close to my own rooms, Abigail Horton had already been placed.

Miss Cranfield's arrival was unorthodox, and so was Mrs Horton's. She had appeared at the gate of Brooke House on her own, carrying a letter from a Bow Street magistrate, Aaron Graham. The letter stated that Mrs Horton should be admitted to the madhouse forthwith, and that all financial matters relating to her care would be met by Mr Graham. I had not made the acquaintance of this gentleman at that time, though I was soon to do so, in the most trying of circumstances.

Mrs Horton was in a state of extreme agitation on her

arrival, though she was by no means as hysterical as
Miss Cranfield. On first coming into the building she
was frantic, saying she had been pursued to Hackney by
a savage woman 'from a Pacific island' (these were her
words), and that this same woman had been haunting
her dreams for a year or more. Mrs Horton's fancy had,
it was clear, become corrupted by some means, and the
exoticism of her story recommended it to me. Mr
Graham's credentials were impeccable, and Mrs
Horton's case undoubtedly interesting. I arranged for
her admittance at once.

Mrs Horton had stood at the door of her own cell as
we placed Miss Cranfield in the strong-room; it was my
custom to leave the doors to the cells open as often as
possible, when the condition of the patient did not
militate against such an approach. Miss Cranfield
screamed terrible obscenities at the matron and the
attendants. She scratched and she tried to bite, and
drew her own nails down her own scarred arms, as if
trying to tear herself into pieces. She uttered one name,
over and over again: that of *Joshua*.

I well remember working with the nurses and
attendants to secure Miss Cranfield against the wall,
dosing her with opium, and then turning to leave. Still
standing in the open doorway of her own cell was Mrs
Horton, her eyes wide at what she was hearing. I gently
took her arm and led her back to her bed, assuring her
that Miss Cranfield would soon be calm and that her
treatment was to begin immediately. She asked for
paper and ink to write to her husband and I was forced,
gently, to remind her that any contact with loved ones
was forbidden, according to the principles of the house.

'You must try and put your husband out of your

mind,' I said to her. 'It may be his presence which is causing you to suffer so.'

It was a hard thing to say, and I would have said nothing like this had my attention not been so distracted by the histrionics of Miss Cranfield. But it had an effect. I remember Mrs Horton looking at me as she sat on her bed.

'If that is so, then I am lost,' she said.

The weeks which followed the arrival of these two women were by no means unusual. One might even have described the time as peaceful, if one had knowledge of what was to follow. Certainly, looking back on that period from the distance of thirty years, those late summer months take on the glow of warm memory, like a holiday taken with a good friend with fine weather and fine food.

There were perhaps thirty inmates in Brooke House at that time, split equally between men and women. Most of them were allowed to walk freely throughout the building, in the cloistered quadrangle, and in the well-tended gardens – though it was our policy, where practicable, to separate males and females. Only a few patients – of whom Maria Cranfield was one – were confined to their cells, and only some of these were secured by strait waistcoats. Again, Maria was one of these, at my instruction.

For Maria was not a settled patient. During her first week in the place, I had ordered a quickened programme of treatments; she was bled three times, and purged twice, and I kept her on a steady dose of opium for her mania. At the end of this week, I ordered that her strait waistcoat be removed. I would not make the same mistake again. She soon scratched into her arms and face with such severity that deep wounds were gouged into them; indeed, such were the wounds on her cheeks that I doubted they would ever fully heal. These wounds ended just before the eyes, and I wondered if that were deliberate or just happenstance. Had she indeed come close to clawing out her own eyes?

I was not going to take the chance that such awful self-mutilation would be acted out. I ordered that she be placed back into a strait waistcoat, and in it she stayed throughout the month of August.

My routine in the asylum was a set one. I would make my rounds in the morning and afternoon, and have individual consultations in the ground-floor room fitted out for the purpose throughout the day. I ate either in my chambers or in the refectory with the nurses and attendants. I encouraged visits from inmates – always assuming they were arranged via a nurse or matron, and that I was available and not engaged in study or correspondence.

It was on one such evening that Abigail Horton visited me in my rooms for the first time. I had made some inquiries into Mrs Horton's circumstances, and had discovered the possible reason behind the munificence of her Bow Street benefactor, Mr Aaron Graham. Mrs Horton's husband, it appeared, was a waterman-constable with the Thames River Police in Wapping, and thus moved in the grimy circles of crime and punishment frequented by Mr Graham. Despite this knowledge I found – and still find – the particulars of Mrs Horton's arrangement with Mr Graham peculiar, but I kept my professional demeanour at all times, despite the very obvious charms of Mrs Horton.

Her husband I knew little of at that time, but a man who had attracted and, it would seem, kept the regard of one such as Mrs Horton must have been an extraordinary man indeed.

Mrs Horton was a particularly handsome and intelligent woman, widely read and possessing degrees of understanding of modern knowledge which I found unaccountable in a female. She had attended seminars at the Royal Institution, had read the latest books on botany, natural philosophy and literature, and was as rounded a woman intellectually as ever I have encountered.

As I have said, Mrs Horton's condition was an unusual one. She had been plagued by dreams of a woman, though not an English woman. It seemed that this woman was a Pacific Islander, and when I questioned Mrs Horton as to why this should be she often became guarded, as if she knew of a reason but did not wish to share it. All she would say is that she thought the dream might relate to a previous investigation of her husband's.

I wrote to Mr Graham regularly with information on the progress of Mrs Horton, and allowed her full freedom to roam the parts of Brooke House and its gardens which were open to patients. We often walked together, and it was during these walks that I discovered Mrs Horton's extraordinarily varied knowledge. Any female of any class would have done well to be as educated as she, but for one of such poor means – her husband a constable, not even a craftsman or a merchant – to have attained such an understanding of the works of mankind and the world around us is, in my opinion, a minor educational miracle. She conversed attentively and carefully, and the time I spent with her was charmed.

On that night, it was Maria Cranfield that was the cause of Mrs Horton's visit. She had, I knew from my own observation and from the report of the nurses, taken a good deal of interest in the condition of her Brooke House neighbour. I had even pondered allowing Mrs Horton to spend time with Maria, in the hope that two women left to their own devices might find ways of communicating with one another. The nurses and physicians, even myself, would be met with either catatonia or a raging terror, which descended on Miss Cranfield with almost visible speed, as if a dark cloud were coming down on her head.

But Mrs Horton had not yet become Miss Cranfield's amanuensis. That would come later. Mrs Horton at that time was still plagued by the visions which accompanied her into Brooke House, and on that August night's visit she told me something that convinced me her condition might be worsening, not improving.

She told me she was convinced that Miss Cranfield had been visited the previous night. She claimed to have heard a woman speaking to Maria and even, at one stage, singing a song to her. I well remember the song Mrs Horton claimed she had heard, as I made some effort to try and discover its origin soon after the events which were about to break over the head of Brooke House. The first verse went as follows:

Ye London maids attend to me
While I relate my misery
Through London streets I oft have strayed
But now I am a Convict Maid.

The song continued in the same melodramatic vein.

My initial assumption was, of course, that Mrs Horton had imagined the whole thing; that this was another species of the visions which already plagued her tired mind. She became quite upset by this opinion, and I well knew why; those whose minds have run away with themselves become terrified lest we, the sane, imagine all their thoughts to be sprites or fantasies. She assured me she felt these things to be true.

'But how can it be?' I said, attempting to reassure her. 'The house is locked up each night. Anyone visiting is noted in the logbook, and no visits with patients are allowed. Maria's room is locked shut at all times. How could there be someone in the room with her?'

She admitted that all this was true, but then turned the question round on me.

'If what I have heard is true, and if what you have said about Brooke House's night-time arrangements is true, is the question of how someone could get into Maria's room not an important one?'

You see the brilliance of the woman. *Assume I am mad, and treat me. Or pretend I am not, and investigate.* Her logic was irreproachable. I promised I would look into the matter. She thanked me, and left.

THORPE

There is a flat, swampy feeling to the land around Thorpe village that gives it something of the flavour of Wapping. Or at least, thinks Horton, Wapping must once have looked a little like this, before the coming of docks and wharves and boarding houses, when there were still meadows instead of walls and warehouses.

Thorpe is set perhaps a half-mile south of the Thames, in a riverine green landscape punctuated by copses which stand as a reminder of ancient forests. There is a sullen order to the topography, which to the interested nose of Charles Horton rather reeks of enclosure. He wonders when these fields were laid out, and what that has done to the local labouring community, and who has benefited.

The Bow Street Police Office carriage rattles down the lane from Weybridge, the river to the right, ever present, sometimes hidden by reeds and willows, sometimes barely a suggestion of open space on the far side of a meadow, but always there, like the soft scent of a rich woman in a Mayfair boutique.

The carriage is driven by an officer from Bow Street, an

older man who introduced himself only as 'Roberts, Bow Street' when he'd knocked on Horton's door in Wapping. He'd waited by the horses, feeding them scraps from his hands. Horton caught him muttering 'fucking animals' in the general direction of a group of dirty, aimless boys who were watching the horses and the carriage. The air had been acrid – it smelled like there had been a fire, somewhere over towards Red Lion Street. Horton had beckoned one of the boys over – he knew them all – and asked him to go and investigate, and to send word to the Police Office if no one had yet done so.

Now, that smoke-stained air and those shit-stained cobbles smack of another world entirely. They turn left off the riverside road and onto a well-maintained track through fields. A house rises up from behind the trees and hedges, an oddly naked structure on the flat meadows surrounding, framed but also exposed by the grey sky and the dense copse immediately behind. The day has autumn in its breath, and though the trees are hanging on to their leaves the coming surrender is palpable.

The house takes further shape as the coach nears: a square, elegant but characterless place. Horton's eyes are untutored in matters architectural, but it seems to him this house has none of the new qualities of the wealthy properties at Wapping Pier Head.

The coach-sweep approach departs from the road and then twists around two sides of the building to the front door, which is set behind four columns holding up a portico. Thorpe Lee House is surrounded by flat grounds which, if need be, could accommodate the entire London Dock. Three or four clumps of trees are set artfully around the place, and although there has been some thought in the past to the design of the gardens, the overall impression is of mild neglect. The woodland Horton saw from the road frames one side of the gardens and from somewhere in the near distance he hears the sound of dogs, a good many of them. Horton recognises how little he knows of country estates, but feels sure they are normally neater than this. The grass is too long, the pathways a little weed-strangled for the artful bucolic polish he has seen along the river at Kew and Richmond.

The driver throws down Horton's bag with no ceremony, and says no farewell as the bag lands with an alarming sound on the gravel of the driveway. With a *hai!* to the horses the coach leaves. Horton experiences another little wobble of dissonance after the sight of the mildly unkempt gardens: the lady of the house is now appearing, unaccompanied, at the door to Thorpe Lee House. Are there no servants?

Horton picks up his bag and walks to the portico where the tall woman waits. She is dressed fashionably if somewhat more plainly than might be expected for a baronet's – what, exactly? There is a sudden and pressing confusion. The wife of a baronet such as Sir Henry Tempest would be greeted as 'Lady'. But Mrs Graham is not Sir Henry's wife. So what *is* Mrs Graham? Companion? *Inamorata?* Concubine? The extraordinary nature of her domestic status is thrown into sharp relief on their first meeting by the fact that he has been sent here by her own abandoned husband. Horton rather feels like the dupe in a Drury Lane farce. The audience is waiting for him to slip on some hidden particle of etiquette.

'Constable Horton?' the woman asks. She has the face of a tired forty-year-old or a well-preserved fifty-year-old. Horton does not know which should apply.

'Yes, ma'am.' He picks the word carefully, yet it feels unwieldy and imprecise on his tongue.

'Welcome to Thorpe Lee House, constable,' she says, adding (to Horton's relief), 'I am Mrs Sarah Graham.' She takes a good degree of care over each word. The word *constable* had sounded foreign and almost insulting when she spoke it. She had shared her own name with some haughty reluctance.

She is polite to him nonetheless, and expresses words of gratitude as they walk into the house, but this isn't enough to hide her apparent distaste at his presence. She had asked for someone to come, of course, but Horton can see his arrival has only served to make real whatever is troubling her. And of course, she had not exactly asked for *him*. She'd wanted a justice of the peace, not a river constable.

Despite the unofficial nature of his visit, Horton sees that he cannot help but represent the encroachment of the public realm into Mrs Graham's confused and confusing household. Mrs Graham is so embarrassed, Horton now recognises, that she has decided to leave the servants out of it for now. She tells him to leave his bags in the vestibule for someone to pick up – she doesn't say who. She shows him into the reception room, where tea already waits on a tray. She has planned everything such that no servant shall see or speak to him before she has taken the chance to do so herself.

He asks after Sir Henry, and is told that the master of the house is up in London and has been for some weeks. Mrs Graham expresses some satisfaction that this is so as they sit down.

'I wish to speak to you of the strangest things,' she says. 'Sir Henry has a different attitude towards them than I.'

'He does not hold with the idea of witchcraft?'

A look of discomfort passes over Mrs Graham's face. Horton's directness is unwelcome.

'Mr Graham has told you everything?'

'Not at all, ma'am. Only the generalities. I carry a letter for you from him.'

He hands it to her and watches her as she reads it. The fire is burning in the cosy grate, above which is a massive painting

44

in oils of the man whom Horton takes to be Sir Henry Tempest. The painting reveals a tall and fashionable figure, standing in a rural scene with several dogs and a gun. His eyes quiver with the zeal of the hunt (the artist's skill is much in evidence around those eyes), and Horton is left with the impression of a determined, almost fanatical individual, full of life and appetite. The figure blazes from its otherwise rather ordinary depiction, the flat oils unable to hold the man's personal force within the frame. Horton keeps looking back at the picture, as if worried that the figure within might leap down from the fireplace and throttle him.

After a minute, Mrs Graham puts her husband's letter to one side. She places her hands in her lap, and looks down at them, as if they might provide a cue for how to proceed. Then she looks up and speaks to him. Her brow is determined, and she speaks with easy authority, inflected by the same clear internal tension which greeted him in the driveway.

'Before we begin, constable, I wish to make one thing perfectly clear to you. We will not be using the word *witchcraft* when talking of the events which have befallen this house.'

'You do not believe that to be the cause?'

Mrs Graham narrows her lips and breathes in heavily.

'I do not know what I believe, constable. But it is of course beyond all rational inquiry that bewitchment has taken place.'

He can see, immediately, that this is not quite the truth, and for the first time Horton warns himself to perhaps take care around this woman. Trusting Aaron Graham at all does not come easily, but Horton had believed him when he'd said his wife believed Thorpe Lee House to be bewitched. She is now lying about that belief to the man charged with investigating its cause. Her dissemblance hangs in the air like the smoke from the fire.

'So your explanation for these occurrences is that they are

mere coincidence? Or perhaps somebody has a grudge against you?'

'Against me? I should hope not.'

She looks to her left, and Horton's eyes are drawn back to the picture above the fireplace.

'Against Sir Henry, then?'

Mrs Graham looks at him directly again, and he feels distinctly uncomfortable beneath her penetrating gaze.

'What have you been told of Sir Henry, constable?'

That he is the worst man in England.

'Very little, Mrs Graham.' The name stings her, slightly. He files that away.

'A great many people have a great deal to say about Sir Henry, constable,' she says. 'Do not believe any of it. They are envious of him and, I suppose, are envious of me too. Envy breeds all sorts of runaway tongues.'

There is something smoothly unpleasant about this speech. Mrs Graham speaks no more of Sir Henry. She tells Horton of the sequence of disturbing events at the house, which began and reached their peak during August and which she had believed were at an end. But now there is the matter of the sudden illness of her daughter, Ellen.

'Does Miss Graham fare any better?'

'Miss Tempest Graham, if you please.'

The correction implies all sorts of questions which Horton does not wish to now pursue.

'Is she better?'

'She is the same, constable. She is very ill but not, her doctor says, in any immediate danger. I confess to having panicked at her first illness, when I spoke to Mr Graham. I may have been premature. You see, I thought perhaps I knew who might be at the root of this matter.'

This is new. Graham had made no mention of it.

'Almost a fortnight ago, I sacked the cook. She is a woman by the name of Elizabeth Hook. The servants, and many in the village, had become convinced that she was the … well, she was the *primary cause* of these incidents.'

'Was there evidence for this belief?'

'There was some. Items related to some of the events were found in her kitchen.'

'That is all?'

'That is all. Also, she became ill during a ceremony performed by two of the servants.'

'A *ceremony*?'

'Yes. They told me about it. A witch-bottle, they called it.'

'Do you know what this ceremony involved?'

'I do not. They can tell you. But it is intended to make the … *perpetrator* unwell. And it seemed to work.'

'I see. And where is Elizabeth Hook now?'

'I cannot say. I presume in the village. Though there was a good deal of bad feeling towards her. She may have left the area altogether.'

'Mrs Graham, you are aware, are you not, of the legal status of accusations of witchcraft?'

'I am. Aaron … Mr Graham … explained this to me. I am choosing my words carefully.'

'I understand. Have the incidents which caused this suspicion been itemised in any way?'

'They have. I have them here.'

She hands him a scroll of paper tied, almost ritually, by a thick black thread.

'Every incident, and its date, is listed therein.'

'My thanks. I would like to read this, and then talk to you again. And the servants as well.'

'Yes. They will be made available to you. Perhaps tomorrow – the hour is growing late today, and we must still eat dinner.'

'And Miss Tempest Graham? May I speak to her?'

'Perhaps, if she recovers a little. Though I confess to being mystified as to why you would wish to.'

'Mrs Graham, I have no idea why I should speak to anyone. I must try to establish whether there is any motive for these mischiefs on your household.'

And envy is by no means sufficient as a motive, he decides not to add.

'Motive? I do not understand.'

Horton is quite familiar with this inability.

'It is my experience, ma'am, that no crime is committed without a motive. Most of the time that motive is personal gain. Sometimes it is petty revenge. It may be fear that forces the hand of the saboteur or poisoner, if such there be in this case. Whatever the matter, establishing the motive always leads to the perpetrator.'

'Ah? Well, as Mr Graham has said, you are the master in such matters. I just wish these things to stop, constable. If you can effect such an arrest, I will be in your eternal debt.'

She looks at him with an expression that suggests her creditors, financial or emotional, are the luckiest people in the world.

Horton is collected from the reception room by the butler, a thin, rather scruffy man of indeterminate age and unknown regional provenance who gives his name as Crowley, but only when asked, and who smells of alcohol and old tobacco. His clothes bear the same tattered air of mild desuetude as the gardens outside; indeed, it occurs to Horton, of the house itself.

They leave Mrs Graham alone inside the reception room, her eyes following Horton out as if he were under suspicion of a felony. From the vestibule a staircase with pretensions of hauteur climbs up to the first floor, and Horton follows Crowley up. There are five doors off the first-floor landing, all but one of them closed, and Crowley leads Horton through into the bedroom beyond. His bag is already on the floor, and he is about to turn and ask Crowley a question when he hears the door close. The butler, without a word, has made his escape.

A small writing table has been placed by the window, and Horton sits at it, leaving his bag to fend for itself. He rubs his freshly shaven face, the skin still itching slightly from the barber's attentions this morning. The view outside is of the lawn to the side of the house, and the dense copse beyond. Another old man, cut from similarly dilapidated cloth as the butler, works away at something in the ground on the edge of the lawn. There is good plate glass in the window, and a small balcony outside.

Horton unties the scroll and folds it flat on the table.

Mrs Graham's handwriting is tidy and, like the woman herself, has the odd property of making him feel rather lacking. The note consists purely of a list of dates, annotated with the events of the day, with no colour or feeling to it:

Aug. 10 – O'Reilly's shed burned
Aug. 12 – milk from Thorpe Lee herd curdled. Remains
*   undrinkable for the rest of the week*
Aug. 13 – dead rat left on dining room table. Rat's blood
*   discovered in kitchen*
Aug. 14 – ring appears on lawn – about 10 feet across
Aug. 15 – words of profane intent discovered in chalk on
*   inner door of linen cupboard; chalk discovered in kitchen*
Aug. 16 – several of Sir H—'s shirts cut to pieces. Scissors
*   with cotton fragments found in kitchen.*
Aug. 18 – cook becomes ill
Aug. 19 – dreadful noise from trees to side of house

Aug. 21 – two of Sir H—'s dogs slaughtered overnight
Aug. 22 – I sack the cook
Aug. 27 – Ellen falls ill, terribly so

He wonders, rather, at the self-discipline which this writing-down must have taken, but then ponders whether he is not making the mistake of assuming a personality where there is none. Even before meeting her, Horton had assumed that Mrs Graham would be a wilful individual. Leaving a husband with Aaron Graham's reputation to take up with a man with Sir Henry Tempest's must have been an act of deliberate will. Or was it? Was there passion involved? Is this precise, calculated handwriting just the careful strongbox within which ardour is chained?

He feels uncomfortable, miserable even, in this odd house. The primary cause is the same as it has been this past month: Abigail's absence, or more particularly his ignorance as to her state. What is she doing now? Who is she talking to? Or is she alone, scared and trembling in some cold cell in that strange building north of London, where he has lingered outside a dozen times this past month, hoping for a glimpse or a clue?

Abigail has been the mournful backdrop of his existence for weeks now. He wonders if Graham had intended to displace it with a change of scene: take Horton out of Wapping, despatch him to this oddly disjointed place beside the river, perhaps he will settle down a bit there. But why should he care about Horton's welfare?

What on earth am I doing here, really?

A knock at the door, and the old butler's voice, asking him down to dinner. He comes back to himself with a start, and sees the shadows have lengthened across the lawn, like bars across a great pit in the land.

*

Dinner is served to him, alone, in the kitchen beneath and behind the main staircase. Mrs Graham will have nothing more to do with him today, it seems. Even the cook is absent. Horton wonders how long the lady of the house can keep up this separation between him and the servants, and what purpose she believes it serves. It leaves him feeling slighted and vaguely disconnected from the real world. Where are the sights and smells of Wapping, the scurrying humanity with its incessant chatter? Here there is only absence and unidentified sounds from unseen rooms.

He finishes his lonely supper, and walks back up the stairs. Crowley, or anyone else for that matter, does not come to meet him. It is as if the house had been abandoned. He takes the opportunity of solitude to give himself a better picture of the house's layout. He looks into the rooms on the ground floor: the reception room, the drawing room, the dining room, the library. All are empty. Behind another door he finds a new water-closet, such as only the newest and finest homes in London have. There is something both daring and strange about it. Is it Mrs Graham's innovation, or Sir Henry's?

He hears movement in the house. The place is haunted by its inhabitants. Or perhaps he is the ghost. He goes upstairs to bed. Behind a door on the landing he hears the sound of a woman weeping. He thinks it is Mrs Graham, but cannot be sure. He contemplates knocking on her door and establishing she is well, but decides against it. Reluctantly he goes to bed.

During that first night in Thorpe Lee House he is constantly awoken by the dreams of those hidden inhabitants of the place. From above him come a variety of moans, shrieks and sobs which are so regular that they give the impression that the house itself is having a particularly bad night of it.

At one point he is woken by howling dogs from somewhere in the blind dark. Sir Henry's pack, presumably, two of whom have been killed. He gets up to look out of the window. A light is shining from a downstairs window – another waker, perhaps? It casts a flickering shadow on the grey surface of the lawn, which is broken only by a ring of freshly dug earth which he had not noticed before.

Wide awake now, he goes out into the hallway. He cannot hear the moans and groans of the servants in the attic rooms above when he is outside the room, and it is as if the house has shushed itself upon hearing Horton's waking. A burst of coughing ending in a rattling sigh comes from one of the main bedrooms.

He hears a clatter of something metallic from downstairs, and a woman's curse. He walks to the stairs and sees an old woman scurry across the vestibule into the drawing room. She is carrying something in a tankard, and from within the drawing room Horton hears the sound of a woman weeping.

He goes down to the kitchen. There is no one there. Three pans and their lids lie on the floor, the source of the noise he'd heard from the landing. A big jug sits by the ugly-looking sink, and finding a tankard he pours himself some water from within it. He sips from the tankard, looking around the kitchen. A scurrying sound from behind the cupboards. He feels watched by twitching rodent eyes.

He waits a few minutes, half-expecting one of the servants to come in and demand an explanation. But no one comes. He walks back up the gloomy stairwell and goes over to put his ear to the drawing room door. He hears a woman talking within, soothingly, her words indistinct.

He senses the great quiet which surrounds the house, so different from London. It seems to squeeze in against the great front door, and he glances through the fanlight at the top of the door, to be greeted only by a flat inexpressive purple, a non-suggestive void.

There is no one out there, he thinks to himself, and after so long as a sailor in crowded ships and a resident of London's scurrying mazes, the thought is a confused and frightening one.

He goes back up to bed.

BROOKE HOUSE

Abigail waits for the night to come once again. Like all her nights in Brooke House, it will be full of sounds and sights which may or may not be true. She no longer has any faith in her perceptions or her understanding.

There is an observing part of her mind that she has started to think of as an anatomist, one such as William Hunter, gazing down at her opened body as she lies on a slab inside some institution or other, the very core of her exposed to men's inspection. This part of her records all the insanities of the previous months inside a doleful ledger, one which she is free to peruse during the daylight when her mind is most at rest.

The ledger is full of the Pacific woman who had pursued Abigail from Wapping to here and who still, somehow, can climb into the madhouse and infect her dreams. The woman's presence has faded not one jot, despite the treatments of the weasel-faced Dr Bryson and his self-important employer Dr Monro.

She has been bled twice, once from each arm. Each time

Bryson watched from the doorway as Brooke House's resident surgeon opened his leather-bound case and made great play of selecting the right instrument 'for such an intelligent and sensitive creature as yourself'. On both occasions he'd picked up a small, beautifully polished scarificator, the tiny blades of which emerged from its metal surface like the teeth of some artificial beast. Once her vein was opened, Abigail watched as her blood dripped into a pewter bowl with numbers marked up the side, until Bryson barked an order to stop and the surgeon covered her new wound with a bandage.

She has also been purged, immediately before each bleeding, forcing down a herbal concoction of Dr Bryson's own devising which, within seconds, caused her to vomit up the contents of her stomach into a different bowl. Each time, Bryson would avidly investigate the contents, like an ancient alchemist discerning the combination of humours from the belly of a duke.

On a half-dozen occasions, Bryson has come into her cell and made her sit on the bed, facing him. Then he has stared at her, his bloodshot brown eyes peering at her as if she were a botanical specimen under investigation by a Kew gardener, and while he stares he has asked her provocative questions about her condition and even about her relationship with Charles. She has answered the questions when she can, and grown angry at the more impertinent of them, but something about her anger seemed to excite Bryson, and he had leaned in and furrowed his brow deeply, never taking his gaze from her, never blinking, nostrils flaring as if he could cast a spell upon her through the space between them.

Each of these strange episodes has ended the same way: Bryson has sighed and looked down at the floor, shaking his head as if she had failed some unspoken examination, then patting her hand and standing. Each time, she has immediately been given some form of intervention: a purging, or a bleeding, or a dose of something-or-other. Some days it is oil, some days opium, some days the juice of an orange.

Otherwise, the only other element of the Brooke House regimen has been seclusion. On this point Bryson is adamant. Abigail cannot write to Charles, nor can she receive any of the letters she is certain he must have sent. She imagines him outside the front of the house, standing under a tree, desperate to catch a glimpse of her. She speaks to other patients of this, and they all confirm it: Brooke House allows no intercourse between patients and their families.

But the Pacific woman endures. The kindly idiot who mans the gate, whose name she has learned is John, may have shut it behind her when she first arrived, but he did not shut out the princess. She came in with her, and most nights she whispers to Abigail, whispers of strange plants and unquenchable thirsts.

The princess has been with her since last year, when the sea captain appeared at her door with a gift of tea for her husband. Tea made from the leaves of an Otaheite tree, a substance full of strange potencies. The Otaheite princess had leaped into Abigail's dreams from the drink she made from that tea, and then she had leaped from her dreams into her waking hours, and now she is a constant dark-haired companion, whispering baleful tales of the crimes of Englishmen and the vengeance of women.

But this is not the only voice Abigail hears. When the old building finally settles into sleep – a fitful sleep, full of creaks and murmurs and audible memories – Abigail listens for the woman in the cell beside hers. And, more often than not, the woman speaks.

Abigail has not seen her since the day she was first brought in, but she has asked Bryson and the attendants about her, and one of them has at least provided her with a name: Maria. For the first few nights, this girl did not so much speak as sob, quite gently compared with the terrible screams she had aimed at the attendants who had tried to calm her on her arrival. The sobs were full of a single name – *Joshua* – and were possessed of the longing of a hundred sonnets.

But sometimes she spoke to herself – spoke of men who'd done things to her, terrible things, of livid indignities and wretched crimes. And then, after perhaps two weeks, Abigail had heard another voice in the cell with her; a woman's voice, its tones soft but its accent harsh. Sometimes it sang to Maria, sometimes it read to her, but when Abigail left her cell the next day, as she was permitted to do, the door to Maria's was firmly shut. No one was getting out, it seemed, and Abigail could not imagine how anybody could have got in.

She'd gone to Dr Bryson with the story of the singing, but had later wondered why she should have done so. He was unlikely to listen to her, she knew. Was she not mad? A female sufferer of terrible visions? What was an overheard voice from a madwoman's cell when there was only a madwoman there to hear it?

Such is how he'd heard her news, that condescending smile on his face, the one he used to calm people, the one which made her imagine his face being ripped into pieces by the hooks of Pacific fishermen. Specifically, Otaheite fishermen and Otaheite hooks.

Ah, she was always there, the princess. Always there to preach violence in the face of men's pig ignorance. Always whispering rhymes of revenge.

She lies awake as night falls. She thinks of her husband, and where he might be, and whether he is sleeping or lying awake like her, their souls intertwined in restlessness. The madhouse seems to possess a different, almost watchful aspect. The house is never *silent*, by any means. It is, Abigail knows, an old, crumbling building which has housed the insane for more than half a century, and such a building is never going to be silent. Nonetheless there is a brooding quiet; even the inmates who contribute to the night-time noise do so with a kind of embarrassment, as if they imagine their quieter comrades turning upon them for their lack of manners. She is aware that she can hear *breathing* from the house around her, the hollow in-and-out of the desperate and the mad, normally inaudible beneath the groans and chuckles and repetitive incantations. Even in a place as respectable as Brooke House, the mad will moan.

The air is cold, and this is also bizarre; summer is still caressing the trees of the gardens, and Abigail had felt perspiration on her face when out walking in the walled garden behind Brooke House that afternoon. Indeed, it is so cold that her breath rises up above her head as she lies on the bed, such that it creates its own little infernal fog.

After supper she'd walked along the corridor that lined the rear upper floor, which looked over the garden. Even in her extremities of loneliness and anxiety this place can please her. She believes it must have once been a grand open gallery of the original house, for its ceiling is lined with ornate carvings which are abruptly cut off by the doors of cells along the corridor, making it clear that a once-open space has been subdivided. She'd looked at the women around her, most of whom were sat down against the walls, and none of them had looked back at her; they were either turned in on each other, or looking into the distance, or closely at the walls or the floor. The windows which ran the length of the corridor looked out onto a grey mist behind the house, as if the place were floating inside a gloomy cloud. Some of the windows had been replaced by boards, and cracks ran down the walls; the building itself seemed to be coming apart under the weight of its own anxiety. Nothing was visible in the gloom.

She breathes on her bed. In, out, in, out. Her smoky breath embraces the air. She holds the book she'd taken from Brooke House's surprisingly good library on her belly, her hands crossed above it, and she remembers the passage she's just read.

My own sex, I hope, will excuse me, if I treat them like rational creatures, instead of flattering their fascinating graces, and viewing them as if they were in a state of perpetual childhood, unable to stand alone. I earnestly wish to point out in what true dignity and human happiness consists – I wish to persuade women to endeavour to acquire strength, both of mind and body, and to convince them that the soft phrases, susceptibility of heart, delicacy of sentiment, and refinement of taste, are almost synonymous with epithets of weakness, and that those beings who are only the objects of pity and that kind of love, which has been termed its sister, will soon become objects of contempt.

She falls asleep with the words on her lips – the same words she'd heard the voice speaking to Maria this previous night – but then something pulls her quickly from slumber. The scream is shocking enough. The fact that it comes from a man is even worse. And worst of all is the nature of it.

It is a low, animal sound, full of terror and anger, and it is quickly followed after a few moments by more screams and shouts, which together form a great chorus of despair and fear. It sounds to Abigail, in her confused just-woken state, as if every man is experiencing the same horror at the same time, like apes hurling noise at an unwanted intruder. She stands up from her bed and opens the door of her cell, stepping out into the corridor beyond. The noise is even louder, and she stands for a moment in shock. The noise is as if the building itself has gone mad.

And for a few seconds which seem impossible, as if they must be happening to somebody else entirely, she *feels* the building go mad. A pressure seems to press against her, an unseen force. She thinks of a diagram for a steam engine she'd once seen at some public lecture or another, the Royal Institution no doubt, and the explanation of steam power: the transition from heat to *pressure*, the way water and air could with the addition of heat be turned into a directional force, shoving machines which weighed more than houses into impossible dances. That's what this feels like: as if Brooke House were a gigantic piston, being pushed slowly and deliberately by an emerging compression.

And then, as quickly as it began, that sense of impending explosion falls away and the terrible noise begins to subside. One by one, the men fall quiet. It is only then that Abigail notices that there has not been a single shout or moan from the women on the first floor. The women's rooms are silent, as if they were all empty. All the noise is male, all of it angry and guttural and terrifyingly desolate, as if each and every man were having a limb amputated on some European battlefield.

The silence grows, as stealthy and gradual as the original shouting had been sudden and shocking. Eventually the last man lets out the last shriek, and Brooke House lapses back into the quiet of midnight. That old sense she'd had – of the house breathing in and out – returns, and a calm lays itself out over the place like a warm blanket.

She goes back to lie down on her bed, leaving the book on the floor. She turns onto her side, her customary sleeping position, facing the wall between her cell and Maria's. She hears a small, scratching, half-buried sound, and moves a little closer to the cold wall, turning her head so her ear is pressed against the stonework.

She can hear Maria whispering, sharply and urgently. Over and over again she whispers the same thing, with a sharply hateful bite, as if she were invoking some terrible spirit with the fury of her near-silent chant.

'Tie his wrists and tie his feet, Spill his guts out on the sheet. Tie his wrists and tie his feet, Spill his guts out on the sheet. Tie his wrists and tie his feet, *Spill his guts out on the sheet!*'

WESTMINSTER

The room into which Aaron Graham is shown by the astonished servant cannot be described merely as opulent. If a man
were to dress in the way this room has been dressed, he would
only be doing so to mock what other men were wearing. Even
Graham, dressed today magnificently but not flamboyantly,
finds the room beyond satire.

But this room, being shut away, has no satirical intent; its
splendour is deliberate and intended only for the one who paid
for it, the one who is now sprawled dead on the purple-and-
black four-poster, his torn silk breeches used to tie his hands
and feet to each of those four posts, an ugly satyr's mask covering his face, his entrails pouring out from him as if trying to
escape the terrible scene, flies buzzing and from one corner of
the room the unmistakable smell of human vomit.

Graham takes one look before turning to the door through
which he has just entered and stepping back onto the landing,
where the astonished servant waits along with William Jealous,
a patrolman from Bow Street. Graham has to fight an urge to
slam the door behind him, as if there were stupid demons

prancing around within who could be banished merely by looking away. He knows the vision of the body on the bed will be one more terrible thing living inside his head, another entry in a catalogue of memories he would sooner be rid of. He also knows he must go back in for a second look if he is going to pursue this matter.

The astonished servant – astonished not by the extremities within the bedchamber, but by his perplexing inability to account for those extremities – steps towards Graham and almost touches his arm, showing such sympathy with the magistrate's plight that Graham thinks he can establish whose vomit it is that now blights the infected air of the bedchamber.

'A glass of water, sir?'

'If you please, yes,' says Graham, and uses the time it takes for the water to be fetched to gather himself for a return into the room. He looks at Jealous. The lad is barely twenty years old; Graham only swore him in last month. And yet he looks completely calm.

'Are you quite all right, sir?'

The lad's London vowels are smoothed down, nothing like as harsh as his father's. Graham nods. He realises something: he is more comfortable with the idea of going back into the bedchamber without the manservant here. There is no need of a glass of water; it was a mere diversion operated by some unthinking part of his brain which wanted to be rid of the presence of the servant.

'I shall go back in for another look.'

'Shall I come in with you, sir?'

'If you please, Jealous, yes.'

With a deep breath, he opens the door to the bedchamber, and they go back within. After a few minutes, the manservant returns with the glass of water on a silver tray. The servant is disconcerted by the disappearance of the magistrate and his officer from the landing, and by the closed door which now confronts him. He knocks discreetly on the door, as if his master were alive and capable of answering. There is no answer, and after a few moments the astonished servant, whose life has been taken into strange new regions by the events of the previous evening and of this morning, places the tray with the water upon it on the floor next to the door, and wanders back downstairs.

After several minutes, Graham re-emerges from the room, and Jealous follows. Graham's face is almost as green as his silk waistcoat. He spies the water and the tray on the floor but does not move to pick up the glass. He pulls the door closed behind him, and goes downstairs, ignoring Jealous entirely for the time being.

Graham seats himself on an especially glorious chair upholstered in the finest chiffon at one side of the vestibule below. The astonished servant reappears, and asks if he can fetch the gentlemen anything. He has not yet allowed himself to be overthrown by any of the men who have burst into the superlative Mayfair residence of which he has been the overseer for a decade now. His world may be in the same wrecked state as the innards of his employer, now putrefying upstairs, but his standards will be maintained.

'You discovered the body of your master?' asks Graham.

'Yes, sir.' The manservant stands with his hands behind his back. He is, Graham estimates, in his middle thirties. He is thin, austere, his shocked face pinched by a rehearsed rectitude.

'At what time?'

'Just after eight, sir.'

'You secured the room?'

'Secured, sir?'

'You made the room safe from disturbance by anyone else?'

'I locked the door, sir. Then I came immediately to Bow Street. Finding no one there, I went to the Brown Bear opposite, as I believe is the custom. It was there I found your officer here.'

He speaks as if he were describing parliamentary procedure, rather than an early morning visit to a Covent Garden inn.

'What time did your master return here last night?'

'It was late, sir. I would say two or perhaps three o'clock.'

'He had been out? Do you know where?'

'No, sir.'

'And you locked up the house and windows?'

'I did, sir. The master was always most particular about that. He said there were any number of footpads and rogues roaming the streets, and a gentleman had to look to his own safety.' Something like a blush washes across the servant's face; he has, after all, just indirectly criticised the magistracy and constabulary, in the presence of two of its representatives. Graham starts to find the man's presence irritating.

'Was anyone loitering when you locked up?'

'No, sir. A few whores. That is all.'

'Whores?'

'Yes, sir. We seem to have had an infestation of them in these parts this past year.'

'Any you recognised?'

'Sir?'

The servant looks as if Graham had suddenly started speaking in German.

'Did you notice if any of the whores were familiar?'

'Familiar to *me*, sir?'

'Then no, I take it is the answer. You may go.'

The servant starts to leave, but Jealous speaks up.

'If you please, Mr Graham?'

Graham nods.

'The mask your master was wearing,' asks Jealous. 'Had he worn it before?'

'I confess to never having seen it before.'

'And you have no concept as to what it might imply?'

'None whatsoever.'

Jealous turns to Graham.

'That's it, sir.'

The servant is sent away by Graham, and resolves to stay out of his way for the remainder of the visit.

Aaron Graham does not say anything straightaway. He stands and walks into the drawing room, where a fire has been set though no master lives to have requested it. He gazes into the flames as if dancing in there he might see the writhing, destroyed body of the poor soul upstairs, and it would speak to him. He feels unaccountably lonely, unable to organise his thoughts. *John Harriott should be here. He would bark at the servants and make a nuisance of himself, but his bluster would hide his thinking. Horton too; the two of them would have a complete picture by now.*

He begins to regret sending Horton to Surrey. He sets himself by the fire, and looks up at William Jealous, whom he'd almost forgotten.

'Any orders, sir?'

Graham considers the question. All he can see for now is blood and red satin. And that awful mask, about which he'd entirely forgotten to ask. Thank God the young patrolman had been here to ask it.

'Yes, Jealous. I want you to gather the servants and ask them some questions.'

'Yes, sir?'

The boy is keen, interested. Graham remembers his father, Charles Jealous. One of the original Bow Street Runners, and one of the most effective, almost a fixed feature at the Old

Bailey. He was in Windsor now, one of several ex-Runners who protected the safety of the Royal Family. Now here was his son, working in the same line, still only a patrolman but already an obvious candidate to be a Principal Officer. Graham thinks of his own son, just made post-captain. This boy looks bright and alert. Perhaps he should introduce him to Horton.

'You know what to ask, Jealous. You just asked yourself. What time Wodehouse returned last night, whether he was wearing that mask when he did, what it might signify.'

'Yes, sir.'

'Also, this matter of whores in the street. Is that a pattern the other servants recognise? I confess, I had not heard that whores were a particular problem on this street.'

'Yes, sir. Anything else?'

The drawing room is longer than any drawing room has a right to be, with six tall arched windows looking out onto Bruton Street. The house, Graham knows, takes up three times as much room as any other of the wealthy properties on the street, but even so its stupendous dimensions amaze him. He finds the self-indulgence rather disgusting; Graham is a self-made man, one who has survived on his own wits and intelligence, and seeing the sumptuousness with which this house garlands itself makes him irritated and rather unwell.

He forces himself to take in the room. His attention is drawn to a scene in a painting on the far wall, facing the door through which he entered. At first he is unable to make out what the scene is, but then with disgust he recognises *Leda and the Swan*, although in this particularly gaudy representation the swan has been given a human face, as well as a crazily engorged phallus, and the face is that of the owner of the house, and the former occupant of the eviscerated vessel upstairs, Edmund Wodehouse, Esq. He turns away from the painting with the same disgust as he might reject an unfashionable cravat from his tailor.

Aaron Graham is known across town for his bonhomie, his charm and his facility with all matters social and sartorial. He is a charming dining companion, a learned travelling companion and a discreetly solid drinking companion. But misery now informs Graham's posture, his expression, even the gaiety of his clothes. His cream tailcoat seems to have no sheen and no joy, and the hat he spins around between his immaculately maintained fingers looks more like a lump of Welsh rock than the latest wonder from his Jermyn Street milliner.

Graham can't even recall the servant's name. How does Horton keep his composure at such times? How can he be so careful in collecting evidence? Graham has seen a good many dead bodies in his time, but the devilish horror of that figure upstairs has, for the moment, temporarily unmoored him.

Jealous is still waiting.

'Yes. I want to know who visits this house. I want to know who his friends were. Now get to it, Jealous. I'll wait for you in here.'

'Yes, sir.'

Jealous departs. Helplessly, Graham's eyes are drawn back to that awful painting.

THORPE

The servants, who had hidden from him the previous day, are brazen in their presence when Horton emerges the following morning. Mrs Graham, though, is nowhere to be seen – 'missus has taken to her bed today, very tired she is,' says Mrs Chesterton the housekeeper, a short bustling creature with a head and body so spherical she looks like a preliminary sketch for a Hogarth caricature. Horton asks if it was she whom he had heard the previous night talking to Mrs Graham in the drawing room. The housekeeper confirms it was with some reluctance and ill-hidden irritation, as if Horton had been spying on the house in its fitful, noisy slumbers. Which, he supposes, he had been.

Mrs Chesterton is one of Thorpe Lee House's seven servants. They have come out into the new day like mice creeping out after the death of a cat. But there is no bustling order to the house as it wakes up; tasks are gone about with indifference. Horton searches the faces of the staff for signs of sleeplessness when he talks to them, but all he sees is a kind of mild defiance in the younger ones, and a puzzled dislike in the older, as if he carries with him a slightly unpleasant smell. And yet last night they had dreamed noisily and restlessly.

Horton finds himself wondering what the staff's ramshackle appearance says about the state of Sir Henry's finances. From his first view of the gardens the previous day, he has been struck by how the appearance of the house itself teeters on the edge of respectability, just as the domestic arrangements of Sir Henry and Mrs Graham teeter beyond the edge of social convention. Abigail would have been as scandalised by the dust as by the relations between the master and mistress of the house, and the food Horton had been served at dinner and then at breakfast was both cold and unappetising.

There is also something pointed about the way the servants talk about Mrs Graham. It is an amalgam of contempt and anxiety. This is personified by the butler, Crowley, who gives as little away on the second day of Horton's acquaintance as he did on the first. Horton speaks to him in the library. The man refuses to sit, despite Horton's entreaties, and remains upright with a wall of books rising behind him. He sweats profusely, despite the lack of flesh on his poorly dressed bones, and his bald head shines and drips like a crystal ball smothered in hot wax.

'How long have you been in Sir Henry's service?'

'Coming up to ten years, Mr Constable.'

Crowley has settled on this appellation for Horton, who has let it pass.

'And Sir Henry has lived in Thorpe Lee House for how long?'

'About the same amount of time, Mr Constable. Before that, Herefordshire.'

'Ah, yes, Herefordshire. Where I understand his wife hails from. It is she who supplied his fortune, yes?'

'So people say, Mr Constable. I do not know nor have any view on the matter.'

'And where is Lady Tempest now?'

'I cannot say, sir.'

'She is still alive?'

'It is not my place to comment on such matters.'

'Well, then, Crowley. Can you comment on the events that have alarmed Mrs Graham?'

'Events, sir?'

A sly look of defiance creeps over Crowley's thin face. It is an expression Horton will come to recognise and despise as the day unfolds. Mrs Graham's name sparks a sour response.

'Yes. The events which have culminated in the illness of Miss Tempest Graham.'

'I don't quite understand the events you speak of. Perhaps you could be clearer about your question, Mr Constable?'

'Well, perhaps this will make it clearer. Do you believe Thorpe Lee House is bewitched?'

'No, sir. I don't be holding with that.'

The man looks offended, as if Horton had accused him of being a Roman Catholic.

'But you must agree there have been unusual occurrences?'

'Aye, there were, sir. August was particularly bad, of course. But there's been nothing for a while now. Not since we got rid of the cook.'

'You think all the events were her doing?'

'Stands to reason, I think, Mr Constable. We found instruments of mischief in her kitchen. She left. The mischief ended.'

'Well, not quite. Miss Tempest Graham fell ill after the cook left, did she not?'

'Oh. Aye. She did. But that's just females, ain't it?'

'In what way?'

'Well, they react in different ways, do they not? Hysterical, some of them get. Some of them get ill. Some of them do lunatic things.'

'What kind of lunatic things?'

'Well, smashing looking-glasses. That'd be lunatic, wouldn't it?'

There is nothing sly in Crowley's face now. He knows he has said something he shouldn't, because he sees the surprise in Horton's face.

'Who smashed their looking-glasses?'

'Well, no one. I was speaking hypothetically, like.'

'Listen to me, Crowley. This is an important matter, and I am perfectly capable of bringing a charge against you, if I am not given the help I need.'

This, Horton knows, is almost certainly untrue, but it works with Crowley. Like most people, he has never been threatened with such a sanction before.

'Someone smashed the lady's looking-glasses.'

'Mrs Graham's?'

'Yes. Every one of them.'

'When?'

'Few days after Miss Ellen fell ill. Perhaps a week ago.'

'And who do you suspect of doing such a thing?'

'I don't suspect anyone, Mr Constable.'

'Could someone have got into the house?'

'Of course, that's possible, Mr Constable.'

'What time of day did this happen?'

'We cannot say. Mrs Graham discovered them just before dinner.'

'She was upset?'

'Wouldn't you be? And I'll tell you this: broken mirrors make for bloody insane women. Bad luck, they all said. Weeping and wailing and gibbering. They wouldn't go anywhere near the glass, neither. Guess who had to clear that lot up?'

Horton ignores the complaining tone in Crowley's voice, and wonders why the broken looking-glasses do not appear on Mrs Graham's list of the miseries experienced by Thorpe Lee House.

Working his way down the list of staff, Horton speaks to the housekeeper Mrs Chesterton ('widder, sir, I was barely married two minutes when the Lord took my Jack from me'), who weeps profusely when she tells Horton of the matters which have taken place, particularly when she speaks of 'the poor hounds' which had been slaughtered.

'Lor', that sent the mistress into a proper frenzy,' says Mrs Chesterton. 'Right disturbed, she was.'

'The dogs were definitely killed? There was no chance that they attacked each other?'

'Well, they might've. But I don't believe that. The bitch killed 'em, didn't she?'

'The bitch?'

'Cook. The one 'oo was sacked. She done it all. Stands to reason, don't it? She wrote those nasty bloody words on my cupboard, 'n' all. Bitch. Devil's bitch.'

Horton is taken aback by the spite in Mrs Chesterton's words. She looks like she might happily snap the neck of Elizabeth Hook, if she were in the same room as them.

'Why is it so obvious to you that Elizabeth Hook did these things?'

'Well, it all stopped after she left, didn't it?'

'Not quite. Miss Tempest Graham fell ill a good few days afterwards. And the looking-glasses . . .'

'Oh, don't remind me of *that*, sir.'

There is no reasoning with Mrs Chesterton. For her, the

sacked cook is at the root of every evil which has befallen the house. The narrative is fixed in her mind. Though Horton notes that neither she, nor Crowley, nor Mrs Graham seem able to understand *why* Elizabeth Hook should indulge in such matters. Crowley seems to be able to hold two opposing ideas at the same time: that Hook is causing mischief to happen, and that there is no such thing as bewitchment.

The lady's maid is a thin, ugly Yorkshire girl who gives her name, incongruously, as Béatrice. She pronounces the word with deliberate emphasis and care, as if she has been schooled in it.

'It's a French name, thou know'st,' she says in her strong northern accent, and Horton acknowledges that this is so before asking her about the house's mishaps. She lists the events already given by the butler and the housekeeper, leaving out the mirrors. When Horton raises this, she looks horrified.

'I am shocked that Mr Crowley would reveal such a thing,' she says, her small eyes opened wide. 'It is a private matter for Mrs Graham, surely?'

'But it happened, did it not?'

'Why, yes, but I assumed . . .' And she stops at that.

'Assumed what, Béatrice?'

'Well, that the mistress had done it herself.'

'Why would she do that?'

'I cannot imagine. But she is not a happy woman, sir.'

'She is not?'

'No, sir. She weeps a great deal. And she is terribly afraid for her daughter.'

'Afraid of what?'

'I cannot say. For me, I think Miss Ellen is a strong girl, and she will overcome whatever ails her.'

'You mean the illness?'

'Yes, sir. You must know what I mean.'

'I'm not sure I do. Is there something more than illness?'

She crosses her arms and draws her mouth into a thin little line and refuses to say anything else at all. Horton does not pursue it; he has no authority to (after all, no felony has yet been committed), and he believes he will be able to talk further to her.

The footman, a lad called Peter Gowing, comes in with the scullery maid, Daisy Webster, and although they sit apart Horton can see that the girl, in particular, is desperate to reach out and hold the boy's hand. Gowing stares fiercely at her whenever she speaks, and even more fiercely at Horton whenever he asks a question, as if he might stand and strike out at anything he perceives as a threat.

The girl acknowledges that all the events described by the other servants – the cows, the dogs, the lawn, the shed, the mirrors – had taken place as described. She becomes particularly agitated when talking about the dead rat in the dining room.

'It was *enormous*, sir. Such a terrible, awful thing. I see it in my dreams, every night. '

'You must have had rats before.'

'Oh, but not like this. We get the occasional one that shows its face, and we have to make sure the cupboards are closed tight at night. Mice, too. But you don't often see these creatures; they're shy, and I don't imagine there's that many of them. So it were proper horrible to see such a monster. And how *malicious* to leave it like that, where she knew I'd see it? I didn't sleep for days, did I?'

This to Peter Gowing, who frowns at her inadvertent revelation, and turns his now-bright-red face to Horton's, daring him to ask. Horton, though, can see all he needs to know.

'And what about Mrs Graham's mirrors? Did you see them?'

'No, sir,' the girl begins, but the boy interrupts.

'They was in her chambers, wasn't they? We're not allowed in there. Only Jane gets in there.'

'Jane?'

'The lady's maid.'

'You mean Béatrice.'

The boy smirks.

'Oh, she calls herself that because the mistress tells her to call herself that. Quite the fashion, French maids, ain't they? But in short supply these days, what with us having been fighting their fellas in Spain and France. Doubtless they'll be flooding over here now it's all over.'

The boy's implication – that Mrs Graham is a somewhat desperate follower of fashion – is clear.

'So her name is Jane?'

'Of course her name is Jane. She's about as French as I am.'

'And she's the only one allowed in Mrs Graham's chambers?'

'Well, apart from Sir Henry.'

'Peter!' This from the maid, who is amazed at her beau's indiscretion. Peter for his part grins and blushes at the same time. The grin is wiped away by Horton's asking about the witch-bottle.

'Witch-bottle?' he says. Daisy looks at her hands, and sniffs defiantly.

Horton says nothing. He doesn't have to wait long, but it is Daisy, not Peter, who breaks the silence first.

'Something needed to be done,' she says, and glares at Horton as if he himself were a consort of the Dark One. 'No one was doing anything at all, and I knew how to deal with such matters. We had a witch of our own, see, back home. You take some of their *piss*, their witch's *piss*, and you put it in a bottle with some hair from her head and you bury it in the woods. So we did. It was my idea. Not Peter's. So if I'm in trouble, it's on my head, not his. Understand?'

During this little speech, Peter leans over to her and tries to place a placating hand on her arm, but she constantly slaps it away, glaring at him as if he were an annoying child.

'And it bloody *worked*, didn't it? It bloody *did*. She got ill, she did. Stomach pains, just like the cunning-man back home said there'd be. Shooting, stinging pains in her stinking witch's belly. And that's when people started seeing her, for the first time, for what she was. But I knew. I knew *all the time*.'

Horton sees there is little point continuing. She is rampant in her determined belief that a witch has been defeated. She is almost exultant. He dismisses them.

The gardener, O'Reilly, limps in next, wincing as he walks, supported by a wooden crutch under his arm. He smells of dung and has a thick rural accent which might be Somerset or Suffolk, but Horton understands enough to confirm the main points about the shed and the dogs. It is he who has dug up the lawn.

'Hag track,' he said. 'Witches on bloody lawn.'

'You've seen such things before?'

'Oh, aye. They dance, don't they? Dance on my bloody lawn. Ruined, it was. Bloody ruined.'

'So, there's more than one witch?'

'Oh, aye. *Always* more 'n one, in't there? That Hook was a bad 'un, she was. Took me in. Liked her, I did. But didn't know her *true nature*, did I? Bitch.'

Finally, the cook, who to Horton's surprise is a man, quite a young man, named Stephen Moore. There is something rather clerical about him. He is precise and quiet.

'Where did you work before here?'

'I worked for Sir Francis Vincent, constable.'

'Is that far from here?'

'It is in Surrey. Stoke d'Abernon.'

'And how did you come to this role so soon after the departure of the previous cook?'

'I understood there had been some dissatisfaction with the woman's performance for some time. One hears these things, even from far away. I wrote to Mrs Graham to offer my services.'

'Is that the normal way of these matters?'

'I couldn't say, constable. It is my way. I have always approached my employers directly.'

'Is it not unusual for a cook in a house such as this to be a man?'

'Perhaps. Though not unprecedented.'

'Sir Francis was happy for you to leave?'

'I doubt he even noticed. He is not yet ten years old. The estate is run by his mother, Dame Mary.'

Horton, no student of the peerage, nonetheless feels Moore's smooth condescension, and it irritates him. And yet this young man is the most intriguing person he has met so far. He is soft-spoken but articulate and, it would seem, well educated. He dresses like a City clerk rather than a provincial cook, and carries with him a ledger – 'I was working on the accounts when summoned to see you, and I don't like to leave them lying around.'

Moore confirms the stories already told, and speaks with unusual warmth – unusual among the other servants – about Mrs Graham.

'It is a pleasure to work for such an intelligent woman,' he says. 'It is not always the case that a woman in her position is so clear and so understanding.'

'What do you mean, "in her position"?'

'Well, I think perhaps it is obvious. She is a wife living under

the roof of a man other than her husband. In those circumstances she runs a formidably well-disciplined household.'

'And yet in recent weeks things have become shakier.'

'Well, perhaps. Though as I have said to her, sorrows such
as these do always seem to accompany each other.'

'You speak to Mrs Graham often?'

'Moderately often, yes. She likes to come down to the
kitchen and discuss matters with me on occasion.'

'And what of Sir Henry? Is he as approachable an
employer?'

'Oh, Sir Henry is cut from unique cloth. I am told he is
fierce and quick to anger, but he is also full of life. But I have
not met the gentleman yet. He has not been here since my
arrival. I am sure his company will be a pleasure.'

He speaks like a politician. Which, for Charles Horton, is
just another word for liar.

A Treatise on Moral Projection

I had experienced nothing like that awful night in my then-short career as a physician. The great asylum of Bethlem, where I had begun my training, was constantly full of the moans and cries of the mad. It echoed with their misery and their complaints, but such was its common state. If it had become suddenly silent the effect might have been as shocking as those awful screams at Brooke House. But I cannot recall such an event ever taking place.

We could find no explanation for the disturbances. On my rounds the following morning, a strange mystery presented itself. I asked each and every male inmate of the hospital what had caused them to shriek so the previous eve, but not a single one of them could remember having made such noises. And there was no guile in their denials; each and every one of them was sorely perplexed by my question. It was as if they had been dreaming, and had (as I have noted often) forgotten the detail of what they had dreamed.

I recall an air of mystery settling itself upon the place. I remember Dr Monro visited us that day, as was his wont once or twice a week, and I told him of what had occurred. He could provide no explanation.

It was while all this was taking place that Mrs Horton

came to see me. Her presence was by no means unwelcome. She had, as I have said, been one of the more interesting inmates of Brooke House, what with her obvious natural intelligence and her more traditional womanly charms. Her dreams plagued her sorely, despite the separation from her husband and her diurnal life, but she did not come to see me for that reason. She told me she had become interested in Maria Cranfield.

I had some suspicion of her motives, of course; had she not already claimed that she'd heard another woman's voice from Maria's cell? She admitted that this must have been only another manifestation of her unquiet mind, and accepted my diagnosis of it as such. But she felt that spending time with Maria would help both her and that poor girl, who was still secured in a strait waistcoat.

With my permission, a chair was placed in Maria's cell, and she sat with her that whole day following the disturbances. She read to her, especially from that volume of Wollstonecraft she had secured from the Brooke House library. I was astonished that such a volume was made available to residents, and while I applauded Mrs Horton's intent in reading to Maria I was somewhat dismayed at her choice of material. After our meeting I quietly made arrangements for the removal of that particular volume from the house's library, at such a time when Mrs Horton was finished with it.

I confess, as I write these words, that my blessing for this new arrangement may be seen as a mistake. The events to come may have been very different – indeed, may not have occurred at all – if I had not permitted these two women to spend time together. Yet I trusted and admired Mrs Horton – and she used this trust against me. I will say only this. As the storm gathered and the terrible events unfolded, I learned a hard lesson: one must never trust a patient. Particularly if the patient is a woman.

WESTMINSTER

It is dangerous, Aaron Graham sees, this feeling of being pulled into a mystery. He has seen it happen to other men, notably John Harriott, his great friend and the magistrate in Wapping, who when he is well is unable to let go of a mystery lest it escape and turn into something else, something that hides itself and festers. That is the feeling he has now: of something awful and half-seen that must be identified.

But then, this is why he joined Bow Street. Old Sir John Fielding, the progenitor of much of what Bow Street now undertakes, had been as bulldog-determined as John Harriott, his blindness by no means disrupting his ability to perceive. But Fielding's *métier* had been the felony of the highwayman and the footpad. He had taken Property as his ward, and had protected her against all villains, be they pickpockets or coiners.

Murder, though, is something else entirely. It is not common for London gentlemen to be murdered in their beds. It is not common for London gentlemen to be eviscerated with no apparent motivation. It is not common for dead bodies to be left in their beds wearing masks. It is not common for all this to have been done with no noise being made, or in any case not enough noise to wake a single household servant.

Those four things are what constitute this mystery, and it is of a very different flavour to that with which Sir John Fielding would have involved himself. Graham throws himself into the heart of it with the full knowledge that this will lead to questions being asked, both by his fellow Bow Street magistrates and perhaps even by the Home Secretary. He is an old man now, semi-retired and only an occasional presence at Bow Street. He no longer sits in the court to hear of the previous night's arrests and charges from the constables and watchmen of the surrounding parishes, and to question those accused. It is by no means unusual for an individual justice of a certain vintage to interest himself in a case, and indeed Graham has been asked more than once by previous Home Secretaries to involve himself in particularly sticky cases, most notably the Ratcliffe Highway killings of 1811. But this case is different. Wodehouse was a gentleman, and the newspapers will no doubt interest themselves in his death, not least because of its melodramatic nature. The Home Secretary may feel that a younger man is needed.

But what indeed would Sir John Fielding have done, in this case? A gentleman has been viciously killed. There is no suspect. There has been, as far as can be ascertained, no theft of property. Wodehouse's chattels will remain within Wodehouse's family. Only his soul has been taken, and what price is a man's soul? If the friends and family do not take it upon themselves to prosecute the case, it is left to the magistrates and their officers. Thus, is he not doing his duty?

And is it not damnably *interesting?*

He decides to proceed and see what transpires. He spends the day learning what he can of Edmund Wodehouse. He is – or rather he was – the third son of Baron Wodehouse of Kimberley in Norfolk. He was born in 1776, making him almost forty at the time of his despatch. No wife, no children, the usual distinguished-yet-disgusting troop of friends and associates. A member, indeed, of one of Graham's own clubs, White's – though Graham is one of those rare London men to hold membership of both White's and Brooks's, disguising his own mildly Tory views in the name of maintaining irreproachable relations with as wide a circle as possible. And it is to that circle he now turns – he would learn more of Edmund Wodehouse, Esq.

Thus, he takes residence for most of the day at White's, talking to as many of the men there as he can politely manage. The news of Wodehouse's death has circulated within the place like blood around the body, and its source is Graham himself. He plants little ingots of fact with various gentlemen, and these are passed around the building like letters between ambassadors. Despite the discombobulating horror of the morning, by the afternoon he finds himself to have learned a good deal more than he might have expected. Unsurprisingly, given the nature of that disgusting painting in the drawing room of Wodehouse's lodging, there is a good whiff of Scandal in the air.

Brummell himself sums it up, waving airily from his table in the bow-window of the club, reserved for years for the most influential and well-connected members. 'Wodehouse? Terrible fellow, terrible friends. But of course, *you* know, Graham.'

This with an elegant wink and the suggestion of a leer. He does know. Of course he knows. For it becomes clear very early in the day that one of Wodehouse's closest friends was Sir Henry Tempest. This one relationship infects every simpering conversation Graham has for the rest of the day, curdling any enjoyment he might have taken in the afternoon. Everyone knows of Sir Henry Tempest's domestic arrangements and how they have impinged on Aaron Graham's. He of course knows how general this knowledge is, and is inured to it. It has been almost three years now, after all. But for this lamentable history to now overlap with the blood-drenched sheets of Edmund Wodehouse is both intolerable and, he must admit, enticing.

The satyr's mask is identified early on in his investigations.

'Ah, the Sybarites,' an elderly baron tells him. 'They wear such masks to their parties, as I understand it.'

He has never heard the name, but a dozen different men allude to the existence of the society. All of them wrinkle their noses in distaste. Some of the more ancient members of White's are old enough to remember Sir Francis Dashwood's Medmenham friars, and many are strangely enthusiastic about gorging themselves once again on stories of devilish parties by firelight in abandoned churches, of despoiled virgins and rumoured sacrifice. Some of the younger members who mention the Sybarites talk of the Medmenhamites as if they were Homeric heroes or even gods, Olympian beings from an older, better time. Byron, it is rumoured, had held devil-worshipping parties in Newstead Abbey, in deliberate homage to Dashwood. There is still talk of Sybaritic meetings taking place in caves beneath the hills of West Wycombe.

The ones old enough to have known Medmenhamites personally (some of them, it occurs to Graham, old enough to have been Medmenhamites themselves) adopt a disappointed air when talking of Dashwood and his circle. 'Selfish men with too much appetite and too little discipline,' says one, and Graham is not sure if he is speaking of Sybarites or Medmenhamites or the members of White's.

Various names are mentioned with regard to this society of

Sybarites: Sir Henry is one, as is Sir John Cope, who is neither a member of White's nor any other club the gentlemen Graham speaks to can recall. 'If Cope was made a member, I would resign forthwith,' says an elderly baronet. His young son smirks at this, and winks at Graham, as if to suggest that Cope might be a scoundrel, but he is also a reliable guide to the source of the brightest entertainments.

Graham does not return to Bow Street from White's until the late afternoon. Several cards have been left for him. Two newspaper correspondents have called at the office, one from the *Times* and one from the *Chronicle*. He will not speak to them – he never does – but it forces him to steel himself for the next day's papers, and for questions from the Home Secretary. A letter has arrived from the doctor at Brooke House, with an update on the progress of Abigail Horton. He reads this immediately, imagining the slightly hysterical little man, Bryson, whose manner is both ingratiating and annoying. The letter is unclear, written hurriedly and apparently without purpose – a cursory update by an uninterested functionary. Its existence worries Graham more than any of its content. Why write at all? He makes a note to visit Brooke House when he can, and perhaps even to consider placing Abigail in another institution – the Hoxton madhouse, perhaps, of which he has heard good things.

There is no news from Abigail's husband, Charles Horton, but it is still early for any reliable information to have emerged. If indeed anything reliable can be perceived within stories of bewitchment and evildoers.

But Horton's presence in Thorpe Lee House has now taken on a different aspect, one that has been apparent to Graham ever since the first elderly gentleman at White's had drawn a connection between Wodehouse and Sir Henry Tempest. In the same week that he has despatched an officer to the country residence of Sir Henry, one of that gentleman's friends has been cut to pieces in his own bed. Horton, it would seem, has inserted himself into another dark metropolitan story, alongside Graham. He notes, somewhat grimly, that the two of them are doomed to be conjoined in such circumstances.

He scribbles a quick letter to be sent to Horton at Thorpe Lee House, asking for information and tasking the constable with speaking to Sir Henry about Wodehouse and the Sybarites. He knows Horton is likely to be lashed by the sharpness of Sir Henry's tongue when the matter is raised, and his relief at not having to raise it himself does him little credit. He takes the letter to Bow Street's Conductor of Pursuits and Patrols, and asks that one of the mounted patrol take the letter directly to Thorpe the next morning.

The light outside is fading. Thinking of Horton in Surrey has injected a new urgency into him. He will visit Sir John Cope immediately.

THORPE

Sir Henry's dogs are kept a good way from Thorpe Lee House for reasons of noise, but still they can be heard barking sporadically from the house, as if a hunt were passing by in the woods behind. Horton asks directions from a tired-looking Mrs Chesterton, who shows him where to go from the kitchen door at the back of the house.

'Are you quite well, Mrs Chesterton?' Horton asks before he leaves. The woman's eyes have heavy bags underneath them. The day has caught up with her.

'Bad night, dear,' she says, the *dear* tacked on with some exhaustion, as if she's forgotten quite who he is. 'All these awful things as have been happening. It's a wonder any of us sleep at all.'

She walks back into the kitchen, closing the door against the September chill.

The kennels are hidden from the house, across the lawn and through a ribbon of ash trees. The structure resounds with howls and barks as Horton comes within fifty yards of it; the noise is sudden and enormous, as if the dogs had been waiting for him. The old gardener, O'Reilly, is limping around to no immediately apparent purpose, but the chorus of barks alerts him to Horton's approach. He stands and watches the constable. The cacophony behind him becomes more feverish; Horton wonders how many dogs Sir Henry has in this place, and this is the first question he puts to the gardener.

'Two dozen,' O'Reilly says. 'Leastways, that's what it was. Twenty-two now.' He, like Mrs Chesterton, seems suddenly exhausted.

'That seems an extraordinary number of dogs,' says Horton.

'Do it? No sense of that, for meself.'

'Would they attack me?'

'Them? Nah, they's friendly. Noisy buggers but friendly. If you war a fox, now. That'd be different.'

'They're kept in there day and night?'

'Aye. I lets 'em out to run around twice a day.'

'Shall we let them out now?'

'Aye.'

The gardener takes a key from his pocket and unlocks the door of the big shed.

'You always lock it?'

'Oh, aye. Sir Henry's very particular 'bout that. Says he's heard as others have had their dogs snatched. We keep a close eye on 'em.'

He opens the door, and a barking, jumping stream of dog bursts from the shed, sniffing round the gardener's damaged foot, running up to Horton and investigating before swirling out onto the grass. The smell of the dogs is rich and, to Horton, unusual. As a city man and a sailor, he is not used to dogs, though he likes them and is comfortable around them. He puts down his hand to allow some curious hounds to sniff, and pats the occasional panting head.

'Tell me about the night the two dogs were killed, O'Reilly.'

The gardener is watching the animals run and fight and shit, and sniffs sadly.

'Found 'em out on the lawn in front of the house. Morning, it was. Early morning. I'm usually first one up. They'd been left dead. Throats cut.'

'So it had happened the previous night?'

'Reckon so.'

'And the dogs had been locked up? The shed was still closed?'

'Aye. All locked up.'

'No one heard anything?'

'No. I don't live in the house, but those as does said they didn't hear nothing at all.'

'Where do you live?'

'Cottage over yonder.' He indicates towards the tree-line, unhelpfully. 'I didn't hear nothin', neither.'

'But the dogs would have had to be taken out of the shed.'

'But that couldn't have happened; no one heard anythin', and you've seen the noise they put up. Maybe those dogs didn't get back in when I let 'em run about. Maybe those two ran off somewhere, and was killed and brought back here.'

'It's possible.'

'Only explanation, to my thinkin'.'

The old gardener sniffs again and wipes his cheek. He considers the deaths to be his fault, Horton can see.

'Did you bury the dogs?'

'Nah. Burned 'em. No good buryin' dogs round 'ere. Some fox will dig 'em up. Vengeful little buggers, they is.'

A small white-and-grey hound runs up to them and barks at the gardener, who strokes its head as it stands up on its hind legs and paws his thigh.

'What happened when you hurt your foot?' asks Horton.

The gardener looks at him, and Horton sees a flicker of anxiety in his eyes.

'What do you mean, what happened? Was an accident, is all.'

'What kind of accident?'

'Was digging, wasn't I? Put the shovel into my foot. Hurt like bloody buggery.'

'Have you had that kind of accident before, O'Reilly?'

'Why no, of course not. I'd have no bloody toes left, would I?'

'So did something distract you? Did you take your mind off what you were doing?'

The gardener starts shouting at the dogs, shaking his head.

'Come on, now! Come back here! Come on, you buggers!'

The dogs start to come back. *Not much of a play for them*, thinks Horton.

'O'Reilly,' he says, having to raise his voice over the growing noise of the dogs again. 'Something distracted you, didn't it?'

'I can't say. Wouldn't be right.'

'O'Reilly, if you saw something, you have to say. This is already a matter for magistrates, O'Reilly. There could be trouble, for you.'

Again, this is probably untrue, but O'Reilly wants to say something, and Horton is determined to midwife it, however difficult it turns out to be.

'Thing is, I don't even know why I was out there.'

'Out where?'

'In the garden. It was bloody well dark.'

'It was night?'

'Aye, it was. It was like I found myself out there. Diggin' up a bloody flower bed.'

Or, thinks Horton, a fairy ring. What had the gardener called it? *Hag track.*

''Twas like I'd been dreamin' and walked in my dream. Thought I was dreamin'. Thought that was the only explanation.'

'Explanation for what?'

'For Miss Ellen bein' there.'

'Miss Ellen?'

'Aye.'

The old man pulls an ancient dirty rag from an ancient dirty pocket and wipes his ancient dirty nose, to no perceivable effect. He looks into the trees.

'In there. She was in there. In the trees.'

'In the middle of the night?'

'Aye, she was.'

'What was she doing?'

'She warn't doing nothing. She was just standin' there, lookin' at me.'

'Did she speak?'

'Not to my recollection, no.'

'Has this happened before?'

The old man frowns, his eyes looking into the trees, as if his memories could be discovered in there among the fallen leaves.

'Not that I can remember, no.'

After lunch Horton walks into Thorpe village to meet with the local vicar. Walking has long been his spur for thinking, and this is a considerable distance, though with rather less to see than the Wapping streets he is used to. He realises as he walks that his eyes and attention are normally occupied by people – what they are doing, who they are talking to, whether they are happy or sad or sullen or angry or afraid. It is in the faces of people that Horton reads the story of his own neighbourhood.

But there are no people at all on today's walk. Thorpe Lee

House and its neighbour (called, mystifyingly and confusingly, Thorpe Lee) are perhaps a mile from the village of Thorpe proper, across the same flat and swampy fields Horton saw on his carriage ride the previous day.

He tries to ponder what the servants told him. His brain is tired; he had slept little the previous night, and not just because of the moans and groans of the oddly haunted residents. He has not slept through the night since Abigail departed, almost a month ago. The sleep he does find is fitful and broken and unsatisfying, and his dreams are of the same nature as his daytime thoughts: random, disconnected, without pattern. Formerly he had been used to pondering on cases in a strange double-minded way. One part of his mind would churn through the information he had acquired, while the other part watched it, seeking out patterns but also monitoring the world around, in touch with its surroundings while its counterpart worried away at facts and evidence like a natural philosopher watching a dying bird in a jar.

But he is even more tired than usual today. He wonders if this, perhaps, lies behind the odd neglect of Thorpe Lee House. Perhaps the servants are exhausted, and if O'Reilly's tale turns out to be true – of Miss Ellen's night-time walks in the woods – perhaps Sir Henry's strange family are tired, as well. O'Reilly's tale is odd, no doubt, but the oddity has no edge to it, is dull and inconsequential, as if it doesn't have the energy to present itself fully.

Thorpe village is a charming place, but to Horton's eyes still strangely devoid of people. Its old redbrick houses, many of them of quite old construction, cluster around a crossroads. A substantial residence, Thorpe House (the naming of houses here is sturdily unimaginative), occupies the north side of the village, behind an opulent red wall which is entirely different in its random curves to the stark commercial walls Horton has become used to in Wapping. The red brick of the houses is matched by the quickening redness of the tree leaves, such that the whole place looks like it is fired from within.

The church, St Mary's, stands some way back from a road alongside this wall, within another cluster of houses and against a bank of trees. Its graveyard is on three sides, the front guarded by an enormous oak. The church looks very old and in places in need of repair; its tower, like all the houses of Thorpe, is made of red brick, and covered in thick ivy. Horton goes inside, but there is nobody there.

Coming out again, he spies another large house nearby, which through a sequence of paths and fencing suggests a kinship with the church. He walks up to the door. His knock is answered immediately by a man dressed all in black, his wispy hair hardly covering his grey scalp. He smiles at his visitor, and his mouth is almost devoid of any teeth.

'Would this be the residence of the vicar of St Mary's?' asks Horton. The man is a butler or steward, he assumes. The local vicar certainly puts on airs.

'It would be.'

'I wonder if I might trouble him for a word or two. My name is Horton. I have been asked by Mrs Graham up at Thorpe Lee House to investigate several incidents up—'

'Oh, you mean the witch. Come in, come in.'

He steps aside, and Horton, somewhat surprised, is let into the house, which is grander than he might have expected for a country vicar.

The Reverend John Leigh-Bennett soon makes an appearance in the drawing room, where Horton waits no more than three or four minutes. He is a genial fellow, dressed in the austere fashion of a country cleric but with a confident air of entitlement. He asks Horton if he'd like some tea and the butler, who comes in with him, leaves to arrange it. He sits opposite Horton in a fine old chair. The room is full of books, and a desk is covered with ledgers and loose papers.

'So Mrs Graham remains adamant about witchcraft?' Leigh-Bennett asks, his eyes twinkling with good humour.

'She has spoken to you of it?'

'Oh, of course. Mrs Graham speaks to me a great deal. And her poor daughter is rarely away from here.'

'Miss Graham?'

'Miss *Tempest* Graham, as I understand we should call her.'

This with a twinkle of good fellowship.

'I have not made her acquaintance,' says Horton. 'She is by all accounts an interesting young woman.'

'That she is, that she is. Very clever, very forthright. Somewhat too clever for her own good, one might say. Now, Mrs Graham did ask me to attend the house. She claimed witchcraft. I pointed out that, officially, witchcraft does not exist, as you yourself know.'

'I do?'

'Well, I had assumed. I am referring to the Act of the last century by which it became illegal to accuse anyone of being a witch. So, as a law-abiding servant of the Church of England in a small parish where, shall we say, superstitious beliefs endure, what was I to do?'

'The villagers still believe in witchcraft?'

'You do live in London, I take it, Mr Horton?'

'I do.'

'Do people not believe in witches in London?'

'Well, I . . . I must admit, I have little idea if they do or they do not.'

'Well, they do in the country. They believe in witches and fairies, in spiritualists and fortune-tellers, in cunning-folk and sorcerers. It's a day-to-day fact of life to them. And I, needless to say, am not to approve of these beliefs.'

'You sound as if you would be minded to believe yourself.'

The vicar sits back in his chair and, pursing his lips, looks hard and long at Horton. His eyes are clear and sharp, and do not shift from regarding him, such that Horton feels forced to look away. He remembers Abigail, and how she chides him often for staring at her, 'as if I were a mouse about to sprout wings'.

'A sailor, Mr Horton. That's it. You were a sailor.'

Horton looks at him sharply.

'There is no mystery about it, Horton. I have known a great many sailors. Captain Hardy himself lives nearby. And I know that once a man has spent more than a few months onboard a ship, it changes his appearance. And, I have observed, it changes his beliefs.'

He leans forward, and almost chuckles.

'Sailors are a big rattle-bag of superstitions and beliefs, are they not? Albatrosses. Umbrellas and playing cards. Leaving port on a Friday. A left-handed captain. Whistling on the quarter-deck. Do you believe in any of these? No, I see you do not. But I see you twitch slightly at some of them. The memory of their power is ingrained, is it not? So it is with witchcraft.'

'But someone is causing things to happen at Thorpe Lee House.'

'You believe that, do you? Well, perhaps they are. Or perhaps the little incidents of the day-to-day have come all in a rush, and someone – perhaps Mrs Graham herself – has wrapped them inside a story which has caused the women of the place to become hysterical.'

'Did Mrs Graham tell you about her mirrors?'

'She did. She did. And let me ask you something, Mr Horton. Is Mrs Graham's conscience as entirely snow-pure as she might wish? Does she have nothing to exercise herself about with regard to her own behaviour?'

He sits back at last.

'If *maleficium* exists, constable, it need not be directed from one to another. Might one not direct it onto oneself?'

Horton is almost back at Thorpe Lee House when he is stopped by a middle-aged woman who is standing by the side of the road just before the inn on the corner of Sir Henry's grounds.

She is, by Horton's reckoning, over fifty years old. She wears clothes which once must have been respectable but which are now threadbare, although care has obviously been taken to maintain their dignity to the extent that such a thing is possible. Her grey hair is almost bald in places, and two or three ugly warts molest her face. But when she speaks out to him, her voice is warm and kind.

'Constable Horton?'

He stops in the road, surprised by the intervention. It is late afternoon, and the fog has lifted, leaving behind an oppressively grey day. The September sky is low over the flat fields north of Thorpe village. A solitary crow squawks from a tree which is grimly holding on to its summer leaves as the temperature falls and the moisture adheres in the air.

'Who is it who asks?' he replies, carefully.

'My name is Hook, sir. Elizabeth Hook. I was formerly the cook at Thorpe Lee House.'

And so, Charles Horton, you find yourself on a country lane face-to-face with a witch. What does one say in such a situation?

'I have been waiting some time for you to pass. I went up to the house and they told me you was in the village. Tell me, sir. Is Miss Ellen any better?'

'Who told you I was in the village?'

'Why ... the cook. My replacement.'

'And are you accustomed to wondering in and out of Thorpe Lee House? I'm surprised they do not run you out.'

'I choose my times carefully. I watch the place.'

'That would, no doubt, be of concern to Mrs Graham. Your watching her house so carefully.'

'I am full of concern for the child.'

'Why so?'

Elizabeth Hook sighs. Her face is as grey as the daylight, and moisture has attached itself to the scruffy ends of her hair. Horton notices her hands – rough, dirty, disfigured.

'Please, sir, do tell me – is she yet unwell?'

Her hands lift towards him, as if she might pray.

'That is what I have heard.'

'Ah, now. I had hoped she might have recovered somewhat since my departure, but it seems it was not to be.'

'I am pleased to have met you, Mrs Hook.'

'Miss Hook, sir.'

'Miss Hook, then. You know my name, and so I assume you know why I am attending Thorpe Lee House.'

'You're investigating the events of August, sir.'

'Yes. Events for which you have been blamed.'

'Indeed so, sir. The village takes me for a witch. The accusations started in the house, and now they follow me wherever I go. Look.'

She pulls up the sleeve of her dress, and Horton feels a queasy rush when he sees the deep scratches on her arms, embedded inside purple-flowered bruises.

'I was mobbed, sir. By villagers. Scratching's a way of fending off a witch. So's beating with wood about the arms and the head. They laid off my head, sir. But they might not next time.'

'And how do you fare now?'

She looks at him, as if surprised by his concern. One dirty rough hand goes to her hair and pulls its moist weight away from her face. She is ugly, Horton sees, as ugly as any woman he has ever seen, but her eyes are sharp. There is a good deal of warmth in them.

'I am getting by. It is hard, but it was already hard. I must try and find work with those who have been successful, but there are so few of them and they are already supplied with cooks. I may have to leave for London, if my fortunes do not change.'

Horton doesn't know what to say to that. One such as her would struggle to find a job in service in London, and she is too old and too ugly to take to whoring. He sees that the woman has something to say to him, and waits for it to come out. He is quite comfortable doing so; he has noticed on many previous occasions that saying nothing can unlock confidences as swiftly as posing questions. Something about this woman's approach, her determination to be heard, makes him trust her.

Perhaps I am bewitched, already.

She looks away from him and up towards the house, the roof of which can just be seen down the road. Men's voices can be heard from the inn. Horton had been intending to stop in there on the way back from the village, to see if anyone has anything much to say about what ails the inhabitants of the estate. He sees three men walking down the road. Elizabeth Hook sees them at the same time, and a new urgency comes into her. She takes a step towards him, as if to create a smaller circle of confidences.

'Whatever you may hear of me, sir, know this: I am a good woman, a good Christian.'

Horton is not surprised by this assertion.

'What am I likely to hear?'

'Whatever stalks Thorpe Lee House is nothing to do with me, sir.'

'And what stalks the house?'

'Something evil, sir. There is terrible evil in that house.'

She looks to her right, towards the men who are coming
down the road. One of them shouts, suddenly, a harsh 'oi!'
which sends the watching crow shuddering into the sky.

'Watch Miss Ellen, sir. Watch her close.'

'What is it that you are—'

'Oi! You! Step away from 'im!'

'And watch yourself, sir. Watch yourself carefully. And do
not believe what they say of me.'

She turns to walk back towards the village. The three men
come up to Horton. One of them, he sees, is Peter Gowing,
the footman at Thorpe Lee House. He is not the one shouting;
that is a fat labourer who smells of beer and tobacco and
cooked meat, and who approaches Horton as if ready to do
violence.

'What's up, eh? Why you speakin' to that witch?' His hard
voice reminds Horton of the street accents of Wapping, its
sinews tight and full of suppressed violence.

'Witch? Why do you say so?'

Gowing puts a warning hand on the fat man's shoulder.

'Easy, Hob, easy. It's all right. This is Constable Horton,
from the docks. Staying at the house, he is. Guest of Mrs
Graham's.'

'*Constable*, is it?' Hob does not seem mollified by Gowing's
words. 'What's Thorpe need with a London constable, now?'

Gowing makes a helpless gesture towards him. Horton turns
to face Hob directly. The third man, dressed in the same
labouring clothes, stands to one side, as if embarrassed like
Gowing.

'Witch, you reported,' Horton says. He draws on the authority his office confers, an authority which he has stood behind
on dozens of occasions, and which never fails to make him vigorous but at the same time disturbed, as if it were a power
guiltily acquired and sheepishly used. 'There's no such thing

as witches, lad.' He remembers what Leigh-Bennett said to him.

'*Lad*, is it?' The fat man is close enough to breathe rancid breath on him. 'This be no *lad*. Visitors from London should take some care over—'

Horton steps right into his face, despite the odour. The fat man's face shows a sudden uncertainty, and Horton pounces on it like a dog.

'No such thing as witches. Declaring someone a witch is an offence, and has been for years, laddie. Want me to put you on a charge? Bring you up before the magistrate? I might come from London, but the magistrate who sent me has a commission for the peace in Surrey as much as he does in London. So shut your mouth, and answer me this: what makes you call Elizabeth Hook a witch?'

Horton's use of the woman's name shakes all three of them, as if it is evidence of local knowledge he is not supposed to have. The fat man steps backwards, submissively. He looks at Gowing for help, and the footman provides it.

'Hob means nothin' by it, constable,' he says, quickly and nervously. 'He is only voicin' the view of many in the village, and you've heard what the servants say.'

Horton looks back down the road to the village, expecting to see the retreating figure of Miss Elizabeth Hook. But the old woman is gone.

BROOKE HOUSE

The matron, who is named Delilah, unlocks the door and shows Abigail into Maria's cell. Abigail stops up short against the word: *cell.* She has not thought of these rooms as such until now, but Maria's situation makes it clear. These rooms are cells, and this is a prison.

The smell inside the cell is terrible. Abigail has managed to keep herself clean and fresh during her time at Brooke House, but it has not been particularly easy, and she can tell as soon as the door opens that no such effort has been made by the woman next door. Then she looks into the room and sees why.

Maria Cranfield sits on the bed, the weight of her body leaning forward over the stone floor, her long black hair drooping down such that it obscures her face completely. She is held to the wall by a chain, itself secured to a thick iron loop in the wall behind her. This chain is affixed to what looks to Abigail like a thick coat made of ticking, only this coat's arms are tied at the back, securing Maria's arms in a cross in front of her. Her hands are invisible, somewhere inside the long sleeves.

So this is what a strait waistcoat looks like. Abigail feels a nauseous anger. It is impossible not to imagine being secured inside that awful thing, strung together like a piece of rancid meat, secured at the back by a single chain, the only way out of it a backwards whip of the head to smash the skull on the metal loop in the wall.

One might as well be dead, after all.

Maria does not look up as she enters the room. Carrying the book, Abigail sits down upon the chair.

'What will you read to her?' asks the matron. Abigail holds the book up to her, but the woman frowns, a big ugly grimace, and looks away, saying nothing. She cannot read, but cannot bring herself to say so. Abigail has seen Delilah's short-handed way with the Brooke House inmates, so is surprised by feeling suddenly sorry for her. The book may have done her some good, after all.

Delilah fusses around Maria's bed for a while, obviously waiting for Abigail to start to read, this being the only way she might be able to identify the book without asking directly, though it will be a great surprise if a woman who cannot read will recognise even this particular volume. But soon another attendant appears at the door and calls for her, and she leaves, glancing back at Abigail once with a sour warning not to fill this poor mad girl's head with even more delusions.

Abigail waits for a little while, listening to the nurses disappearing down the corridor, looking at Maria as she does so. The girl is silent, her breathing regular. It occurs to Abigail that she might even be asleep. After some minutes, she opens the book to the title page.

'*A Vindication of the Rights of Woman. With Strictures on Political and Moral Subjects. By Mary Wollstonecraft. Third Edition.*'

Still, Maria says nothing, but Abigail thinks she can detect a shift in her breathing, a new inflection suggesting attentiveness.

She skips the dedication to M. Talleyrand-Perigord, late Bishop of Autun, and the Advertisement, and begins reading from the Introduction.

> After considering the historic page, and viewing the
> living world with anxious solicitude, the most
> melancholy emotions of sorrowful indignation have
> depressed my spirits, and I have sighed when obliged to
> confess, that either nature has made a great difference
> between man and man, or that the civilization which has
> hitherto taken place in the world has been very partial.

She pauses after the long sentence, and before continuing asks:
'Did she already read you this, Maria? The woman who comes in the night. Did she already read this?'
Maria lifts her head. Her face is beautiful yet ghastly, young yet old, mad yet quiet. Her blue eyes suggest both frenzy and a despairing attentiveness. Her nostrils flare; she is breathing heavily now, as if she had just run into this place wearing that awful strait waistcoat.
Abigail smiles at Maria before her head falls down again.
After a little while, Abigail continues to read.

WESTMINSTER

Graham walks down towards the Strand in the approaching twilight. He turns into Adam Street, pondering on the arrogance of developers as he goes, and then turns onto the Royal Terrace, its thirteen houses presenting their elegant windows to the scurrying river.

Suspended on the steep slope between the Strand and the Thames, on the river side of the Adam brothers' great Adelphi development, it strikes Graham as appropriate that the building was finished with funds raised by a lottery. There is something showy and unlikely about the place, an element of the impossible about the design and situation, an impertinence in the way it blocks the old riverside processional of the Strand from its historical view of the Thames.

He pauses for a look at the river, hearing a buzz of diligent commerce from the arcaded warehouses beneath his feet, despite the late hour. Lighters and wherries fill the river's surface, reminding him of the view from his friend John Harriott's window at the River Police Office in Wapping. There, the vessels entering the new dock system and disgorging a world's harvest are massive and slow-moving, mammoths of wood and cloth and rope. The boats on the Westminster river are smaller and cleaner, as if the Thames itself were refining goods as they head upstream, turning barrels into bottles and boxes into bags.

He turns and walks along the terrace towards number thirteen, remembering suddenly that Dr Thomas Monro, the owner of Brooke House, resides behind one of these doors. Before he can ponder on which door Monro can be found behind he is accosted, loudly, by an old street woman whom he takes, on closer inspection than he would like, to be a gypsy.

'Fortunes told, noble sir! Fortunes told! I shall consult the Dreaming for you, sir, if you so please! Or perhaps the Tarot? Or a little love magic? Though one so well set-up as thee surely requires no such assistance?'

She coughs and laughs and wheezes, performing as if on the stage. She is quite the most charismatic street woman Graham has ever come across and, as is his way, he finds himself delighted by her. She is a repulsive thing, of course, her face disfigured by a terrible scar, her black hair tumbling down across her filthy head, her dress torn but still artfully made.

'Are there rich pickings for you hereabouts, woman?' he asks. She chuckles meaningfully.

'Richer than you'd ever think, fine sir, richer than you'd think. These houses contain clever gentlemen and willing women, as you know – but there's a good many people within who believe in the power of my people.'

'Indeed so? Servants, I take it?'

'Servants is people, sir.'

'And women, of course. Women are credulous of these things.'

There is something about this gypsy which makes Graham talk to her as if they were in on a shared joke, one at the expense of the maids and cooks within the houses behind them. She seems intelligent and speaks to him as an equal, not a potential client. This makes him uncomfortable, suddenly.

'Women sees things, sir. Women sees a great many things.'

'Well, now, be away with you. You'll be telling me this ground is a fairy graveyard before long, and I should return with money to talk to them.'

'No fairies at all, fine sir. None around here. But horrible large numbers of devils.'

And with that she walks away, chuckling to herself. Graham thinks of his wife and her superstitions, and finds himself considering the gullibility of females. He turns back to the house of Sir John Cope.

All thirteen houses on the Royal Terrace are identical. Their tall, elegant windows reflect the fading yellow light back on itself, creating an impassive secrecy. The houses remind Graham strongly of Wapping Pier Head where Harriott lives and, just now, recuperates. He is somewhat exercised by thoughts of Wapping today.

Thirteen black doors gleam with identical paint, their maintenance presumably enforced by some complex property regulation. Number thirteen is different to the dozen other houses for only one reason. Its curtains are closed to the world, on every floor.

Graham knocks on the door, and waits. A moment or two later, the door opens, and he is shown in to a wonderland.

The exterior of number thirteen may be austere and in keeping, but the interior is an impertinent phantasmagoria of colours and textures. The hall is lined with rugs and hangings such that every sound is swallowed up by densities of wool and cotton and silk. Where most English gentlemen would line their walls with portraits Sir John has opted for pure decoration, a riot of colour, purples peeking out from behind reds, blues muttering at greens, shrieking oranges and yellows which announce themselves so directly that one expects them to detach themselves from the wall and take wing. It is less an English gentleman's house than a Caliph's tent.

From somewhere inside the house, music is playing. A piano, tinkling as if from behind a waterfall in a Chinese valley.

The place looks, it occurs to Graham, like a magnificent bordello.

He presents his card and is shown into the drawing room, off the vestibule. The room's effects are more muted than the hallway, but only by comparison. Patterned rugs festoon the chairs in the room, and the bookshelves glitter with painted spines, like expensive courtesans standing in London clubs. The smell in here is almost overpowering – a thick, potent combination of tobacco smoke, spices and something else, an intoxicating vapour which for a moment makes Graham's head spin. He thinks about the young men he has seen taking the *hookha* at the Hindostanee Coffee House.

He ponders sitting down, but looking at the furniture he worries about doing so, lest he be sucked down into it. As in Wodehouse's drawing room, he ponders the art on Cope's ostentatious walls. One painting in particular is deeply familiar: a copy of Hogarth's famous depiction of wicked old Sir Francis Dashwood, who is turned into a parodied St Francis of Assisi, gazing not upon a bible but on an erotic novel, the *Elegantiae Latini sermonis* edition of *Satyra Sotadica*. From his halo peeps the wicked old face of Lord Sandwich. And lying on his palm is the wanton figure of a naked woman.

The picture still has the power to appal. Graham is amazed at himself, and at his recall of the details of the picture. Such is the hold of Dashwood and his acolytes on the English imagination, even at a distance of a half-century. And is Royal

Terrace really the headquarters of a new society of Medmen-hamites, modern acolytes of Sir Francis Dashwood's legendary band of hedonists? Has Dashwood's Cistercian monastery by the banks of the upper Thames been transplanted here, to this elegant terrace by the same river? Graham has no illusions as to the appetites of society gentlemen, having witnessed them first-hand on too many occasions.

And then Sir John arrives.

He is wearing a dressing gown and slippers, of a piece with the rampant opulence of his house. The dressing gown is fashioned with stars and comets streaking through a purple-blue Void, and his slippers curl up at the toes as if eating themselves. On his head is a cap, the point of which leans over his eyes. He is a fat man with a young face, hooded eyes which flutter with exhaustion and a thick, sensuous mouth which puffs, intermittently, on a pipe as big as a baby's arm.

'What is it?' he asks, in a quiet whisper. He does not offer Graham a seat.

'Sir John Cope, I take it.'

'You take it, yes. What do you want from me?'

'You have not heard?'

'Heard what?'

'Heard of the fate of your friend Wodehouse.'

The man frowns through his pipe smoke and sits in one of the chairs. Graham, considering it unlikely that he is ever going to be invited, sits down anyway. Cope does not seem to notice.

'I have heard nothing of Wodehouse,' he says.

'He is dead, Sir John. Murdered in his bedchamber.'

'Dead?'

'He is an acquaintance of yours, is he not? A fellow member of the Sybarites?'

Even under the effete exhaustion of those hooded eyes, Graham can see he has struck home. Cope holds the pipe in

SAVAGE MAGIC

his hand and his voluptuous mouth hangs stupidly open.
Graham is beginning to feel an impatient anger.

'Before you say anything, Sir John, I should say that I have
information that connects the deceased Sir Edmund
Wodehouse with a society called the Sybarites. Wodehouse
was found wearing the mask of a satyr. I understand that
members of the Sybarites wear such masks at their evenings.
The pursuit of pleasure is the primary purpose of these gatherings. Am I correct? Wine and, perhaps more pertinently,
women. London's nymphs, pursued by a group of hedonistic
men. Sir Henry Tempest is another member. Is he not?'

It is a calculated risk, playing his cards so very early in the
rubber. But Graham can see that Cope is intoxicated in some
way – or at least very profoundly hung over – and a man in
such a state cannot play games. He must push Cope into
revealing something.

'There is no ... *law* ... against parties.' Spoken slowly and
carefully. Graham begins to see there is no mystery to Cope's
demeanour. The man is, to put it simply, drunk.

'No, Sir John, there is not. But whoever killed Sir Edmund
meant it to be known he was a member of the Sybarites. Why
would he do such a thing?'

Cope looks at the pipe in his hand as if seeing it for the first
time. Graham decides enough is enough.

'Call your manservant, Cope. Maybe I'll get some more
sense from him.'

Cope's manservant is austere, alert and sanguine – everything
his employer is not. He is also, notes Graham, deliberately and
almost defiantly close-mouthed. If Cope's reputation is anything like Graham has heard, he would need a reliable and
discreet man to look after him. Discretion clothes this man as
neatly as his well-pressed coat.

The servant stands in the drawing room, his back to the fire-place, his hands clasped in front of his stomach, looking at Graham with the neutral half-smile of a curate. Nothing perturbs him. He doesn't once look at his employer.

'Now, sir, my name is Aaron Graham. I am a magistrate at Bow Street.'

'Indeed, such is as I understood from your card, sir.'

'And your name?'

'Burgess, sir.'

'Well, as I have been saying to Sir John here, there has been a terrible slaughter. A man called Sir Edmund Wodehouse is dead.'

'Indeed, sir.'

'Do you know of this man?'

'Yes, sir, I know of him.'

'Has he attended parties at this house?'

'Parties, sir?'

'Yes, parties, Burgess. Gatherings of people for the pursuit of pleasure.'

'Is his own manservant not able to answer this question?'

'I am asking you, Burgess.'

'Well, then, sir. I am not sure I am at liberty to say.'

'You may consider it the case that you are. Sir John here has agreed to help me with my inquiries.'

'He has?'

'Yes, Burgess, he has. You are required to answer my questions. Any refusal to do so may lead to me charging you for obstructing the course of justice.'

'Well, then, sir. You have made the situation quite clear. Yes, Sir Edmund has attended parties at this house.'

'Thank you. And when was the last of these parties?'

'The night before last.'

'I will require a list of names of those attending.'

'As you wish, sir.'

'How would you characterise the party, Burgess?'

'I'm not at all sure I take your meaning, sir.'

'Was it a dinner party? A drinks party? How many people attended?'

'It was the usual kind of thing.'

'The usual? And what is the usual kind of thing?'

'A small group of men. No more than a dozen, sir. They were served food and then retired to the salon.'

'The salon? Another room in the house?'

'Indeed, sir.'

'Will you take me to see it?'

'As you wish, sir.'

'Who else was in the house during the party, Burgess?'

The smile on the servant's face opens a little wider, the eyes narrow a small way, the nostrils flare almost imperceptibly. Burgess, sees Graham, is about to lie.

'Only the servants, sir. I can provide you with a list of those, as well.'

'That will be for the best. And what about women, Burgess?'

'Women, sir?'

'Burgess, obstructing the course of justice is a crime. A very serious crime.'

'Yes, sir.'

'Were there women at the party, Burgess?'

Again, the eyes flick to Sir John. Again, there is no help there.

'Yes, sir.'

'There are always women at these parties, are there not?'

'Yes, sir.'

'And you acquire them, do you not?'

It is a chancy question, a gamble, but as often happens it pays off immediately.

'Yes, sir.'

'From where?'

'I have an understanding with a fellow at the Bedford Head Tavern.'

Discretion is falling from Burgess's shoulders like a loosened robe. It piles up at his feet. His misery is apparent in the set of every limb. The name of the Covent Garden tavern depresses Graham profoundly.

'Talty?' asks Graham. He spits the name, with the same distaste he might say *Bonaparte*.

'Aye, sir. Talty.'

'And he supplied women for the party two nights ago?'

'Aye, sir.'

'Well, then, Burgess. You have been most helpful. Now, the salon, if you please.'

'Yes, sir.'

Burgess, without once looking at Sir John, leads Graham to the door. The baronet, notes Graham, appears to have fallen asleep.

He walks out of the Royal Terrace house and up towards the Strand. It has grown late and dark, and the streetwalkers are out in force. He thinks of Sarah, and how this night-time display of sexual commerce upset her. Dozens of prostitutes line the pavements, overflowing from Covent Garden, in and out of the lights from the main thoroughfares. The Garden trades around the clock: fruit and vegetables and coffee during the day, gin and beer and sex at night.

He turns left at Drury Lane, and walks up past the theatre which has consumed so much of his time for so long, the surrogate wife which filled the void left behind by Sarah's departure. The theatre attracts whores and their gulls like a naked candle attracts moths. There they are now, flirting and spinning down the pavements, seeming to bounce off one another like those same moths frantic for the light, peeling off to attach themselves to silhouetted men in newly fashionable top hats, disappearing into the lodging houses and so-called hotels of the side-streets.

Like so many magistrates before him, Aaron Graham had once believed that all it would take to clear the streets of these countless members of the Cyprian corps would be determination and application. But like all those before him he has been frustrated in his efforts. The desperate painted jades always return, their thuggish bullies watching in the shadows, and the men streaming into Covent Garden every night with their shillings and their hot desires.

It always makes him mournful, this thought. He has desires of his own. He would wish for a clean, honourable stretch of street hereby. It shames him that his beloved Bow Street office sits at the centre of a disgusting cobweb of street vice which, like a disease, seems to replicate itself in other venues in the metropolis. St James's is now as bad, and Farringdon Without even worse.

But Covent Garden is the original, the definitive neighbourhood of disgust. He walks up Drury Lane and right into Great Queen Street, the enormity of London's degeneracy heavy on his shoulders, his own degeneracy black in his belly.

THORPE

It is evening. Horton contemplates Sarah Graham's scroll while sitting at the rough kitchen table where he is being served dinner by the cook Stephen Moore, who has already made several attempts to read the scroll over Horton's shoulder. Each of them Horton has prevented.

What to call this note, now, after such a strange day? A mere list does not seem to do it justice. It has been given to him, but now the woman who wrote it has disappeared into her room and will not, it seems, come out. On returning from Thorpe he had found Jane Ackroyd and asked to speak to Sarah Graham, but she had shaken her head and said Mrs Graham was unwell and unwilling to discuss matters. He had also asked after Miss Tempest Graham, but was told the young miss had also taken to her bed, and her mother had instructed the servants that she was not to be disturbed.

Why call him here and then hide? It seems the strangest behaviour of all.

Horton is used to strangeness. He has seen a great many puzzling things. As a Navy seaman he has seen the bodies of comrades blown to pieces, the glowing smoke from fireships off distant capes, the eyes of savages rolling with despair and hatred. He has hidden from the searching eyes of spies and judges, betrayed fellow mutineers, discarded friendships and abandoned family. He has married beyond all his expectations, but even this solid thing has been tarnished by insanity, his adored wife now an inmate of an asylum, dozens of miles and an entire metropolis away from here. And in his last years as a waterman-constable he has seen and heard such things which, did he but admit to them to a third party, would be nourishment for his own incarceration.

So it comes as a surprise to him that he does, when all is said and all is done, find Thorpe Lee House very odd indeed.

The servants themselves are not notably unusual, with the exception of the cook Moore, who stands out not just because of his gender but also because of his easy, accustomed manner.

No, it is the stories and the situation that create the strangeness. Mrs Graham's larcenous, near-incestuous relationship with her cousin fractures the air of normality which should exist in a house like this, situated on a mid-sized estate in a pleasant position in the orbit of London. Sitting in this kitchen with the sound of rats in the walls, watched over by a strange young man with too much interest in his business than is right for a cook, Horton finds himself wondering if a place can indeed be bewitched, not by witchcraft or cunning-folk, but by the people who live in it and their behaviour towards one another.

He looks at the scroll, and he remembers Elizabeth Hook's bruised and scratched arm. He wonders at how the scroll and the arm relate to each other. He notes to himself a curious fact: that Mrs Graham has called out to her husband for help from a witch, even while her servants imagine the witch to have been banished. Do they fear Elizabeth Hook – fear what she might do, now her living has been taken from her, her fellow-villagers turned against her?

One thing seems overwhelmingly clear: not all the strange events in Thorpe Lee House can be ascribed to Elizabeth Hook. She did not smash the looking-glasses in Mrs Graham's room. And she did not stand in the woods looking at O'Reilly as he dug his hag track in the darkness.

Outside, the flat muddy fields, the surrendering trees, the whispering river.

Eventually, Moore makes himself scarce, muttering a surly 'good night' as if offended that Horton hasn't shared the mysterious document with him. Horton merely nods back, fighting an unaccountable dislike for this young man. Upstairs, he imagines, Mrs Graham is finishing her own supper, alone in the dining room, watched over by the servants who seem, in some unaccountable way, to despise her. And what do they make of the humble London constable, no better than his village counterpart, who is no doubt even now sitting in a Thorpe alehouse, hearing the local chitter-chatter of the arrival from London of a lonely pale-faced man in dark clothes who asks a great many questions? And who seems not to believe in witches – this accompanied by contemptuous chuckles.

He finishes his meal, rushing rather when he once again imagines hearing rats scurrying behind the cupboards. He has always hated rats. He remembers the first time he saw them at sea, aboard the *Apollo*, running in a line from shore-to-ship along a rope, looking as if they were speaking to each other as they stowed away.

And then the ghost of Thorpe Lee House appears.

'You are alone? That is unkind.'

A girl stands at the door into the kitchen, a wispy thing

dressed in a simple white nightgown, her hair loose and dishevelled.

'I wanted something to drink,' she says. 'I thought Stephen would be here to supply it.'

'Well, allow me, Miss . . . ?'

'Miss Graham.'

Not Miss Tempest Graham? Well, then.

'Of course. Do sit down, Miss Graham.'

'Thank you.'

She sits, wrapping the robe beneath her legs as she seats herself, exposing the angular shape of her legs and rear, and he watches her from the corner of his eye as he fetches her something to drink. She gazes round the room searchingly, perhaps looking for the same rats as he. She is thin, terribly so, her chest almost completely flat, the angles of her jaw visible along the edges of her face. How old is she? He has forgotten to ask this obvious question. This thin ghost could be anything between ten and fifteen years. She arranges her hair behind her ears, and he notices that some parts of her scalp are completely bald. Her arms are bare to the elbows and as substantial as the dry twigs of a dead tree. He brings over her drink, and sits back down, pushing his plate away.

'No, please, finish your meal, sir. I do not wish to disturb you.'

'I have eaten enough, thank you, Miss Graham.'

'I do not believe we have met?'

'No indeed. My name is Horton. I am a constable from the River Police Office. Your father asked me to visit you here.'

She frowns.

'Forgive me, Mr Horton. But by "my father", you mean Mr Graham?'

Horton frowns in bemusement, though a sudden understanding then comes upon him.

'Oh, Miss Graham, forgive me. I imagined . . .'

'Please. There is nothing to forgive. It is Sir Henry that I am to call *father*, these days.'

What an odd construction that sentence seems to Horton.

'Mr Graham is concerned for me?'

'Very much so. And your mother, too.'

'Ah yes, my mother. She believes the house to be under a spell of *maleficium*.'

'It is an odd word to use, is it not?'

'It's what they used to call the curses old witches once put on families. It means *evil thoughts*.'

'Do you believe in such evil?'

She ponders the question.

'I believe this is an evil house.'

The answer is surprising.

'Evil? In what way?'

'The villagers came, you know. They stood outside the house one night, and they banged pans and shouted. *Rough music*, Mrs Chesterton called it. To drive out the witch.'

'You believe there was a witch here?'

'Oh, perhaps. Perhaps not. Witches may come and they may go. Strangers may teach us forbidden things, and we may act upon them.'

'Strangers came here?'

'Why not? It is a place of evil spirit and evil intent.'

'In what way, Miss Graham?'

'I believe the people within this house have done and continue to do evil things. My mother left Mr Graham and came here. I am too young to understand such matters, but she is still married to Mr Graham, as far as I can see. So she lives in sin here at Thorpe Lee House. And I now carry the name of the man she lives with. Her cousin, no less.'

'You speak very freely, Miss Graham.'

'Do I? Well, I will die soon. That rather loosens one's tongue.'

'Who said you will die soon?'

'Oh, no one. They do not wish to upset me. But I am ill, and I know why. My sin is as great as anyone's in Thorpe Lee House, constable. My death may redeem it or it may not. I admit to feeling terrified lest what comes after my death is infected with the sin that came before it. But I have made my penance, and God must decide as he sees fit.'

'What is your sin, child?'

'Do you know the old story of Rynadine, constable?'

'I do not.'

'I read it in a broadside I bought from a gypsy woman in the woods. The song tells of a young girl meeting a stranger in the woods, who seduces her. It ends like this:

When I had kissed her once or twice, she came to herself again, And said, kind Sir be civil and tell to me your name. Go down in yonder forest, my castle there you'll find, Well wrote in ancient history, my name is Rynadine: Come all you pretty fair maids, a warning take by me, Be sure you quit night walking, and shun bad company, For if you don't you are sure to rue until the day you die, Beware of meeting Rynadine all on the mountains high.'

The girl's voice is whispery and as dry as the rats' feet in the cellar walls.

'It is a warning, you see. A warning about meeting strangers.'

'Like the strange woman you bought this broadside from, perhaps?'

'Yes, like her.'

'Do you ever go outside at night, Miss Graham?'

'I dream I do. Perhaps I dream of something I have done in the real world. It is often impossible to tell.'

'You have been seen. Standing in the woods.'

'I have? Well, then, I must have been. Or perhaps the one who saw me dreamed. I have dreamed some terrible things.'

'What sort of things?'

'I am tired now, constable. You should pay no mind to me. My mind is as broken as . . .'

She holds up a plate, and drops it to the stone floor, where it obliterates itself.

'. . . that.'

She stands, and walks gingerly to the door, her feet terribly fragile on the stone floor. Before she leaves she stops and turns to him.

'You asked me if the house was bewitched, constable. It is a blasphemous, heinous question. God has made his judgement on we who live here. For my part, you can see of what that judgement consists.'

She turns, and abandons him to the unseen attentions of the rats.

The second night is as the first, his sleep disturbed both by the moans and cries of the residents of Thorpe Lee House, and by his own wild imaginings, which take the form of terrible dreams and wake him several times. Each time he wakes he goes to the window to look outside, onto the lawn, as if it were a stage on which a drama might be played out.

He wakes from one dream of being pursued through an old, evil ship by a hungry, ageless creature and he gets up and goes to the window to see a tall man in a pea-coat limping across the lawn. The figure is horribly familiar and when he gasps it turns and looks at him, an old-young face he recognises, and then he really wakes up, sitting upright, a bellow caught in his throat, his heart crashing in his chest.

The house's residents walk up and down the corridor in

different combinations or alone: Mrs Graham talking to Jane Ackroyd; Mrs Chesterton coughing; Crowley the butler whistling incongruously; Peter Gowing and Daisy Webster whispering. He listens carefully whenever he can, but can detect no obvious pattern in their movements, beyond the odd restlessness of the house itself.

BROOKE HOUSE

Abigail reads to Maria for three hours. Not once does the girl raise her head again, nor make any sound. Only the regular breathing interrupted by an occasional pause, usually at some particularly perspicacious slice of prose from the book, suggests she is paying attention at all. But the timing of those pauses suggests to Abigail a good deal more than attentiveness; there is intelligence there, and understanding.

The matron, Delilah, comes to fetch her, saying that Maria 'is to be visited by the doctor', and suggesting that Abigail take some time to eat and perhaps walk in the garden. Her face suggests that she hopes a tree might fall on her.

She has a surprise in the afternoon, as she sits in her cell reading the Wollstonecraft volume. John Burroway, the happy and kind idiot who serves as a sort of gatekeeper cum manservant cum factotum for Dr Bryson, comes to her cell with a card. He hands it to her and she reads it with him watching. 'I'm to wait for your answer,' he says.

The card has the name of Dr Bryson etched in florid type, and beneath it the doctor has written in a crabbed and untidy hand, 'I would like to discuss the case of Maria Cranfield with you over supper in my rooms this evening. 6 pm. Please confirm to Burroway.'

A great many odd things have happened to Abigail, before she arrived at Brooke House and since, but in some ways this is the oddest. It seems both an impertinence and a curiosity, and yet she feels unable to resist. Dr Bryson had refused to indulge her stories of women speaking to Maria in her cell; perhaps, in a more congenial setting, she may discover whether these are phantoms or facts. The measuring anatomist in her head points out, of course, that this behaviour is unacceptable, both Bryson's invitation and her acceptance of it. But she disregards those thoughts. Surely social niceties can be suspended within the walls of a madhouse?

She says yes to Burroway, and he looks oddly pleased, like a child being told he can stroke an animal.

So she cleans and dresses herself, taking some care over it. There is no looking-glass in her cell, nor has she seen one anywhere in Brooke House. She does not let this worry her. She wants to look nothing more than presentable. Or, more accurately, sane.

Burroway comes to fetch her at six, walking her down the stairs and unlocking the door at the bottom. Bryson's rooms are in an annex joined to the main building, and as she enters she realises she may be making a terrible mistake. Something about the set of the candlelight, the care around the table setting, the way Bryson stands, self-consciously, by his hearth, as if he had practised the position which set him off best.

Is this, then, a seduction?

She feels suddenly and sharply angry, and yet this helps. Her mind clears. The doctor's impertinence does not change what she wishes to do – to help Maria, and to understand her mystery.

'Mrs Horton, I'm very pleased you agreed to dine with me.'

'I wish only to discuss Maria, doctor.'

Her tone is sharp, and he blushes.

'I think, perhaps, you find this setting inappropriate, Mrs Horton.'

'I do.'

'It is by no means unprecedented. I have dined privately with inmates before. A great variety of people come through Brooke House, Mrs Horton. A good number of them are both distinguished and, despite their illness, entirely lucid. I feel it is important to have this private time with them, to speak to them freely and generally about matters cultural and scientific. It aids my diagnosis and my treatment, this attempt to understand the person in the round, as it were.'

'You dine with women as well as men, doctor?'

'Of course!'

Bright and brittle. A lie.

He asks her to sit down, and she almost does not. She nearly turns round and walks out. But this would be a retreat, and would set her back – she has Dr Bryson's trust, for now, and would like to keep it.

'Please, Mrs Horton, I understand that you are an exceptionally honourable woman. I admire you for that. But let me make it clear to you that my only wish is to discuss your treatment.'

'And that of Maria Cranfield. I would like to discuss her, as well.'

'Of course. Of course!'

He gestures to the table, his squirrelly face trying hard to be charming. She sits.

The food is by no means distinguished and she refuses wine; Bryson, however, drinks fairly freely of it. He asks her about her education and interests, and seems surprised (as most men are) to hear of her reading, as she discusses the latest texts on natural philosophy and describes some of the lectures she has watched at the Royal Institution.

As his wine bottle empties and his face reddens, though, Dr Bryson turns his attention to a subject he obviously finds particularly fascinating: himself. Or more particularly, his views on mad-doctoring, and on the *problem of women* (his own phrase, which he apologises for and then uses continuously).

'The mental fragilities of women are a social issue of enormous import. Take, if you will, the rampant problem of prostitution in the metropolis. At this time there are brothels and bagnios and bawdy houses throughout Westminster; on one little street south of St James's Square, called Kings Place, every single building houses a brothel. In my days working at Bethlem I would often walk into Westminster, but venturing outside on any day would lead to pestering from a half-dozen or more different women, some no more than children. Children, Mrs Horton! Without shame men would pull their emaciated frames into doorways or cellar rooms and enact upon them awful degradations.'

He pours another glass of wine.

'Most of these women became ill – and, mind you, for these women, falling pregnant was no better than succumbing to disease. And a great number of them went mad. Who would not flirt with madness amid such misery? At Bethlem we helped those whom we could, but that place had long become little more than a prison for the mad. Dr Monro's *therapeutic philosophy*, such as it is, involved little more than separation from society, rest and, once a year in the spring, a regimented blood-letting of all the inmates which I found awful and pointless.'

'But Dr Monro owns Brooke House, does he not?'

'Oh, he *does*, he certainly does. But I am trying to move us on here. Monro's attitudes are already old-fashioned, scandalously so. Blood-letting, emetics, opium – these have been the tools of mad-doctoring for a century or more. During the Restoration, madmen would be ignored, tolerated or, in the worst cases, beaten. Thankfully that barbarism had given way to more humane attitudes. No, I prefer a new way, a modern way.'

'And what does this approach consist of?'

'It *consists* of *moral therapy*, Mrs Horton. I am an admirer of the Reverend Dr Francis Willis, who cured the King of his first bout of madness at the end of the last century. Willis achieved his success by asserting his *will* over the patient – in this case, over His Majesty himself. The physician's mind becomes locked with the mind of his patient, and within this mysterious relationship a cure might be affected.'

Abigail thinks of those odd occasions when Bryson had sat in front of her and stared, to no perceptible effect.

'And this is the approach you have adopted here at Brooke House?'

'It *is*, it is *indeed*.'

'Yet I have been bled, and purged, and given medicine.'

'You have, that is true. Dr Monro is still the master of the place, after all.'

'Are we merely specimens then, doctor? Instruments on which your theories can be tested?'

'Come now, that is an unfair conclusion.'

'But Dr Bryson, have you not tried this so-called *moral therapy* on me already? Yet I can recall no such *interplay* as you described between yourself and myself.'

'That's because you are a *woman*, Mrs Horton! And, may I say, a very attractive one.'

He giggles, slightly, very drunk now. But she will not leave. This has become interesting.

'It works on men, Mrs Horton. Oh, I have had great success with the men. I can project my will upon them after only one or two sessions, and I can calm them. Other approaches are needed as well, of course; I am particularly proud of the spinning chair. Have you seen it? No? It is magnificent. It is *moral therapy* that informs *all* my work with the men. But the problem with women is this . . .'

He stands and makes his way to the hearth again, holding the mantelpiece as if it were a piece of wreck-wood above a sinking ship.

'I can't make it work! I have tried. The techniques I use on men have no impact on women. The frenzied stay frenzied, the sad stay sad. You have barely even noticed when I have attempted it, and you have certainly not responded. Neither has that poor madwoman Maria Cranfield.'

She tries to speak now the subject has turned to Maria, but he will not be stopped.

'So I fall back on Monro's ways with the women. I bleed them, I purge them, I dose them. Their minds are closed to me, so old approaches have to take the place of new ones. Separation from families. Quiet and rest. The occasional emetic, a dose of opium. It's all so damnably *old-fashioned!*'

He smacks his fist into the mantelpiece, and a small dish upon it jumps into the air and falls back down with a sharp crystal crash.

'Britain has fallen behind, Mrs Horton.' He is not looking at her; it is as if he is addressing an invisible lecture hall. 'During the previous century, all of Europe regarded England as the maddest nation on Earth, such that lunacy was known, far and wide, as the *English disease*. And of course, in 1814, we have a figurehead for our insanity: a mad King, of all things!'

He sways slightly before the fire.

'This is not medicine. It is not treatment. It is no better than the savage hiding in his cave until the rain passes. There is a madness loose in our society, a kind of perversion of moral sense which is visible wherever one looks. Robberies and violence stalk the streets of the metropolis. And worst of all – an epidemic of *whores*, a screaming barrage of *female vice* in the face of every decent man living!'

She has had enough. She stands and demands to speak of Maria Cranfield. He turns his eyes on her as if he were surprised to find her standing there in that imaginary lecture theatre, long after all the distinguished men who had been hanging on his words have left.

'Maria Cranfield? Why do you care, Mrs Horton? What is Maria Cranfield to you?'

'I have tried to tell you, Dr Bryson, that Maria has been visited by another. Someone who has got into her cell and spent time with her. Why will you not believe this?'

'Because you are *mad*, Mrs Horton!'

Her cheeks blush red as if he had stepped across the room and slapped her. He continues.

'You are *mad!* You see visions of . . . what? Of some savage Pacific princess? Someone who is not there? And yet you expect me to believe your tale of mysterious night-time visitors. What kind of mad-doctor would I be, if every madwoman with a frightening tale were able to gain my credence!'

'Then I shall return to my cell. I wish to contact Mr Graham, my benefactor . . .'

'No! Oh, bless me, no.'

He walks towards her unsteadily.

'Mrs Horton, my apologies. I have consumed more wine than was good for me. Your company is charming, and I have lost hold of myself.'

And then he darts towards her, as lithely and unexpectedly as a leopard leaping on the back of a zebra. His fingers are at her wrist. Claret fumes rise from his mouth which, with no more warning, he presses against her.

She shoves him away, and with as much force as she can find she slaps him in the face. He falls to the ground, but rises immediately, hand held to his face.

'You will hear more of this,' she says. 'A good deal more. You are a disgrace, Bryson.'

'Burroway!' His call is surprisingly loud and strong and clear, as if her blow had knocked the wine from his veins. The idiot appears.

'Take Mrs Horton to her cell, Burroway. She is to be locked in tonight.'

Abigail turns away from him, and leaves.

CANTERBURY

The hops are fat and green on the poles, and the hoppers' huts are going up alongside the fields. The hop garden at this time of year is like a heavily pregnant woman, blooming with life but also terribly tired, ready to relieve herself of her burden. Soon the huts will fill with poor folk from London and Kent, ready to work through the deep golden days of September and on into October, pulling the hops down from up high and carrying them over to the oast house for drying.

Henry Lodge sees this coming birth but cannot settle upon it. Indeed, he has not been able to settle since returning from Deal in April. His skittishness has not yet quite affected the business of his hop plantation – his diligent manager, though alarmed by his master's sudden lack of application on horti-cultural matters, is by no means obstructed by it. The hop garden can run itself. Such is the achievement of this man of means.

If he had a wife, she might have gently suggested some time ago, perhaps over dinner one fine evening as the sun set over the oast house and the hops quivered on their poles, that the pattern of his interests has become obsessive, that it is one thing to pore over the Lloyd's Register of Shipping with the same avidity as his fellow gentlemen farmers pore over live-stock prices, it is quite another to take his rickety old carriage to Deal just to take a look at a ship. And to return with nothing on his mind but transport ships and unfulfilled promises.

Ah, but my dear, he would say, *I am what I am and I can be nothing else. I am the man who grew from the little thief. I am the man who was taken from a Portsmouth hulk onto a naval frigate, a convict-gardener for Parts Beyond The Seas. I am the man who hit an iceberg and was taken to New South Wales on a convict transport full of women.*

But he has no wife, nor children, nor family of any kind. He has no one to hear his story, or at least no one to understand it. He has pondered writing a book: *My Shipwreck on HMS Guardian and My Years in Sydney Cove.* It would sell, he thinks. But he has no patience to write such a book, and he has no facility for words. He was a poor thief and then a poor convict-gardener. What words he has are functional and suited only to the running of his business.

And the hops continue to grow, two hundredweight to the acre, to be despatched to London, there to be transmuted into the staff of a working man's life.

Maggie Broad has returned to Britain. This thought is the root of all his restlessness. Her presence on the old island fills his imagination and, if he cares to dwell on it, fuels his discomfort. She is back, at long last she is back. Her return has been the continuing obsession of his life ever since he returned to England. It has been a species of madness, this inability to leave Deal unwatched, this humming mania to be there when she returns.

And after all those years of waiting, he missed her arrival. The thing he has anticipated has happened, but the mania endures, along with a nagging anxiety that the woman may be angry with him.

'Did she say where she was going to, after she left the ship?'

He'd asked the young boys on the *Indefatigable* this, and they had said nothing, but the little girl, so careful to hide behind them for protection but also so determined to help, had spoken up.

'She said she was going to London.'

She might as well have said 'she is going to the Moon'. He had, nonetheless, given serious consideration to travelling to London, speaking to his contacts among the merchants and agents of Wapping and Limehouse. But any questions he would ask would only fizz into further questions, like yeast being added to wort. They would grow beyond his capacity to control them.

Why are you looking for this woman? What concern is she of yours? Is it true what I hear – that you regularly go to Deal and pretend to be a ship-owner's agent? What are you about, man? What are you about?

And what is he to say to that?

Everything he is, everything he now possesses, results from a small founding kindness of Maggie Broad. It was she who gave him work as a farmer in New South Wales and she who had given him his first tiny parcel of land, out of her own grant. She became wealthy, in ways which should have been impossible for a woman with a drunk for a husband in a penal colony. Henry Lodge became self-sufficient, his hard work building on Maggie's kindnesses, until one day he had enough to pay for his passage home. When he returned, he acquired some land for himself, and over the last decade he has built what he has built. But he owes it all to her. And so he looks for her.

He has told this story to some, and he can see the dissatisfaction in their eyes. It does not explain his mania, the care he takes to visit every returning transport. It is such a small part of the explanation, indeed, that the story might as well be a lie. He does not understand the full explanation himself; his obsession with convict transport ships runs, he well knows, outside the bounds of any wish to repay a favour.

Perhaps, he thinks, all he seeks are answers. He had asked her two questions on his final night in the colony, two questions that a great many others were asking.

How did you come by that hundred acres?

And how did you – a woman with a drunk for a husband – keep it?

He had asked her the questions, and she had looked at him, and of all the expressions and glances and glares of others staring into his eyes, it is that look he remembers. It was as if she had opened up the front of his head and stamped an instruction on his mind.

I will answer your questions when I return to England. And you, Henry, will watch for my return, for I will need your help when I come.

It had been an instruction, and that is why his life consists of only two things: hops, and the watching of transport ships. One he does for himself. One he does because he has been told to. That is the truth of it. He can tell himself that he only wants those questions answered. But it is that glance on that long-ago evening on the far side of the world, the way her eyes burned into his understanding: that is what has driven him down to Deal three or four times a year this past decade.

How can he explain such madness to anyone sane? *I do it because a woman told me to.*

So he is mad still. She was not on the *Indefatigable*. His instruction has not been obeyed. He waits as he has always waited, in his Canterbury hop plantation, somewhat afraid, watched by his half-amused servants and his exasperated manager. And somewhere out there in England, the woman he has waited for might be found. He wonders what she might be doing.

Until, one day in the middle of July, with the Kent sun high in the sky, she appears at his door. Older than he remembers her, but otherwise the same. Deliberate and determined, and unashamed in asking for the help she once promised him she would need.

And with her, deranged and raving, her damaged daughter.

PART TWO

A Guiding Consciousness

Johnson. 'Sir, I am not defending their credibility. I am only saying, that your arguments are not good, and will not overturn the belief of witchcraft. And then, sir, you have all mankind, rude and civilised, agreeing in the belief of the agency of preternatural powers. You must take evidence: you must consider, that wise and great men have condemned witches to die.'

Crosbie. 'But an act of parliament put an end to witchcraft.'

Johnson. 'No, sir! witchcraft had ceased; and therefore an act of parliament was passed to prevent persecution for what was not witchcraft. Why it ceased, we cannot tell, as we cannot tell the reason of many things.'

James Boswell, *Journal of a Tour to the Hebrides*,
entry under Monday, August 16

WESTMINSTER

Graham dreams of Sarah, as he often does. As always, the mood of his dream is elegiac, purged of anything lustful, suffused with sadness. There is never any narrative to these dreams of his departed spouse. There is a lake, around which she walks and walks, and Graham walks behind her. From the lake comes the sound not of water, but of Purcell. Always the same strange sad music. He never speaks to her, and she never turns. They just walk round and round and round.

He is disturbed from his slumber by his manservant, who has long been under instruction to wake Graham if any urgent word comes from Bow Street. There is a young officer outside in Great Queen Street, demanding Graham's attendance. There has been a murder. He hears the word 'Cope' and rises to dress himself. He takes his time. Aaron Graham will not be seen out and about in untidy garments, even at six in the morning.

William Jealous, the young patrolman who had attended with him at Wodehouse's residence, waits for him outside.

'One of the St Paul's constables just come to the office, sir,' he says, his breath clearly visible in the cold early morning air. 'Says someone's done away with Sir John.'

'What were you doing at the office at six in the morning, Jealous?'

'Raids last night, sir. Warrant from Sir Nathaniel, sir.'

Graham scowls at the mention of his fellow magistrate. Why organise a raid at a time such as this? Or is he jockeying for some kind of advantage? Graham's finely tuned political instincts twitch, even as they turn to walk down to the Strand.

The metropolis is quiet at this time, though he can hear the costermongers and barrowboys manoeuvring themselves into the Piazza for the early trade. Some whores can still be seen on the pavements, looking worn-out and disconsolate, their only customers at this time of day either gentlemen too ine-briated to do much more than molest and insult them, or early morning husbands looking for escape before another day of work.

The sun is creeping into the sky above the City and beyond as they walk down the hill towards the Strand. Graham speaks to the young patrolman, learns that he is in fact a member of Bow Street's mounted patrol, though he hopes to follow his father 'into a more *investigative* line, if you get my meaning, sir'. Graham looks at him with some surprise, and thinks of the lad's father. Charles Jealous, it is said, could scry the difference between city dirt and country dirt on a highwayman's boots. Perhaps such facility runs in the blood.

They turn left into Adam Street, and the vacancy of air above the river opens out before them, revealing the timber yards and manufactories of the Surrey shore. Like the Piazza, the river is opening for trade, flexing its wherries and stretch-ing its lighters into a new day.

There is a small group of people outside the door to number thirteen. He recognises two parish constables from St Paul's; the others seem to be servants of the house, many of them in night attire underneath coats and capes, some of the women weeping, the men staring open-mouthed into the gaping wound of the front door. The house has been disturbed in its sleep, and looks embarrassed and ill-prepared.

Graham steps through the crowd and into the hallway, greeted again by that splendour of draperies and rugs. The lonely, astonished figure of Cope's manservant, Burgess, is standing at the bottom of the stairs waiting for him. His face has the same disbelieving pallor as that of the servant of Edmund Wodehouse.

'You discovered him?' asks Graham, after a nod of greeting.

'Yes, sir.'

'At what time?'

'It was just past five, sir. I alerted the watch immediately.'

'Why did you attend upon him so damnably early?'

The question does not sound quite as he intended it, and Burgess is surprised. He blinks, raises his eyes to the ceiling, and frowns, as if someone had just asked him to explain how his Mind perceives of Itself.

'I . . . I hardly know, sir. Perhaps I heard a noise?'

'Were any of the other servants disturbed?'

'None, so far as I believe. I have not had time to question them minutely.'

'And there was no one else in the house?'

'No, sir.'

'And the door was locked?'

'Yes, sir.'

'Have all the windows been checked?'

The manservant blinks again, and that same puzzled look. Young Jealous coughs, and says he will himself check all the windows, and see if they are secure. Graham nods.

'Well, then. Please show me up, Burgess.'
'Yes, sir.'

Sir John Cope's bedchamber carries the house's theme of Eastern opulence to new extremes. Draperies cover the walls and windows and bed, and Graham sees depicted upon them various exotic scenes which cause his heart to stop in its chest. He remembers that awful version of *Leda and the Swan* in Wodehouse's drawing room, but that was a child's picture-book offering compared with the devilish depictions of Cope's drapes. He catches glimpses of tigers and lions astride the naked forms of women, and priapic satyrs binding women together, of whips and branches and desperate chains, and for a moment this half-seen whirl of debauch almost distracts him from the figure on the bed.

Sir John's arms are secured behind his back using a strait waistcoat of the kind Graham has seen at London madhouses. He thinks, incongruously, of Abigail in Brooke House. The waistcoat has been tied to the frame of Sir John's bed. He is on his knees, leaning forward, his weight supported by the waist-coat and the bed frame. His face hangs down, something raw and indescribable hanging from the mouth which Graham cannot quite perceive. Sir John is naked apart from the waist-coat, and the area below his stomach is an unholy red mess which seeps out from beneath the heavy canvas. The bedding is purple and red and black and silken, so the blood and other matter which has fallen down upon it appears only as a darker stain.

Graham can smell the sweetly acrid odour of human vomit, but does not ask where it comes from. He can probably guess. Even now his own stomach is twisting and forming its own wet release.

He stares at the body for an unknown stretch of time. 'What

is in his mouth?' he eventually mutters, to no one in particular. With a small cough, Jealous steps from behind him and into the room – he has finished checking the windows, then. He walks up to the side of the bed, stepping around something on the floor, and then grabs Sir John by the back of the head and lifts up his face to Graham. At which the senior Bow Street magistrate turns and divulges the contents of his stomach to the elegant rug of the dead Sir John Cope.

THORPE

Given the odd neglect which rests over Thorpe Lee House like a layer of dust, Horton feels he perhaps should not be surprised by the condition of the shed. Its burned-out remains have not been cleared away and they remain an untidy memorial to the recent unpleasantness. What had once been a shed is now a large black square at the side of the lawn, at the rear of the house and almost within the trees which line one side of the open lawns. Half-burned timbers are piled in the middle where they have fallen in upon themselves. A sturdy-looking well stands nearby. The grass all around is long and wet and almost muddy as it prepares for autumn. A few curled leaves lie on the ground, the harbingers of falls to come.

Horton looks at the charred ground around the sorry remains of the shed, and feels an old familiar itch. He can smell a narrative here, and the smell is as vivid as the black odour of smoke that still hangs in the air. The previous day's interrogations and encounters have been swirling around his head all night, louder even than the sleeping moans of the servants which must, he thinks, be a permanent feature at Thorpe Lee House.

It seems obvious to him – so obvious, indeed, that he wonders that others have not seen it – that Thorpe Lee House has been targeted. He will have no truck with witchcraft, and cannot help but feel that those who do are laughably primitive. Can it really be that here, only a few miles from London, people still scratch the arms of women and bang their pots and pans in the woods to drive away supposed hags and brides of Lucifer?

No, indeed. The itch tells him there is mischief here, and it is mischief of an everyday nature, grounded in motivations which he has not yet unpicked. Elizabeth Hook may be involved, but she did not smash Mrs Graham's looking-glasses. Ellen Tempest Graham may be involved, but having spoken to her Horton believes the girl to be authentically unwell and possibly even deranged. Some or all of the servants may have undertaken some or all of the petty mischiefs – the curdled milk, the rat in the dining room. And someone killed Sir Henry's dogs.

Indeed, the only member of the household above suspicion is Sir Henry himself. And that only because he does not seem to have been here when any of these things were taking place.

The questions he must ask himself are not supernatural, after all. They are capable of being answered. They are the same questions as always: how, and why. And they will lead him to who.

The fire which took the shed must have been rapid indeed, as it has consumed almost all the wood that the structure contained, leaving only the black ground, a few black bits of timber and a half-dozen big pieces of smoothed-down stone, on top of which the old shed had stood. Nature has already begun to make her presence felt; small green shoots can be seen within the sooty surface of the ground, revealed to the sunlight again after who knows how long. And that ugly dead smell of smoke in the air.

The distance from the remains of the shed and the well is perhaps fifty feet, and with an old familiar calm which encases a galloping excitement Horton notes a long thin channel which has been gouged out between the two, perhaps an inch-and-a-half wide. At one point this channel disappears, and here the grass is disturbed differently, as if something large had been dropped upon it and then dragged back up; the grass has been ripped up in a couple of places.

He hears a carriage approaching down the road from the river, the same direction from which he travelled. He puts the noise out of his mind, and walks over to the well and looks in. The noise of his own excitement subsides and a crystal concentration takes its place. The water level in the well is higher than he expected; it is perhaps only a few feet beneath the lip of the well. He remembers how swampy the surrounding fields had seemed on his journey here.

The well is a good fifteen or twenty feet from the tree-line, and there are no leaves on the ground around it. So it is surprising to him to see the vast quantity of fresh-looking leaves and twigs which float on the surface of the well's water. Big clumps of material swirl only inches below the lip of the well, like leaves in a giant's teapot.

And did this well not have a lid?

He hauls down the bucket on its chain which rests on the winch above the well. He doesn't have to go very far. The bucket comes back up, full of water and the dark green-and-black stuff which floats on top of it.

Horton lifts some of this stuff out of the water, allowing the liquid to run through his fingers and back into the well. He is left with a handful of small limp leaves, like old rotten cabbage.

He sniffs at them but detects no odour. He squeezes the remaining water out of them, and folds them into a handkerchief and puts them in his pocket.

He stands up from the well, and looks back towards the burned-out shed. He looks to the trees lining the lawns. He looks towards the house, which is quiet and still and watchful, waiting for the next calamity.

The sound of a carriage is growing louder and louder. Soon, he can hear it turning into the driveway of the house, and he sees it as it drives around the far side of the house and turns back to face the front portico. One of the two men on top of the carriage jumps down, the door is opened, and a large man in hat-and-greatcoat climbs down.

'*Gowing!*' he yells at the house.

Horton walks towards him, pictures of conspiracy sharpening in his head.

WESTMINSTER

There is a frenzy of letter-writing. On reaching Bow Street, Graham calls to ask if the note he wrote to Horton the previous eve has yet been despatched. It has not. He amends it hurriedly and is about to give it to Jealous for delivery when he pauses. In the matter of Thorpe, he finds himself infected by a strange frenzy; like a rope slowly turning on a rope-walk, Thorpe Lee House and the events in London are becoming more and more bound together. He is aware of a great and growing anxiety for his estranged wife and the young girl who shares his name with her. Sir Henry Tempest carries a new stench with him; the stench of the targeted.

But Jealous can be of use to him here in London; indeed, he has a job in mind. Any of the Bow Street horse patrol can safely deliver a letter. In the end it is Roberts, the man who delivered Horton himself to Thorpe two days before, who is despatched to Surrey.

There are several possible avenues of inquiry, and he sends Jealous off to chase the most nebulous of them. It is perhaps an indulgence to send Jealous to enquire of the gypsies in

Norwood. It may turn out to be thus, but the old woman out-side Royal Terrace had already seemed possessed of some quality of significance even before he had spoken to Sir John's butler, Burgess, who said she had been seen around the house on half-a-dozen occasions. So off Jealous goes to Norwood.

That business concluded, he must write to the Secretary of State at the Home Department. It is his second missive to Sidmouth on sanguinary matters in days; he had already alerted his lordship to the death of Edmund Wodehouse, it being such an unusual event, but no reply to that letter had been received. Perhaps Sidmouth is otherwise engaged. Graham feels this second killing may change matters. A gentleman's death may not exercise the former prime minister. A second death, with the same ritualistic marks, smacks of something more sinister.

Extraordinary, how the second identical killing establishes a pattern. He has seen this before – during the Ratcliffe Highway killings of three years earlier, it was the second atrocity which sharpened the national panic, which gave the killings a sense of implied purpose. It changed them from random acts into deliberate ones, from violence into obscenity. A guiding con-sciousness, however dark and vicious, could be perceived within the blood-splattered scenes.

Such a consciousness is at work again here, and it was partly visible in that first murder. The careful placing of the mask on the dead body, like a signature of intent. And now this, an extension of that first killing, a new chapter in a book which someone, somewhere is in the business of writing.

This is the import of his letter to Sidmouth: that the second killing implies a pattern, and that within the pattern the future can be descried. Cope was a member of this party of Sybarites; somebody is killing those same Sybarites. The *why* is still unanswered, but will have to wait now that the *what* presents itself.

The letters are barely on their way when the gentlemen from the *Chronicle* and the *Times* reappear at Bow Street, and are rebuffed. They are accustomed to this game. They will write their story anyway.

Next, Graham summons the Bow Street principal officers and as many parish constables as can be found – a good number of them are already in the Brown Bear with their Bow Street colleagues. He tells them to bring him the senior household servants from Sir John Cope's residence, Burgess the butler and the housekeeper. If they refuse to come, they are to be arrested. He feels a twinge of guilt at this imposition of authority – he suspects neither of the servants, or at least has no reason to as yet – but he must now base himself at Bow Street and its court. He wishes never to see the inside of Sir John's house ever again. He informs the other magistrates of the office that, for the time being, his attention must be wholly on this particular matter. They seem strangely willing to remain uninvolved, as if the case is already infected and capable of transmitting that infection to the unwary. Graham has the same sense himself, but an old magistrate on the cusp of retirement is somewhat immune to such contagions.

THORPE

In the time it takes him to reach the house, the freshly arrived carriage in front of Thorpe Lee House has been completely unloaded. The driver is preparing to take the carriage round to the rear of the house, where there is a small stable-block and carriage house. As Horton climbs the steps to go within, he hears the driver crack his whip and the crunch of wheels and hooves on gravel.

Inside, the previous atmosphere of impatient quiet has been shattered. The exhausted servants dart up and down the stairs. Crowley the butler is barking orders, seemingly at random, while Mrs Chesterton scurries around with what looks like a huge ostrich feather, flicking it at random items as she goes. Jane Ackroyd (or *Béatrice*) the lady's maid shouts something from the upstairs landing and moments later Daisy Webster the scullery maid appears on the stairs, rushing down to the kitchens below. She catches a glimpse of Horton as she goes and nods politely, but her face is red and flustered. The only servants not on view are Peter Gowing, who is presumably performing some task for his master elsewhere in the house, and Stephen Moore, who must be in the kitchen.

A male voice yells 'CROWLEY!' from the drawing room, and the butler, caught in mid-flow remonstrating with Jane Ackroyd at the top of the stairs, dashes downstairs and into the room.

'I take it Sir Henry is returned,' Horton says to no one in particular, and everyone ignores him in the same way. He leaves the servants to their scurrying, and heads upstairs to his room.

He had been thinking of writing to Abigail, as he has done multiple times since she left for the madhouse. He knows his letters are almost certainly not being read. During the empty days of August, while his beard grew and their apartments congealed under neglect, he had often walked up to Hackney, always demanding to be let in to see her. On one occasion he had managed to speak to the resident doctor, a weasel of a man called Bryson who seemed to have taken an unaccountable dislike to him.

This mad-doctor had explained, superciliously, that Brooke House patients were allowed no contact with family or friends during their rest. He had used the word 'rest' as if it had some magical resonance, like an elixir of life hidden in a Florida jungle. Horton had complained – indeed, by the end of the short interview he had been shouting – but his complaints fell on deaf ears. He had insisted that, as Abigail's husband, he had final legal redress over her, that she was, to all intents and purposes, his property, and she was being held against his will. Such had been the extremity of his dismay that such thoughts came willingly; he would have said anything at all to have Abigail come out of that place.

And when it came to it, Bryson had in any case backed down, agreeing with him that, yes, as the woman's husband, he had every right to withdraw her from the asylum. He would arrange for the nurses to make her ready. Following which, with bleak acceptance, Horton told him to wait. For the terrible truth which awaited him always presented itself: Abigail had chosen to go to Brooke House. No one had spirited her away.

Abigail had chosen to cut herself off from him.

It is this empty, bleak and unavoidable truth which has haunted him these past five weeks. It is what always prevents him taking her away from that place. He is too much afraid of what would happen if he did.

That fear comes back to him now, but its return makes him realise that he has not thought about Abigail for some hours now. Something about Thorpe Lee House has arrested his self-consuming obsessions. After that investigation of the well – and the discovery of the vegetation within it – perhaps he is beginning to feel haunted by something else.

He settles down to write a letter, much different to the one he might have composed to Abigail. One he had not anticipated writing when he first woke this morning.

It is a new feeling, this writing-down of things. He has never before now been a man of letters, even private letters. He has been on the ground in Wapping, surrounded by his network of small boys, always watching and aware. He is able to attend, in person, any event he desires.

Besides, he has hoarded too many secrets and carried too many disreputable histories to feel entirely safe when writing them down. He knows how important the letters of the Nore mutineers were to their deliberate destruction at the hands of the Establishment, assisted by one Lt. C. Horton. A great deal of agony might have been avoided if some of his fellows had avoided prolix celebrations of success in letters to loved ones which had only been intercepted by the government's spies in

Sheerness, and had later served to incriminate their verbose creators.

Horton had bought his freedom – and a life with Abigail – by turning evidence against his fellow mutineers, and has ever since been rehearsing a kind of running away, though from what exactly and to where precisely is unclear even to him. Better to think of him as hiding in plain sight, operating and breathing and living but never revealing himself more than he has to. And what could be more revealing than an ill-considered letter to an indiscreet recipient?

But Horton is a quick if deliberate thinker, and a highly creative one – he knows this of himself perfectly. Writing things down slows down his mind, gives him the time to delineate his thoughts precisely and with care, and he has found in consequence that light falls on dark matters in a different way. Sometimes a more revealing way.

So, while he waits for the chaos downstairs to cease, and while the thoughts of his sojourn in the garden are fresh in his mind, he begins to scribble. A rather preposterous idea has occurred to him. Soon, the thoughts and the ideas coalesce themselves into a new letter. He looks at it for some moments before folding it and placing it in an envelope. He leaves it open. A knock comes on the door.

'Come in,' he says.

The footman, Peter Gowing, looks round the door. There is a sheepish look on his face, as if in acknowledgement of their previous encounter.

'Constable, the master would like to see you. He's waiting in the drawing room.'

Horton stands. He leaves the letter on the desk.

'Certainly. I have left some leaves drying by the window – could you tell the other servants to leave them as they are?'

WESTMINSTER

Sir John Cope's housekeeper is an Irish woman who is unexpectedly calm in the face of the events in the house under her keeping. She informs Graham, when she is brought to Bow Street, that Sir John was always likely to come to a bad end. She'd only been with him three months, and in that time she'd seen 'matters such as I never thought to see, and never wish to see again', her fat face aquiver with indignation and disgust. She tells Graham who the household staff are, and which of them were under Sir John's roof this last night. She heard nothing, and reports that none of her staff heard anything either.

One by one the other servants of Sir John Cope are interviewed, as in the wings the other arms of officialdom wait to take the stage: the reporters, the coroner, the undertaker. No doubt somewhere, even now, someone is preparing for the sale of the lease to 13 Royal Terrace, and lawyers are dusting off legacies. Sir John Cope was a rich man, by all accounts, though Graham notes how the legacies of the so-called rich like Sir John often melt like river fog upon their death, subsumed into lawyers' correspondence and the dozens of unpaid tradesmen's debts accrued over decades of living in a certain fashion.

So, as Westminster begins to swarm over the literal, legal and metaphorical carcass of Sir John Cope, Aaron Graham reads the depositions of the dead man's servants. All agree on the dates of parties, all tell of the nature of them. Burgess had told him of the procurer for these events – Talty, the pimp of the Bedford Head, the present day's very own Jack Harris, upon whom a visit will shortly be paid. While there is some suggestion that Cope believed his parties to be operating at a different level – one of spiritual resonances and ghostly recurrences – Graham thinks he knows the kind of parties the Sybarites enjoyed. Parties where men devoured drink and food and then devoured women, made beastly by their own appetites and desires, whatever mysticism Cope believed himself to be practising. It is clear, in the testimony of the servants, that they saw the parties in the same light as Graham.

Burgess is a different matter. That air of shocked stillness is still upon him when he is brought into Graham's office by one of the constables. He surprises Graham by telling him he had been Sir John's butler for the best part of two decades, and Graham wonders how a character such as Burgess could last in the company of a man such as Sir John. When he puts this question to him, the butler seems not to understand it. He is like a dog that has been badly treated for so long it has forgotten what kindness is like.

Graham asks for a list of the attendees of Sir John's last party, and Burgess unfolds a piece of paper from the inside pocket of his coat and hands it across. A list of names presents itself, some of them very recognisable to Graham, either from acquaintance or report. He asks Burgess if these men have attended parties at Sir John's before. Burgess replies that they are, indeed, regular attendees, there being two of what he calls 'Sir John's special parties' a year.

The name Sir Henry Tempest is in the middle of the list, picked out, as it were, in flashing personal significance.

Did Sir John always host these parties? he asks Burgess. No, comes the reply. Sometimes they were held at far-flung venues, chosen, says Burgess, by Sir John Cope.

Graham asks: chosen for what reason?

Burgess looks unable to answer for a moment, struggling in his shocked state to find the right words. He says, eventually, that Cope believed these venues to have some kind of significance.

Graham asks, what kind of significance?

Burgess looks embarrassed now, for the first time. Even on Graham's first visit to 13 Royal Terrace, Burgess had feigned distance, not shame, at his master's behaviour. But now he seems gripped by a deliberate and deep remorse. It is as if his true feelings were resolving themselves back into expression. He says, eventually, that Sir John believed certain places carried resonances from previous things that happened there; that the past could be drawn back into the future by the performance of certain rites and ceremonies in those same places.

There is silence for a moment, as Graham digests that. It smacks of a different flavour of lunacy. He does not care for it. He asks, eventually, for an example.

Well, sir, says Burgess, and now he is squirming like a naughty schoolboy in front of a headmaster. Like Medmenham.

The name squirms into the room like a serpent.

Sir John held parties at Medmenham? He struggles to keep the disbelief – almost the mockery – out of his tone.

Once, says Burgess. This time last year.

'And what happened?'

'Very little. Nobody died.'

THORPE

Sir Henry Tempest stands in front of his portrait with, Horton presumes, no satirical intent. But the juxtaposition of the idealised portrayal with the fat, angry and contemptuous reality is too stark to be ignored. Horton, after a mere three minutes with Sir Henry, thinks he can picture a small army of servants stood here where he is now, inwardly smirking at how far the real man falls from the man in oils up there on the wall.

He is not offered a seat, a cup of tea, a walk in the garden. No, none of these would be in keeping with how Sir Henry so obviously sees him: as a kind of manservant to Aaron Graham, the man he has cuckolded. Paid for by the Bow Street magistrate, sent by him, and told what to do by him. Horton does not find this description to be wholly inaccurate.

'So here's the *witch hunter*,' says Sir Henry, thumbs hooked into a stained silk waistcoat, hat thrown onto a nearby chair, one leg bent at the knee, the other ramrod straight. His breeches are tight, far too tight for a man of his girth, and his face is blotchy. The finer things in life have caught up with Sir Henry Tempest.

'Sir Henry,' he says, with a slight dip of the head which he tries to invest with as much insubordination as he once used to mock the admirals of His Majesty's Navy. 'If I may intro-duce—'

'Do not bother yourself,' Sir Henry barks, reminding Horton of those dogs out at the back of the house. 'I know who you are. Graham has written to me about the unspeakable witchfinder-generaling you're wasting my cousin's time on.'

My cousin. No anxieties over nomenclature for Sir Henry. Mrs Graham might be his lover, but she is primarily his cousin. Presumably Sir Henry thinks this reflects upon her rather well. Also, Sir Henry must be deliberately trying to avoid ever referring to Sarah Graham by her married name.

An answer is expected, even though no question was asked and only derision was offered. Horton has become used to being shown respect by his betters – John Harriott and Aaron Graham, senior magistrates both, are comfortable deferring to him. It is rather a shock to experience this pressing disgust, this bullying derision, from a man who so obviously considers Horton to be almost semi-human in his inferior position.

'Sir Henry, if you would rather I left this house and returned to London, I will be on my way immediately.'

'In defiance of Graham? You should know your place, sir.'

'And you should know, Sir Henry, that Mr Graham may be my social better but he is not my superior. That position is another man's. Mr Graham has asked me here as . . .'

He stops. Calling this mission a *personal favour* would be too much. He has already gone too far, and he can see it in Sir Henry's face.

'There are, I believe, things to be investigated here,' he says, as neutrally as he can.

'How so?'

'There may have been crimes committed.'

'Crimes against my property? Or crimes against the Heavenly Host?'

'Against your property. I trust you have been kept appraised of events?'

'You may assume I have, yes.'

'Well, then. I believe your shed may have been burned down deliberately. Your dogs were, clearly, slaughtered by someone who wishes this household malice. These seem to be matters worthy of investigation.'

The mention of his dogs does not improve Sir Henry's rough mood; though Horton rather thinks nothing much can achieve that.

'It is my understanding that the cook – what is her name, Hook is it? – has been accused of these things.'

'Accused by some, indeed. But without any real evidence or motivation that I can find.'

'Evidence? Motivation?'

'I mean, why would she do things like this?'

'Malice. I would have thought that was obvious.'

'Malice with what foundation? Does she have reason to resent you or Mrs Graham, Sir Henry?'

'Are you interrogating *me*, now, constable?'

'I am attempting to explain my approach to this matter.'

'You are stating, then, that there is nothing to suggest Elizabeth Hook committed these crimes.'

'Nothing I can as yet discover, no. And then there is the matter of Miss Tempest Graham.'

He says the name carefully, and he can see the charm it weaves. Sir Henry's face softens, and for a moment his cantankerous carapace is pulled aside, revealing a man with some great anxiety beneath.

'My daughter's illness should not be confused with this stupidity of her mother's.'

And yet she is not your daughter, thinks Horton, and wonders at this obvious affection.

'Perhaps not. But Miss Tempest Graham has alluded to matters which ...'

He stops because Sir Henry has stepped towards him, newly enraged. He swings one arm behind him as if he might strike Horton, and another side of the man's essence is revealed for a moment. For a country baronet, Sir Henry looks more than capable of playing the part of a street brawler.

'Alluded! Alluded *when*, constable? You were given *no permission* to speak to my daughter!'

'She spoke to me in the kitchen, this past night. I sought no interview with her.'

'You should have sent her away!'

'She seemed disturbed. Sending her away would have been unkind.'

'So she comes to you in her night attire, indecently dressed and dizzy with sleep and illness, and you have no compunction in interrogating her with the same impertinent material you have offered me?'

'No, Sir Henry. It was not at all like that. She seemed genuinely distressed by something ...'

'Of *course* she is distressed! Her mother has been chattering about witches and demons and all sorts of Godawful nonsense, and she has brought a strange man – an *impertinent* man – into her household, as if he were some gypsy cunningman from Norwood with a book of spells and curses. For God's sake, man. This must cease!'

'Very well, sir. I will pack my possessions and have a carriage ordered ...'

'No. Wait. *Wait.*'

Sir Henry puts his hand to his forehead and closes his eyes. The other hand he holds up to arrest Horton. He sits down on an elegant chaise longue, his fat breeched legs splayed wide, his belly hanging down. His blotchy face has gone grey, as if the richness of the previous night's food has come back to him.

There is silence for a moment. From somewhere within the house a woman shouts. Horton looks at the window and sees O'Reilly passing with a shovel over his shoulder. He thinks of the leaves drying in his window, the open letter waiting to be sent. He thinks he will go to the inn to eat and drink tonight.

'It's a bloody stupidity.' Sir Henry mutters this while his eyes remain closed, and then he sighs and opens them to look at Horton.

'Is there anything to be discovered, Horton? Is there something peculiar happening here?'

'There is something happening, Sir Henry. As to its peculiarity, I will not say.'

And he finds he doesn't want to leave this place, after all. Not while something remains unresolved. And certainly not while Abigail isn't there to welcome him home.

A Treatise on Moral Projection

And so we come to it: the heart of the matter, and the
rationale for this paper you see before you. The events I
am about to describe have been the object of decades of
my personal consideration; barely a day has gone by
these last thirty years when I have not given them some
thought, as if by turning them over in my mind I can
accommodate some explanation for them. I do believe,
now, that there is indeed a scientific rationale for them;
but when I first experienced the episodes I am about to
describe, the theoretical tools for understanding them
were either absent, or severely misguided. These are
matters I shall return to.

So here is the substance of it: having spent a month
trying to establish some connection or rapport with
Maria Cranfield, and having failed utterly in this matter,
I was visited that September morning by Miss Delilah
Underwood, the matron of the female part of the
Asylum. There had been more disturbances during the
night; for the second eve in a row, the men of Brooke
House had made a fearful commotion, raised to it by we
knew not what. I assumed she had come to speak with
me of this, or perhaps of Mrs Horton, whom I had had
occasion to lock in her cell the previous evening when
she had become frenzied during a consultation with me.

Like Maria Cranfield, I did not see Mrs Horton making any progress whatsoever. She continued to have the same visions as when she first entered Brooke House, and I had tried out a whole barrage of remedies on her. At that time, my preferred regime of *moral therapy*, while highly effective on the male inmates, was proving less so on the females, and for this reason we also maintained a more traditional regimen of quiet solitude, mixed with vomiting, blood-letting and even the occasional opium dose when it was required. We had installed a new circulating swing chair on the ground floor, and this had proven very effective with certain male patients, but I believed the female frame to be too weak for this kind of physical intervention.

By this time I had become disheartened, but both the women remained subjects for study. When Miss Delilah came in to my consulting room, I was glad to see her; I asked how Mrs Horton was that morning after a night spent in isolation. This had followed an episode the previous evening in my consulting room when Mrs Horton had temporarily lost her wits, as if to demonstrate the lack of progress she had made in Brooke House. I was told that she was quiet, although there had been a good deal of weeping during the night. This saddened me, but I hardened myself in the knowledge that what I did was for the benefit of her own mental state. There had been too much wandering around the place for the woman's own good; too much stimulation of the fancy was, no doubt, in some way preventing my effecting a cure.

However, this was not why Miss Delilah had come to visit me. She wished to speak of Maria Cranfield, she said, and I detected a certain tension in her manner when she spoke of that creature. I asked what she wanted to say of Miss Cranfield, and she responded by requesting that the patient be moved out of Brooke House forthwith.

I was shocked by this suggestion. It was of course wholly inappropriate for a mere matron to be recommending any course of treatment to a physician, but to insist on a patient's removal! This was so unprecedented as to be scandalous. I responded with a good deal of anger, and demanded to know what in Maria Cranfield could have sparked such an outrageous demand.

I well remember, even today, what Miss Delilah said at that point.

'She gets in your head, sir,' she whispered, and to my great astonishment she began to weep as she spoke. Miss Delilah, who had calmed lunatics and sewn up wounds and faced down violent men in the extremities of a fit, was crying!

'She gets in your head, and once she gets in there, you can't get her out.'

I was thunderstruck. For a moment I could think of nothing at all to say. My head was, I recall, a little sore from wine I had drunk the previous evening, and I had been suffering from that torpid sense one suffers under the day after liquor has been consumed. I may also have been tired, my sleep having been disturbed by the disturbances among the male patients.

But I was firm with Miss Delilah, saying she was overwrought and suggesting she might need to go home and rest. She refused, saying her day's work had barely begun. There was something of the old, familiar and solid Miss Delilah in this reply, forthright and slightly irritated. She could plainly see that I was giving no countenance to what she said, despite that shivery sense of familiarity I had felt. I agreed to go and visit with Maria Cranfield, and Abigail Horton, immediately.

'Take an attendant with you, sir,' she said, and a pleading tone had re-entered her voice. I asked why I should do such a thing. 'T'would ease my mind if you did, sir.'

'Well, we are in the business of easing minds, are we not, Miss Delilah?' And I smiled. I may even have laughed. How innocent of the truth I was.

I called for an attendant to come with me to Maria Cranfield's cell. His name is one I shall be repeating often, for despite his mental incapacity (he was an idiot, with the conception of perhaps a ten-year-old boy) he was to play a central part in the horrors to come.

He was called John Burroway. He came from somewhere on the south coast. He was a young man, big and strong, one of several of that type we kept in our employ in order to be able to deal with some of the more excitable males in Brooke House. John was, as I have said, simple, unable to write much more than his own name, but capable of basic menial tasks and instruction. He lived with a sister in Hackney, who also worked in the house. He did not speak unless spoken to, but with my head as sore as it was, the last thing I wanted was conversation.

I had no particular reason for choosing John Burroway to attend with me that day. Indeed, I was a good deal irritated by Miss Delilah's insistence that I take a companion. John was simply the first attendant I came across. But oh how things would have been different if I had not taken him with me!

We walked past the chapel and up the stairs to the women's floor, to those two rooms together: Mrs Horton's cell, and the strong-room which held Maria Cranfield. Both doors were shut. I decided to look in on Mrs Horton first, and required Burroway to open the cell.

Mrs Horton was lying on the bed, and raised her head when I entered the cell. Seeing me, she sat up. She looked pale, and tired, and, to my great consternation, she looked afraid. I asked her how she was, and she said she felt unwell that morning and that she had slept little. I asked her what had disturbed her, feeling I knew what she would answer. She told me Maria had been disturbed in the night, that she had been shrieking in her sleep, and that she believed Maria had been visited once again by an unseen female. And that, of course, the male inmates had made such an infernal noise.

My response to this was complicated. I pitied her, but I also found myself becoming angry at this woman's seeming unwillingness to cooperate with me or with my methods. I had shown her nothing but kindness and consideration, and could not comprehend her persistent refusal to accept that the voices from Maria's room were in her head, and in her head only. I spoke to her for some time, expressing my sentiments with some force, and as I spoke she shrank back against the wall behind her bed. We left her there after a time, locking the door closed behind us, and went on to visit Maria Cranfield.

Maria was not sitting on the bed, as Mrs Horton had been. She was standing and, to my surprise, staring intently at the door as we entered. The chain which held her to the wall was stretched tight as she stood in the middle of the room. She looked alert and aware, by no means lost in herself as she had wont to be throughout her stay. When I spoke to her, she looked at me, though she made no sign that she understood what I was saying.

I sat down in the chair in the room – that same one we had provided for Mrs Horton to sit in. I felt quite sharply unwell. My headache became suddenly acute, and it was accompanied both by a tightness of the chest and a sudden nausea. The room seemed to swell around me, and I felt as if I would lose consciousness if I did not secure a seat. John stayed by the door.

Maria's eyes followed me as I sat down and tried to recover myself. She ignored my entreaties to sit down upon her bed. She remained standing above me. As I spoke, she said nothing. I don't remember, today, what I said. No doubt nothing of great import. But what I do remember is how terrible I felt under her gaze, how unwell. I had always been a hearty fellow, and while the occasional headache inevitably accompanied me in my work, what I felt that morning was like nothing I'd experienced before or since. I felt as if a knife was being turned slowly inside my skull. But that was not the worst of it.

The worst of it was that when Maria turned her eyes away from me, and to Burroway, my headache ceased. It went away instantly, like a candle being snuffed out. My eyes widened with the shock of it. I stopped speaking, and for a moment there was silence in Maria Cranfield's cell.

What happened next chilled me, and chills me still.

Without warning, John stepped backwards out of the cell. I had given him no instruction, yet he strode away. I called after him, demanding he come back, but he made no reply. It was an act of staggering disobedience, but I was only angered by it for a moment, for Maria now turned her eyes back to mine, and that terrible pain swooped over me once more. It was as if Maria's eyes were causing that pulsating, queasy agony.

Then it switched off again, because Maria had looked away. Someone had come to the open door of the cell. It was Abigail Horton. Burroway stood behind her, the key to her cell in his hand. He had opened her door!

I began to shout at this egregious insubordination, but my yell was stifled as Maria's eyes locked back onto mine, and the pain returned, stronger and more deliberate than anything that had gone before. I felt at that moment as if the pain might overcome me, might drag me down into a state of dreadful oblivion, but then Mrs Horton stepped into the room and walked up to Maria. Not once looking at me, she began to speak in Maria's ear, putting her arm around the young woman's shoulders. My head hurt so much that I was unable to listen to what she said, but I thought I could feel the pain lessening, bit by bit, and as it did so Maria's fierce frozen stance seemed to soften under the emollient effects of Abigail's words. Slowly, the two women sat down upon the bed, and then Maria looked down at the floor, and I was released.

I stood at once, and began to remonstrate with Burroway and with Abigail, conscious of the terrible breach of behaviour I had just witnessed. But my words were stopped in my throat, when Abigail looked up at me and said, with great anger in her voice: 'Leave us.'

The impertinence of this was shocking to me, but I had little time to consider it, for then Maria too looked up at me, and again that great pain returned to my head, accompanied by a fierce entreaty to leave the room.

It is impossible to describe how I felt this. It was rather as if my own mind was issuing instructions to itself, forcing its will upon its will. Is that not a flavour of lunacy itself? How recursive might such a concept become? A mind talking to a mind talking to a mind, onwards and downwards to the unplumbed depths of the imagination. Few if any other physicians of the Mind can have experienced what I did in that room. I felt as if my sanity was snapping itself in two.

And more than this: I felt myself leaving the room. Burroway waited outside, and as I stepped into the corridor beyond the cell, he reached past me and closed the door, as if following the stage direction of an invisible playwright. We walked down the corridor, down the stairs, and into my rooms. I came to myself again therein, sat in my old leather chair, John Burroway before me, with no conception at all as to how I had arrived there.

For the attention of ROBERT BROWN
% Sir Jos. Banks
Soho Square
London

Sir

*I have a most unusual request to make of you, but following
our meeting last year during my investigation into the
Solander affair, I trust that oddities might at least pique
your interest.*

*I am currently in attendance at a fine house in Surrey
which is plagued by a number of odd incidents. Following
what I take to be one of these occurrences a shed has been
burned down to the ground. The shed is next to a well,
which supplies the house with drinking water. From my
examination of the house, it would appear that something
was dragged from the well to the shed. This thing, whatever
it may have been, burned in the fire which consumed the
shed.*

*It is perhaps little more than speculative fancy, but I have
imagined a circumstance wherein the shed was burned to
conceal the burning of something else; in this case, the
wooden lid which protected the water in the well from leaf-
fall and other elements. Having pondered this, I looked into
the well and saw a good deal of green matter floating on the*

surface of the water, in a huge clump. It looked nothing like the leaves or twigs on the trees which surrounded the well. And so, following my thoughts, I conjectured that someone had removed the lid to the well, and had then added something to the water.

I have taken a sample of this material and dried it, as I believe is the way. This is enclosed with this letter. I wonder if this little tale might have piqued your interest, and if so whether you might feel compelled to investigate the dried matter I am sending you. You might, perhaps, even be able to tell me what the substance is.

I would be obliged by any help you could provide on the understanding, of course, that you are not yourself obligated to assist me in any way. But, as you can see, there is perhaps an interesting story here, and it may be one you would consider helping me compose.

Please send any response to my name at Thorpe Lee House, Thorpe, Surrey.

I remain
Yours
Horton, C.
Waterman-constable, River Police Office, Wapping

THORPE

Horton takes the dried leaves and twigs and places them carefully inside the envelope, and is sealing it when there is a knock at his bedroom door.

'Yes?' he shouts. Nothing happens for a moment. 'Oh, come in, then.' He is not used to being waited on so.

Peter Gowing puts his head around the door.

'Pardon me, constable, but there's a horseman just arrived for you.'

Horton thanks him and heads downstairs; Gowing disappears into whatever part of the house the servants scurry away to. Outside on the drive he finds Roberts, his baleful driver from the day before last.

'Letter for you,' Roberts says, and half-hands, half-throws the letter down to Horton. He is about to turn the horse and leave, in his customarily charming way, when Horton stops him.

'Wait a moment, please. I may need to answer.'

Roberts snorts, and his horse snorts, and the two of them wait for him to read.

Horton says nothing for a moment, then:

'A moment, please. I shall return immediately.'

He runs up to his room, and fetches the letter to Brown. This he hands to Roberts.

'This letter is to be delivered to the man on the envelope, or his manservant, at the Soho Square address written. To no one else. Do you understand?'

Roberts looks at him as if weighing up how sharp a knife would need to be to run him through.

'I ain't no bleedin' ticket porter, son. I'm an officer at Bow Street.'

'And this is Bow Street business. If the letter is not delivered, the magistrate will hear of it. Do we understand each other, Roberts?'

Roberts snatches the letter from him, and turns away. His horse snaps its tail in contempt.

Horton goes inside, and tries to speak to Sir Henry again about the contents of the letter. But the master of the house is locked in his room, and has left explicit instructions not to be disturbed. Horton is left to wonder how the murky events at Thorpe Lee House might overlap with the horrors taking place in London, as described by Aaron Graham. The itch he'd felt at the well now feels like a fever.

WESTMINSTER

Aaron Graham has made his home on the fringes of Covent Garden, so its stenches both physical and moral are as familiar to him as the pain in his calves and the growing tightness in his chest. Like all gentlemen that choose to live in this extraordinary place, Graham steps out of his home on a daily basis and is near-overwhelmed by the stench from the open drains, the mud and shit which cake the cobblestones, the torrent of shouting noise: the calls to trade of the fruit and vegetable sellers, the curses of the carters, the caterwauling of the ballad singers, the knife grinders and the milkmaids.

The physical stench can be overcome with nosegays, and the better sort do indeed wander the Piazza with various items held to their faces to ward off the odour. The moral stench, though, is of another kind, and deepens at night, when the whores and the constables take over the pavements. They dance in front of the elegant Tuscan portico that Inigo Jones built on the front of St Paul's, and the classical architecture puts Graham in mind not of God but of Derangement, for when comestibles give way to sex as the main item on sale,

Covent Garden does seem to him to become Mad. Its covered walkways are cloisters for the insane, where whores who give their names as 'Ann Nothing' or 'Mary Knowbody' or 'Kis my Comekel' grasp at the sleeves of men and where pox surges through the blood of an unknown number of them, such that it may as well be all of them, an infected Body Erotick, shrieking its appetites to the sky.

Consider, then, how Aaron Graham functions in a place such as this. For Graham buries his appetites beneath his great professionalism. He is universally admired for his application. His practised ease in society presents to the world the face of a man who knows everybody, is known by everybody, and is one of those two or three hundred ordinary men in London, neither nobility nor criminal, around whom the daily round circulates.

So what is one to make of Graham's life here in the Piazza of the Mad? What does it say of such a man that he chooses to make his home in a street that maintains its elegance, but nonetheless sits squarely between the rookeries of St Giles and the darkened doorways of Parkers Lane, now the most notorious whoring street in London? Does he hide behind his curtains at night while the street circus plays itself out? Or does he watch it, hungrily and bitterly, a lonely man abandoned by his wife, a man who like any other such man will, on occasion, present himself to a panderer in one of the coffee houses or taverns and ask to hear of the proclivities of their List? *Why, here's a young maiden, not yet broken in. And here's one expert in the ways of* bizarrerie, *she will break your skin in ways you will never forget. And here's one who weeps, and here's one who laughs, and here's one who never speaks but who has entered the dreams of Dukes and Viscounts* ...

These whispered conversations in the corners of taverns are one element of the unconventional drama that plays out behind Aaron Graham's careful eyes. But it is Sarah Graham who takes the biggest role in the masque. The anger towards Sarah leached out of her husband many months ago, though her motivation for taking such a scandalous course remains opaque to him. Sir Henry is a baronet with a fortune (though even that has attracted society gossip as to its provenance and its extent), but how can his social status accrue to a woman who had become, effectively, his concubine as well as his cousin? And yet somehow it does. The social sphere accommodates and, to a great extent, it forgives. Sarah may have married a well-regarded yet common professional, in truth a very rarefied kind of clerk, but she lives with a baronet.

Is it enough? Was it worth it? Graham, who only speaks to his wife by letter and only, until recently, on dry matters such as estates and inheritance, cannot supply an answer. Sarah has taken with her their youngest child, their daughter, sweet Ellen, the girl he has not seen these past three years and now, it appears, has been rechristened *Tempest Graham*, as if she were a cow to be rebranded by her new owner. And that rebranding has implanted a question which dare not be asked and which Graham constantly recoils from: is he Ellen's father, or is Sir Henry? Did this dalliance begin years before Sarah left Covent Garden for Thorpe?

A year after her mother took her away, Ellen began secretly writing to Graham in Covent Garden, telling him of the comings and the goings of Sir Henry Tempest, and the growing dismay of Sarah Graham. He had written to her, though carefully, never alluding to Ellen's own letters lest others read what he wrote and took action. It was the cessation of Ellen's letters – which had become almost fortnightly affairs – which had made him particularly amenable to Sarah's request for an investigation into the recent mysteries.

And if Ellen Graham – Ellen *Tempest* Graham – is in danger, what then? How much would he risk for the wellbeing of a girl he does not see? Is this not another unconventional ingredient in the surprisingly complex stew that is Aaron Graham? A man with a daughter he never encounters, and yet a daughter that he loves. A daughter that may not even be his.

Such a man lives in Covent Garden, the madhouse open to the sky.

It is past eight when he finally leaves the Bow Street office. The inmates of the Covent Garden asylum are out in force in the late summer twilight. There is still a good deal of heat in the air, and the streetwalkers own the pavements along the length of Drury Lane, from the Strand and into the dismal rookeries of St Giles. He turns south down Bow Street and then into the great prostitutional artery, Russell Street, which connects the Piazza with the Drury Lane theatre. Here the streetwalkers are sometimes two or three abreast on the pavement, approaching all passers-by with their proposals. Even men walking with female companions, or children, are propositioned, and a good many of them have their refusals greeted with a volley of abuse. The trade is blatant, open and violent. And through it walks one of the magistrates who are supposed to deal with it.

Or at least such is the belief of those polite people who are scandalised by the prostitutes' behaviour. The reality, as Graham knows, is somewhat different. The law is by no means clear on which constituent part of itself is being broken by these women. Magistrates such as Graham are often reluctant to do little more with these streetwalkers when they come before them each morning than tick them off and quietly suggest they go about their business with a little more surreptitious care. The occasional unfortunate will get sent down to Bridewell, and until recently she may even have been flogged, but the pursuit of a case against a prostitute in the criminal court of the Old Bailey is rare indeed, at least in comparison with this heaving reality of the street. Graham has even heard tell of parish officers in some parts of the metropolis refusing poor law relief to young women, arguing that such as these can always go whoring to feed themselves. The law concerns itself primarily with Property, not Propriety, and as a result there must be two hundred whores on this street alone; a busy night, indeed, but by no means an exceptional one.

Graham is no wide-eyed fool when it comes to these women. He knows they are trading something, and for many of them the thing they trade is the only thing they have. A good many of them will have been in service or in work as milliners or haberdashers or mantua-makers, but when a woman's labour becomes surplus to the requirements of polite society, she must resort to other assets. Defoe had called this the *amphibious lifestyle* – the need for women to drift in and out of prostitution according to the tenor of the economic times. At the end of the last century, it is said Pitt himself created 10,000 whores by the simple expedient of taxing maidservants.

This is understood by the magistrates, and it is understood even more instinctively by the men who are charged with arresting these women and bringing them before the magistrates – the parish watchmen and constables and beadles, the men who must share the pavement with these street women.

The night watch is just now being set. Graham walks past the watch house, and nods to the head constable for the night, a man named Larkin who is no better or worse than any of the other men who fulfil this role. Larkin will tonight supervise perhaps two dozen watchmen, who are charged with patrolling their beats and making arrests as they see fit. Any women arrested will be locked up in the watch house and brought before the sitting magistrate at Bow Street in the morning. But even an arrest is a comparative rarity, for in truth the constables and watchmen tolerate the prostitutes. The gin-money bribes the whores pay out may protect this tolerance, but in truth it comes from a deeper source. The whores and the constables come from the same families. They have, in certain ways, been forced to trade on their last remaining assets. Where the women trade caresses and permit violations, the men have little left to sell but their eyes and their fists.

It is, supposes Graham, a kind of equilibrium. It is perhaps the only possible balance left to the chaotic, disordered mechanism that is London law and order. What else can be done? The watchmen and constables are responsible to the parish authorities, who pay their wages. Those wages are tiny, and subject to a battalion of back-handed benefits. The magistrates, their own stipends paid by the Home Department, have only a supervisory role over the men of the watch, and in any case there is a well-understood set of priorities for those magistrates. Nowhere is it written down, but the statutes and the lists of offences make it clear to any man with intelligence and the wit to look that London's magistrates concern themselves first with crimes against property. They are the line between the monied classes and that enormous seething mass of criminality which the lords and merchants perceive as swilling up to their doors, its hands in their pockets and rifling around in their drawers. Perhaps, the wealthy might argue, it is better to tolerate prostitution, for at least it gives these vicious females a means of supporting themselves that does not involve theft from us.

And indeed, look at all the fine gentlemen parading on the pavement tonight! Why, there is the third son of the Earl of W—, a notoriously vicious abuser of whores whose whip has marked dozens of backs on these streets. And there, disappearing around a corner pulling a girl by the hand who cannot be more than twelve, is Sir P— himself, whose tastes run young indeed. These men are beginning their night early, and are unusual – most of their peers will never be seen grabbing females on the street, unless it is their own particular predilection to do so. Most men of means will end up in the serails and nunneries of St James, where the polite doors of King's Place open into elegant chambers of pleasure, sweet-smelling and clean, where the essential transaction between cully and whore is masked by suffocating sophistication.

These are at either ends of the social scale of whoring: the street, and the salon. But in between are the hundreds of whores in lodging houses and the new breed of hotels, paying for their rooms by the hour, turning buildings with short leases into effective brothels, though with no presiding Madam or Mother Superior. These women can be accessed in two ways: they can be encountered on the street, or they can be hired through the offices of a panderer. Every tavern or coffee house around Covent Garden has at least one of these, a man who can be found either working as a waiter or perhaps just sitting and waiting on himself, a man who knows the names and prices and predilections of dozens or hundreds of whores, and is able to accommodate any dark desire or perverted passion. Such a man is Albert Talty, and he can be found at the Bedford Head Tavern, once owned by Talty's illustrious predecessor in pimping, Jack Harris himself.

Maiden Lane runs from east to west between the Piazza and the Strand, and is as disgusting a river of human vice as any in the metropolis. The Bedford Head lies about halfway along, and is one of the largest establishments on the tight little street. Graham is buffeted and knocked as he walks along, though here the bulk of the passing trade is male not female. A stream of very drunk costermongers heads from tavern to alehouse to inn, pouring the takings of the day down their throats, investing in tomorrow's hangover.

After some shoving and shouting, he makes it to the door of the Bedford Head. He does not feel uncomfortable or out of place, even though his outfit – a duck-egg blue frock coat, a white silk waistcoat, and silk breeches – would have paid the wages of one of these barrow-boys for a year. He carries no money on his person, so his pockets can be picked again and again with no fear of loss. Seeing the small dark scurrying heads of children in the crowd, he knows that the pockets of those less careful than he are now being gently decanted into the purses of dark unseen gentlemen, through the medium of fast-fingered small boys.

The inside of the Bedford Head is as raucous and crowded as Maiden Lane. A thick smoky fog passes for air inside, while almost eighty years of ale has given the floor and the walls the stench of hoppy vinegar. Waiters scurry from table to table with vast jugs of ale and endless bottles of wine, no doubt consisting as much of Thames water as of Burgundy grape. There are whores here, too, as there are whores everywhere; in one corner of the place he catches a glimpse of a posture moll, kneeling naked upon a table over a shiny pewter tray. Such things used to be the preserve of the Rose, next to his beloved Drury Lane; since the immolation of that place, they have clearly made their way south of the Piazza.

But, Graham knows, the Bedford Head has a long tradition in such matters. The Society of Dilettanti, Sir Francis Dashwood's prototype for the Medmenhamites, had met here regularly during the last century. In one of the rooms inside Dashwood and forty other men had dressed up in robes, hidden pretend books of magic inside a casket called 'Bacchus' tomb', and had appointed an Archmaster of Ceremonies to sit on a throne, wearing a robe of crimson taffeta. Graham thinks of Sir John Cope and his ludicrous robes and furnishings, and wonders at the silly games of idle men.

He feels an arm, deliberately, on his own, and looks down and to his right. A young girl of perhaps eleven or twelve looks up at him, her face thick with slap, a wig almost as big as her upper body tottering on her head, a leer in her eyes which looks as practised and alien on her young face as his own wife's expression once appeared when he asked her if she was happy.

'You're the lucky one, tonight,' she says, and the voice that comes from her lovely mouth is cracked and appallingly ancient. 'You'll be my first, sir. 'T'would be most fine, would it not, to be my first?'

He smiles down at her, and pats her hand in acknowledgement of a fine performance.

'First *tonight*, perhaps, my dear. You'll need a more amenable gull than I. Now, tell me – I wish to speak with Talty.'

She snatches her hand away from his, and her painted face hisses. She swears, words which would shame a boatswain, her eyes black and furious.

'Hold your tongue, trollop. And tell me where Talty is, lest you spend the rest of this night in the watch house.'

She swears again, but at the end of a run of curses which would have had that same boatswain blushing and taking holy orders, she flicks a tiny hand to a far corner of the bar, and then she is gone, off to pawn her already abused maidenhead to some other willing gentleman.

Talty is on his own, a small circle of quiet in the chaos of the Bedford Head. It appears that the landlord has accorded the panderer special status; he is, after all, one who brings steady custom into the tavern, and Talty's clients (both the whores he advertises, and the culls who seek them) make regular use of the rooms upstairs. And by giving Talty this little franchise, as it were, the tavern keeper avoids any potential accusation of keeping a bawdy house. If attention is paid to him, as it is unlikely to be, he will simply move Talty on to another tavern, and look back on a happy trade which had to come to an end.

It is, of course, a shock to see him there. Graham can see it in the panderer's eyes. Magistrates are not people of the street – engaging with the pavements is the job of watchmen and constables. Justices sit in their offices and have the bad and the depraved brought to them, and from there pronounce judgement. This is the model for most London magistrates. Graham, though, is different; he has been inspired by another approach, that of John Harriott of Wapping.

'You are Albert Talty?' says Graham. The panderer, still in a state of mild shock, just nods. He is dark-featured and younger than Graham expected. Graham tries to suppress his instinctive dislike of the man and his profession; it will cloud his judgement.

'You know who I am? I see from your face that you do.'

'And what do you want from me, magistrate?'

Graham is aware of two large figures standing up from a table to his right, and feels an intense ripple of fear. He has stepped into a region where he is resented and incapable. Social conventions exist to prevent these icy moments. He should not be here.

Talty sees the fear in his face, and smiles – a yellow-toothed, baleful grin. He hisses at the figures, and they disappear into the crowd. An equation has been set, Graham sees. He on one side, Talty on the other. As of now, the equation does not balance.

'Will you sit?' Talty points to the chair opposite him, and Graham takes it, aware of sitting in the same position as hundreds of men before him, all of them seeking release. Perhaps he is no different.

A waiter appears, but Talty waves him away. This will be a short interview, the gesture says. Thinking he should have brought a constable – or a dozen of them – with him, Graham begins.

'I seek information on whores supplied to a particular group of gentlemen for their use at parties. I have been given your name by a servant to one of these men.'

The pimp says nothing. Yellow teeth are still visible through his lips, but they no longer form a smile. They look like they might bite.

'The men call themselves the Sybarites.'

The smile comes back. A wolf, sharing a splendid story.

'I know of the men. I have supplied them with no women. Why would I have done?'

The lie is splendidly relaxed, and Graham ignores it.

'Women were supplied by you to a party recently at the house of Sir John Cope. Also in attendance was Edmund Wodehouse, another gentleman. Both Cope and Wodehouse are now dead. They have been murdered in such a way that suggests a connection to these parties I have mentioned. I will be speaking to the other gentlemen concerned. I also wish to speak with the women who were there.'

As he speaks, he is aware of Talty's countenance changing. That theatrical, spiky grin eases, and is replaced by a face of concentrated thought. Graham knows what is happening. The world of society, the world of propertied men, the world which the magistracy was established to protect, has been threatened by the perpetrator of these killings. A justice has ventured out into the streets to investigate, an unprecedented event serving to emphasise the severity of matters. The comfortable balance between magistrate and pimp, between constable and whore, is being endangered. Refusal will make that danger intensify; Talty only has one option.

'You think the women killed these men?'

'By no means. I have no indication of such a thing. But the circumstances of Cope's killing, in particular, lead me to think there may be some association between what the women were paid to do, and the deaths.'

Talty allows that grin to reappear.

'You mean, they were killed for fucking whores.'

'Not just killed, Talty. Cope's cock was severed and pushed into his mouth. Perhaps before he was killed.'

The sight of this had made him vomit copiously in 13 Royal Terrace. And yet now he can use it to extract information from a pimp. A wondrous recovery.

That grin has gone again, but will return once more. For now, Talty is professional again.

'I don't keep records, magistrate.'

'I expect you don't.'

'But I do happen to remember who the whores were at that last party. Rose Dawkins was one. Elizabeth Carrington was the other.'

'How do I find these women?'

'Not my problem, that, is it?'

Graham acknowledges this. Talty is a businessman. He can hardly be expected to send his women into the arms of the authorities. He decides to push Talty's sudden cooperation a little further.

'Any other names, Talty? These men have regular parties.'

Talty breathes in through his nose, narrows one eye, runs one finger along his chin. Decides.

'Rose has been to the last few. She'll remember more names. I can only recall two. Jenny Larkin and Maria Cranfield. Jenny's long gone, left London months ago. Maria's disappeared. Last I heard she was pleading her belly down in Southwark. Shame. Popular girl, she would have been.'

Graham, his pockets strategically empty, has nothing on which he can write the names down. The four names are simple and unmemorable in their way, so he forces himself mentally to repeat them a half-dozen times. Then, he stands.

'I'll issue a warrant for Dawkins, Carrington and Cranfield. You'd best warn them if you see them.'

'Treat them right, magistrate. Word'll get back to me if you don't. And we've all got our own information to trade, don't we?'

The grin reappears for its final performance. Graham, his blood temporarily frozen, stares at the panderer, but avoids the obvious question. He doesn't wish to know what the information Talty might have would be. Replacing his hat, he turns back into the rank mass of the night-time Garden.

CANTERBURY

For two weeks during that hot July, the hop garden was haunted by Maggie Broad's daughter. Maria wailed and moaned, and the women who worked on the farm would mutter prayers to themselves whenever they walked beneath her window. The men were angered by the sound, and complained to the hop garden's overseer, who passed their complaints on to Henry Lodge, with no expectation that anything would change.

And while the girl made these sad noises, her mother sat with her, sleeping when she slept, holding her hand and stroking her brow when she woke, feeding her and showing her to the farm's water-closet, a recent addition to the property which Maggie Broad had stared at in frank amazement on the women's first night in the farmhouse.

'Do you remember the heads on the *Lady Juliana*?' she asked. 'Do you remember sitting out there above the waves, shitting into the sea, waiting for some bloody sea serpent to leap up and tear off your arse?'

She laughed, and the sound was hard and savage, and the man of means felt a terrible discomfort.

He had not known she had a daughter. There'd been no mention of Maria during their time in the colony. He asked about where she had sprung from. The answer was brusque.

'I had her before I was transported. She was raised by a farmer and his wife in Suffolk.'

This was where Maggie had disappeared to upon leaving the *Indefatigable*. She had travelled to Suffolk to find her daughter, but the daughter had gone. The farmer and his wife were dead of some disease or other. There had been no mention of Henry's failure to meet Maggie, and somehow this made the man of means anxious.

'So how did you find her?' he asked her.

'I asked people. I'm good at asking things of people.'

This was not how he'd pictured their reunion. He'd imagined them sipping claret as the sun went down over the hop poles, he telling her of the success he'd made of himself since returning from the colony. He had no ambitions to court her; only to justify himself, to say he'd made the most of the beginning she had gifted him. He wanted to impress her, not woo her.

But her desperate daughter was all she cared for, and there were no comfortable drinks on the terrace behind the farmhouse. Whenever he alluded to New South Wales, he received a hard and cynical response, as if she despised him for sentimentality.

This dismissive contempt began immediately. She asked him the name of his farm, and he was reluctant to share it, but that reluctance was obvious and only inflamed her curiosity, such that she insisted.

'I named it *Juliana*.'

She stared at him.

'You're a bloody fool. Let me tell you about the *Lady Juliana*.'

She turned away from him. He noticed this a good deal. She rarely looked directly into his face.

'The *Lady Juliana* was two weeks out from Cape Verde when she crossed the equator,' she said. 'I'd been a prisoner on that bloody ship of fools for a year. The whores on board had been allowed to ply their wares at the places we docked; the pox in their loins was traded from Plymouth and Portsmouth and London and beyond, and sold for pennies and pounds to take up residence in the loins of men in Tenerife or on slavers off the coast of Africa. By the time we reached the Line, almost every seaman, including the officers, had selected a woman to share his hammock or his cabin. The captain and the master approved of it, and these women – the ones who did not call themselves whore – were glad of it. A good many of them were pregnant.

'But on the night we crossed the Line, one of those doomed unborn souls died.

'A sailor harpooned a dolphin, and skinned it, and one of the seamen wore the skin as a costume. He was Neptune, and two of his shipmates wore long wigs made of seaweed. They were his attendants. The men were all drunk, and they cheered when Neptune pointed out the sailors who'd never crossed the Line before to be part of their ceremony. The women watched, but then Neptune rushed at them, and they panicked. Many of them fell, and one – I do not remember her name – was by then heavy with child.

'She screamed, and then she wept, and the older women knew what was happening. They took her below, and screamed for the barber-surgeon, but he was drunk and playing Neptune's games. So the women had to do it, while the men played their games abovedecks, and down at the bottom of the ship the rats hid in the piss and shit of the bilge.

'They talked of bleeding her, as someone had seen a

surgeon do this once, but she screamed at that, and then the decision was made for them. The baby was dead. I put my hand on her belly, and there was no life in there. It felt as dead as a cannonball. We gave her China tea with opium drops, and the older women worked away at her stomach and slowly – it took an hour – she pushed out the body. We gave her laudanum, wrapped the baby in sailcloth, and threw it into the sea. The men did not even notice us. The father must have been among them.

'But they were all its father. Every one of them, even Neptune himself.'

The next day, he took down the sign with the hop garden's name on it down.

When he could, he asked her questions. So many questions: about the state of the township at Parramatta, about William Bligh and the Rum Rebellion, about the savage natives he still thought of as 'Indians'. But she was reluctant to talk of any of these things, saying she'd left New South Wales behind, that she'd come back to England to rebuild a life with her daughter, now she had the means to do so.

But the daughter was quite mad. He could see it. His overseer could see it. The men and women of the farm could see it. She shrieked and shouted, she tore at her hair and dragged at her forearms, her nails leaving long ruby-red tracks.

This was his life for two weeks. Until at the end of the fortnight she came to him and asked for a favour. She didn't mention his failure to perform the last task she'd asked of him. She didn't have to.

'Anything. I'll do anything.'

'Well, then, sir.'

She stared at him, and he felt a strangely familiar squeezing touch on his head, a sense that his temples were being pushed together.

'You do not need to demand anything of me,' he said, with some effort. 'I am in your debt.'

'Perhaps you are, Henry. But I owe no one, and I would have no one owe me. So do this one thing for me, and we will part as equals.'

'Anything that is in my power, I will do.'

'Maria has lost her wits, Henry. She is quite out of them. She needs treatment, and she needs to be cared for. And more than this, I am not able to watch over her for a time. I must settle a certain matter which will take all my effort for the coming weeks. I need to find an appropriate place for her.'

'You mean a madhouse?'

She looked away, and that pressure on his head subsided.

'I . . . I am sorry. I meant . . .'

'No.' She looked back at him again. 'You are right. A madhouse is what she needs. And she needs to be hidden from sight during what comes next.'

He knew nothing of madhouses. He recognised the name of only one: Bethlem. But was Bethlem not a Gehenna of madness? A palace of lunatics, throwing their excrement from one to the other, undressing themselves for display to a gawping public. How could he possibly send the daughter of this woman to that place?

But after consulting some of the professional men in the nearby village, he had learned that Bethlem's chief physician, one Dr Monro, had a private madhouse of his own, in which he treated the well-to-do in a more congenial atmosphere. The madhouse was in Hackney, a long way from Canterbury. But Maggie said she had her own business in Wapping, and that Hackney was by no means too far from there.

So it was agreed. Henry would take poor, desperate Maria to Brooke House in Hackney. Maggie would not accompany them, and she added a condition: that her name not be linked to Maria's. As far as Brooke House was concerned, Maria was the ward of the man of means. He asked her why this should be, and all she said was this: 'She cannot be associated with what is to come next. She will recommence her life with no stain. No one can know she is my daughter, Henry. It must be as if I were never here.'

She looked at him, and his head felt squeezed once more, and he agreed, adding that he would visit London every week during the stay of her incarceration. As July finally gave way to August, the three of them left the hop garden for London, leaving the relieved overseer to make arrangements for the coming picking season, with the blight of the mad girl lifted from the place like poison lifted from a well.

PART THREE

Do What You Will

CHARCOT: Let us press again on the hysterogenic point. Here we go again. Occasionally subjects even bite their tongue, but this would be rare. Look at the arched back, which is so well described in the textbooks.
PATIENT: Mother, I am frightened.

Jean-Martin Charcot, *Charcot the Clinician:*
The Tuesday Lessons

THORPE

The Pipehouse is at the south-eastern corner of the Tempest estate, at a fork in the road. It is a relatively nondescript place, and is quiet tonight as Horton approaches it in the September twilight. The sun is setting behind him, silhouetting the copses of trees and the partly hidden buildings of the fine houses which dot the swampy land. An owl lifts itself from a tree by the side of the road and flies off across a field, its long wings twitching gently in the evening breeze. There is a warm sympathy to the evening air.

The warmth dissipates when he steps into the Pipehouse, and he wonders for a moment if he has made a terrible mistake. The interior is cramped, by the standards of London's larger inns – the place is barely as big as the Town of Ramsgate in Wapping. It houses perhaps a half-dozen old tables and a dozen stools on its uneven wooden floor. A middle-aged woman is scrubbing down one of these tables, her bulky figure partially obscuring two men sitting behind her. There are five other men seated at different tables, none of them speaking to each other, most of them looking at their jugs of beer with the same mournful intensity they might adopt when watching a pet die. Several of them smoke pipes, and the air is thick and grey with tobacco odours. The fat woman stands straight as Horton steps inside, and he sees the two men sat behind her. He recognises them from the road the previous day, the friends of Peter Gowing. The labourer who had reproached him, and his embarrassed friend.

'Good evening to you,' he says, to the woman. She nods and walks to the little wooden bar. He follows her, ignoring the stares of the men around him. No one says anything. He asks for a tankard of ale, and she pours him one from a big brown cracked jug. From somewhere inside the place he hears a distant crash and a shouted profanity, and the woman stares at him coldly, as if daring him to mention it. He thanks her, turns, and sits down at the same table as Peter Gowing's friends. He doesn't look at them at first, staring carefully one by one at the other men in the bar, but it only takes a few moments for a hand to put itself on his shoulder and suggest, impertinently, that he turn his head.

He does so, sipping from his tankard as he goes, and faces the angry red-faced labourer from the road.

'You make very free with your hands, sir,' he says, softly. 'Do you need reminding of my station?'

Hob smiles, and leaves his hand on Horton's shoulder. There is an intensity to the colour in his cheeks. He is drunk.

'I would like,' he begins, then stops, frowning slightly. He belches hugely, then starts again. 'I would like to know what you think you are doing.'

Horton smiles, mildly.

'I am drinking ale, sir. And if you do not remove your hand, I shall shortly be arresting you.'

The other man at the table reaches over and pulls the red-faced man away. There is no complaint. Hob looks at his friend as if he were some species of elephant, belches again, and looks back at Horton, happily. More than drunk. Incapacitated.

Horton turns to the man's friend, who looks as miserable as he did on the road yesterday. He is narrow, red-haired, his hands small but roughened, his face as pocked as the wall of Newgate. Horton nods at him, and the man nods carefully back.

No one in the place has anything to say, so Horton fills the silence himself.

'My name's Charles Horton. These two men have already met me, but you others have not, though you may have heard tell of my visit. I am looking into the recent events at Thorpe Lee House.'

'The witchery, you mean,' says the fat woman at the bar.

'I mean no such thing,' says Horton. 'There have been episodes of trespass, damage to property and even attempted murder at Thorpe Lee House which I am seeking to uncover the cause of.'

''Tis done,' says one of the men at the tables.

''Twas the witch, Elizabeth Hook,' says another.

'Witchery,' says the fat woman, again, emphatically.

'And yet – why?' says Horton. No one answers that. 'Why should anyone wish mischief on Thorpe Lee House?'

'Witches need no reason,' mutters another man.

'Do they not? I have heard it differently. Those accused of witchcraft in the past did not do so out of pure malice. It was always in response to a slight, a refusal of help, a dismissal from a kitchen door. Is this not true?'

No reply comes to that.

'So why should it be that Elizabeth Hook wanted mischief done to Thorpe Lee House? To Miss Tempest Graham?'

'It's a rotten, wicked place,' said the woman.

'How so, madam?'

She scowls at being addressed directly.

'They live as man and wife up there. Him and her and that poor girl. 'Tis a bad place.'

A few of the men nod. Horton thinks that the villagers probably all agree on this.

'But a witch is evil too, is she not? Why would something evil visit mischief on another evil? What is the motivation?'

Hob belches again and giggles slightly. Horton looks at his short friend, who is staring into his tankard as if it held cosmic truths.

'But he seen 'er!' says one of the men. 'Bill seen 'er!'

'Bill?'

There is a shrinking of the small man's shoulders, almost involuntary, that gives him away. Bill is the man sitting beside him, it would seem.

'What did you see, Bill?'

No reply.

'Bill, if you saw something, you are bound to . . .'

'I didn't see nothin'. Not a bloody thing.'

His voice is unexpectedly deep in one so lithe and sinewy. His slight hands are clenched into rough-red balls.

'Well, let us start with where you were when you didn't see anything.'

'In the vicar's field, just down the lane.'

'So you did see something?'

Bill's uneducated face is angry and weak and confused.

'I saw 'er bloody fly, didn't I!'

Bill spits it out, straight into Horton's face, as if he were reacting to a taunt from a child.

'She flew along the top of the 'edge, all the way back into the village. She's a bloody witch! Elizabeth 'ook is a bloody witch!'

*

A little the worse for ale, Horton walks down the lane a way, towards the village, leaving Thorpe Lee House behind him. Bill had calmed somewhat once his revelation had been extracted, enough anyway to describe the spot he'd sat in when Elizabeth Hook had flown through the air above his head. He finds it shortly – an open section of hedgerow, giving onto a fallow field. It is full dark now, with no moon, but the sky is astonishingly clear, such that the stars cast their own light, enough almost to make a shadow. He remembers standing outside a Ratcliffe Highway house, reading the markings on a coin in the moonlight.

He almost falls as he steps into the field, which is somewhat below the level of the road. It is as if a ditch has been dug all the way around the place at some point in the preceding centuries, and has been slowly filled in, leaving only a declivity in the ground as an echo of former works. He steadies himself. He has drunk a good deal of ale, and has become something of a friend to those men in the Pipehouse. Only Bill remained sullen, embarrassed by his outburst, determined to prove his own sanity but equally determined not to be drawn into Horton's dealings. His fat friend Hob had slept with his head on the table, snoring out clouds of beer fumes into the crowded saloon.

He walks a way into the field, and kicks around with his boots for a moment or two before hearing the sound of glass knocking against stone. He squats down and picks up an empty wine bottle. So, the first part of Bill's story is confirmed, at least potentially. Someone has at some point sat here drinking wine and looking at the stars. Horton sits down himself and looks back at the hedgerow, as Bill claimed to have done.

It is true – the dip in the ground here does give the impression that the hedgerow has great height. Not even trees are visible on the other side, only stars. He can imagine, rather more vividly than he would care to, the silhouette of a witch skittering across the sky along the top of that hedge, her dark skirts fluttering behind her. He can almost hear a malicious chuckle floating down from the night sky as she watches him, sitting there in the field, beer in his brain and a sudden, inexplicable, inescapable belief in the possibility of *maleficium*.

He shakes his head to restore himself, but is then shaken once again as a shape does, in fact, fly across his vision, scudding across the top of the hedge. For a moment he has a view of outstretched arms, of a gleeful gliding, and then he recognises another owl, perhaps even the same one as before, entertaining itself on the warm night's updraughts.

Mistaken identity, then? Had Bill just seen a bird?

But no. Bill had *spoken* to the witch. Or at least, she had spoken to him. She had stopped her flight and turned back, and hovered on top of the hedge with impossible intent, and had mocked his cowardice.

Look at you, little fool. Look at you. Pity the man sitting in the field drinking cheap wine and spying on witches. Elizabeth sees you, little fool. She sees you. And she remembers.

She had laughed, then, and turned back on her course, flying off into the night, leaving Bill chattering with fear, full of his story, desperate to unleash it upon his fellow villagers. He'd run back to the Pipehouse, and had burst in with the news that there was indeed a witch at Thorpe Lee House, he had seen her and she had spoken to him, and her name was Elizabeth.

Horton stands up, somewhat shakily, and makes his way back to the road, clambering up the steep little bank at the edge of the field. He turns down the road towards Thorpe village and walks a little way in the starlight, glancing back towards the Pipehouse once or twice, unable to shake the overwhelming feeling that he is being watched.

After perhaps fifty yards, he stops, and turns back. It is

impossible to see anything, even with the starlight. He will return in the daylight on the morrow; besides, the night-time has lost all its congeniality. He feels more than ever the watchfulness of unseen entities, and walks back to Thorpe Lee House, considerably faster than he left it.

It is impossible to sleep, even with a great quantity of ale in his belly. Horton feels himself prey to an itching discomfort which reminds him of childhood fears. The horror of what might wait behind his closed eyelids. He leaves his candle burning for an hour or more, listening to the sounds of the house and those within it: a light step-step-step somewhere nearby (Ellen?); a giggle followed by a shush (Peter and Daisy?); a muttered prayer. The previous two nights these sounds were intriguing; tonight, for no reason he can account for other than the Pipehouse's ale, they carry malicious intent.

The old house has thin walls, or its cavities carry sound peculiarly clearly. Or perhaps the house itself has things it wishes to say.

He steps to the window half-a-dozen times, looking out onto the lawn before the house, the swoop of the driveway, the shadowed fingers of the trees. The noises of the house recede, and a great and, to Horton, shocking silence wells up. Never such a silence in London, where the river breathes in creaking masts and illicit splashes. The silence is strange beyond words, stretching out over the lawns to the flat fields behind, as if waiting for something to happen.

And then, something does.

A figure appears from the house, walking out onto the lawn. A woman, dressed for sleep and not for garden walking. Sarah Graham. She walks out towards the middle of the lawn and then stands, perfectly still, watching the trees that ring the lawn.

Nothing happens. The moment stretches out. Horton breathes quietly, as if he were standing behind Mrs Graham, looking over her shoulder into the unresponsive trees.

After a while, he begins to count, slowly and deliberately. He reaches a hundred, then two hundred, three, four, five hundred. And then, as six hundred goes by, Mrs Graham turns and walks back to the house. Her face is up and her eyes open, and she looks directly in front of her, but in the same unseeing way as a blind man walking across an empty room. She disappears below the line of the house, and he hears (because he is waiting for it) the door close, with a clandestine thud.

He walks to the door, and opens it slightly, and sees Mrs Graham in the gloom of the hallway appear at the top of the stairs and then turn into her chamber. At no point does she look right or left. She is, it seems, unaware of her surroundings, yet she opens and closes her bedroom door without mishap.

Horton closes his own bedroom door, and walks back to the window to close the curtains. But he stops there.

Another woman is standing on the lawn.

She is at the edge, just in front of the ring of trees, as if she has just stepped through them. Unlike Mrs Graham, this woman is agitated; she takes little steps to and fro, and keeps walking towards the house, and back again. As she comes closer on one of these little attempted visits, Horton sees her face clearly.

It is Elizabeth Hook.

He ponders opening the window and then calling down to her, but cannot bring himself to do so. It is as if she were floating above the hedge on the road, waiting to speak to him. But this is not in keeping with what the woman herself does. Elizabeth spends five minutes (he counts them, again) in agitated movement on the lawn before turning around and walking back into the trees.

The enormous still silence descends again. From somewhere he hears an owl, as if it were calling to him like one of his watching Wapping boys, alert to Elizabeth Hook's progress.

She's here! She's here! She's here!

A Treatise on Moral Projection

To find oneself sitting in a chair and to have no idea
as to how one arrived there – such a feeling is almost
indescribable. But to be one such as I – one who has
made the examination of mankind's impulses and
perceptions his lifetime's work – is to be more than
confused. It is a moment to shake one's own mind like
the earth is shaken by a violent quake. Suddenly,
one's own Mind is an Entity, something to be
observed and even feared. For how can one's
perceptions work so counter to one's reality? Was I, in
short, going mad?

   I sat in that old chair, staring at John Burroway. What
was he doing there? How dare he come into my rooms?
I asked him how I had come to be there, and I was no
doubt forthright in my irritation with him. I well
remember the look of confusion on his face as I spoke
to him, and I know now it must have mirrored the
picture of complete consternation that had been on
mine own.

   Tears sprang into his feeble-minded eyes, and he
begged to know why I should speak to him like this. He
had walked to my rooms with me. We had come there
together. Why was I now asking how he came to be
there? Had I forgotten?

Now we come to the heart of the matter. And it is a dark heart, one which many of my readers will find it impossible to account for. For I had, indeed, forgotten all that had transpired immediately before finding myself in my old chair.

I have told you of my visit to Maria Cranfield's cell, and of the strange sense of *compulsion* that I experienced there. I have told of how I was forced from that room, seemingly without any volition of mine own, and only came to myself once I was outside.

But I must tell you now: in the immediate aftermath of these events, I had no recollection of them at all. I remembered leaving my consultation room to go to Maria's cell – but the next thing I knew, I was sitting back in that room, in that old chair, staring at John.

It was this one moment that shaped the next thirty years of my life. It is my attempt to understand what happened in that cell with Maria Cranfield, and the way that my mind responded to it, that is the reason for this paper. I will try to explain what actually happened, and from this draw out my own theories.

John Burroway was, as I said, tearful and scared in the face of my anger with him. Thankfully I have learned how to act in such situations, and I fell back on the techniques of moral therapy to deal with his weak mind. He needed to submit to my mastery, but he also needed to be made comfortable with that submission. My mind was beginning to clear by this stage, and I was able to assert myself in a more helpful manner.

Slowly, over perhaps an hour, John told me, in his own rambling way, what had taken place in Maria Cranfield's cell. John's own memories were impressively sharp, given his hitherto blunt faculties. As my chain of thought reasserted itself, I perceived something within my own mind: a blank spot, at the centre of my thoughts. I realised there was a distinct empty space in the pattern of my memory.

I still did not precisely picture the story I have described here; it relies strongly on John's own recollection. But as we talked, I began to perceive that empty spot filling up again, not with the solid shapes of a well-educated mind, but more with shades and impressions, perceived as it were through a fog. These memories had not been wiped away like dirt on a glass, I began to see; they had rather been obscured by some intervention into my own mind.

Maria Cranfield had, it seemed, reached into my head and obscured me from myself. I thought back to what Delilah Underwood had said to me before I went up to Maria's cell: *she gets in your head, and once she gets in there, you can't get her out.* This did not quite describe what I was now experiencing, but the symptoms had some close association.

I felt I had stumbled upon some huge hidden truth about the mind of man. From this point on, I became obsessed with the matter. I recorded every single detail relating to Maria that I could remember. I wrote down *everything*.

Including, of course, the peculiar case of John Burroway. His simplicity – the damage done to his brain in childhood, which had reduced his faculties through some kind of physical injury to his brain – in some way protected him from whatever it was that Maria had done to my own memory. But it did not prevent Maria from forcing him into actions against his will.

What was this power? Where did it stem from? These questions began to haunt me, and have obsessed me ever since. I shall now turn to what I believe that power to be, which is the substance of my contribution to human knowledge.

BROOKE HOUSE

'What did you do, Maria?'

They are the first words Abigail speaks once the two men have left the room – or rather, once the two men have been *pushed out* of the room, by whatever force emanates from the dark-haired slender frame which now sits hunched against the wall, uncomfortably so, the harsh line of the chain presumably biting into her back.

Maria does not answer for a time. Her breathing is ragged, as if she has run a great race. Abigail asks the question again, trying to keep the galloping panic out of her voice, trying to stay calm.

'What did you do, Maria?'

She had moved from the bed to the chair, once Bryson and John had left the place. When she'd first come into the cell, and seen Maria's eyes locked upon Bryson's – but, more than this, seen the look on Bryson's face – when she'd seen that, she'd sat down on the bed without thinking, her old training as a nurse coming back to her. There was frenzy in the air, and it poured out of Maria like heat from a stove, and it needed to be calmed. Whatever else was happening, that needed tending to first. So she sat on the bed and put an arm around Maria and whispered consoling words to her, meaningless words, full of empty comforts. But it had calmed Maria and whatever hold she had on Bryson – however that hold was expressed over the gap between them – was dropped.

And then the two men had left, their eyes confused and angry, unable to understand what compelled them. And Maria never said a single, solitary word.

I did, though. I said, Leave us. *And they did. As if I had commanded it.*

Imagine. Having such power over men like Bryson.

Or, to put it better: imagine if the hating rage she felt towards Bryson after the previous evening could be turned into something *tangible* . . .

'I don't know what I did.'

The first words Maria has ever spoken to her are quiet, precise, in a strong accent – Suffolk, perhaps? She does not raise her face when she speaks. But then she does. And any fear Abigail might have felt towards her, and towards what she can apparently do, cannot survive that look. The girl's eyes are full of longing, no madness in them at all, like the clear windows onto a workhouse, with children in rags inside licking out filthy bowls.

'When he came in here – the doctor – I wanted him to feel some of the pain I feel. I wanted to *hurt* him. And I wanted you to see me hurting him, so then I made the other man go and fetch you. You were crying last night, you see. You cried, and you said his name – perhaps you were sleeping, perhaps not. His name, and Charles's name. You say Charles's name a lot, don't you? I would like to meet Charles.'

Abigail moves back to the bed. She is not a doctor, and Maria is not a patient. They are women, on their own, facing – what, exactly? The indifference of men? The cruelty of fate?

'But, how did you do it?'

'I know not. I did it. That is all.'

'The woman who visits you, the one I hear through the wall. Did she tell you how to do it?'

Maria turns her head to look at Abigail, and Abigail feels something between her temples: a slight tightening, as if an old sponge were being gently squeezed between unseen fingers. And then it is gone. Maria looks away. Abigail cannot help herself; she inches along the bed away from the other woman.

'I must go and speak to Bryson,' says Abigail. 'And I must fetch my husband.'

'Bryson will not remember what happened for some time.'

Abigail frowns.

'How do you know?'

'It is something I have been told. And besides, the door is locked.'

Maria smiles, as if at a little private joke.

'I made John lock the door. Until he comes to unlock it, we must stay in here.'

And then the smile disappears, and misery takes its place.

'What has happened to me?' she whimpers. 'Surely some demon has come into me. Why hast thou forsaken me, Lord? Why hast thou forsaken me?'

Abigail reaches out, instinctively, to take the girl's hand, forgetting that her hands and arms are bound inside the strait waistcoat. Maria keeps her eyes averted.

'I saw it,' she says. 'I saw it all. They were cutting him to pieces, there, in his bed. I saw it all. What are these visions? What are these terrible visions?'

She looks at Abigail then, and her eyes show no power of persuasion or suggestion. They are only full of despair, and loss, and agonising fear.

'Why has my God abandoned me?' she says.

6 September 1814
Bow Street Public Office, Westminster

Dear Sir

This letter is being sent, immediately and by hand, to a number of gentlemen. I must beg your forgiveness for the forthright and impolite nature of the communication, but feel it is essential to warn you without delay that your life may be in some considerable danger.

You may have heard, from any number of sources, of the recent terrible deaths of Edmund Wodehouse and Sir John Cope. Both of these men have been killed, we do believe, by the same person or persons unknown. Although we can find no immediate motivation for the deaths of these men, we are conducting an investigation based upon a particular theory; that both these men were members of a society calling itself the Sybarites, and that their membership of this society was in some unknown way connected with their deaths.

It has come to our attention that you, the recipients of this letter, are members of this society. I make no judgement on this situation. I simply warn you that, if our hypothesis proves to be correct, it may become dangerous for you in London. While we seek to clarify this matter, it may be a sensible precaution for you to leave the Metropolis for the country, while we continue this investigation.

In the meantime, the constable who has carried this letter to you will remain, this coming night, in observation of your household. Please allow him to investigate the premises, and to check all points of entry. He will remain outside your residence for the night, and ensure no intruder creeps inside.

Please note, however, that this arrangement can only possibly be preserved for two or perhaps three nights. My resources do not stretch themselves to providing individual guardianship of all the houses of those receiving this letter. For reasons of individual privacy, I am also not revealing the full list of those receiving this letter to anyone on receipt of it. No doubt, though, if your Society is still extant, communication will occur between you all.

I remain
Yours sincerely
GRAHAM, A. – Magistrate, Bow Street Public Office

NORWOOD

The coppice at Norwood is thick and ancient and now, thanks to the ministrations of ministers and commissioners, almost entirely enclosed. Land now owned by Lord Thurlow pinches down from the north, while the trees which once whispered within the Great North Wood are now the property – roots, branches and memories – of the Archbishop of Canterbury.

Within the trees, in clearings and under shadows, live the gypsies of Norwood.

Aaron Graham's carriage makes its way into the coppice, along the road which took its name from the local residents. Maggie Finch, the Queen of the Gypsies at Norwood, had made the area famous almost a hundred years before, and her niece Bridget had become Mother Bridget, the most famous gypsy in Britain, her name associated with two books she almost certainly never wrote: *Mother Bridget's Dream Book* and *The Norwood Gypsy*. The woman herself died in her hut here on Norwood Common more than thirty years before, but her name – and the reputation of Norwood itself – still holds sufficient allure for printers to exploit it on their chapbooks.

William Jealous had visited the place yesterday, on Graham's orders. Jealous now rides alongside Graham's carriage, which is driven by Roberts. The young patrolman is as alive and aware as any human Graham has ever seen, clearly relishing the opportunity to involve himself in an investigation which is already the talk of London. He will take Graham's letter to the Sybarites on to Thorpe once they have spoken to the gypsies. It is time to warn Sir Henry of the danger he is in, Horton or no Horton.

Sir John Cope's death has filled the second and third pages of the morning's newspapers – the front pages continue to support London's commerce. It would take the death of a monarch or a declaration of war to shift the advertisements. But none of the stories printed by the scribblers have made any connection between Sir John and Edmund Wodehouse, other than the plain fact that both murders have happened and both victims were men of quality. There is some mild speculation that the ritual nature of Wodehouse's death might have been repeated in Sir John's despatch, but Graham has been careful to warn Sir John's staff, via Burgess, that any discussion of the case with the press will lead to unspoken punishment.

Graham has attempted to lead the press by publishing his own version of events in the *The Hue and Cry and Police Gazette*. It is the first time he has done such a thing. The newspaper had been John Fielding's invention, as *The Quarterly Pursuit*, a mechanism for alerting the public to recent robberies and assaults as means of generating information. It had been notably successful in this, going through several changes of name. By using the newspaper to address the public directly about the circumstances of Sir John's murder, Graham is seeking to do something new: to guide the emotional responses of the street, to assert his own will upon their panic, to *calm them down*. Whether this will be effective, it is too soon to tell.

*

The main gypsy encampment is at the foot of the hill that rises up to Upper Norwood. It presents itself to the little road almost blatantly; this is, after all, a public attraction, a spot for those wanting their fortunes told and their palms read. Graham knows how malevolent the promises of these people are; he has arrested and locked up a half-dozen of them for the *hokkano baro*, their 'great trick' of taking valuables from the gullible with the promise to return them multiplied. In one case he had prosecuted, a man from Covent Garden had given one of these people eleven guineas, having been promised that two nights later three white doves would come to him and place 200 guineas, as well as a watch and a gold ring and (the detail Graham found particularly clever and pernicious) some silver buckles and shirt buttons underneath his pillow. When brought before Graham, the gypsy concerned had muttered something in the strange half-invented language these people used, and when Graham insisted he repeat it in English, the gypsy scowled and said words to the effect that non-gypsies were fools to believe their money could be multiplied, so why should gypsies not exploit the gullibility of fools? The man had been sent to Newgate to await trial in the Old Bailey; Graham assumes he is by now dead or practising his art on the shores of New South Wales. Perhaps the fools are made of sterner stuff in those parts.

Such stories as these are the common currency of folk suspicious of gypsies, yet still people flock to Norwood. They come not to have their money multiplied (though lottery predictions remain popular), but to have their fortunes read. Fortune-telling methods are varied and complex: a mermaid-shaped piece of catgut held in the palm, which will curl up and indicate the nature of a future husband; an egg white dropped into a glass of water, its shapes full of meaning; fate read in the features of a face; the patterns of the stars and planets in the night sky, used to tell the most propitious time to marry, to invest, to harvest. For sixpence a time, a whole panoply of mischievous fiction can be invoked.

The huts and tents and carriages of the gypsy encampment are quiet this morning, though a gaggle of small children sees their carriage approach and runs into the wood, shouting in some tongue which sounds vaguely, but only vaguely, English. By the time Graham has climbed down from his carriage and Jealous from his horse, half-a-dozen gypsy women have appeared, all offering their own version of the timeless promises of their kind. These women are young and, presumably, inexperienced. Their older sisters stay within the trees, wary of the arrival of three men, one of whom seems dressed with obvious authority. This is not the time of day for wealthy visitors from town. They must be up to no good.

Jealous ignores the women who approach them, and heads into the woods. Graham follows him, and some of the women shout abuse and threaten dark curses. Jealous leads him to a hut next to a particularly ancient carriage, in front of which a black horse stands and waits, seemingly rooted to the same mysterious earth as the old trees of the North Wood.

Jealous raps on the hut, and from within a cracked female voice shouts angrily in return.

'Come out, Mother,' the young officer shouts. Graham is once again impressed with him. He acts as if he has been a resident of the Norwood gypsies his whole life. 'It is the patrolman from Bow Street, come with the magistrate.'

More mutterings from within, but after a few seconds the top half of the door of the hut swings open, and a dark-skinned face surrounded by grey gorse-hair emerges, the face narrow and obscurely beautiful, the eyes as black as the wood behind them. The old eyes narrow as the gypsy sees the man with Jealous, and Graham sees her calculate the situation –

and her likely benefit from it – within half a second. A movement behind the hut disturbs him momentarily, and he sees, with a well-dressed shiver, that the gypsy's horse is glaring at him with the same deliberate calculation. Her old husband, perhaps, transformed into a beast by some ancient Balkan curse.

'Mother Marcus,' says Jealous. 'This is the magistrate of Bow Street, Mr Graham. He wishes to hear what you told me yesterday.'

'Ah, do he?' asks the gypsy, and her voice is as smooth as milk warmed before a fire. Graham wonders how many fortunes have been coaxed out of how many pockets by that voice. 'And he knows my trade, I take it, patrolman?'

'He does,' says Jealous, and he is smiling. It seems he, too, has been somewhat charmed by this woman, old enough to be his mother, seductive enough for his dreams.

'Then perhaps he can demonstrate his knowledge.' She smiles, and waits. Graham steps towards her. She watches his approach with the welcoming charm of a fatally attractive cobra.

'Mother Marcus, I have questions I wish to ask you.'

'Ah, questions! Well, questions cost no money at all, comes the time. But answers is not free, magistrate.'

'You must answer my questions, madam. The law requires it.'

'Does it, now? Then you would not be a magistrate who prints handbills and asks for statements, then? You'd be a special kind of magistrate, who doesn't give rewards? Is that it, magistrate?'

'There is no reward for information in this case.'

'Is there not? Then I can see how you afford such fine clothes, magistrate, and I hope you enjoy your journey home from our little enclave. I see sadness in your face, magistrate.

You must take it with you, along with your empty purse and your ignorance of what I know.'

Her face begins to reverse into the dark of the hut behind her, and the effect is eerie indeed. She is like a Delphic oracle in a cave, stepping backwards into the gloom, until all that is visible is the forest glinting back from her eyes. The horse makes a sound like an amused *harrumph*.

But she does not reverse all the way in. She waits. Graham can smell the game on her, as strongly as the stench of her old horse. Well, then. He will play.

'A guinea, then. A guinea for what you know.'

Her face remains where it is, almost entirely obscured, but the warm-milk voice floats from the hut.

'Ah, the guinea is a social bird, magistrate. She is never happy on her own. At least a dozen make a happy brood.'

'Perhaps. But London guineas are made of sterner stuff. They become impatient with more than two companions.'

'Is that indeed true? 'Tis new knowledge to me. Here in the forest, three guineas would be defenceless. Six would make a happy band.'

'Well, then. It is your forest, madam. If six guineas are needed to protect each other, six guineas it shall be.'

He takes out his purse, counts out six coins, and lays them on the lip of the hut. One brown hand, its fingers long and narrow, its nails painted black, emerges from the gloom and pulls away, sweeping up the coins without, it seems, even clenching its fingers. Mother Marcus floats back into the light.

''Tis an elegant magistrate,' she says to Jealous. 'As you promised.'

Jealous blushes. Graham speaks.

'Jealous described a woman to you. A gypsy woman.'

'No gypsy she.'

'How can you be sure?'

'She offered you the Tarot?'

'She did.'

'No gypsy would offer the Tarot. It is not in our lore. It is a disgusting invention of Swiss priests and Italian charlatans. No gypsy believes in it.'

'This seems unusual to me, woman. The gypsies of my acquaintance would offer their own children if there were money in it.'

Her eyes settle on his, and in their dark circles he sees the promise of something awful and something majestic.

'You are well acquainted with my people, magistrate?'

'They make free with my officers' time in Covent Garden, woman.'

'Perhaps. But never with the Tarot. Never.'

'Then who is this woman?'

'I may know her. But I am interested in something she has promised people. In addition to the Tarot.'

'And what is that?'

'I believe she calls it the Dreaming.'

Graham recalls this from his own encounter with the gypsy.

'And what is that?'

'I have no idea, magistrate.'

She smiles, and Graham finds himself waiting for her to lick her lips. She does no such thing.

'But it is intriguing, is it not? Why does she offer such a thing, if it does not exist? Or perhaps it is her own invention.'

'And what if it is?'

'We are a creative people, magistrate. We cherish the new.'

'Meaning new ways to wrest people's money from their purses.'

'Perhaps. But this woman, and her Dreaming – she interests me.'

'This woman has been described to you?' Graham asks.

'She has.'

'And what was the description?'

'Dark hair. Dark skin. Dark eyes. And . . .' The gypsy runs a finger along one cheek and jaw, mapping out a scar. Graham instantly recalls the damaged face of the old gypsy woman.

'And do you know where we might find this woman?'

'Find her? I do not. And you have had good value from me today, magistrate. You should be on your way.'

'But you have seen her?'

'Aye, I have seen her. She was here.'

'When? When was she here?'

'Oh, she stayed a good while. In the spring it was, and when the spring turned into summer. She didn't have much to do with the people here, magistrate. Kept herself to herself.'

'She was alone?'

'She was not alone, magistrate, no. She had a young woman with her. A sad and beautiful thing, she was. The image of her mother. But without . . .'

Once again she draws a black-nailed finger along her jaw.

'Did you speak to them?'

'I spoke to the mother. But not to the daughter. She was a deranged girl, magistrate. She screamed and she shrieked and the mother could not keep her quiet. I had to ask her to leave us.'

'Where did she go?'

'She did not say. Or at least if she did, no one here remembers.'

Graham frowns at this.

'Why do they not remember?'

'I know not. *I* remember her. But she,' nodding towards one of the younger women who stand waiting, 'she may not.'

'I do not understand.'

222

'You do not? Well, the guineas have spoken, and they promised information, but not understanding. Perhaps you should
consult this Dreaming?'

She smiles at him.

'As for you, magistrate. I see in your face what you desire,
and some of it you will get. You will rise to the pinnacle of your
profession. But you will only stay there for a day or two. And
with that, farewell.'

Her face goes back into the darkness, and the shutter of the
hut falls down with a slap.

A Treatise on Moral Projection

As my mind cleared, and as I spoke to John Burroway, some of my memory returned. Perhaps all my memory came back to me, but it was impossible to be certain of this, for how could I know?

It became clear to me that my patient Maria Cranfield had exhibited two extraordinary abilities. One of these was to force others to do her bidding, even against their own will. The other was to persuade their memories to forget certain events. The effect of this latter ability was to prove to be temporary, but how much *long-term* destruction of remembrance is occasioned by this ability it may prove impossible to fathom.

In other words, Maria Cranfield was able to step inside the conscious mind of another, and adapt that consciousness to her own will – either by *enforcement* or *deletion*. She possessed the ability – it seemed to me then, as it does today – to *mesmerise* others.

I use the word *mesmerise* deliberately in this case to evoke a concept which has fallen out of fashion but which, at the time of the events described in this treatise, was still very much discussed and debated in Europe. I speak of course of the techniques laid out at the end of the last century by that brilliant son of Swabia, Franz Anton Mesmer.

In Mesmer's original conception a *universal fluid* existed within and between living beings which was subject to an external force, called by Mesmer the *animal magnetism*. He believed that it was possible to manipulate this magnetic force, and thus manipulate the flow of that invisible fluid through the human body. He applied this theory to a whole range of diseases and afflictions, arguing that a great many of these were caused by blockages or misdirections of the fluid.

Of course, this *mechanical* explanation of bodily functions was soon discredited. It smacked too strongly of Galen's concept of the intermixture of the *four humours* being at the root of physical and mental wellbeing. Surely we had moved on from such mistaken ancient theories? What continued to be true, however, was that even after this dismissal of the *explanation* of his technique, Mesmer *continued to have significant therapeutic success.*

Even as late as the time of which I write, Mesmer was still practising, in quiet semi-retirement amidst the uproar of war and revolution. People continued to come to him for treatment. Even those who had investigated his theories at the request of France's doomed Louis XVI, and had found Mesmer's magnetism to be little more than charlatanism, did not dispute the effectiveness of his methods.

After three decades of reading on this subject, it seems clear to me why Mesmer was able to succeed. One must put aside his own notions of *universal fluid* and *animal magnetism*. They are a discredited set of terms from an outmoded medicine. One must instead look at *what Mesmer did when he treated patients*.

Some of Mesmer's cures were on the surface

sophisticated and even bizarre. For instance, he would connect as many as a dozen patients to a vessel via iron rods, and seek to make of them a kind of *electrical circuit* through which he could manipulate the magnetism between them and thus their universal fluid. I do not speak of these techniques. I speak only of the most familiar of Mesmer's approaches, the one with which he had the most success of all, which involved only him and the patient, with no intervening device or mechanism.

Mesmer would sit before the patient and look deeply into the man or woman's eyes. At the same time, his knees would touch the knees of the patient, and he would take the thumbs of the patient in his hands. After holding this position for a time, Mesmer would move his hands from the shoulders of the patient, all the way down their arms. After some time doing this, he would then press his fingers into the patient's upper stomach, in the region of the *hypochondrium*. He was known to hold his hands sometimes for hours in these positions.

Does this not smack strongly of my own *moral therapy*? For what is this but the creation of a strong emotional bond between the doctor and the patient, through which something powerful can be transmitted? Might it indeed be that moral therapy was working through precisely the same medium as mesmerism? Had we mad-doctors, without even knowing it, been practising a species of mesmerism? Had the Reverend Willis *mesmerised a King*?

When subjected to these treatments of Mesmer's, patients reported convulsions, either mild or severe, and it was believed (indeed, it is often believed still) that these convulsions were a kind of crisis of the body, during which the patient's ailment was corrected, or perhaps forced out. What was firmly believed, both by Mesmer, his patients, and the army of physicians and charlatans who claimed to provide similar treatments, first in France, and then throughout the whole of Europe, was that some kind of *transfer* was taking place. Mesmer's power, in this theory, was the ability to manipulate the *animal magnetism* between himself and the patient and thus change the flow of the *universal fluid* within his patient.

In other words, Mesmer claimed the ability to change the internal arrangements of his patients – either in their heads or in their bodies – *through the power of thought alone*.

As I sat there on that long-ago day in my consulting room at Brooke House, my memories fading back into my mind, these thoughts started to come to me. I had long held an interest in Mesmer, and his ideas came to me with some force on that fateful day. I was willing, you see, to countenance Maria Cranfield's abilities, because I seemed to have come across something like them before in my own practice of moral therapy.

In the months and years that followed that extraordinary episode, I attempted to synthesise these three strands into the concept I now present to you. The first strand was the *moral therapy* I sought to engage in at Brooke House – the interplay between a doctor and his patient, the ability of the doctor to impose order and calm on a frenzied mind. The second strand was *mesmerism*, though even then I found Mesmer's concepts of *universal fluid* and *animal magnetism* unconvincing; it was his method, and his success with it, that attracted me. And the third aspect, the final cog in this little machine, was what I had just experienced; Maria Cranfield reaching into my mind, compelling me against my will to perform a task, and then wiping my memory of it.

These three elements combine to form my new conception, which I now send out into the public sphere for the first time. I have named it *moral projection* and I believe Maria Cranfield represents the first documented case of its demonstration. Of course, if I am right about this being an ability of the human brain which, to some extent, we must all share, then moral projection has always been with us. Have we not all known people who were peculiarly able to influence others, to have them behave in ways they wanted? And have we also not all experienced that odd, unaccountable inability to remember a simple experience from a week, a day, even an hour ago? Have we not, then, all experienced moral projection working in the real world?

I have much more to say on this matter, and I have many notes. This concept does, of course, require more research, more experimentation, more observation. But I feel a great urgency to present these ideas in the face of those new theories delineated by the Manchester physician James Braid. He has conceived of ideas based on his theory of *hypnotism*, which themselves build upon the original conception of *mesmerism*.

When I read Braid's work *Neurypnology* I recognised straightaway a kindred spirit. But I believe Braid fell into error in disavowing Mesmer's concept, that to send someone into a state of hypnosis meant transferring some unseen charge or power from the object to the subject which affected a change within the subject. Instead, Braid asserted that a state of *hypnosis* could be created by inducing *fatigue*, through forcing the subject to stare fixedly at a bright object. In Braid's conception, *hypnosis* is actually a form of *sleep*.

But how can this possibly be? It is clear that Maria Cranfield did not cause me to *sleep*. She caused me to perform actions of her own desiring, and to forget about them. At no point did I fall asleep – such a thing would have been nonsensical!

What Braid did was to assert that it seemed to be possible to deliver another human into a state under which their consciousness might be manipulated, or *projected upon*. But he disagreed that this involved an intervening substance such as the *animal magnetism* mentioned by Mesmer. No, in Braid's hypothesis, the mind of the subject is put into a receptive state of *hypnosis* by exhausting it. Once in this state, some kind of projection of will becomes possible; I may, if I so wish, put thoughts and wishes into the mind of another. But only if they be asleep.

Nay, I say. The power exhibited by Maria Cranfield was not that which Dr Braid describes. It was (to use my own term again) *moral projection*. Miss Delilah came closest to it with her own demotic description: she said Maria 'got into people's heads' and once there could do as she wished.

How did she do this? Through the same techniques I used to assert my own moral control over patients: through arresting their attention, focusing it entirely upon me. The eye is the window to the soul, but it is also the gun-barrel for this kind of projection. There is no need for any kind of universal fluid, but there is a kind of magnetism at work: the magnetism of one man's *moral will* over another's.

But these are the thoughts of a man who has wrestled with these ideas for nigh on half a century. On that day in September 1814, I had no conception of these matters, even as I tried to rebuild my memory of the events in the cell. I had an understanding of the writings of Mesmer, but his techniques were not used by Doctor Monro, in Bethlem or in Brooke House. They smacked of French Tricks, and in any case they ran counter to Monro's own view that madness was a temporary thing, which would expire before long if the patient was separated from their daily routine. This was the core diagnostic rock on which all Monro's practice rested. Touching patients to shift their magnetism? Why, such a thing was almost blasphemous!

But Monro was wrong, as were we all. Mesmerism did have results, and did have obvious correlations with practices which were already in use as moral therapy. We were all, in some way, mesmerists.

THORPE

Am I awake?

He can feel the soft cotton of Thorpe Lee House's pillows on his face, but he can also see dark figures dancing on the lawn outside. He can feel the fullness of his bladder underneath him, but he can also hear the sound of rough music from the woods. He can taste the dry insides of his mouth, but he can also smell burning.

Am I awake?

He watches Elizabeth Hook appear on the lawn. A witch watching the house?

He watches Sarah Graham appear on the lawn. A witch leaving it?

He sees Ellen Graham's – no, Ellen *Tempest* Graham's – sad, disturbed eyes, hears her surrender to the strange rhythms of her own head.

He sees the cook. The male cook. Stephen Moore. Watching him as he eats his dinner.

He sees Abigail, and she is in terrible danger. She has her arm around a serpent.

A shape flies by the window. Then another. Then another. Dark flying shapes circling Thorpe Lee House, their skirts trailing behind them, and each of them looking in at his window as she passes. Women in the air, watching him.

And thus, Charles Horton's strange night comes to an end.

He sits up in his bed, still light-headed with exhaustion. He drinks from the cup beside his bed, the lukewarm well-water sluicing his parched mouth but bringing no satisfaction at all. There are so many questions in his head that they have over-lapped themselves, a chattering flock of mysteries and unseen narratives. He has written to Robert Brown to try and unlock the mystery of the material in the exposed well. He has, it seems, been forbidden to speak with either Miss Ellen or Mrs Graham.

Very well, then. He will follow another trail. Today, he will try to learn more about Thorpe Lee House's unusual new cook.

The servants' quarters are in the top of the house, squashed within the roof, the stuffy enclosed air reminding Horton strongly of a Navy frigate. A narrow passageway follows the line of the house. There are six doors off it, all of them shrunken copies of the majestic doors of the main house. Horton has to stoop slightly to walk across the landing.

Breakfast is being served downstairs, and all the servants are about their business. The attic passageway is silent – much quieter and stiller than it had been during the night, when the giggles and murmurs of the staff had echoed down these corridors, down the stairs and into Horton's half-sleeping fancy.

He knocks at each door, and when no answer comes he opens it and peeks within. There are no locks on any of the doors – no privacy is allowed the servants of Thorpe Lee House. There are male rooms, and female rooms. The male rooms are austere, almost empty – beds, drawers full of clothes (no wardrobes in any of the rooms, the ceilings are too narrow), candles, chamber pots and washstands. The female rooms are frillier and warmer, edged with lace and drapery, the claustrophobic edge taken off them by decoration.

There are two of the male rooms. One must be for Crowley, the butler and senior male servant. The other, assumes Horton, must be shared by Stephen Moore and the footman, Peter Gowing. There is little, on the face of it, to distinguish this room from the butler's, save the additional bed and the crowding. Horton carefully opens the drawers, finding nothing but clothes, and looks underneath the beds. There are so few places for a servant to tend any private materials. Moore, if he has a secret to hide, must be hiding it elsewhere. There is only one other room over which he has dominance.

So Horton heads down for his breakfast – as ever, it is served in the kitchen, though this is now where he wishes to be. Moore is down there, and he turns his calm eyes to Horton as the constable steps into his domain.

'Good morning, constable,' he says, once again with that easy lack of deference.

'And to you, Moore,' says Horton, careful to keep some social distance. 'Did you rest well this past night?'

Moore does not answer at once. He looks at Horton while he weighs up the question and his answer. He is, Horton can see, as careful in such matters as himself.

'I think the house does not sleep as well as it might,' he says. 'Nor those within it.'

'You think us haunted? By witches, perhaps?'

Moore smiles at that.

'Well, by the fear of them, perhaps.'

He turns back to his task – washing dishes, quite fine ones, presumably used by Sir Henry and Mrs Graham for their own breakfast, in that part of the house to which Horton is only granted invited admission. It has been three days now since he spoke to Mrs Graham; since then she has been perceived within night-time rooms and even outside on the lawn. She is like a tired haunting spirit, one to whom Horton can have no access. When he asks to speak with her, the servants say only that she is keeping to her room, and that Sir Henry has ordered she is not to be disturbed.

A prisoner, perhaps, rather than a spirit.

Horton sits himself down at the kitchen table, on which is laid out bread and cheese and preserves and butter. He begins putting together a plate of food, and without warning Moore walks over with a jug of freshly made coffee.

'My thanks to you,' says Horton. Moore smiles that non-deferential smile, and walks back to the sink. Horton eats, and looks.

The kitchen is a large room, rectangular, with a long table down the middle, at which he now sits. It is well lit by external windows, high in the walls yet substantial in size. Horton tries to picture the topography of the house, eventually estimating that the kitchen must run front-to-back almost at the middle of the house, beneath the main hall. So there must be considerable vacancies on either side – storage rooms, a cellar, but what else? Doors on either side of the kitchen lead to these rooms. Otherwise the kitchen contains nothing that could be thought out of the ordinary – a large fireplace, a brick hearth from which dozens of pots and pans are hung, a sturdy stone sink, some shelves fixed into the bare brick walls.

'I would think this kitchen very similar to the one at Stoke d'Abernon,' says Horton, thinking nothing of the kind, as he has no view of what that other kitchen would be like. Moore does not look at him, keeping his eyes on his task, but he does answer.

'It is larger at Stoke d'Abernon, but also more crowded. There are half-a-dozen kitchen servants there. The head cook is a terrible tyrant of a woman named Mrs Thomas. She is Welsh, as wide as she is tall, and I have seen her bring grown men to tears. It is a relief to have my own kitchen, and to not be subject to such a woman.'

A full answer, thinks Horton. A rounded, detailed, evocative answer, as if from the script of a play.

'Who taught you to cook, Moore?'

'My mother, Constable Horton. A remarkable woman, if I may say so. I grew up in a village near Northampton, where she was a cook to a great house. I helped her in the kitchen. It was my education.'

'You did not go to school?'

'I did, yes. There was a charity school in Northampton. I went there every day. All the children of the servants did. The master of the house demanded it.'

'Where was this?'

'Lamport, constable. The estate of Sir Justinian Isham.'

Horton files that memorable name away, though it had not been requested.

'Did your mother go with you to Stoke d'Abernon?'

'Yes, constable. She went to work in the kitchens there, and I followed her. And then I came here. Now, is this interrogation over?'

Moore does not look at him when he says this, and Horton does not reply, munching contemplatively on a thick hunk of bread.

'Then, if you'll excuse me, I need to go and check if all the kitchen items have been returned from the dining room.

Gowing and Mr Crowley are not always as thorough as one would like in such matters.'

Moore leaves, and still Horton says nothing. When the cook has gone, he stands and tries the doors leading off the kitchen. Both are locked. He returns to the table to finish his breakfast.

He goes in search of Mrs Chesterton, the housekeeper. There are noises from the dining room, where he presumes Sir Henry and Mrs Graham have finished their breakfast and retired elsewhere. Or perhaps only Sir Henry ate here, leaving Mrs Graham to the prison of her bedchamber. He steps into the room to see Moore, again, and Mrs Chesterton. She is telling the young man off.

'I've told you, now, haven't I? You don't need to be in here. Peter'll collect all the bits an' pieces. You need to stick to the kitchen, and not be poking around the house all the time, as I've told—'

She stops when she sees Horton. Moore, he notices, has not even been listening to her, and simply carries on scooping up the remaining detritus of the breakfast, oblivious to Horton.

'Mrs Chesterton, might I have a word with you?'

'Now? I'm particularly busy just now, constable.'

'If you please. It will only take a few minutes.'

She frowns and makes a harrumphing sound, and with a final glare at Stephen Moore she walks out with Horton into the corridor.

'Shall we step outside?' Horton suggests. She nods, curtly and almost rudely, as if she finds the whole thing an impertinent imposition. They walk through the front door and down the steps, onto the lawn. Mrs Chesterton looks suddenly lost and fragile, extracted from her domestic empire within.

'Will I be able to talk with Sir Henry today? It is on a matter of some urgency.'

'You'll have to speak to Crowley about that.'

'And might Mrs Graham be available?'

'She might, she might not. Jane says she's no better, and is keeping to her room.'

'Indeed? I imagined I saw her walking on the lawn last night.'

'Well, the imagination's a funny thing, ain't it?'

Her face is defiant, but there is something else beneath her words, a little wobble. Perhaps Mrs Chesterton's imagination has been capering as much as Horton's.

'Then I would like to talk to you about Stephen Moore, Mrs Chesterton.'

She perks up a bit at that, suddenly interested.

'Why? What's 'e done?'

'As far as I know, nothing. But I wondered if you could tell me the circumstances of his hiring.'

'Well, he just showed up, didn't he? The old cook was sacked, her as we all think is behind all this nastiness, and Mr Moore was here two days later. Said he'd heard there was a vacancy for a cook, and he had excellent references, and could we give him a chance?'

'Had you advertised the position?'

'Lor', no, no. Had barely the time to think about it. Saved me a job, didn't he?'

'I suppose he did. Did you check his references?'

Her face scowls a little at that, and Horton thinks he gets a flavour of the woman in that scowl. An essentially lazy person, one comfortable in her position, loathe to generate fuss where there is calm. He can see she did not check Stephen Moore's reference, because to do so would have been additional work, but also would have exposed her to the task she thought she'd avoided: that of advertising for a new cook. Moore was a short cut, and she'd taken the short cut, and had thought nothing of it. Horton thinks he sees why Thorpe Lee House has an air of untended shabbiness about it. Its housekeeper does not do her job.

She does not answer his question, turns that scowling countenance away to the garden, and Horton can see – if he had not done so before – he has made an enemy. He ponders asking to see the letter from Stoke d'Abernon, but she would take that as a direct attack, and might make things difficult. In any case, he does not need to see it. Moore is a careful and assiduous person. If the reference has been faked, it will have been faked well.

'No matter, Mrs Chesterton. I'm sure it was in order. My thanks to you.'

'Will that be all, then, constable? I am *particularly* busy.'

Such people are always busy, reflects Horton. He thanks her again and says no, that will be all. She walks back into the house.

The day stretches out before him. He thinks of Abigail, and her own day, and what may be in it for her. But that thought is, his guilt tells him, subsumed in the familiar itching belief that something is here to be discovered.

He walks back to the house. He will write to Dame Mary Vincent at Stoke d'Abernon. There is little other option available to him, unless he can get into those rooms off the kitchen.

He hears the sound of hooves, and turns to see a rider coming up the drive, the horse breathing heavily as if after a fierce gallop.

The horse arrives at the front of the house ahead of Horton. Its young rider climbs down and removes his hat to expose a shock of bright-red hair. Steam rises up from the horse's back and sides, and it puffs and shakes its cheeks with recent exertion. Mrs Chesterton and Crowley scuttle out of the house and talk to the rider, and as Horton comes close they are followed, at speed, by Sir Henry, accompanied by Peter Gowing. O'Reilly the gardener stands to one side, looking at the horse as if it were an elephant.

Sir Henry strides past his servants, brushing Horton's arm out of the way as he does so, and the servants around the rider give way to his approach.

'Well, then,' he says to the young rider. 'You have something for me?'

'Sir Henry?' asks the rider.

'Of course I am Sir Henry. Who else would I be?'

'Well, sir, I bring an urgent letter for you from Mr Graham, the . . .'

'I know who he is, dammit. Give me the letter.'

As the rider does so, Horton watches the other servants. At the mention of Aaron Graham's name, Crowley raises an eyebrow towards Mrs Chesterton, thinking himself unwatched. She smiles back at the butler. To Horton's left, Peter Gowing is himself looking at the ground with the kind of smile on his face which suggests he and the ground have just shared an amusing story. They look like a crowd of smirking children who have just heard an adult say something rude.

Sir Henry rips open the letter and throws the envelope onto the ground behind him. Gowing picks it up while Sir Henry reads. Horton watches him closely, as do all the servants. The urgency in Sir Henry's frame tightens unbearably, and when he looks up he appears a man ready to strike out.

'You came straight here?' he says to the rider.

'Yes, Sir Henry. As ordered by Mr Graham.'

Sir Henry says nothing else. He turns and glares at Horton, who looks back mystified. Then Sir Henry clatters back into the house.

'I've also been asked to speak to Constable Horton,' says the rider, and Horton turns back to look at him as Sir Henry walks away.

'By the magistrate?'

'Yes. Are you Horton?'

'I am.'

Horton looks at the servants, one by one.

'If you please. I wish to speak to this man on a policing matter.'

Gowing looks annoyed, Mrs Chesterton outraged and for a moment Crowley looks like he might pull out a stiletto and plunge it into Horton's side, there and then. Horton waits, and eventually they do move away. Only O'Reilly remains, his mouth agape, and soon he too walks back to whatever gardening mystery he had been engaged upon before the rider's sudden arrival.

The rider climbs down, holding the reins of his horse, and indicates to Horton that they should walk a little away from the servants.

'I'm to give you news of the investigation, from the magistrate.'

'What is your name, officer?'

'William Jealous. Of the Bow Street mounted patrol.'

The name is familiar. Horton frowns in recall.

'Jealous. Are you of the same family as Charles Jealous?'

'He is my father.'

The young man looks pleased. Horton feels he has made an ally.

'A good man, your father. Now, tell me.'

'All the members of the Sybarites have been warned that they may be potential victims of this killer. Sir Henry has just received that letter.'

'Ah. Well, then. Perhaps he will talk to me now.'

'Also, we have investigated the gypsies of Norwood.'

'Gypsies? Why on earth is Graham talking to gypsies?'

'One was seen outside Sir John Cope's house.'

'But gypsies are almost as common in London as whores.'

'I know not the magistrate's reasoning.'

'Did you learn anything in Norwood?'

'Only that there had been a strange woman there, with a younger woman, earlier this year. She matches the appearance of a gypsy woman seen several times outside the home of Sir John Cope.'

'But this is hardly evidence of foul deeds. Women come and go from Norwood all year round.'

'I cannot say.'

'Anything else?'

'Constables are being sent to the London homes of all the Sybarites. To keep watch.'

'What has been learned from the houses of the two dead men?'

'Nothing. There are no signs of any forced entry. All the doors and windows were secured. None of the servants heard or saw anything during the night. It is as if the men were done away with by spirits.'

The young man's face is excited. The thrill of investigation is written in his eyes. Horton tells himself this boy may be of use.

'That is all?'

'Yes, constable.'

The young rider shifts position, and climbs back on his horse.

'Wait,' says Horton, tearing himself away from his thoughts, which is considerably harder than he might have expected. 'When are you expected back?'

The rider looks down at him, perhaps not as impatiently as Horton might have imagined.

'I was given no specific duty today beyond informing you of developments.'

'Well, I have something I'd like you to help me with. But it'll be a long ride.'

'Raven here likes a run.'

He pats the side of his horse proudly.

'Does he? Well, perhaps you both would appreciate an even longer run.'

'Perhaps. Where to?'

'A place called Stoke d'Abernon. It is not quite a dozen miles from here. I need you to deliver a letter, and bring back a reply.'

WESTMINSTER

The letters he sent out the previous evening have already sparked a reaction by the time Graham returns to Bow Street from Norwood. Six letters in all have been sent in London, to six of the seven names on the list provided by Sir John Cope's manservant, Burgess. The seventh name is Sir Henry Tempest, and that matter, Graham trusts, is already in hand.

Of the six letters, two provoke a direct response. Sir Thomas Mackworth sent Graham's constable back with a terse note saying any further association of his name with the Sybarites will lead to an immediate suit; he even intimates that to preserve his honour he might threaten a duel. He adds that no Bow Street 'meddler' is going to be loitering outside his house, and damn the consequences.

The other note does not come back with the constable; it appears that John Cameron, the youngest of the supposed Sybarites, is going to cooperate with Graham's request. His note simply thanks Graham for the attention, and informs him that he will be returning to his father's estate in the country.

The note asks for Graham to kindly keep the reasons for his return secret; the Earl of Ruthin and Flint, Alexander Cameron, has an upright reputation (the letter does not say, it only implies, as such letters tend to do), which would be tarnished by Sybaritic associations.

Three of the other letters have met with no response at all, only a silent and presumably rather embarrassed acquiescence, and so Graham's constables spent last night in attendance at the residences of Samuel Lake, the second brother of Viscount Lake (who claims direct descent from Lancelot of the Lake), Algernon Lincoln (son of Hugh Lincoln, the Duke of Handforth) and Henry Harcourt Palmer, son of Sir Charles Harcourt Palmer.

The sixth letter, not to Graham's surprise, sparked the biggest response of all. An hour after his return from Norwood, the Bow Street servant brings him a note. Graham is required to attend the Secretary of State for the Home Department, Viscount Sidmouth, immediately. Graham is not entirely surprised, and decides to walk, and to think.

It is the afternoon, and the fruit and vegetable stalls in the Piazza are being cleared away. The streets have an air of preparedness about them, hung between the clattering commerce of the day and the illicit trading of the night. He tries to clear his mind of what is to come with Sidmouth, using a technique he learned from a courtesan who'd once been kept, for some months, by Charles James Fox. 'He always said, the only way to stay sane is to turn off your thinking,' Miranda had said, one night as they'd sipped wine in her rooms off Maiden Lane. 'And the only way to turn your thinking off is to open your senses – your ears, your nose, your eyes – to everything that is around you *right now*.' And with that, she'd moved her hand down beneath the bedclothes, and Aaron Graham found that, indeed, one's senses could overwhelm one's cares.

He thinks back to what Talty had said, the previous night. 'We've all got our own information to trade, don't we?' Had that been a threat? Did he know, then, that Aaron Graham, magistrate, was an infrequent but long-standing customer of some of Covent Garden's finest jades? But surely such knowledge was immaterial; it would have been more of a matter for gossip if a man in Graham's circumstances did *not* partake of such pleasures, even before his wife departed to usher in his singleton existence on the fringe of Britain's most scandalous district. But this only makes Talty's implied threat more disconcerting; does he know something else? Has Graham said something to one of those women – said all manner of things, tenderly over the pillow in some candle-lit bedroom – which has been passed down and across and into the hands of Maiden Lane's primary panderer?

The avenues for investigating the Sybarites are closing up, at least in London. The trip to Norwood had generated intrigue – a mysterious woman, apparently the same one he encountered at Sir John Cope's, and her daughter, living among the gypsies. But however theatrical Mother Marcus had been, it leaves him with nothing: just another gypsy living among gypsies. The six guineas he'd left with Mother Marcus could have been better spent.

The previous night has brought no new developments. The six members of the Sybarites he had contacted had all been made aware, all (even the angry Sir Thomas Mackworth) would have had an eye on the street and on their doors and windows. Even John Cameron, who is presumably even now in a coach clattering to a country redoubt, may have been looking to his coach driver and imagining riders approaching the windows.

Meanwhile, other constables have responded to the search

warrant he has issued, demanding the immediate arrest of any or all of the three whores mentioned by Talty: Rose Dawkins, Elizabeth Carrington, Maria Cranfield. Jealous has promised to take up this search himself when he returns from Horton.

And then there is Horton himself, and Thorpe Lee House. The case is obscure, but nowhere is that obscurity deeper or more distressing than in Thorpe. Graham had considered ordering Horton to return to London, in light of the most recent death. He is impatient for news of the place, and for the results of Horton's interview with Sir Henry. The more he thinks about matters, the more Sir Henry's timely flight to Surrey seems significant.

He reaches the Home Department with barely a thought for the meeting with Sidmouth. He has his own method for avoiding thoughts of an unpleasant meeting, it would seem; replace those thoughts with ones which are even more unpleasant.

Henry Addington, the Viscount Sidmouth, is the most powerful person with whom Aaron Graham has any personal dealings. The younger Graham, working away on legal and judicial matters in Newfoundland, would have been astonished by the prospect of such an association as the one the magistrate now has with the former prime minister. It would indicate how far he had risen, how much he had made of his meagre family resources. That younger man might even have traded his future domestic happiness for the prospect of such advancement. That younger man, Graham reflects, was a naive fool. For one, he had never lost a wife.

Sidmouth's lean, sensible, dull face is poised over a letter when Graham is shown into his office. He does not ask Graham to sit down, nor would Graham expect him to. He does not even immediately acknowledge Graham's presence, but finishes his letter and puts down his quill. He breathes in through his nose and closes his eyes, as if resetting his thoughts, and then looks at Graham.

'The Sybarites, Graham. Tell me all you know of the Sybarites.'

'A private society, your Lordship. A small group of men. It appears to be an entirely hedonistic enterprise – no political intent whatsoever, as far as I can garner.'

'And two of them are now dead?'

'Yes, your Lordship.'

'I know neither name – Cope, was it? And Wodehouse?'

The Home Secretary looks at no paper when saying his name. He has, it would appear, read carefully over this matter.

'Indeed, your Lordship. Wodehouse is the third son of Baron Wodehouse of Kimberley; a young man, of no significant achievement. Sir John Cope was the heir to Sir Richard Cope's title. A rector, I believe his father was.'

'The circumstances of their deaths, if you please.'

'Both were killed in especially violent ways. Their bodies were much mutilated, such that it is almost impossible for the coroner to be entirely certain of the cause of death. Wodehouse's stomach was opened, and his entrails were partially removed. Cope's manhood was severed, and the surrounding area eviscerated. The member was placed in his mouth.'

The Viscount blinks, mildly. He has long made it clear that this kind of dispassionate summary is his preferred mode of discourse. The man lacks imagination, it is well known, but in counterbalance he possesses sense, calm and propriety. Sometimes, he reminds Graham of his friend Sir John Harriott, in that gentleman's quieter moments.

'You are making something of a habit of these bizarre

episodes, Graham. The Ratcliffe Highway murders. That odd occasion around Sir Joseph Banks's vessel last year. And now this. You have a suspect?'

'No, your Lordship.'

'You have arrested no one?'

'No, your Lordship. There is a warrant in place for the arrest of three Covent Garden prostitutes.'

'You believe them to be the killers?'

'Not entirely, sir. But we believe they may help us to establish a motive for the killings.'

'A *motive*? Hmm. Well, I have received a letter.'

He picks up the paper from his desk, for all the world like an absent-minded professor referring to a note from his sister. Graham imagines it is anything but.

'It comes from the Earl of Maidstone. I understand you wrote to him.'

'Yes, your Lordship.'

'You have accused him of membership of the Sybarites.'

'Does he deny this?'

'Ah, not quite, no.' The Home Secretary smiles, a knowing little expression, and Graham relaxes a little. 'He does rather resent your bringing it up, however. You perhaps should have contacted me before writing to one such as this, Graham.'

'There was little time, your Lordship. I was acutely concerned that these men might be threatened this past night.'

'That is as it may be. But there is form and there is etiquette, Graham. The Earl is the son of the Marquess of Tonbridge. His mother is the daughter of a Viscount. This is a significant family, and it would seem from his letter that the Earl is most aware of that.'

'Does he require anything of me?'

'He does. He requires four constables.'

Graham frowns in some confusion. That little smile reappears on the Home Secretary's face.

'Yes, Graham. He resents your intrusion onto his personal sphere. But he also rather thinks you might be right. Do you have the men available?'

THORPE

After Jealous has left, promising to return when he has an answer from Stoke d'Abernon, Horton tries to speak to Sir Henry right away, but there is little immediate chance of that. The baronet has locked himself in his library and has left instructions with Crowley that he is not to be disturbed. *By that bloody officer in particular* is the unspoken additional command which Horton sees in the old butler's eyes.

Stephen Moore has retired to his kitchen, so there is little to be done with regard to that line of inquiry, either. A growing sense of frustration comes over Horton. More hours are to be wasted inside this odd house and this odder investigation. The master and mistress of the house are locked in their respective rooms, like sulking children. He feels himself to be waiting for something to happen – a letter to be answered, or an opportunity to let himself through a locked door. And suddenly, his mind is full of Abigail and London, of Covent Garden constables and Hackney mad-doctors.

It is another sunny day, so he resolves on a walk around Sir Henry's estate. He heads for the trees at the edge of the lawn –

the direction, he's been told, the rough music came from that August night weeks before. The phrase had been unfamiliar to him at first, but then he'd recalled it: rough music was the sound made by people shouting and banging anything that came to hand to try and drive out a maddened witch. The people of the village had been standing here, in these woods, with their pots and pans and their fear, shrieking in hate at the poor old cook.

Yet it was out of these woods that Elizabeth Hook stepped last night. Perhaps this is really why he gravitates towards them. He has no means of finding her, and he would very much like to speak to her again. Perhaps the woods will offer a clue.

The ground is dry and soft beneath his feet. It has been a hot summer of little rain, and within the trees the air feels dry and exhausted. Abigail had spoken to him of air once, of how it was not a single thing, but compounded of multiple gases laid within and on top of each other (he forgets the precise mechanism). What was the word for the most vital of them? He forgets that, as well. He tries to imagine this vacant air containing matter, or something like matter, but fails. Why can he see through it if it consists of something else? It is like the inverse of the events of Thorpe Lee House, which obfuscate and cloud and interrupt and through which nothing can be perceived.

A white shape, dancing through the trees. He stands still, as if he were hunting a stag.

No, not a stag. A white hart, dressed in night-clothes. Miss Ellen, running through the woods. Singing. She seems to be running in a circle, around where he stands. A step in any direction would take him towards her. So a step is what he takes. And another, and another. She does not heed him, and then she does, when he is only a half-dozen yards away.

She is dressed in the same white cotton shift as the night he met her in the kitchen, and this time the sunlight pierces it obscenely, picking out the angular shapes of her childish body, even displaying the small malnourished circles of her unformed breasts. She might as well be naked.

O'Reilly's voice in his head. *She warn't doing nothing. She was just standin' there, lookin' at me.*

She says nothing, and her glare is surprising. She looks angry.

'Miss Tempest Graham. We met in the . . .'

'I know who you are, constable.'

'Well, then. Are you well enough to be running so through the woods? Dressed in . . . so little?'

She looks down at herself, and her face changes. Anger rushes out and embarrassment courses in. She sits down on a log, tucking her cotton shift beneath her backside, covering her chest with her arms as she leans forward, closing herself in tightly against his male gaze. It is the action of an older girl, almost a woman, who is beginning to understand the attentions of men.

He hears a sound – that of a carriage pulling away, somewhere at the outer edge of the copse, where a wooden fence cuts through the trees, separating one piece of land – Sir Henry's estate – from another. He can spy the edge of a field through the trees, its wheat recently harvested, and along a track between the two estates an old wagon is making its way. A woman sits atop it, higher up than normal, dressed in gypsy rags.

'What are you doing in the woods, constable?'

She asks the question quickly and almost too loudly, as if to distract his attention. And for a moment he is distracted, turning his gaze back to hers, and feeling an odd sensation in his head – a squeeze, a tension – before pulling his eyes back towards the gypsy on top of her wagon, as it rolls away beyond his line of sight, too fast to follow.

When he looks back at Ellen, there is such a look of anger and hatred in her face that he feels momentarily afraid, as if she might lunge into the trees towards him, tearing at his face with her long fingernails, her white shift flowing behind her like wings.

'I was out walking, and thinking,' he says.

'Ah, walking and thinking. Yes. Men do a lot of walking and thinking.'

He is terribly confused. It is like talking to a different girl. The sad, gnomic skeleton of the kitchen two nights before has become an irritated, sarcastic shrew.

'You seem quite the Forest Sprite, constable. A Manly Apparition!'

He feels a sudden quickening pressure in his temples, the beginnings of a headache. He is tired, bothered by the terrible visions of the previous night, by his complete inability to rest in that strange chattering household. He feels compelled to end this conversation, and yet Ellen's appearance in the woods is at the same time extraordinary and in keeping with what has passed before.

'This is not the first time you have run through the woods, I think, Miss Ellen.'

His head feels suddenly released, the pain scudding away. What on earth is wrong with him?

'What do you mean by that?'

'The gardener saw you. O' Reilly. He saw you running in the woods.'

'He is a *liar!*' She spits like a cat with its feet in hot water. 'I have seen the way he looks at me. He is a disgusting *liar* and my father will have him *dismissed.*'

'Which *father*, Miss Ellen?'

Pleasure, anger, embarrassment, rage and now confusion. Miss Ellen's emotions dance around her face like a hart she must herself chase down. The intermixture is too much for her. She begins to cry.

He does not know what to do or what to say. He feels he should comfort her, but to approach her when she is dressed – or, rather, undressed – like this would be a step too far. Yet she is distraught.

'I was so angry! I was so scared!'

'Miss Ellen, please. You must not . . .'

'I didn't know! How could I have known?'

'Known what, Ellen?'

'I dreamed he killed the dogs. I dreamed I made him. Like *this* . . .'

She is glaring at him, and suddenly his head hurts tremendously, and that sense of his temples being pinched between the thumb and forefinger of a giant returns, but multiplied a dozen times. He winces with the feel of it, and closes his eyes against the pain, and then it is gone as quickly as it came, like a candle being snuffed out.

Leave me alone. The words appear in his head, unbidden and clear, and he feels a great urge to do so, but at that moment, and as if they had emerged from a tunnel beneath the ground, Sir Henry's dogs surge out of the forest, frantically barking and banging into each other in their frenzy. Behind them comes Sir Henry, riding a chocolate-coloured horse in a similar frenzy to that of his dogs. Horton leaps out of the way of the surge, but this only puts him in the line of Sir Henry and his horse.

'Out of the bloody way, you idiot!' the baronet shouts, and Horton scrambles to get behind a tree. As it is, the horse passes less than two feet from him, its eyes white with terror and excitement, long red lines down its flanks from the slashing of Sir Henry's stick.

Then the baronet and his dogs are in the field behind the wood, where he had seen the gypsy wagon. They rush across it in a seething, demented rush.

Horton looks after them, and then looks around him. He is in the woods. He cannot remember at all how he came to be there.

His head hurts a little, but it is a different pain to any he has felt before, that of a tired limb recovering after hard work. He walks back to the house, eyes to the ground as if he could trace the memory of the past few minutes there. The headache starts to clear as soon as he steps out of the woods. He wonders how tired he must be, to be so confused. He remembers leaving the house, and then there are only shadows. Had he spoken to someone? He vaguely recalls seeing a carriage.

At the house, he goes looking for Crowley the butler or Mrs Chesterton the housekeeper. He finds neither, because to his very great surprise he comes across Mrs Graham dusting plates in the dining room, singing a song of wandering soldiers and lovelorn lovers. She stops when she hears him step into the room.

'Constable Horton. Good day to you.'

Her face is tired and pale, and her good cheer somewhat enforced. He wonders if she has been waiting to speak to him.

'And to you, Mrs Graham. It is a fine day.'

'It is, constable, it is. And how goes your *investigation*?'

She says this with a small smile, as if they are sharing a huge joke at someone else's expense; he cannot imagine whose.

'Mr Horton, I fear I may have been wasting your time, summoning you here.'

'Really, Mrs Graham?'

She winces slightly at the name. Her own name.

'Yes, I fear so. You see, I have not been well. I am concerned that these fancies of mine may have been the fruit of a fevered imagination.'

'And yet you sacked your cook.'

'Yes, I did indeed do that. I wonder if I was perhaps not a little hasty. You have met Elizabeth?'

'I have.'

'And she denies any mischief?'

'She does.'

'Well, then. I shall reinstate her. This nonsense must come to an end.'

'Do I take it that Sir Henry wishes me to leave?'

'These are my wishes, not Sir Henry's.'

She disguises the lie beneath a particularly vigorous bout of dusting. She polishes with some skill, Horton notes, and he wonders if this is something she has to do a good deal, and whether the servants resent it and despise her for it.

'Well, I cannot stay if you do not wish me here, Mrs Graham.'

She looks at him directly, and with some puzzlement. She had been expecting an argument, of course.

'You agree with me, constable? That these matters are fanciful?'

'By no means, Mrs Graham. Something is happening in this house, and some people within it have secrets they do not wish me to discover. Miss Tempest Graham continues to be ill, inexplicably so. And I doubt your new cook is all he says he is.'

She puts down her cloth, the ruse of cleaning forgotten.

'You surely cannot ascribe all these events to Stephen. Why, most of them took place before he even arrived.'

Mrs Graham, he notes, still thinks of *these events* as needing explanation. He is being removed for other reasons – presumably, the wishes of the master of the house. He thinks he can see why she has not appeared these past two days. They have been arguing about his presence. She has refused to dismiss Horton, while Sir Henry has insisted she does not speak to him. This new fabrication is her surrender.

'I do not believe Stephen Moore to be responsible for the events which preceded his arrival.'

'Then what do you accuse him of, constable?'

'I accuse him of nothing at all. I merely state that he is not all he seems to be, and I would recommend you take references for him, unless you plan to reinstate Elizabeth Hook. I will plan to make my leave, but may not be able to do so until the morning. Will that be quite acceptable, Mrs Graham?'

She looks back to her crockery.

'Quite acceptable, constable.'

One more night, then.

'Then I will leave you with one final question, if I may.'

'Always asking questions, are you not, constable?'

'It is a habit I find impossible to break.'

'Well, then. Ask your question.'

'Would it be yourself who holds keys to all the rooms in the house?'

Her smile, which had been barely there and which was ill-meant in any case, vanishes at that. The question is serious and perhaps has an intent she cannot unpick.

'Why, yes. It is normal for the mistress of the house to keep keys.'

'So you have the only full set of keys?'

'Yes.'

'But surely those who need to get into certain rooms must hold their own keys. Does Jane, for instance, have keys to your bedchamber?'

'She does.'

'And O'Reilly, he must keep the keys to the outbuildings – the destroyed shed, for instance? The dogs' kennels?'

'Without keys, they'd not be able to do their jobs, would they?'

'Of course not. And what about the rooms in the basement? Does anyone else have keys to those?'

'Why, the cook, of course, in addition to me. She ... or rather, *he* ... uses those rooms to store things. Is this relevant to anything, constable?'

He uses her own tactics. He obfuscates.

'It is merely a matter of personal interest. If I may, Mrs Graham, I will return to my room and prepare my things. I would like to visit the village a final time, to speak to the rector. He is a man of some distinction, and I have enjoyed his conversation.'

'Why ... yes. Yes, of course.'

Mrs Graham is now the picture of confusion, and Horton, having done what he came to do, leaves her to recover. But as he goes, he asks another question.

'Your looking-glasses, Mrs Graham. Was it you that broke them?'

She looks shocked and then angry.

'How impertinent! Why on earth would I break my own property?'

'Perhaps you saw something in them you did not care for.'

She gazes at him open-mouthed, her face white apart from an angry blaze on each cheek. Then she turns away, and Horton does not speak to her again.

The first room off the cellar contains nothing of immediate interest. It is easy to get into – he secures two knives from a drawer in the main kitchen, and after half-a-minute of manipulation the simple old lock gives way and the door opens. He has always been able to get into locked doors, normally without even damaging the mechanism. He learned the trick as a boy in Margate, where the back streets were almost heaving with locked doors behind which smuggled goods swelled in barrels and crates. Fully a quarter of all the boys in Margate could navigate their way past any lock; it was fear of the terrible smugglers that stopped them, in most cases, not the mechanical barrier. And when they did force their way in, it was vital that the door remain unscathed, lest their incursion be discovered.

After passing his candle over the first room's unsurprising, and uninteresting, contents – flour, vegetables, fruit, a barrel of salted meat, a dozen loaves of sugar – he decides the room will yield no information. He backs out, and locks the door behind him, and turns his attention to the second door.

Almost immediately he senses this incursion will be more fruitful. The lock, for one thing, has been changed, and pretty recently, too. He puts his finger into the keyhole and feels fresh grease inside. Mrs Graham had mentioned no such thing, and there may well be no reason why she would have done. But he rather suspects Mrs Graham's keys no longer work in this particular door.

The lock yields a little more reluctantly than its companion, but eventually the door does fall open. Taking up his candle, he walks into the unlit interior.

At first sight, all is much the same; jars and barrels and crates of foodstuffs line shelves. But along the far wall is a bench with a sink within it, suggesting this room would normally be a more common part of the kitchen than the locked door now implies. He walks over to the bench, and finds a gas lamp sitting upon it. He lights the lamp from the candle in his hand, and Stephen Moore's little laboratory opens itself to the light.

He does not recognise it as such immediately, but after a minute or two of gazing he comes to the inevitable conclusion.

A dozen large bottles of liquid – some clear, some opaque – line a shelf alongside one end of the bench. The labels upon them are written in Latin, or sometimes in French. He recognises none of the words. A pestle and mortar sits, clean and smelling of nothing in particular, beside these bottles. Several books sit on top of one another on the other side of the bench; Horton opens the top one. It is a herbal, apparently in German, richly decorated on every page with colourful illustrations of plants.

He flicks through the other volumes: an edition of Linnaeus, no less; he recalls a conversation with Abigail about botanical matters. A freshly printed edition of something called *The Secret Commonwealth of Elves, Fauns and Fairies*. An older book, called *The Problems of Aristotle*. A chapbook, a cheap and ugly thing, called *Mother Bridget's Dream-Book and Oracle of Fate*. Horton recognises none of these books, but he wonders why a 'cook' should be consulting them.

He stands for a while at the bench, settling his thoughts, trying to imagine that he was Stephen Moore standing here, consulting these odd dark little books, swirling liquids into one another, gazing by the shadowy light of the gas lamp into alchemical secrets. A hobby, perhaps? Or something a good deal darker?

He hears the urgent sound of a horse approaching up the drive of Thorpe Lee House, breaking his concentration. He puts the books back as he found them, extinguishes the gas lamp, and makes his way out of the gloomy room and back into the kitchen.

The approaching rider is, as expected, William Jealous returning from Stoke d'Abernon. Horton hurries out to meet him before any of the other servants can do so, and Jealous stays in his saddle while Horton reads the note.

Stoke d'Abernon, September 7
To Whom It May Concern
At the request of Patrolman Jealous of Bow Street, to whom
this letter is given, I confirm that no one of the name
STEPHEN MOORE has been in the employ of Stoke
d'Abernon during my own employment at the House, which
encompasses some twenty years.
Watson, P., Butler

'Is it what you were expecting?' adds Jealous. Horton can see
in the young man's eyes that he has read the letter. He does not
blame him for it. He would do the same.

'Almost entirely,' he replies.

BROOKE HOUSE

John Burroway opens the door of Abigail's cell.

'Doctor would like to see you, miss.'

She puts down her book on the bed.

'I have not eaten, John. Not since breakfast. When may I eat?'

He does not answer because, she can see, he does not know. Before yesterday's events he would speak to her excitedly and with an extraordinarily detailed completeness, every yarn and anecdote spun with the finest thread, with no regard for the attention or patience of his listener. Now, he is silenced. Has Maria done something terrible to him, without knowing?

She stands up and smoothes down her dress. He steps aside for her, and she waits in the corridor beyond for him to lock the door – again, that maddening attention to detail, for there is no one in the cell to be shut inside. He takes his time over the lock, for his hands are shaking. To his left is the closed door of Maria's cell, from where he'd retrieved Abigail the night before, his hands shaking even more than they are now, his eyes on the floor, avoiding Maria's gaze like a dog terrified of punishment.

Again, Abigail worries what Maria may have done to John's mind, as she follows him down the stairs. She shivers as she passes the door to Bryson's apartment, in that part of Brooke House which the attendants call the Cottage. Her skin is still alive to the disgusting memory of the dinner she'd shared with him. But they are not going to Bryson's apartments. They walk on down the corridor, towards the front entrance to Brooke House, and John opens the door to Bryson's consulting chamber. She turns her head to the floor, and goes inside and sits in the nearest chair she can find, not once looking up.

She is terribly, terribly afraid.

She will not look at him, even when he speaks.

'Mrs Horton, I owe you a sincere apology.'

The words are kind, as is the tone. And yet she still does not look at him.

'I have treated you terribly, and have in addition behaved like the worst kind of St James roué. Please forgive me.'

She glances up, then, disgusted with herself for being so afraid, disgusted with him for what has passed between them, and she sees the little smile on his face and looks down again, suppressing the urge to stand and drive the letter-knife he holds in his hands into his leering eyes.

What is wrong with me?

She holds her hands, left in right, right in left. To stop them shaking.

If he stands I shall scream.

'I need your help, Mrs Horton. Your help with Maria. I have given it much thought. And I believe she is the most extra-ordinary specimen I have ever come across.'

At the word *specimen* her shakes come to a sudden stop. She places her hands on her lap, and looks up at him, head on one side.

Well, then.

'We need to talk to her, Mrs Horton.'

He sits at his desk. The letter-knife held between his fingers spins in the light from a gas lamp. He is smiling. Of all things he is smiling. The vengeful, angry, spiteful creature she'd expected is not in the room. She thinks of an expression of her mother's. *He looks like a cat that swallowed a canary.*

'I have not eaten, Bryson.'

The deletion of his honorific causes that self-satisfied smile to falter somewhat, but it soon comes back.

'No, that is an oversight. I will arrange for food to be sent to you.'

'So I am still to be locked in my cell, am I?'

'By no means. You are to sit with Maria again, Mrs Horton.'

Am I, indeed?

'To what end?'

'To calm her. To soothe her. To make her realise that this place, of all the places she could be, is best suited to her.'

'I am to convince her of this?'

'No, I do not think convincing will do much good, do you?'

His smile now says he knows a good deal more than he once did. That he has some understanding. Still the subject of what took place in Maria's cell the day before is not mentioned explicitly. It is a huge creature – an elephant, perhaps – that sits in the room beside them, about which neither is allowed to talk.

'May I write to my husband?'

The knife catches the light, causing her to blink.

'Perhaps tomorrow.'

Well, then.

THORPE

Horton must find Moore, immediately and before he can speak to anyone else of what he has learned. Telling Crowley or Mrs Chesterton will certainly lead to Moore's immediate dismissal; to his being thrown from the house. Sarah Graham has implied that the cook may soon be departing in any case. But Horton would know more of that strange little collection of jars and jugs and liquids before any such action is taken.

The problem is, no one knows where Moore is. It is by now mid-afternoon, and surely he must return soon? Horton finds himself loitering at the bottom of the main staircase, when he hears a bark from the library. It is Sir Henry. He would speak to the constable now, it appears.

Sir Henry is reclining on a splendid chaise longue which has been placed before the window facing the lawn from the library. He makes no effort to rise from his prone position as Horton walks into the room. He does not look up at the constable. Only a waved hand and a grunt acknowledges Horton's presence. The hand returns to its place against Sir Henry's chin, as he ponders the view outside. He looks rather as if someone were coming to do his portrait – a very different portrait to the active huntsman that hangs on the far wall. *Sir Henry Tempest, Composing Poetry by the Window.*

Horton clears his throat (wondering, as he does so, when he began this servile affectation), and begins.

'Sir Henry, Mr Graham has asked me to discuss with you some matters relating to events in London.'

Sir Henry breathes in through his nose, slowly and deliberately, but otherwise makes no response.

'I believe you have already been told of the deaths of two gentlemen, who, it is thought, you may have some acquaintance with.'

'Oh, stop it, Horton. Stop talking like a bloody politician.'

Sir Henry speaks mildly, and still doesn't look at Horton.

'Well, then, sir. Did you know the two gentlemen?'

'Yes, I knew them. Of course I knew them. You bloody well know I knew them.'

'And will you confirm your membership of this society to which they both also belonged? The Sybarites?'

'It's not a *society*, Horton. It's not even a club. We have organised some parties under that name. There is nothing more to it than that.'

'And you were at the most recent party?'

'Yes.'

'Where and when did that take place?'

'You are not as well informed as you sometimes suggest, constable.'

'Perhaps not, sir. But I have been here at Thorpe Lee House while events have unfolded.'

'The most recent party was at Sir John's residence on the Royal Terrace. It was a matter of a few days ago. The fourth of the month, I believe.'

'How many attended the party?'

'*Attended?* There were perhaps ten of us there.'

'Servants, as well.'

'Of course.'

'And . . . women.'

Now Sir Henry does turn to look at Horton, and the poetic aspect of his repose is broken. He now looks like what he is: a fat, middle-aged man lying down on a scruffy sofa, leering at the impertinence of an inferior.

'We ate. We drank. We fucked. Will that do?'

He turns away again, a hard smile on his soft face. The spat-out syllables bristle the air like the pikes of infantrymen.

'Were there any others there? Other than servants, and whores.'

He says the word with soft emphasis, his own spear pointing towards Sir Henry, who looks at him with contempt.

'There were no others, constable.'

Horton pulls Graham's letters from his pocket. Some names have been scribbled in the margins of the original.

'We have been given names of whores that have been . . . *supplied* to your group, Sir Henry, for previous parties. Can you confirm whether Rose Dawkins, Elizabeth Carrington or Maria Cranfield were at the most recent party?'

A wistful smile now, almost a twinkle on the tired fat face.

'Ah, Rose, well now. Yes, Rose was there. And Lizzie too. They are quite a pair, those two girls. Sir John kept Lizzie, as I understand it. She certainly was particularly attentive to his needs.'

'And the third name? Maria Cranfield?'

'There was a Maria, at a party last year. I don't recall her surname. She never returned.'

'Any other names?'

'Do you mean any other whores, constable?'

Horton says nothing, waits. Eventually, Sir Henry sighs, and looks back out of the window.

'The Sybarites are not what they were, Horton. Even when we started, we had none of the magnificence of the old clubs. We were no Medmenhamites.'

'Medmenhamites, Sir Henry?'

'Sir Francis Dashwood's crowd in the last century, constable. The Hell-Fire Clubs. Men with money and a certain debauched elegance. I have heard tell that *their* parties would have made the likes of Brummell and these so-called renegade poets run home crying to their mothers.'

Sir Henry sighs, in mourning for a better past.

'As for the Sybarites? Well. There used to be more of us – two dozen to a party, at least. And a whore to every man. But those days are long past. There were only two whores at the last party, Horton. Lizzie and Rose. No more.'

'You know where these women can be found?'

'I have no idea whatsoever. Sir John sorted the women out, and the other essentials. He was very much the master of our ceremonies. Now he has gone, I suspect the Sybarites are no more.'

Sir Henry sounds almost wistful.

'The other members have been told to take precautions. If someone is targeting the members . . .'

'Oh, I understand very well, constable.'

'If you wish, I could remain here to maintain an eye on things, until Mr Graham requires my return.'

Sir Henry turns those fat old eyes on him again.

'How useful do you believe yourself to be, constable? If whomever is doing this comes to Thorpe, will you be able to stop him?'

Horton says nothing.

'I thought as much. Do as you will. I will return to London on the morrow.'

Horton, nonplussed, can think of nothing to say to that.

'If I am to be *hunted*, I will not be hunted here,' says Sir Henry. 'It may endanger Ellen. And Mrs Graham, of course. And besides . . .'

He frowns at the garden, as if a mystery were walking across its lawn.

'Thorpe Lee House . . . disturbs me.'

He has no power to keep Sir Henry at Thorpe Lee House, short of arresting him. He writes a note to Graham, but has no means of getting it to him quickly. He has no riders with which to send messages like Graham does.

He ponders going back with Sir Henry – insisting on accompanying him, and thus solving two problems at once: how to preserve Sir Henry, and how to alert Graham to the change in circumstances.

But then there is Stephen Moore.

It is impossible for him to leave the house, he realises, before he has established what Stephen Moore is up to. A dark suspicion unfolds. It is one which he cannot afford to leave uncovered.

He feels temporarily helpless in the face of the problem. London, he realises, presents opportunities to hide and to watch which Thorpe will never supply. He cannot follow Moore safely, cannot observe him without being himself observed. He has seen Moore's secret kitchen. Is it perhaps time to have him arrested and interrogated, perhaps with the aid of a local magistrate?

The memory – or rather, the non-memory – of that strange episode in the woods comes back to him. Now it seems he can recall speaking to someone. But who? The

question scares him. Charles Horton has the same relationship with his mind as a clockmaker has with a mechanism. It
is a reliable object, which can suffer occasional discombobu-
lation through anxiety (for Abigail, for his work, for his past)
or through alcohol. Such breakdowns can always be recovered. But this strange absence in his recollections feels peaky
and different.

He walks up the stairs from the library after his conversation
with Sir Henry, and opening the door to his room sees a note
left there on the desk.

Meet me at the church at 4 o'clock.

Moore.

The cook, it would seem, has discovered Horton's entry into
his secret room. There is no need to chase after him.

There is a light rain in the air when he walks into Thorpe village for the second time, and it has the chill of autumn in it.
Horton turns up the collar on his old sailor's pea-coat as he
walks down the lane.

The red-bricked walls and little thatched houses gather in
around him once again, and soon he is at the church. It is
quiet, the door closed. There is no one in the churchyard. He
opens the door, and almost walks directly into the rector, the
Reverend John Leigh-Bennett.

'Ah, constable!' he says, with a polite delight at reacquain-
tance. 'You are welcome!'

'My thanks for that,' says Horton, and is then unsure what
to say or do next. He feels vaguely caught out, and wonders
why Moore would choose the church as a place to meet, given
the danger of observation. Or perhaps he has secreted himself
in the churchyard? Should Horton have checked first?

While these worries occupy him, he sees Leigh-Bennett pick
up a coat and hat from hooks near the church door. The rector

ignores him as he dresses himself for the rain outside, and then smiles again as he makes his leave.

'I must apologise for leaving you *unattended*.' The word is given odd emphasis. 'I am needed elsewhere, and I'm sure you will relish the privacy solitude can afford. And, my dear Horton,' this with one hand placed carefully but deliberately upon Horton's arm, 'do recall our conversation. Superstition and belief, you see. They revolve around one another in a place such as this. Like the Earth and the Moon.'

And with that, Leigh-Bennett leaves.

Horton watches the door close behind him. Its mild Anglican slam echoes around the empty church interior, seeming to pick up volume as it does so, until it sounds like rocks pouring down the roof. His head gives one internal swirl and he sits down heavily. Something flies past the window, then the next, then the next. A figure on a stick.

A woman laughs. He feels his heart beat in his chest, and turns towards the sound of steps. Elizabeth Hook walks out of the gloom.

'You!' he gasps, theatrically. He is unable to stand. That headache swells between his temples again, and his body and his mind seem to be in disjunction.

She walks to his side, her height increasing until it fills the hall, her fingers growing into claws, her mouth opening to reveal sharp yellow teeth, her breath as fetid as an ancient cave ...

And then she is sitting next to him, a concerned middle-aged woman, one hand on his arm, the other on the back of his neck, in the honoured pose of the nurse.

'It will pass,' she says, gently. 'It will pass. Just wait a moment or two.'

The women on sticks fly away. The booming rocks fall into silence. His head makes one final reel and then settles back into place.

'The enchantment fades,' she says. 'It was the same for me, when I first walked away from the house and came here. A powerful, final vision, perhaps brought on by the church. This is the building in which we contemplate such things, after all. But it fades with time.'

He is himself again: a middle-aged guilty man, a mutineer and a constable, abandoned by his wife and deserving nothing better. A great urge to weep comes over him, but he pushes it away, just as he pushes Elizabeth Hook's hands away, and stands.

'How did you come to be here, woman?' he says, feeling anger bubbling. 'You cannot have sent me the note. Who is your accomplice?'

Another set of footsteps, another figure walks out of the gloom. Stephen Moore.

'So.' Horton looks at the two of them, and says nothing more, since nothing more needs to be said.

'Stephen is my cousin,' says Elizabeth Hook, after a few moments of churchy silence. 'I asked him to come here. He is of the cunning-folk. I asked him to work to lift the enchantment that sits on Thorpe Lee House.'

Horton looks at Moore, whose face has remained in that supercilious, comfortable mode in which he first encountered it. A peevish sense of irritation fills his head. He waits again.

'The house is clearly under a spell of *maleficium*,' Moore says, finally. 'When my cousin Elizabeth approached me and told me of the episodes which had occurred, the diagnosis was clear. It is one of the worst cases of bewitchment I have heard of. It is made more horrible by the vehicle through which the bewitchment is carried through the house. The girl. She is at the root of it.'

'Miss Ellen, Mr Horton,' Elizabeth Hook whispers from the

bench in which she is sitting. 'The bewitchment sits upon her, and from her visits itself upon the rest of the house.'

'When I arrived here, the girl was not herself,' says Moore. 'During the days, she slept. During the nights, she walked the house and the grounds. She was seen – by the gardener, and by me – running through the woods that surround the house, inappropriately clothed. I do believe it was she that killed Sir Henry's dogs, though I did not see this myself. When questioned on these matters, she affected not to understand. My cousin tried to discuss this matter with her, and she was greeted with hysterics and accusations. It was Ellen's testimony that led to her being sacked from her position.'

'And you are feeding her poison.' The truth, when Horton realises it, is like a draught of sweet, cool, untainted water.

'No, constable. I am curing her. It is what we cunning-folk do.'

'This is madness.' Horton says it, but he is thinking something else. He is thinking of the things he has witnessed these past two years. He is thinking of Abigail, pursued through her dreams by a woman of the South Pacific. He is thinking of a sea captain, young yet old, howling from the hold of a doomed ship. 'This is madness,' he says, again.

'No, constable. This is witchcraft.'

'There is no such thing! There is a law!'

Moore laughs at that, an unpleasant laugh, the laugh of a corrupt minister jeering at the indignities of his constituents. Elizabeth Hook flashes a glance of dislike at him, stands, and faces Horton.

'These things are true, and they are real, constable,' she says, her face kind but serious. 'Some of us grew up surrounded by the truth of these things. You did not. But we cannot deny what has happened to us. You yourself have experienced that house. You know something evil poisons men's minds up there. I can see in your face that I speak truth. What have *you* seen, constable? Why do you deny what your eyes have seen?'

Horton looks at Moore, and then clearly and suddenly he remembers. He was speaking with Ellen in the woods. The gap in his memory fills smoothly and with a sense of cleansing, like water rushing into a well.

'This will end. This will end today.' He steps to the door. 'I will consider what to do. But you, Moore, will tender your resignation immediately. I am going to seize the materials in the basement rooms for investigation by those who understand such matters. I will alert Thorpe's constable as to what you have told me, and you will present yourselves to him this afternoon, or a warrant will be issued for your arrests. Good day.'

WESTMINSTER

Graham stands at the window of his drawing room, looking out onto Great Queen Street. It is almost midnight. He nurses a glass of Tokay, and waits for something to happen.

Five houses are currently being watched by his patrolmen and officers, one of them secretly, for the second night. Sir Thomas Mackworth, he of the furious threats of a duel, is watched without his knowledge; Graham hopes he can trust the patrolman concerned to stay in the shadows. James Blake-Slater, the Earl of Maidstone, along with Samuel Lake, Algernon Lincoln and Henry Harcourt Palmer are all cooperating. Each of them has a patrolman at his front door, charged with walking around the house every hour. The Earl has insisted on an additional three men to watch his house. The final Sybarite, John Cameron, should be well away from London by now.

Jealous, his promising young patrolman, is out there somewhere looking for the whores Rose Dawkins and Elizabeth Carrington. Indeed, all the Bow Street patrolmen not concerned with watching the houses of the Sybarites, along with the watches of St Giles in the Fields, St Paul's Covent Garden, St Clement Danes, St Maria le Strand, St Martin in the Fields and even St Anne Soho have been issued with warrants for the two women, an unprecedented show of cooperative determination by the magistrates and the parish watch committees.

Most of his time since returning from the interview with Sidmouth has been spent organising this, a tiresome interlude indeed. His old friend John Harriott would not have had the patience; but then Harriott believes London and Westminster needs a unified policing system, with central control, not this hotch-potch of parishes, magistrates and aldermen which currently subsists. Graham himself is unconvinced of the need for centralisation; how much power would they give to a single man to control such a force? He would be as a monarch.

And yet, by God, how ridiculous, this twisted inheritance of watch committees and assizes, remnants of a Saxon past filled with villages, by no means fit for purpose for a swarming, gargantuan metropolis which swells with evildoers! The boundary between two of these ancient parishes passes through the foyer of his beloved Drury Lane Theatre Royal – a whore could stand on one side of this foyer and be immune to arrest by a watchman of the wrong parish on the other side. Insanity!

And after all, the truth is this: the women might not even be in the area any longer. They might have wandered a mile or two, into the City or over to Lambeth, and be in an entirely different jurisdiction, one with no interest in Sybarites or their whores.

He thinks of Horton, out there in the Surrey darkness. Has he spoken to Sir Henry yet? Is Sarah safe? And what of little Ellen, that dark half-daughter, barely seen but, in a twisted, sardonic paradox, deeply loved? She is not even his daughter. And yet, she is.

A whore walks past, screaming at an unseen fellow. Somebody's daughter. Perhaps, God help her, somebody's wife.

The night-walking women of London, screaming from the streets, owned by no man but subject to all men.

Aaron Graham sips, and waits for something to happen.

THORPE

Charles Horton finds himself lying in a field in the dark. The earth is wet against his cheek and edges his mouth, which drools into the soil. He is as one with the field, as damp as an old leaf, as tired as a winter tree, as confused as a lunatic.

First things first. Who am I?

I am Charles Horton.

Well, then. And where am I?

I am in a field.

And where is the field?

Thorpe. It must be in Thorpe. I was in Thorpe.

And how might I have arrived in this field?

He turns his cheek, and a stab of pain as bright as lightning supplies part of the answer. Still lying in the soil, he brings one hand to his face and presses his cheek, releasing another crackle of pain, as vivid as the spark from a Leyden jar.

I have been assaulted. I have been left here.

But by whom?

He remembers.

After leaving the two cooks in the church – the woman, and her cunning nephew – he'd gone looking for the village constable to make arrangements for their arrest. He'd begun with the Rev. Leigh-Bennett, who as rector of the church must know of his parish's constable. Leigh-Bennett had not been at home, but his manservant had willingly given Horton the name of the constable: Benjamin Ridley. Where might Ridley be found? Either at home, or in the Pipehouse. The manservant's grimace suggested to Horton that Ridley would most likely be in the latter, presumably already drunk, in keeping with the tradition of many rural constables.

It had been late afternoon, getting on towards evening, when he'd made his way to the Pipehouse. He'd planned to arrange things with Ridley (the constable's state permitting) and then head straight for Thorpe Lee House. He would begin clearing Stephen Moore's secret chamber of cunning potions, and would demand an immediate audience with Miss Ellen Tempest Graham.

Ridley had indeed been in the Pipehouse, and was indeed drinking, though he was still largely sober. He was sitting with four or five other men, none of whom welcomed Horton's attempt to extricate their friend from the inn. His old fat friend Hob, the labourer from the road who'd seen him with Elizabeth Hook days before, had also been in the place, and was drunk, though not as incapacitated as on Horton's first visit. No, Hob was this time more than capable of expressing violent disapproval of Horton's return to that place, and made physical threats as soon as he saw him.

'Oi, here he is!' Hob had shouted as Horton stepped in. 'The London Bloody Wizard! Have you arrested her then? That witch? Is she going to bloody burn for all this?'

Horton had tried to ignore him, and had asked whether

Benjamin Ridley was in the place. A few fingers pointed at the surprisingly old, shrinking figure sat drinking with half-a-dozen others, and Horton went to speak to him directly. But Hob got in his way.

'I'm a-talking to thee, Constable Bloody London!' he said, stepping in front of Horton and pushing him in the chest with a pewter tankard. 'Is that fucking witch under lock and key? Or am I to go out and drag the bitch out to a tree now?'

Horton, in full knowledge that he was here to arrange exactly what the fat labourer was demanding, nevertheless pushed him out of the way. He was not about to discuss his plans with one such as he.

'Ridley,' he began, 'I am Charles—'

He was grabbed from behind and whirled around, and a fat but solid fist collided with the side of his face. He felt something crack, and the pain brought back hard memories of naval splinters and naval bones cracking under enemy attack, and barber-surgeons below-decks snapping damaged limbs in twain. But he did not go down. No, he swung his own punch, and felt the labourer's own face give way beneath it, and then the fat man was lying silently on the floor, and every face in the Pipehouse was on him.

He spoke, and every word brought agonies in his face, but he spoke still.

'Ridley, I am Charles Horton of the Thames River Police Office. I am sent here by Aaron Graham, magistrate of Bow Street and a justice of the peace in Surrey as well as in Westminster, to investigate certain events at Thorpe Lee House. I need you to arrest Elizabeth Hook and her nephew Stephen Moore immediately; I believe they can be found at Thorpe church, if you be quick.'

No one said anything for a moment, then two of the men

with Ridley laughed. Neither sound was pleasant. Ridley himself looked miserable, and sunk his old, bearded face into his beer, and refused to look at Horton directly.

'It's no use arresting Elizabeth Hook,' a voice said, but Horton could not identify from where it came. His head was beginning to feel light and airy, and he felt the floor shift slightly beneath his feet.

'She's a witch,' said another voice.

'That she is. No sense in arresting a witch.'

'She wants drowning.'

'Nah. That's for testing what she be, drowning. We know she's a witch. She needs burning.'

'That's it. Burning.'

'My Janey always said we'd have to do this, one day soon.'

'She's a witch. No doubting she's a witch.'

One by one, the men in the room stood up from their chairs, said their piece, and waited for their comrades. Horton watched them as they did so, saw the manifestation of a brave battalion, a regiment made fearless by drink and fellowship and made drunk by fear and ale.

'No, no, no, you cannot.'

His voice seemed to him to come from one of the other men, not from him, so separate from himself did he now begin to feel. He lurched to the only man in the room left sitting. Benjamin Ridley, the constable. He fell onto the solid table before him, unsettling the drinks on it, casting two jugs to the floor, and leaning across it grabbed Ridley's ancient labourer's jacket, the smell of fields and shit threaded through its ancient stitching.

'Ridley, stop them! They must not!'

Ridley looked like he might cry, shaking his head, helpless. He never spoke a word, as one by one the men walked out, in silent determination.

Horton followed them out into the road. The stars danced in the sky, whirling and collapsing to their own silent music. Horton half-ran, half-stumbled through the crowd of men, grabbing shoulders, twisting arms, cajoling and pleading and shouting and threatening. But before long they became tired of him, and two of them grabbed his arms and span him through a gap in the hedgerow, such that he fell down a small inclination in the ground and collapsed, face down, into Thorpe's newly enclosed earth.

And now he finds himself again, here in the fallow earth.

How long has he lain here? Have they already found Elizabeth Hook? He manages to lift himself onto all-fours, his face hanging down like a cowed dog, and then, the pain from his cheek now infecting every part of him above the waist, he turns to sit and face the hedgerow.

He recognises it immediately. The same place as he sat in, the place where the man from the inn – Bill, had it been? Yes, Bill – had seen the 'witch' flying through the air.

Can he smell burning on the wind? Can he hear men shouting?

No. But he can hear a horse approaching down the road. And then, to his surprise, he sees a witch flying along the top of the hedge. She appears from his right – from the direction of Thorpe Lee House – and she is going fast. The sound of horse hooves fills his ears. Her black hair is streaming behind her, and her face is set towards the village. The high wagon she sits on looks like the one he'd seen her on earlier today, behind the woods at Thorpe Lee House, during his encounter with Miss Ellen. The wagon is so high that only its driver can be seen along the row of the hedge, such that she might look to one with too much alcohol in his blood to be flying.

She flashes before his eyes, along the line of the hedge,

powered by the sound of hooves. The unknown witch from the woods rushes away from him and into the darkness, towards Thorpe.

She is, thinks Horton, riding away from Thorpe Lee House.

WESTMINSTER

The woman is running, running hard, but her skirts and her shoes make things difficult for her. Even through the noise of Covent Garden's streets, William Jealous can hear the noise of her frantic breathing, an urgent three-four waltz of half-swallowed shrieks and desperate swallows, so much more weary than the hearty two-four march of his own powerful lungs. As she runs, she calls out helplessly to others on the street, begging their help.

'He's upon me! He's upon me! Help me! Help me!'

But they are going too fast. Even when a bystander tries to help – when a streetwalker sticks out a boot, or a pimp emerges from the shadows with a cudgel, or a gentleman out for the theatre or for whoring raises a gloved fist – it is a mere matter of swerving and avoiding before continuing the pursuit.

He is ten yards away. Nine yards away. Eight yards . . .

Whoomph.

He sprawls onto the cobblestones, horse-shit and worse squelching up his hands and arms. He just avoids putting his face down into the mire, when an unknown number of feet start kicking his legs and sides.

'What's it about, eh?'

''What you up to?'

'Fucking bastard.'

'Leave 'er alone.'

He springs up in half a second. The voices are all female, the faces angry but now afraid, because he is standing before them, young and strong and unaffected by their pathetic violence. A pimp begins to appear behind them, so he casually slaps one of the whores, hard, around the face. They turn to their screaming companion, and he turns as well, back to the pursuit.

Twenty yards now. Not much ground lost. Nineteen. Eighteen.

She stumbles momentarily, her side caught against the arm of a costermonger's barrow. He is almost upon her. She screams, but almost silently – there is no air left in her lungs. She runs again, but within twenty steps he has her. Now things could become difficult. They have stopped running, so it is easier for bystanders to intervene, to knock him about the head and try to release her. So he must think quickly.

A door opens onto the street. Light floods out of it. He wraps his arms round the whore's shoulders and lets their momentum carry them into and through the door, knocking down the old man who had been on his way out, sending him back into the house.

She struggles, but he holds her and with a foot slams the door closed. Jealous hears people knocking at the door, he hears the old man start to shout, and he hopes what he says next will calm the situation.

'Bow Street officer! I am a patrolman! I have a warrant to arrest this woman!'

He shouts it at the old man, and hopes it is loud enough for the women in the street outside to hear.

'Rose Dawkins,' he says to the woman lying on the floor. 'I've a warrant to arrest you.'

She bites and scratches and screams, but eventually Rose Dawkins relents, after a fashion. It takes ten minutes to extricate themselves from the old man's home. When they finally emerge onto the street, Jealous notes that his pursuit of the prostitute has taken them deep into St Giles.

This brings its own troubles – St Giles is notoriously poor, and vicious – but also a respite from the more crowded streets around Covent Garden. No one comes to St Giles for entertainment. The only people here are the ones who live here, a dozen to a room, crowded into buildings which were built for the rich but which the rich slowly abandoned as they moved west, allowing landlords to steal in and partition rooms and seal off hallways, squeezing every rentable bit of value out of every nook and cranny.

William Jealous grew up in St Giles. His father, the Bow Street Runner, had been a hard man. St Giles had held no fears for him, and it holds none for his son, either. And a whore is a whore.

She has stopped struggling, at least physically. But St Giles holds as little fear for her as it does for Jealous – and her words are spiked with defiance.

'Fucking constable. Fucking nonsense. You're no fucking constable. What are you, fifteen? You ever fucked a woman, you ginger shit? Have you? Want to fuck me now, I can see it in your piggy little ginger eyes, you dirty fucking pig. Come on then. Do me here. Do me. I'll cut your fucking prick off, you dirty—'

He slaps her, hard, with his free hand, never letting go with his other. He is panting and, yes, astonishingly aroused. He could fuck her. He could take her, here, down this alley, up against the wall, a quick one while no one's about, and then get on with business.

She starts speaking, and he slaps her again. He feels something in his head – a definite force, pushing him away, as if someone had grabbed the back of his collar and was yanking him backwards. She is staring at him, her green eyes full of hatred and intense concentration, and he replies with violence. He shoves her against a wall, and, spitting into her face with the passion of it, tells her the story of the Sybarites, of the men being guarded in their houses this very night, and of his search for her companion in whoring, Elizabeth Carrington. And at the end of it, he slaps her again. That feeling of being pulled away switches off like a candle in an open window.

When he lets go of her, she slides down the wall to sit on the turd-encrusted cobbles. Her old tart's skirts ripple around her knees like uneaten vegetables thrown on the ground. She puts her head on her arms and knees and stays like that for a while, not crying. She has never cried, not once, during this whole performance.

She sniffs, loudly, and then she looks up at him.

'Come on, then,' she says. 'I know where she is.'

She stands.

'But if you hit me again, I'll kick your prick off.'

The lodging house where Elizabeth Carrington lives is on the borders of St Giles and Covent Garden, in that area which still retains some gentility, where whores can take a room for relatively little money and bring back gentlemen without having to climb over dirty children and begging adults on the stairs. Beds can be paid for by the hour, 18d. to 2s., in this part of town.

Rose hasn't seen Elizabeth since the Sybarites party. She refuses to speak of the party other than to confirm her attendance, and Lizzie's. She's been down in Kent the last two days, had been planning to pick hops, needed to earn some money, but they're not ready for pickers yet. How long is this stupid jaunt going to take, anyway?

The house is on Brownlow Street, just around the corner from Drury Lane. It's not an enormous place, probably no more than fifty years old, and may at one time have housed a lawyer or a doctor. Now, its half-dozen rooms house four whores and a pimp while the sixth, according to Rose, is let by a peer of the realm who brings whores back here, three or four at a time, undresses them, and paints on their skin.

The door to the street is open, and they go inside. The vestibule is scruffy and noxious, the shit of the street trodden through onto the stone floor. Vestiges of the house's former status remain: the line of the dado rail, the unbroken panelling at the back by the stairs, a painting, hung askew, of a fat man and a horse. Rose leads them upstairs.

She waits while he knocks at Elizabeth's door. There is no answer, so he knocks again. Still no answer. He tries the door. It is unlocked. Rose tries to stop him (out of fear or propriety, he cannot tell), but he opens the door and steps inside.

The room has been emptied by persons unknown. All that remains is a bed, its linen stolen, a chest of drawers, opened and ransacked, a chair and, in the chair, the stiff, lifeless body of Elizabeth Carrington. Rose, as she turns to walk into the room, stifles a cry and backs away from the open door. He grabs her arm and pulls her into the room.

'What? No, not here!'

But he shakes his head, pushes her against the wall by the door, and closes the door. He pulls a bolt across.

'Stay there.'

He turns back to the room, and approaches Elizabeth. He walks carefully, as if trying not to wake her. Her hands are drooped over the side of the chair, and something white reflects what little light there is. A cut-throat, dropped on the floor beneath her right hand. Which means . . .

Yes. The left wrist and hand are darkly smeared, as if she'd sunk her hand in oil up to the wrist. A puddle of this dark stuff swells on the floor beneath this hand.

Self-destruction. And not too long ago. But long enough for the locals to have heard of it, and to have let themselves in, and helped themselves to whatever goods poor Elizabeth Carrington had managed to secure. And then let themselves out again.

From the next-door room, a slap, a gasp, and a deep, male chuckle.

THORPE

The witch is not on a broom, of course. She never was. He realises this as he half-walks, half-runs to the house, his cheek seemingly full of knives and needles. She is riding a wagon. Sitting on top, riding along, she appeared from where he was lying to be flying along the top of the hedge. Such must have been Bill's view, and his mistake. Appearances can deceive. The mind can play tricks on the understanding.

It seems to represent something important, this thought. But he has no time to interrogate it, for a glow appears at the side of the lane where the house is, and shouts are growing in volume, and then he stumbles into the gardens of Thorpe Lee House and upon a scene from another century.

The burning of a witch.

The fire has been set in the middle of the lawn in front of the house; at the centre of this lawn, incongruously, stands a lonely beech tree. Its straight, thickish trunk has been dressed all around with wood from other trees. Its branches have lost a few early leaves, with gaps showing against the moonlit sky; a giant scarecrow which is losing its hair.

At the bottom of the tree, tied to the trunk and with wood gathered up to her waist, is Elizabeth Hook.

Do they mean to burn the tree, and her?

The glow he'd seen from the road does not, yet, come from the pyre. A dozen or more men are standing around the tree, shouting, and each of them carries a torch which blazes with medieval intensity. They wave these torches at Elizabeth, and then, one by one, they hold their torches to the wood. The flames from the torches dance across the front of the house, as if the building itself were goading them on.

He shouts at them, and the effort seems to rip his cheek bone in two. He begins to run, thinking as he does about the woman on the wagon riding away.

She was here, she started this.

Elizabeth Hook screams, and he thinks of the gun deck in a naval battle, of wood chips flying through the air and into skin, eyes and mouths, of enemy cannon balls connecting with the blood and bone of his shipmates, of the screams of pain, the agonies of heat, and he can feel that heat on his face as he draws near to the pyre. His stomach, empty of food, turns over and he vomits up bile and bitterness into the earth, and falls to his knees, shouting at the men to stop, desist, or face the consequence.

He pukes again, and again, and again, as if he could expel the sight of that burning, the smell of the old cook's flesh blistering in the flame, until his belly is only emptiness, and he pukes up even that, pushing the hollowness out of himself as if he could turn himself inside-out and show his corruption to the world.

And then there is nothing left, and he looks up again.

The beech tree stands solitary and untouched in the centre of the lawn. The air is cold, and damp, and resolutely unburned. He is alone.

For a moment, his brain is as empty as his stomach: a void, in which understanding can gain no purchase.

A vision. A phantasy. A view of the unreal.

Am I then indeed mad?

A shout from Thorpe Lee House, or more of a scream. But not the scream of a frightened woman; this is the angry, pained shout of a man.

Given how filled the air was with screams and angry shouts just minutes before, the countryside is now silent, and the shout from the house is thus shockingly loud.

Did his brain really invent all that has just transpired? The fire, the smells, the shape on the carriage? Did he see the woman from the woods (the *witch*) riding along the road, or did he not?

The empty darkness of the lawn gives no answer. It seems to contain more fear, even, than those blood-drenched visions. There is a thick possibility to the shadows within the woods behind the lawn, drawn deeper by the sudden uncertainty of his own perception. Is he still dreaming? Is he still asleep? Where might he be?

He walks up to the front door of the house and finds it open. Servants are milling about the vestibule in night-attire and he hears a woman – he thinks it must be Sarah Graham – wailing and shouting from the drawing room. Horton thinks what lies before him must be of the same species as the witch-burning. A phantom of perception, painted beneath the flickering eye-lids of a man who is even now asleep in his own bed. Perhaps not even here. Perhaps in Lower Gun Alley, Wapping, his pretty, clever wife asleep beside him, and not in a madhouse, far beyond his reach, the warmth of her body as familiar and comfortable as the shape of his own face.

But his own face is misshapen. His cheek is swollen and full of agonies. He did not imagine that. His mouth is full of the sour taste of choked-up bile. As he steps into Thorpe Lee House, his knuckles smack into the doorframe (he is by no means steady upon his feet), and the pain – low, sharp, definitive – is as real as real can ever claim to be.

He wishes to go to bed.

Jane Ackroyd rushes past him, fetching something from the kitchen for her wailing mistress in the drawing room. He grabs her by the upper arm, and she shrieks. He notes that no one, until now, has realised he has returned.

'What is this commotion, girl?'

She stares at him, her eyes wide and red and exhausted of the tears she must already have shed.

'The constable!' she shouts. 'The constable!'

From somewhere in the house, a roar. Sir Henry is still here.

'It's Miss Ellen, sir,' says Jane, and he drops her arm immediately. 'She's tried to do away with the master!'

PART FOUR

The Woman of Means

We may without exaggeration assert that a common
Prostitute is, in a Community, an Evil, not dissimilar to
a Person infected with the Plague; who, miserable
himself, is daily communicating the Contagion to those,
that will propagate still wider the fatal Malady.

An Account of the Institution of the Lock Asylum
for the Reception of Penitent Female Patients when
Discharged Cured from the Lock Hospital,
ANON, 1792

WESTMINSTER

The regularity of Westminster's finest houses, it occurs to Graham, is worthy of a book.

What else can explain the fact that five astonished servants have appeared at Bow Street, accompanied by officers, within the space of an hour? Between 7 am, when he is woken in Great Queen Street by one of the officers, and 8 am they show up, one by one, their pale astonished faces disbelieving of the stories they bring.

The butler to Algernon Lincoln, son of the Duke of Hand-forth, was the first to arrive, accompanied by a patrolman, Daniel Bishop.

Something has happened to my master. Something terrible. He is dead in his bedchamber.

Was he wearing a satyr's mask? He was.

Within ten minutes, a footman appears from the house of Sir Thomas Mackworth, Bt, despatched to Bow Street with a Runner, John Nelson Lavender. Sir Thomas, he who had angrily refused any protection from Bow Street, is currently lying face down in his room, his head staved in by a small marble statue from Tuscany of two entwined naked women.

Is he wearing a satyr's mask? He is.

Representatives from the houses of Samuel Lake (second brother of Viscount Lake, and a claimed descendant of Sir Lancelot) and Henry Harcourt Palmer bring their shocked faces to Bow Street at the same time, both accompanied by patrolmen. Lake is currently pinned to the wall of his bedchamber by a spear from Guinea, secured for him by a slave-trader relative, and now securing him through the throat. Harcourt Palmer is unmarked but dead, apparently smothered, on his bed.

Satyr's masks? Yes, in both cases.

The final arrival is the valet to James, Earl of Maidstone, the only son and heir of the Marquess of Tonbridge and the only one of the Sybarites to be married (to Miss Fabbiano; they have two daughters, who are currently residing in Sissinghurst in Kent). The Earl is a late riser, hence the tardy discovery of his body, its throat slashed, sitting on a commode in the corner of his bedchamber. His hands have been cut off and left by his side.

He was wearing a satyr's mask.

Outside the Bow Street office, Graham can hear the metropolis waking up. It will be a loud, bursting, vicious sort of day.

BROOKE HOUSE

It has been another bad night in the madhouse. Abigail thinks of her bed in the adjacent cell. It is amazing how attractive something so ordinarily awful can be after hours spent in an uncomfortable chair in a different room.

Maria is sleeping, lying on her side, the strait waistcoat forcing her into an odd position. How can she sleep with that awful thing holding her? It has been a month now since the two of them arrived at Brooke House. Maria has been enchained like this for the whole of that time.

She had been reading to Maria when the night turned bad. Reading aloud is the best way of calming the irregular motion of her own thoughts, never mind those of Maria. Food was brought to them by John Burroway. No other nurses appeared, nor did Bryson. They had been placed in a weird isolation. Abigail half-suspected they were being watched and listened to, though how this can be she could not imagine.

She read, dozed, ate, drank. Maria remained calm. Abigail herself became agitated as darkness began to fall, because for a terrible few minutes she saw the Pacific princess, removed from her own skull and sitting on the bed beside Maria, watching them both, and then whispering into Maria's ear.

'What does she say?' Abigail had asked, her voice stretched, her blood cold. Maria had tipped her head onto one side, and had spoken one of the very few sentences Abigail heard from her that day; the first sentence she had spoken directly to her, unmediated by some lunatic raving.

'You see things too, I think.'

She sounded like a milkmaid: a beautiful, slender Suffolk milkmaid with rough hands, exquisite hair, and eyes as old as driftwood.

'But the things are not real. Not like the things I see.'

Night deepened, and then the bad things started again, in the exact same way as they had three nights before. Abigail had fallen asleep in the chair. She was awoken by a single, sharp scream, and again it was the horrific, unexpected yell of a male patient, from the ground floor.

That single scream had been followed by Pandaemonium. She ran to the open door of Maria's cell, and poked her head out. The corridor was empty, but it sounded like an agonised shriek was rising from the cell of every male patient, a shriek which wrenched sympathetic horror from the breast – for what kind of terrible fear could be sparking these cries? And how could it be seen from within the four solid walls of an asylum cell?

She turned back into the room, and a vision of a man in a mask being run through with a spear slashed before her eyes and was gone. Maria sat on her bed, upright as a piano, her eyes wide and unseeing, her breath pumping in and out like a bellows. She was chanting something, something quiet and repetitive and hurried, and it was so hard to hear that Abigail took some time to make it out. It was a familiar chant.

'Tie his wrists and tie his feet, Spill his guts out on the sheet. Tie his wrists and tie his feet, Spill his guts out on the sheet. Tie his wrists and tie his feet, Spill his guts out on the sheet.'

'Maria? Maria, my dear? What is this?'

She might as well have been speaking to a machine. Maria's voice and her breath were as regular as a steam engine, and as remorseless; there was no change in emphasis to her words. She remembered what Maria herself had said about the demon that dwelled inside her.

And she heard it from outside, as well. Standing there in the open door of the cell, she heard the shrieks and cries of the men begin to fall back into one another, until a single rhythmic chant thrummed through the stone floors of that rambling old building, every male patient's scream turned into the same marching tune.

Tie his wrists and tie his feet, Spill his guts out on the sheet. Tie his wrists and tie his feet, Spill his guts out on the sheet. Tie his wrists and tie his feet, Spill his guts out on the sheet.

Like slaves on a galley, she thought.

It went on for some time, this incessant chanting. And then, suddenly, Maria stopped. One by one, the male voices accompanying her fell away, until silence once again made its residence in Brooke House. Abigail remained standing, not daring to approach Maria.

'Maria. My dear. Was that you?'

The girl had looked at her. She had started to cry.

'Oh, my dear Lord. Oh my God. What has she done?' Maria asked. 'And why can I see it so clearly?' And she fell into exhausted, whispering prayer.

Dr Bryson appears at the door of Maria's cell. He looks exhausted, as exhausted as Abigail feels. He also, notes Abigail with some grim satisfaction, looks afraid.

When he sees Maria is sleeping, his pointed little face eases slightly, but not entirely. He does not step into the cell. Abigail notes all these things, and remembers them. She has much business with Dr Bryson, and one day soon she may be able to transact it.

'She slept throughout the night?' he asks, not once looking at Abigail, his face set towards Maria, watching for any flicker of the eye, any sign of approaching wakefulness. 'Throughout that terrible disturbance?'

He does not know what she did. He did not hear her.

Like any practised natural philosopher, Abigail feels a mild contempt for Bryson's failures of observation and imagination. She realises, fully, why he wants her to keep watch over Maria. He knows that Maria was able to force him to do things against his will – John Burroway, also. But he has not made the connection between the three disturbed nights at the madhouse and the sleeping girl who rests, held in place by that dreadful prison canvas.

'She slept,' Abigail lies. She is not his experimental assistant.

'You heard the disturbance?'

'It was terribly loud.'

'And yet she slept.'

It is a question, but Abigail does not answer it. She will not be interrogated.

She is about to ask if she might write to Charles, but she knows what the answer will be. Bryson is losing his grip on whatever is taking place inside these walls. He has little conception of Maria or of her capacities. And the events of the last night had badly scared her, not least those muttered questions that followed the cessation of that awful chant.

What has she done? And why can I see it?

Who was she speaking of?

'Dr Bryson, Maria's sheets need changing, and she needs to

be washed. As do I. It begins to smell in here, and that will not make either of us comfortable.'

He looks away from Maria for the first time, and back at her. That flat lustful sheen comes back into his eyes. She throttles an urge to spit at him.

'I will send John Burroway up shortly.'

He turns away, and she smiles for the first time in days. A stupid man will always be vulnerable to a clever lie.

THORPE

The sunlight falls across his bed, a blade of white light enclosed by two dark parallelograms. He nearly wakes, but then subsides again, sliding down that blade of light and off into the darkness at the side.

He is climbing a rope ladder lashed to the side of a black ship, but the gunwale never gets any closer. Somebody up on deck is letting the rope ladder out, hand-over-hand, and he climbs and climbs and climbs but never gets any higher, suspended against the hull of the black ship. Inside, he can hear men and women moaning.

He is in a corridor in an old house. Doors run off the corridor on one side, and windows off the other. The windows look out onto tidy gardens. There are women in the rooms, and one of them is Abigail. He runs up and down the corridor, opening doors, and in every one of them he sees an older woman with long black hair and green eyes and a snake-like scar running down her jaw.

He wonders if he is, at last, going mad.

He cannot wake up.

But then he does, and remembers.

He remembers it all.

He emerges from his bedroom into the swirling, half-real morning, his cheek feeling like it has been cut with a hot poker, and immediately encounters Crowley, the butler.

'A letter has been delivered for you.'

The butler, like the house itself, has a sheepish air.

'May I have it?'

'I left it for you in the kitchen. You may help yourself to some food. The servants are occupied, and we no longer have a cook.'

'My thanks to you.'

Crowley walks on down the landing, slowly and carefully, as if he were on hot coals. Horton follows him down. He stops at the front door of the house, and steps outside for a moment, giving no immediate thought to the diversion. He sees the lonely tree, the one that had been aflame last night, though only in his addled mind. He sees a darker patch, to the right of the so-called hag track which O'Reilly had dug up, how many days before? An extraordinary dream, from last night's black, bubbles up to his sense. Crowley and Moore chopping up a deer on the lawn. They were both naked, and laughing.

In the kitchen, the letter sits on the big central table, but his stomach demands feeding. His breakfast consists of bread, cheese and milk. It looks like it has been standing there for a good deal of time. He imagines something asleep inside the milk jug, the top of one claw visible above the surface.

Mrs Chesterton bustles through the kitchen, saying nothing to him, shaking keys as she goes. Another memory from last night: Mrs Chesterton singing something in Latin on the landing, and banging the walls as she did so.

He pours himself a glass of water from a jug and opens the letter. It is from Robert Brown.

32 Soho Square, Westminster
Sept. 7

Horton
I acknowledge receipt of your note, and the materials contained within it. It was fortunate that it reached me – I am shortly to travel to Paris with Sir J—, to investigate the current state of France's botanical facilities following the cessation of hostilities with that nation.

Given the imminence of that trip, I have had little time to inspect the material you sent to me, though I suspected instantly what it might be. If the plant is what I believe it to be, it is passing strange, the coincidence of it – for I believe the plant to be of a kind the aboriginal people of New South Wales call bedgery *or* pitchery. *I have only seen it on two previous occasions, both while travelling in New Holland and New South Wales on the voyage of the* Investigator. *On both these occasions I did not see the plant in the wild, only in the state in which it is consumed by the natives. It may well be the same plant as I identified in my 1810* Prodromus *as* Duboisia myoporoides, *though I suspect not. I believe the plants may be related, but are not the same species.*

It is a mysterious plant, and I wish I might have done more to investigate it. All I know is this: the aboriginals use the plant for purposes of intoxication, of themselves and of animals. It is said that the plant plays some part in their strange religious practice, called the Dreaming, of which we know very little. It is also used for hunting, or so I am told – it can be added in quantities to a waterhole and will stupefy the animals, particularly the Emu, such that the creatures become easier to catch.

I took several sketches of the dried plant when I came across it in New South Wales, and have consulted these. Your leaves certainly appear to be remarkably similar. I admit I am as much struck by the situation in which you found it as by the morphology of the leaves themselves. Dropped in quantity in a well, or so you said – which appears to be similar behaviour to an Aboriginal adding it to a waterhole. If the quantities were such as you described in your letter, and if this well was the primary water source for the house, I can say only that the effects on the house's residents might be odd indeed. As I say, the aboriginal usage of the plant in religious practice suggests that it must have some kind of hallucinatory property.

The question presents itself, does it not? If someone did add this strange plant to the well at this house you are investigating, why did they do so? And whom were they hunting?

It is a question as strange as any we confronted together during the Solander *matter, and I admit to still being disturbed by the events of that time. I trust your current situation is less serious, and I hope I have been of some help.*

I leave for Paris tonight. I would hear more of this matter on my return, if you are willing and able.

Regards
BROWN, R.

He reads the letter three times, each time as slowly and carefully as the last. Then he stands and pours the water in his glass away, and heads upstairs.

*

Horton has only seen tenderness in the frame of Sir Henry Tempest twice: once at the mention of his daughter Ellen during their first interrogation; and now. The man sits at the girl's bedside, his arm in a sling fashioned by the physician who came the previous night, and who was told only a fraction of what had occurred. Sir Henry had fallen upon a decorative suit of armour, it was said, the sword piercing his upper left chest just below the shoulder. Ellen had swooned at the sight of the blood and fallen into a faint which had endured the whole night.

The house is quiet – quieter than it has been throughout Horton's strange visit. After the terrible commotions of last night, it is as if a convulsive maniac has been subjected to a suite of cures – bleeding, electrical shock, emetics, restraint – and has finally surrendered to exhaustion in the face of the onslaught.

Sir Henry looks up at him as he enters the bedchamber.

'My God, man,' he says. 'Your face looks as if you had swallowed a cannonball.'

It is meant, Horton notes, sympathetically. Sir Henry is a calmed man, indeed.

'How does the girl?' he asks.

'It is impossible to know,' says Sir Henry, looking down at her. 'She sleeps peacefully, and that is a blessing, for God knows she has not done so for weeks.'

'It is certainly for the best.'

'No doubt. But neither of us is a physician, constable. Nor a mad-doctor.'

This last is whispered, fearfully, lest it awaken demons in the sleeping girl's head. So different, that face, from the snarling fury upon it last night when Horton had come upon them in the drawing room, Sir Henry pale and nearly gone on that elegant chaise longue, bleeding from his wound; his daughter restrained by Crowley and Gowing, the sword with which she had speared her father on the floor between them.

'Sir Henry, I have received a letter that casts some light on what has been taking place here. I also have intelligence on your cook, Stephen Moore, and his relationship with your former cook, Elizabeth Hook. May I share these things with you? And then, I believe I should repair to London again, for these facts may have a wider bearing on Mr Graham's investigation into the deaths of your . . .'

He stops. Your what? Fellow debauchees? Fellow Medmenhamites? Fellow fornicators? Sir Henry does not notice the pause, or if he does he takes no note of it.

'Can you answer me why my daughter attempted to kill me?'

'I believe I can, yes.'

'Then continue.'

Horton constructs his tale as well as he can, although parts of it are dark and obscure, and the whole is inflected with such lunacy that it can scarcely be credited. How the house has been, since the burning down of the shed almost a month before, under the influence of a drug in the form of Brown's New Holland leaf, left to soak in the water supply and replenished, as far as Horton can see, at least once. How this must account for the visions of the people within the house, and the suspicions of witchcraft. How Elizabeth Hook brought Stephen Moore, a self-professed cunning-man, into the household in the belief that Ellen was herself the source of the bewitchment, and that he has been steadily poisoning her in an attempt to treat this bewitchment. How Ellen herself has come to believe herself bewitched – to *be* a witch, almost.

He does not say it all, for he does not quite believe it all. He does not mention that strange pinch in his head when Ellen had encountered him in the woods, nor does he describe that odd temporary loss of memory, nor does he speak of his own visions of the previous evening – the burning, the mob, the witch flying along the hedge. And he does not mention his darkest thought: that the sour events which have blighted Thorpe Lee House have been perpetrated by the residents themselves, under the influence of the drug in the well and, perhaps, something else even more wicked.

Did the one who killed the dogs know what they were about? Was it Ellen herself, or someone under her influence? And what is the nature of that influence?

These are lunatic questions for which he can yet supply no sane answer.

Sir Henry says nothing during this recital. Nor does he look at Horton. His eyes remain fixed on the still, pale face of his strange daughter, as if he could reach into her mind through the force of his own will and untie whatever knots bind her serenity. When Horton finishes, he says two words only.

'Why? How?'

They are indeed the only two words that matter. Why this lunatic plot? And how can the plot explain the manic occurrences? The dead rat, the poisoned milk, the destroyed shirts, the profane message, the fairy ring, the dead dogs. Horton cannot explain this mechanism. The why, though, may be clearer, and it is from motivation that explanations will spring.

'The Sybarites, Sir Henry.'

At this, whatever his newfound calm, the old Sir Henry reasserts himself. His head snaps up, and his eyes when they look at Horton are as cold and as angry as a judge sentencing the murderer of his own children.

'Ridiculous. You are being ridiculous.'

'Sir Henry, there is no other explanation. Thorpe Lee House has been visited by what appears to be a campaign of sustained malevolence and mischief, which has ended in an attempt on your life. Two other Sybarites have been killed, sir. The coincidence is beyond possibility.'

'My daughter tried to kill me because I am a member of a dining society? It is preposterous.'

'I cannot yet explain the mechanism, Sir Henry. But I believe the motive is clear. This is why I must return to London. I believe what is happening there can only be connected to what is happening here. Your household will be safe – I will request that men be sent here to watch over you. But I must return.'

'Graham has sent for you?'

'No, Sir Henry, he has not. But still, I must go.'

'You are mad. And you are arrogant, to think one such as Graham deserves or needs your assistance.'

Horton says nothing to that. It may, indeed, be very true.

'Then go. Leave us. And take your insane ideas along with you.'

'Yes, Sir Henry. But I must ask you – is there no event in the history of the Sybarites which might draw the anger of someone in this way?'

'Impertinence! Leave now, sir, before I raise the sword that almost killed me last night and inflict its edge upon you.'

Horton leaves. He packs his bag in his bedroom, and makes his way downstairs. Crowley, the old butler, stands in the vestibule like an exhausted stork. He is holding a small notebook, which he hands to Horton.

'Sir Henry has asked me to give you this.'

Horton, astonished, puts down his bag and begins to open the book.

'Not here!' And Crowley's hand snatches the book back. His other hand grabs Horton's arm, and he leans in, his breath smelling of dry cabbage. There is nothing to drink in the house yet, following Horton's instruction that no one drink the water from the well.

'Read the book in private, and then destroy it,' says Crowley, barely in a whisper. 'Promise me this, Mr Constable. Or I won't give it to you, whatever Sir Henry's command.'

Horton nods, and the book is pushed back into his hands.

'Then on your way, Mr Constable. We shan't be seeing each other again, I expect.'

He turns to walk away, but Horton speaks to him, and he turns.

'Make sure the well is drained, Crowley,' he says, lifting up his bag again. 'And keep a close eye out for a gypsy woman on a tall wagon.'

And with that, Constable Horton exits the madhouse.

The quickest way to get back to London is via Staines, on the far side of the river to Thorpe. He walks the half-mile from Thorpe Lee House to the river. A stone bridge crosses the water here, and he walks over the calm, broad stream into the pleasant market town to enquire after a coach.

Coaches come on the hour heading out west and eastwards into London. He has some time to think over matters on a stone bench in the pretty market square, which looks to have been the subject of considerable improvement in recent years, and notes that he feels, for the first time in days, a considerable sense of calm. His senses are clearing, as if he had been intox-icated this past week – he rather supposes this is exactly what has happened. Those strange nights and eerie visions are the result of poisoned water.

And nothing else? He is clear that the material in the water might explain dizziness, loss of perception, oddities of vision. But it doesn't explain dead dogs and hag tracks. Something else is at play here. He climbs into a coach twenty minutes after arriving in Staines, and begins the seventeen-mile journey back into town. The further he travels from Thorpe Lee House, the clearer his analysis of what that something might indeed be.

He knows there are untied knots still in Thorpe. Elizabeth Hook and Stephen Moore will need to be found and arrested. But such matters can be arranged with Aaron Graham, and they represent, for Horton, answered questions. Ellen's illness is the result of Moore's quackish interventions. Elizabeth Hook is not a witch. There are no such things as witches.

But there are still hag tracks, and dead dogs, and rats on dining-room tables. There is still *maleficium*. But what is the wellspring of it?

He opens the notebook given to him by Crowley, but reading the first page he closes it again, his face hot. He will not read the contents in the confines of a coach; not with two women in it who already seem terrified by the prospect of a shared journey to London with a man of pale skin, intense eyes and a cheek swollen beyond the size of a fist and as black as pitch.

But the book now feels hot in his hands, its contents as fierce as a forge. Part of the answer lies within its pages, he sees immediately; he would be disappointed, indeed, if this were not so, so melodramatic was Crowley's behaviour when handing it over. He can no longer think clearly about the case, not with this material on his person.

And so the miles stretch out, and the three-hour journey feels as long and unending as a Pacific crossing. When the coach finally pulls up at Whitehall, Horton steps out and into an alehouse – his mouth is parched, and he needs a clean, unsullied drink of something. He orders an ale, takes it to a secluded corner and, to prepare himself for his arrival in Covent Garden, looks into Sir Henry's little book.

*

The book has perhaps forty pages, all written in a neat but purposeful hand, presumably that of Sir Henry himself. On the first page a kind of frontispiece has been constructed by the same hand.

The Testimony of the Sybarites
An Account of the adventures in pleasure
of the Sybarites
The Heirs of Dashwood and of Harris,
whose famous LIST this book replaces
A Guide to the Cargoes of Covent Garden's
Pleasure Ships
'Square stern'd, Dutch built, with new sails
and rigging'

Horton does not recognise the quotation. On the next page is the first of the material that makes up the book: a sequence of descriptions of whores, written in a deliberately arch and inflated style. The first entry is thus:

CHERRY COOPER, Covent Garden, March 1808
We did make our acquaintance of the celebrated
Cherry Cooper on the occasion of our first Meeting.
Her first name is one to be reckoned with, and its
origins are both mysterious and (as the Swiss doctor
would have it) mesmerising. 'Tis most likely that the
name is a most fitting response to her red cheeks, her
red lips and her red something else. She is a most
agreeable girl, one for whom we were to a man
grateful for her attentions, but she was so frolicksome
and so noisy during our attentions that a neighbour of
our host was heard to shout, What a blasted house is
here!

All the entries have dates, and all are written in this style, suggesting a single author. So, have the Sybarites been holding their parties since March 1808? It would seem so. Horton turns to the end of the book, reading the last few entries in reverse order.

Elizabeth Carrington (July 1813)

Ah, fair Lizzie: a woman of the strictest honour and secrecy! Upright and reserved in public, agreeable and convivial behind the locked-up doors of pleasurable society! She was educated in the rudiments of erotic knowledge by a certain well-established Bird of Paradise, is about twenty-eight, is slim and tall; has a fair complexion; brown hair; good teeth; and is upon the whole a very pretty woman. She does not give her company widely now, but agreed to return to the stage on which her talents are most valued for our particular party. We shall long remember the pretty little show Miss Carrington performed for us with her talented friend Rose Dawkins. We hope she may be persuaded to return!

Rose Dawkins (July 1813)

Miss Dawkins is one of those rare friends of the Sybarites whose company is so cherished, and whose character is so prettily debauched, that a return visit was agreed by all members to be desirable. Miss Dawkins is a mistress of the bizarrerie, and is a patient and attentive practitioner of such; one amongst our number is a connoisseur of such matters, and notes to us that Miss Dawkins's hand is as firm and as sordid as any he has before encountered. She is also a noted performer of the Duet, and introduced us to her friend Miss Carrington in the most delightfully vivid way imaginable.

Maria Cranfield (July 1813)
What are we to say of Miss Cranfield? She is an odd fish indeed, yet an enticing one. She has joined with us but once, and presented a strange conundrum indeed: a fresh-faced novice, her sanctity still intact, and not in that way which so many young girls of the Plaza claim, passing for a maidenhead two dozen times to the gullible culls who appear there. We did much enjoy her introduction to the Sybaritic arts, and her natural fresh bloom did darken exquisitely with each additional transaction she did enjoy with the members of our members. She has eyes clear and as fine-coloured as the azure blue, and her dark hair curls in a thousand artless ringlets down her snowy neck. She is tall and has a beautiful complexion; her meretricious performances were transporting and extraordinary.

Finishing his ale, Horton leaves the place, and walks up to Bow Street.

Covent Garden has a different air with the book in his pocket. Horton, like any Londoner, knows of the illicit trade that suppurates through the streets around the Piazza and the theatres, the dark counterpoint to the licit business of fruit and veg. But he has never taken a whore – in England, anyway. So the Covent Garden whoring has been of the nature of a story told to him over a pint of ale.

He recalls an incident with Abigail, some years ago. They had been to a play at the Theatre Royal in Drury Lane. They had only been married a short while, and Horton was still navigating an understanding of this strange woman who had nursed him back to health in St Thomas's hospital and who, she said, had come to love him. This single extraordinary fact had made it preposterously difficult to understand her, for how could any woman – especially one as clever and enchanting as Abigail – have come to love one such as he? And yet she said she did, and he had begun on his project of unpicking her, of gazing at her from infinite angles, holding her up to the light of his intense view as he tried to make sense of this development.

They had exited the play – it had been one of Sheridan's, he remembers, though he cannot recall which – and the whores had been there on the pavement, dozens of them, grabbing the arms of men, and some of the women, offering all sorts of bizarre and oddly worded services, a screeching bazaar of the profane.

Horton's own arm had been grabbed, as it was bound to be, and Abigail – calm, clever Abigail – had lashed out a hand and slapped the whore who'd grabbed Horton. So powerful had been Abigail's blow that the whore had stepped back three or four paces, her hand to her cheek, a look of shock on her face which took a second or two to transform into a pavement rage.

The whore threw herself at Abigail, who snarled back at her with astonishing anger, and if Horton had not succeeded in getting between the two of them the picture may have become grim indeed. As it was, he'd shoved the whore away and pulled his wife through the angry crowd of debauched women, desperate to haul her away before their anger grew and focused itself in a way that might become truly dangerous.

They walked back to Southwark, where Abigail still worked in the hospital and Horton did bits and pieces around the ship-yards. Horton had tried to discover what lay behind his wife's sudden violence, it being so uncharacteristic. But Abigail's face had set into a stubborn, sullen refusal, and it was never spoken of again.

Pondering Abigail and whores and his own personal history, Horton finally reaches Bow Street. And finds uproar.

WESTMINSTER

When Westminster society – its politicians, its peers, its scribblers and its gossips – turns its attention onto a single event, it is wise not to be the one fellow on whom responsibility for that event can be said to rest. It is a terrible word, *responsibility*, and though it is not one from which Aaron Graham has previously flinched, its dreadful weight is upon him today.

His polite but firm interview with his Lordship, Viscount Sidmouth, now seems to have come from an earlier, calmer time. Today, Sidmouth came to him – a sign of the terrible urgency of the morning, but also a sign of Addington's common sense. Graham needs to be at the heart of whatever investigation is now emerging into the previous night's deaths. He has no time for perambulatory visits to government ministers.

Tomorrow's papers will be full of it; there may even be stirrings in whatever printed matter Grub Street and its environs shits out today. And it will not be the number of deaths that the story emphasises; instead, it will be that an Earl has been taken from this earth, accompanied by the sons of a Duke and two

Baronets and the brother of a Viscount. Debretts will be thinner come the next volume, while London's reputation as a pus-filled sewer of terrible violence has been encrusted still further. And all beneath the supposedly watchful eyes of the famous Bow Street magistrates.

Graham has not even been able to visit the murder scenes; were he to walk away from Bow Street, he feels the office might be invaded by a screaming horde of rumourmongers and muckrakers, his fellow magistrates collapsing under the attention. He now knows how the magistrates of Shadwell must have felt as the shockwaves of the Ratcliffe Highway murders rattled against their windows. He'd despised them before. He thinks he understands them rather better now.

You will have whatever you need, Sidmouth had said, and his uninteresting face had been set into a mask of such fearful determination that Graham had felt not comforted but positively afraid. A killer must be found.

More than one killer, almost certainly. But how many? The great mystery at the heart of this horror rises up again: five men killed, in their beds, locked up in their houses. Outside those houses had stood Bow Street officers and patrolmen, not to mention parish constables and watchmen. It is almost satirical in its devilishness.

The morning passes in a blur of coroners and constables. He despatches riders from the horse patrol to all five addresses, charging them with guarding the front of the houses and keeping crowds away. The other Bow Street magistrates make comforting noises but, he notes, keep out of his way. They sense a terrible fall and reckoning. He believes they may be right.

In the secure room over at the Brown Bear waits Rose Dawkins, brought in last night by William Jealous, who has himself been despatched to the scene of the most important crime, at least in the eyes of society, and these are the only eyes that Graham currently cares about. Jealous is at the home of the Earl of Maidstone, and Graham awaits his return to the office. The only other man who could be of any use is, maddeningly, away and cut off from the stream in Surrey.

But then, in that mysterious way he has, Charles Horton appears, shown in by William Jealous, who has himself just returned from the residence of the Earl of Maidstone. Despite everything Graham finds enough of his old self to be both annoyed and bemused by the maddening way Horton has of appearing when he is least expected – with the least-expected news.

The stories tumble over themselves in the Bow Street parlour which doubles as a kind of office for the magistrates. Graham is put in mind both of a basket of puppies and a nest of snakes. There is a playful oddness to what he is being told by the two officers. But there is confused danger, also.

He hears from Horton first, his attention firm despite the growing clamour in the vestibule outside his office. If Sidmouth were himself sitting here, he'd be asking calmly but dangerously why strange tales of visions and poisonings from a debauched house in Surrey could possibly be relevant? Horton can say little about this, beyond his belief that there is deliberate foul play involved, and that it is aimed at the Sybarites.

'But, Horton. A mysterious substance in the well? Visions of witch-burnings?'

'All I know is this, Mr Graham. Ellen tried to kill Sir Henry on the same night that the other five remaining Sybarites were despatched. Does this not strike you as redolent?'

'What are you suggesting?'

'I know not. Not yet. But then there is this.'

Horton shows Graham the book he had been given by Crowley the butler. Graham opens it and immediately raises an eyebrow.

'Sir Henry wrote this?'

'So it would seem, sir.'

Horton watches the magistrate flick through the pages, sees him work out that the entries are dated and turn to the closing pages of the book, which he reads closely. It is a close facsimile of what Horton himself had done. When he looks up, his face has lightened a little of its previous cares. He hands the book to Jealous, open at the back pages, and speaks to Horton.

'We know of the last two women. Carrington is dead, apparently by her own hand. Dawkins is locked up over at the Brown Bear.'

A look passes between the three men, and Horton knows what meaning it carries. The connection between Sir Henry, the Sybarites and the woman downstairs draws tight. But how does it connect with the previous night's deaths?

Next, Jealous describes the scene at the Earl of Maidstone's residence, just off Piccadilly. He confirms the house was locked, from the inside, during the night. The Earl was found in the morning in his bed, his throat slashed and his hands cut off and left by his side. The aspect of ritual is clear. Graham updates Horton on the other deaths, watching him as he does so. Horton's head is turned slightly, his eyes are pointing into a corner of the room, but they are not seeing whatever rodent or insect may be there. He seems to be staring into a middle distance, an unspecified realm of revelation. Graham waits for a moment.

'Horton, do you have a suggestion as to how we proceed?' he says eventually. The constable looks at him.

'I would like to talk with this Dawkins woman, firstly,' he says.

'Of course. You may do so immediately our current con-versation is finished.'

'And there are some questions I would have asked of every servant in every residence where there has been a killing.'

'Jealous may deal with that. What are the questions?'

'Have they been visited by a gypsy in recent weeks? Have they experienced any strange visions? Has there ever been a suspicion of bewitchment on their houses?'

It occurs to Graham that in any other public office in Westminster or Middlesex – or in the chambers of aldermen in the City – such a set of questions would be met with angry amusement. But not here. Here, oddness is neither here nor there; it is fitness which matters.

'And the houses should be searched for bloody clothes, and for the implements of the killings. The beds of all the servants should be checked for bloodstains. Their means for washing themselves should be investigated.'

Jealous is staring at Horton.

'You suspect the *servants*?'

Horton looks at him.

'No one went in. No one went out. Who else can it be?'

After the clamour of the Public Office, the Brown Bear is rel-atively calm. Horton and Jealous had shoved their way out of the office, forcing a way through a clamour of newsmen, patrolmen, constables and watchmen and Covent Garden street-folk, all merrily getting in the way and taking part in the disarray in the manner of gawkers throughout the ages.

The Brown Bear has for decades been the traditional meet-ing point of the Bow Street Runners, and the place has kept its reputation as a semi-official adjunct of the office. People may come here to seek a Runner or a patrolman – indeed, those who know of such matters tend to come here before they try the Police Office. The office is the province of magistrates; the Brown Bear the kingdom of their officers.

Such is the tavern's status that a number of secure rooms have been fashioned within it, to be used by Bow Street officers as temporary cells. This is where Rose Dawkins is being held.

Jealous walks over the road with Horton. The lad is quiet, almost reverential in his tone, but Horton scarcely notices. Since stepping away from the madhouse at Thorpe, and presumably from its surreptitiously intoxicating well-water, his head has been clearing but also churning.

He checks the details of Elizabeth Carrington's death with Jealous as they walk. The constable seems in no doubt that the woman killed herself. He seems abashed by the scene he'd found in Carrington's lodging, and it is this which causes Horton to notice him properly. The lad has a tough London exterior and looks like he could handle himself in a brawl, but there is an obvious sympathy and natural intelligence there as well. For the first time Horton sees some of what Graham has already seen in the boy. Jealous's father has a colossal reputation as a taker of thieves, but Horton knows nothing of his character. Perhaps at least the father's ability has rubbed off on the son.

Jealous opens Rose Dawkins's cell and lets Horton in. He hesitates at the door, but then Horton asks him to give him the keys, and to go and speak to the servants of the murdered men. He steps inside.

Rose Dawkins is a short woman, a fact emphasised by the enormity of her red hair. Everything about her is red: her dress, her hair, and her angry face, which is particularly ugly. She stands when Horton comes in, but then sits back in the corner of the cell like a malignant dwarf. The smell of shit and piss rises from an un-emptied chamber pot in the opposite corner.

'Who the fuck are you, then?' she says, her troll's face sneering.

'My name is Horton. I am investigating these terrible events.'

'Done away with them, have they?'

'Done away with who?'

'Those so-called Sibarits. Wondered when things'd catch up with those scandalous bastards.'

Horton passes her the book, open to the page containing her description. She doesn't take it from him.

'This isn't a fuckin' school, is it? I don't read, constable.'

He takes it back, and reads her entry back to her. She grins wider and wider as he reads, the gaps between her teeth showing black in the red ruin of her face.

'Well, someone fancied themselves as an artist, didn't they? Proper little portrait, that is.'

'I believe it was written by one of the Sybarites. A gentleman named Sir Henry Tempest.'

'Oh, it would be him. He was a rum cove, he was. Arrived all screaming and shouting, but once I got to work on 'im he was as gentle as a lamb.'

'What is the *bizarrerie*?'

'Fuck, you're a little innocent abroad, aren't you? The whip. The slap. The scratch. Even a bit of the blade at times. Sir Henry liked me to go to town on him, he did. Not as bad as that other one – Sir John. Oh gods, he was as soft as an old washrag until we started knocking 'im about.'

She cackles, but it's a practised sound, not a genuine one. She is putting on a show, he realises, and he wonders where the genuine Rose Dawkins might be found, if indeed she is still alive inside this cauldron of inflamed amorality.

'And the Duet?'

She frowns at that, and looks away, and Horton sees he has unexpectedly broken through the gutter-theatrical mask.

'Fuck off.'

'But it was something you performed with Eliz—'

'Performed!' She stands and takes a step towards him, so furious that he actually steps away before remembering himself. 'Like a pair of fucking Barbary apes, a-kissin' and a-touchin' and . . . and . . .' She takes in a great sobbing gulp of air, and then goes quiet, standing in the middle of the cell, looking at the floor.

'Elizabeth Carrington. The woman who took her life. You knew her well.'

'Yes.'

'She attended these parties with you.'

'Fucking says so in there, don't it?'

'And Maria Cranfield? What of her?'

'She's in there?'

'Yes.'

'Read me what it says, then.'

He does so, and still she stands, facing the floor. She does not even look up until she finishes. But she does speak.

'Awful, horrible, vicious bastards. The fucking lot of you.'

She turns back to the corner, and sits down. She lifts her head and rests it back against the wall behind her. Her eyes are closed.

'Maria . . . well, Maria was not like the rest of us. She wasn't even a whore.'

'Then what—'

'Oh, she *said* she was a whore. I don't know where she came from, or anything about her. So don't ask me, right? She showed up at that party, and she was like a boy sent off to march with Wellesley. She didn't know one end of a gun from another. If you take my drift.'

'Then why was she there?'

'Who am I to say? Go outside now and ask them women on

the pavement why they're there! You'll get a dozen different answers from a dozen different women. Some of them was gulled into it. Some of them ran out of money, or lost their job, or got thrown out by their father, their brother, their husband. Even their mother, some of the poor cows. I don't know why she started. But starting with the Sybarites was a mistake.'

'Why?'

'Because – if you hadn't cottoned on to this by now – they're a bunch of vicious, nasty thugs. That book might be full of pretty words, but it doesn't describe what happened at their little evenings. Not even half of it.'

'Describe them for me, then.'

'Drink, food, and whores. In that order of importance. They spent more time choosing the wine and the meat than they did the girls. Even though we were little more than meat to them. But when they saw Maria, they could smell it on her. She was like the choicest cut of veal you could imagine. You could see them sniffin' round her, like dogs round a ham.'

'What could they smell?'

'Her rose.' She frowns, and for a moment he wonders why, but then remembers her name. 'She'd never been with a man before. Her first time. Her first fucking time. She must have been older than I am, and she'd managed to keep it under lock and key. When Talty found out, he must have thought every fucking ship in the world had come in.'

'Who's Talty?'

'A panderer. Works out of the Bedford Head on Maiden Lane. Thought you lot had spoken to him.'

'Perhaps. Not I.'

'Well, there's nothing worth more to a panderer than a girl with everything intact. But they're usually young 'uns – twelve or thirteen. And they usually get sold a dozen or more times as being intact. But Maria – well, there was something exotic

327

about a girl like that still being intact. And it was genuine. You could see the filthy swine knew that. They were clambering over each other to be her first. She was terrified.'

Horton doesn't say anything. He doesn't know how to ask what needs to be asked. But Rose Dawkins is now lost in the memory of that night.

'They drew lots. There was eight or nine of them, and they couldn't decide. So they drew lots. An order was agreed upon. Your Sir Henry. He drew the first one. He was her first. And then they took her. One by one, they took her.

'She screamed at first. But that only ever inflamed them. Lizzie was particularly good at that – pretending to be scared, to be in pain. Brought them off in a minute, that did. But Maria wasn't pretending. She screamed and cried and struggled, and they held her down, and they took their turn.

'She went quiet for a while, and then she started laughing. Now, laughing's not appreciated by the men. They don't like it at all. It disturbs them. So the last two or three who had her, they didn't like it one bit. But they went ahead. Knocked her about a bit to try and shut her up. Part of the game, wasn't it? Couldn't be seen to be weak or letting the good name of their society down.

'She had beautiful clear eyes, did Maria. I saw that in her straightaway. I asked her, what you doing here, love? And she turned those beautiful clear green eyes on me and she smiled a bit. It was a lovely smile. Dark hair in ringlets down her neck. Smooth skin. She looked like a lady. A real fucking lady. What was she doing there?

'I looked in her eyes after, when they threw her out. Her mouth was bleeding, but she was still laughing. That's why they threw her out, see. She was laughing fit to burst. And I saw her eyes when they threw her out. They weren't shining any more. They were as dead as my old man.'

He turns to leave.

'Constable?'

'Yes?'

'What will happen to Lizzie? Will she be buried?'

'That's up to the parish authorities.'

'I can pay.'

'You have money?'

'Oh, I've got *money*, constable. It's Lizzie I ain't got no more.'

Horton looks at her. She can be no use to her dead friend in here.

'I will arrange for your release, immediately,' he says as he goes.

He walks back over the road to the office to arrange for Rose's release. It is by no means straightforward. The pressing crowd inside the office has not thinned one jot; indeed, a few additional bystanders may have been levered into what little space there is. Horton recalls the crowds outside the River Police Office in Wapping in the aftermath of the Ratcliffe Highway killings; how they had clamoured and shouted, but how they had been kept outside. John Harriott, his magistrate in Wapping, is rather more forthright when it comes to dealing with crowds.

And scribblers, also. A man from the *Chronicle* recognises Horton from that earlier investigation and shouts his name, drawing the attention of a half-dozen others, like a wolf spotting a lone kid. They immediately surround Horton, barking questions and demanding answers, their dirty clothes reeking of desperation. But he ignores them, and forces his way through to Aaron Graham's office.

Graham is readying to venture outside, saying he has been called to speak to Viscount Sidmouth and pointing Horton towards the Bow Street register clerk, who is sitting in the same room and keeping his head firmly down while whatever storm is lapping at his shores subsides. Graham leaves, and Horton arranges with the clerk for Rose's release. He also asks the clerk to check Bow Street's famed register of thieves, receivers and pimps for the address of one Talty.

Minutes later, he is shooing away a cat, but the cat keeps coming back, silently and deliberately, to lick at the thick pool of blood which lies half-under the chair. It's entirely black and almost invisible in the half-light, and Horton only notices it when the cat's tongue starts to lap and lick again, breaking the silence of the Bow Street room.

The address had surprised him. Talty, the panderer of Maiden Lane, has lodgings only five doors down from the Bow Street office. He had not paused in coming here. His blood is up.

Unlike Talty, whose blood is down and defiantly outside his body, a body which sits, strangely upright, in an old armchair. Talty's head is down on his chest, and his two hands grip a sword which has been shoved deliberately into his stomach. The position of the body, the hands, the head, leave Horton in no doubt that Talty inflicted this terrible wound upon himself.

The room is a comfortable one, decorated sparsely but with some taste. Horton walks through into a bedroom, which has a similar feel of mild opulence and unaffected sensibility. Talty has made a good living from pimping and procuring. Horton has heard tales of girls being lured from small towns in the North of England by procurers such as Talty with promises of marriage. Once in the metropolis, a sham ceremony will be arranged between the pimp and the girl, who will then be brought back to a room such as this. What happens next depends on the pimp and the circumstance. Sometimes, he will take her himself, before revealing the truth and sending her out – bereft of all her hopes – as a streetwalker. Other times, he may turn out the lights and welcome in a customer, who will pretend to be the supposed 'husband' and will consume the girl's precious maidenhead for good money. Rarely, the girl will have been procured on the demand of a rich man – he may have seen her at a ball and become determined to have her, or he may just bark 'get me a girl from Leeds'. It will be he who then takes the place of the pimp when the light is turned out.

All the scenarios lead to the same place: a girl dishonoured, shamed and cut off from her family. A girl who can be sent out onto the street as the only choice for one so besmirched, humiliated and alone.

A good life, Talty's body seems to say to him, its hand gripping the helm, the blade pinning him to the chair.

Someone disagreed, he says back to it.

Talty and Elizabeth Carrington: two actors in this worrying drama, both dead by their own hands.

He wonders if that poor Maria Cranfield's life ended like this: alone, maddened, suicidal. All she is to him is a name and a story, and her role in these melancholy transactions is still unclear. Her role may already have ended. He hopes it has not, and that he may yet find her alive.

His only remaining clue is the plant which Brown identified – the *pitchery* from the well at Thorpe Lee House. The substance must have been brought to England from New South Wales, and in significant amounts – he doesn't know how many times it was put into the well, but the stuff he pulled out was somewhat fresh.

He goes back to the office, and once again – the third time in less than an hour – fights his way through the throng. He

LLOYD SHEPHERD

walks into Graham's office without knocking, and gives the register clerk a fright. He asks to see the office's copy of Lloyd's List of shipping, and his question is met by a blank look of incomprehension. No such copy exists. Why on earth would a Covent Garden police office need to know about shipping?

And, of course, why would it? There will undoubtedly be other places he could view the List, but he only knows of one place where it will for certain be available to him. He needs to go back to Wapping.

332

WAPPING

So eastwards he goes, like a dog returning to its kennel. The Bow Street mounted patrolmen are all occupied with keeping the peace in the immediate vicinity of the office, or by the houses of the dead Sybarites. No matter. He gets a hackney carriage, and within an hour he is back in his own neighbour-hood, under the eyes of familiar gaggles of boys.

He does not go into the house in Lower Gun Alley, but he does stand outside it for a moment, his bag over his shoulder, looking for signs of Abigail. Perhaps she has returned from the madhouse, as he has done. Perhaps her mind, now stilled and emptied of its visions, is even now turning itself to a book on natural philosophy or exploration or medical matters, while a meal cooks in the hearth. Perhaps she is waiting for him to return.

But there are no signs. The curtains over the windows are half-open and untidy, just as he had left them. Abigail would not have been able to leave them thus. She is not there. He cannot stand to go in.

He is barely noticed when he returns to the River Police

Office, but then this is hardly unusual. He continues to be resented by most of the officers and attendants within; they remain unclear as to the precise role of this quiet man with his odd methods, and they resent the magistrate's pugnacious protection of him.

It is troubling, then, that John Harriott is still absent from the office due to illness. Horton seeks news of him from his attendant, who confirms that Mr Harriott has spent some time at home and some time at the London Hospital in White-chapel. He is now staying with friends in Essex, with his wife, in the hope that the country air will revive his spirits and his health. Horton raises an eyebrow at the use of the word 'spirits' – is Harriott also suffering under some mental disturbance? But the attendant will say no more. He disapproves of Horton as much as anyone.

Horton goes downstairs to consult the office records of shipping, which are collated from records supplied by the dock operators, the Port of London, Trinity House and, of course, Lloyd's List. None of these records is, by itself, complete, so the River Police record seeks to combine them to draw a detailed picture of the comings and goings on the Thames. It is, supposes Horton, the Wapping equivalent of Bow Street's famous register of receivers and thieves.

He starts at August 1814 and works his way backwards a few months, looking for ships arriving from New Holland and New South Wales. It has been a busy time, with many fleets of transports going to and from England to Bordeaux, to Gibraltar, to Lisbon and Oporto, with regiments and prisoners of war. The news from Lloyd's List tells another, ongoing tale – of ships and privateers doing battle off the eastern seaboard of the United States, the conflict continuing even while Europe's wars fall away now Bonaparte is safely imprisoned on Elba. Massive fleets still come and go to the

West Indies, huddling together for protection in the face of American aggression. The remainder of the lists show the continuing tale of English commerce, hundreds of ships coming and going.

The lists serve to show how cut off New South Wales is from this world; a distant colony, fit only for criminals and the soldiers who watch them. He finds a perplexing array of ships coming, going, disappearing, reappearing – the lists seem to tell the story of the uncertainty of sea, a story he recognises from his own past. He flicks through records for the *Emu*, a transport full of women convicts captured by Americans and then abandoned on St Vincent for a year, the women eventually being returned to a prison hulk in Portsmouth harbour, and then another transport.

But it is the records for the *Indefatigable* that register his attention. She left for Van Diemen's Land on 4 June 1812, accompanied by the *Minstrel*. She arrived, alone, at Hobart in October 1812 – the first convict ship to sail directly to that place. Digging further, Horton discovers that she sailed back to England from Port Jackson, via China and St Helena, arriving at Deal in April of this year. He finds a list of passengers, a random selection of names, including Mr and Mrs John Simpson, Mr Michael Michaels, George Mason and Lawrence Drennan, a Mrs Broad, and a Mr James Gardener, accompanied by his wife and child.

The ship is owned by James Atty and Co. of Whitby, whose London storehouse is right here in Wapping.

There is a faint smell of smoke in Red Lion Street, and for a moment Horton is arrested by this. The smell that had hung over Wapping on the morning he departed for Thorpe must have had its origin here, at the storehouse of James Atty and Co. A harassed and exhausted clerk is keeping a kind of guard over the place, but its contents are gone, replaced with a black void. It had been one of the hundreds of little warehouses that dot the alleys and squares of Wapping. Whatever had been stored here is gone.

The clerk shows Horton to a small door at the side of the blackened shell, and a flight of stairs takes him up to the administrative office. The smell of smoke is thick and disgusting inside the building, and Horton wonders how anyone can work in here. Another harassed clerk asks him his name and his business. When he explains, the clerk goes to fetch Mr MacDougall, the London agent for the firm.

MacDougall is true to his name; a large Scot with a red beard, like an actor playing the part of Highland Chieftain in a Drury Lane comedy. He shows Horton through to his little office, stating in a rich brogue how much he admires the work of the River Police, and how he has had the pleasure on several occasions to converse with the magistrate, Mr Harriott. When Horton asks him about the *Indefatigable*, he frowns.

'What business do the River Police have with the *Indefatigable?*' he says, his Celtic bonhomie suddenly absent.

'Am I required to state my business in detail, Mr MacDougall? I would like to know what the cargo was, where it was stored, and what information you hold on any passengers who returned on it.'

'We had a fire, last week.'

'So I understand.'

'The storehouse which was burned down contained the items which we had shipped back from New South Wales. They are all gone.'

'Well, that is as may be. I only want to see the records.'

'There are no records.'

Horton can see now that MacDougall is not irritated by his request; he is embarrassed by it.

'Is that not unusual?'

'It is unprecedented. We have spent much of this past week trying to establish where the records may have got to. Until they turn up, I can do nothing to help you.'

'The records are normally stored at this office?'

'They are. All our other records are complete and up to the current date. The only ones missing relate to the *Indefatigable*. I have never experienced such a failure of a clerical nature.'

'How might you account for it?'

'I cannot account for it. If I did not know better, I would say that one of the clerks had deliberately removed the records.'

'You do not suspect them?'

'I do not. I trust them as I would trust myself with these matters.'

Horton wonders how far to pursue this. The man is clearly flabbergasted by his firm's failure in this matter. But the coincidence smacks of something bigger and unseen, a rock below the surface at the entrance to a harbour.

'And what of the people who were on the ship?'

'Well, I can help you with that matter. Those records were also destroyed, but another contractor was responsible for the passengers, and I was able to request copies of their own records.'

He calls out to a clerk, and a minute or so later the man appears holding a piece of paper. He hands it to MacDougall, with a formal deference, and the merchant hands it to Horton.

The letter lists the same passengers that Horton had seen in the records at the River Police Office, only this time with full addresses in England. Four of the names have addresses in London: two in Southwark, one in Spitalfields, and one in Ratcliffe.

Ratcliffe. Two syllables, hard on the mouth, rigid and ominous. The last time he was in Ratcliffe he was looking at the bodies of three dead men in an empty boarding house. The place is just downstream of Wapping. It takes him barely a quarter-hour to walk there.

RATCLIFFE

The Gardeners live on George Street, a raggedy little alley off the Commercial Road. The address from the shipping agent is for a boarding house, and Horton begins to tell their likely story as he ascends to their rooms: was Gardener a convict? Or did he travel there with his wife in order to make a living? Had he failed or succeeded? Why have they returned to London?

A tired, small woman opens the door on the first-floor landing when he knocks.

'Mrs Gardener?'

She nods. From behind her, he hears the sound of children shouting at each other, of furniture being run into. The sound must be terrible for her – he projects it back into the days and weeks and months before this encounter, as something about it suggests an uninterrupted cacophony.

'My name is Horton. I am a constable of the River Police Office in Wapping. I would like to speak to your husband, if I may.'

'My husband is dead.'

She says it with no emphasis, no emotion. She might just

as well have been describing the finish on the floor or the weather.

'Ah. My apologies, madam.'

'I thank you for that.' Her face shows no thanks at all. 'Why would a constable wish to talk to my husband?'

'I wished to ask him about your voyage back from New South Wales. On board the *Indefatigable*.'

She raises an eyebrow – the first sign of animation in her exhausted face. She looks back into the room behind her, towards the noise, as if looking for a question to be answered. Then she looks back at him.

'Come in, then. You can ask me.'

The children are bigger and older than he was expecting, two boys and a girl. They fall silent when he enters the room, become solemn, as if they were afraid of him. The girl stands behind the boys, as behind a wall. The room is devoid of furniture, but for an old armchair and a table by the window.

'This is a constable,' the woman says to them. 'He wishes to talk of our sea voyage.'

'Why?' says the smaller boy, defiantly. The woman turns to Horton, as if to repeat the boy's question.

'I am investigating a matter which I think may have involved someone on the ship with you. A woman.'

'The witch?'

The larger boy speaks this time, and the matter-of-fact way he says the words almost causes Horton to laugh out loud. An extraordinary thing to hear, moments after stepping into this little room. He looks at the boy's mother. She says nothing, but a look of sour amusement has come into her face which he does not care for.

'What makes you say there was a witch?' he asks the boy.

'The sailors said it. They wanted to leave her in China.'

'Why did they think she was a witch?'

'They said she had the master in her ... what was the word, Emily? You remember it.'

The little girl, hiding her face, says simply 'thrall'.

'Yes, thrall. They said she had the master in her thrall. That she could make him do anything she wanted. They said that's why he wouldn't put her off. She had stuff in the hold, they said. Witch's stuff.'

'Did they say what this stuff was?'

'Are you hunting for a witch, then?'

This from the woman, with a sneer of contempt.

'Witches do not exist.'

'They do, though.'

This from the little girl, quietly, into her brother's back.

'What was this woman's name? The one the children speak of?'

'She was called Broad.'

'Did you speak to her?'

'During a voyage of five months? Yes, I spoke to her. I spoke to everyone. What else was there to do?'

'May I ask why you were on the ship?'

'My husband took us out there, ten years ago. He said we would make our fortune. A farm, he said. Feeding the soldiers and convicts. Said it would transform our lives.'

'It failed?'

'Yes, constable. It failed. The soil was barren. The natives hated us. The soldiers were more corrupt than the convicts. We watched while the governor made his farm profitable with free labour and seed while we toiled in the face of floods and fighting. Then he attempted to take our leases from us. When the soldiers rebelled against him, things got even worse. I wanted to leave years ago. We came back here to start again, but then James died. I have sold all our goods.'

'What will you do?'

'The workhouse for these. For me? What does it matter? Perhaps the street.'

He wonders, now, how he could have found the sneer on her face unpleasant. The despair in the room is as thick as river fog. The children are so silent, having been so loud. Guilt, who stalks Horton like a persistent old friend, taps on his shoulder once again.

'I will do what I can.'

'And what can you do?'

'Very little. Perhaps nothing.'

'Well, then.' She sits in a chair, and the three children look at her as if she were a marionette with invisible strings, interesting yet none of their concern. The smaller boy pokes the larger in the arm, and then without warning they are off again, running around the empty room. The woman speaks to him over the noise, as if it were an act of God or a freak of the weather, and none of her concern.

'Mrs Broad was a wealthy woman, constable. She said she had owned a farm in Parramatta, though I had not heard of it.'

'What was her appearance?'

'Impressive. She was tall, strong, brown-skinned, well fed. Black hair which she always wore loose; I remember admiring her for that. But her face was ugly. It was disfigured by a terrible scar along her jaw.'

One of the boys falls, and his siblings fall on him like wild dogs.

'Did she say where she would be staying, in England?'

'She did not. She said she had come from Suffolk, originally. She did not say where and when.'

'And why was she returning, if she was successful in New South Wales?'

'Oh, I asked her that. Over and over again, I asked her. She had done what we had failed to do, and I couldn't understand her. She said she had served her time. That was her phrase.'

The woman looks sadly on her shrieking children, as if they were a story that had happened to someone else.

'It is odd. You are the second man who has come to ask me about Mrs Broad.'

The shrieks of the children subside, and Horton, who had been on the point of leaving, feels his heart clench.

'Who was the other?'

'He came twice, which is why I remember. He visited the *Indefatigable* in Deal; came on board the ship, spoke to my husband. And then he visited us here, just yesterday.'

'Did he state why he wanted to find Mrs Broad?'

'He said he was an old friend of hers. I didn't think much of it when he came to Deal, but when he came here . . . I mean, it must have taken some effort to find us, must it not? Though you found us. I think he's a well-to-do man. A man of means. Perhaps he can help us?'

'Who was this man?'

'He gave his name as Lodge. Henry Lodge. He said he could be found at the Prospect of Whitby.'

THE PROSPECT OF WHITBY

As a man of means, Henry Lodge can afford better accommodation than that offered by the Prospect of Whitby. But he likes taverns and alehouses and inns. They are his business, after all. The hops which climb up his poles in Canterbury end up here, in the tankards of working men and women. He likes to see the alchemy his trade weaves: the cuttings he plants in the Kent soil becoming the balm for men's souls here in London.

He should not be here, of course. The hoppers' huts will soon be filling up, as the picking season approaches. He does not even know what pulled him back into London. He feels the same compulsion that once dragged him to Deal three or four times a year. He has not been sleeping well. The newspapers are suddenly full of blood and murder. Gentlemen are being killed in their beds.

He'd promised Maggie Broad that he'd visit Maria weekly, but even that has proved impossible. The madhouse does not permit such interaction with its inmates; the anxious-faced little doctor who'd accepted Maria had made that clear, and he'd taken the information back to Maggie, and she'd scowled and said she would see her daughter herself, rules or no rules.

And then she had disappeared.

That had been five weeks ago. He has not seen her since. During these anxious weeks he'd felt a growing pressure, like fermenting beer ready to explode from a glass bottle. His mind is confused and unhappy, and he haunts the Prospect of Whitby like a faithful dog unsure of its purpose. He wants to leave and go back to Kent. He finds he cannot.

He sits and he drinks and he thinks, but then he is interrupted by a tall, pale man with exhausted eyes who walks up to his table, and asks if he is Henry Lodge.

'Why yes, I am. Who is it who asks?'

'Charles Horton. Sir, I am a waterman-constable from the River Police Office, here in Wapping.'

He cannot help it – his whole body clenches itself, ready to pound and punch and forge an escape. Once a convict . . .

'I am looking for a woman called Broad.'

The stomach stays tight. The constable's eyes may be tired and supported by grey-black bags, but they are searching. Does he not blink?

Fly or fight. Fly or fight.

But Henry Lodge has been a man of means for a decade or more. He is a convict no longer. He needs not such violence.

'Well, sit down, constable. May I buy you an ale? It is quite excellent here.'

'I am given to understand you have been looking for Mrs Broad,' the constable says, after the maid at the bar has brought them ale.

'You are? By whom?'

'Are you looking for her?'

'In a manner of speaking.'

'And have you found her?'

'May I ask why *you* want to speak to her, constable?'

'First I would like to know more about your interest.'

Henry sips at his ale. He must choose his words with care.

'Well, then. It is no great secret, I suppose. I knew her in New South Wales.'

'You were a farmer there?'

'I was. Before that, I was a prisoner.'

He can see it in the constable's eyes: *he thought I was one thing, and I turn out to be another. A more difficult thing.*

'I see.'

'You do? Well, I was a convict. I went out on the *Guardian*, and was later transferred to the *Lady Juliana*.'

The constable frowns. Henry can see him trying to remember. Ancient history now, he supposes.

'HMS *Guardian* was cut open by a spur of ice in the South Seas, constable. You may or may not remember. We made it back, eventually, to Cape Town, and I was taken aboard the *Lady Juliana*. A transport for women convicts.'

'For what reason were you transported?'

'Picking pockets. I was fourteen. But that was only part of the reason.'

Lodge sees the constable is a man of some imagination, and is now conjuring with that thought. *A fourteen-year-old boy amid the ice mountains.*

'The penal colony needed farmers and gardeners, constable, and I was one of them. I was raised on a farm. We volunteered, after a fashion. Go out on a transport in what became known as the Second Fleet, or go out on the *Guardian*. I knew nothing of boats, but I knew about numbers. Twenty-five convicts on a naval vessel, or hundreds on a privately contracted one. It wasn't a difficult decision, volunteering.'

He is enjoying telling the tale, but an internal voice warns him: *keep the secret you have pledged to keep*. It is Maggie Broad's voice.

'We were sent to help the colony grow its own food, but the scheme ended when the ice tore a hole in the *Guardian* and ripped off its rudder. Thanks to the good sense of the captain, and a passing whaler, we made it back to Cape Town. I was shipped off with the *Lady Juliana*. It was on that ship I met Maggie Broad.'

'Was her husband also transported?'

'She had no husband then. She found one on the ship. A good many of the women did. He was a marine. They married in Sydney Cove soon after we reached that place. For a woman, it was the only way to avoid being shipped to Norfolk Island.'

Henry Lodge sips some ale. This is his third pint of the stuff today. He is feeling dangerously loquacious.

'She took her husband's name?'

'Aye, she did.'

'And what was her unmarried name?'

He nearly says it, but when he goes to fetch the name, when he turns his memory around in his mind, there is nothing there. It is like looking for a key he has set down on a table moments before which has now disappeared.

'I know not,' is all he says. The constable sniffs. Henry Lodge goes on talking, as much to fill the silence as anything else.

'The man she married – William Broad, his name was – he served out his own time in the marines and then in the New South Wales Corps, and he was given a fair parcel of land in Parramatta, where the soil was at least decent and didn't run away whenever it rained, like in Sydney Cove. And before long the Broads' farm was the richest in Parramatta. The most successful farm in the colony. Even the Governor's soil didn't sing the way Maggie's did. And he took the best bloody land of all.'

'Maggie's soil?'

'Yes. Her soil. Broad was a useless drunk. Maggie did everything. But the women of New South Wales were of a particular stripe, constable. Some of them were vicious, some of them were sly, some of them would open their legs and then shove a knife in your back while you were enjoying them. But the ones that survived the voyage, and then survived the living? They weren't women like the women in this fine place, constable. They became something else. The men did, too. Hard lives back here, they'd lived. And even harder lives over there. And yet they'd survived.'

Henry finds himself feeling wistful, thinking of the boy becoming a man, the boy who'd survived a shipwreck but the man who'd nearly succumbed to New South Wales.

'And Maggie Broad was the toughest, cleverest, most powerful of the lot of them. There were a good many tales doing the rounds about her. How she'd killed her husband back in Suffolk, and that was why she got transported. How she'd caused women to miscarry on the voyage out. How she'd sent a man overboard as the *Lady Juliana* crossed the line, for forcing himself upon her. But the strangest story of all was about how she was friends with the savages. She could speak their language, people said, and they taught her things. She had power over the soil, people said, though the savages didn't grow anything of their own and lived on fish and what grew wild, so how much power did they have? And she had power to make people do things they didn't want to do. There were tales aplenty about the magic of the savages: how they could point a bone at you and you'd drop dead within a day, how they could pull out your soul on a white cord while you slept. And Maggie Broad, it was said, had learned their tricks. And that was why she could make stuff grow, where others could not.'

Another sip.

'Toxic brew, it was. Jealousy of a woman. Hatred of the savages. Put them together, and you've got a barrel of something that's bound to explode. And one night, it did. The Broads had about a hundred acres in Parramatta at that time. Not a great amount by the standards of this country, especially now the enclosures have come in, but she made the very best of it. She could grow anything in that cursed bloody soil. Grapes and figs and oranges and pears. Rich stuff. Stuff that made poor convict men and women think they could live like kings and queens, out there where the rock was just beneath the soil and snakes dropped out of trees and bit you on the bloody head.

'But she's surrounded by men who can't make the soil sing in the way she can. So one night one particular group of dullards decided that Maggie Broad was, beyond the bounds of doubt, a witch.'

The constable looks surprised.

'A witch? They called her a witch?'

'Oh, yes. And as such she needed to be taught a lesson. So, off they went, carrying torches and unpleasant dispositions. They marched to Maggie Broad's farm. The ringleader was a thug called Longman. Birmingham man, he was, and he'd just finished a stint in the Corps. He was a brutal, vicious bastard, but so were all those Corps fellows. Longman had his own tract of land near the river, and like all the Corps men he'd been able to choose it himself. Helped themselves, did the Corps, always. But his plot kept flooding, of course, and it brought him to the brink of ruin. It drove Longman into a rage. How could a woman know more about land than an officer?'

'And for that she was called a witch?' asks the constable.

'It's the way of these things: when a woman bests a man, witchcraft must be at the root of it. So Longman and his band marched on Maggie Broad's property. She was waiting for them, unaccompanied and unarmed. William Broad was nowhere to be seen; she chained him up, some said, and made him sleep in the yard. And Longman strode up with his knife, and said the quickest way to draw a witch's power was to scratch it out of her, and he cut her cheek. She made no sound, I was told, but just tore the bottom off her skirts and held it to her cheek, turned her back on Longman and his men and said she would like a private word with him. He refused, saying he wouldn't be going off anywhere with a witch, but she said they would not be going out of sight of his companions. There were secrets she wished to share with him, she said, *horticultural* secrets which would help him be as successful in his planting as she had been. And Longman, being a greedy and stupid man, said he would like to hear these secrets.

'So they stepped to one side, out of earshot of the other men, and she spoke to him, it was said, for twenty minutes. When they returned, Longman insisted that the men walk away from Maggie Broad's little plantation and return to their homes. Enough time had passed for the fires in their bellies to extinguish, and they were willing to do as he said, and to leave Maggie Broad alone.'

'They left her alone for good?'

'Yes. All was quiet for a month, during which time Longman neglected his own farm and consumed dangerous quantities of liquor. He got into fights with other men, and one night he was found weeping by the side of the road, unable to explain himself. His decline was precipitous, and I saw it myself, going to visit him on three separate occasions. I wanted to try and discover what ailed the fellow, because I had my own idea that

Maggie Broad might help me to understand the soil. Seeing him almost put me off the scheme. His life was as unproductive and barren as the fields he planted, he said. All that was left to him was drink and despair. And then, about two months after the encounter with Maggie Broad, Longman took his own gun and, placing it in his mouth, blew his head off.'

Lodge's throat is quite dry – both from the storytelling, and from his own memories. He sips from his ale again. He wonders why this story should be coming out in such detail, and then he sees the constable's eyes again. Searching, asking, examining. Those eyes, and this ale.

'Now, I saw all this, because the fact of it was Maggie had done me a great kindness. I'd presented myself to her when I got my ticket of leave, and she remembered me from the *Lady Juliana*, and she gave me work. And I worked hard, and well. She trusted me, I think, in a way she didn't trust any others. After a time she gave me a plot of land, part of her own grant, and lent me seeds and seedlings and tools. She advised me on planting, and cultivation, and harvesting. Though she did not seem old enough to be more than a sister to me, she did mother me. And while the stories surged and ebbed in the shacks and houses and dormitories of the colony, we became almost friends.'

'What of the husband?'

'A sad tale. Threw himself off the rocks at the entrance to the cove.'

'Killed himself, you mean. Like Longman.'

The words *like Longman*, in the constable's mouth, become dire.

'I suppose so, yes.'

'And then you left the colony.'

'I did, constable. I always had that in mind. I wished to make enough of myself to get away from that place, awful as it was.

It took me four years, but I earned enough to pay for my passage home and for a small plot in Kent, where I grow hops. I took what Maggie Broad had taught me, and I applied it here in England. And here I am today. A man of means. A pickpocket become a gentleman-farmer. Is it not a miraculous transformation? Sometimes I think that witchcraft must, after all, be at the root of it.'

'Perhaps it is.'

The constable doesn't smile, and Henry Lodge doesn't reply.

'Did you expect Maggie Broad to return, one day, as you did?'

'She said she would come back when she had served her time, and she had made herself.'

'Why are you here, Mr Lodge?'

Henry Lodge may grow hops but, he tells himself, he cannot take his ale. His tongue is too loose. Somehow another ale has appeared in front of him; when did the constable order that? He takes a slug of a quarter of it, and it is comfortable, delicious, English. It tastes of home. But he must be careful. The daughter must be protected.

The constable's eyes are fixed on him, and for a moment it is like sitting opposite Maggie Broad. The power of her expression, the way she is able to pour herself into his thoughts, that strange sense of the front of his head swinging open and his mind being revealed, though for the constable this is for revelation, not manipulation.

'Your story has been a fine one, Mr Lodge. Still, I fail to see its relevance to your attendance here in Wapping. You have seen her. Have you not?'

He asks himself an odd question: *Am I allowed to answer this?* No answer comes.

'Aye, I have. She came to me, during the summer. She had found my hop garden, and she visited to wish me well.'

'She had no other reason?'

'None that I can fathom, constable.'

'And where did she go then?'

'I know not. Perhaps to Suffolk? She said once that she hailed from there.'

The constable's eyes are, if anything, colder and harder than ever. A little shiver of anxiety in Henry's stomach, soon drowned in another slug of ale. The constable takes a little black notebook from his pocket, and turns to the back pages.

'Does the name Rose Dawkins mean anything to you?'

'No, I do not believe. I do not quite recall . . .'

'Elizabeth Carrington?'

'It does not strike me as familiar.'

'Maria Cranfield?'

Oh God.

He imagines Maggie standing at the bar behind the constable, turning her face to his, and remembers that pinching sensation in his head. He has felt that sensation before. His ale-drenched head begins to ache, suddenly. He feels afraid.

'No, constable. None of these names mean anything to me at all.'

'Why are you here, Mr Lodge?'

The repeated question.

'I . . . have business here.'

'I think not.'

The constable leans forward, and makes a strange dipping action with his head, as if he were trying to look under Henry Lodge's face to see what might have been buried there.

'No, I think you're here because you were told to be here. I think Maggie Broad has been telling you to do things for years. I wonder whether she even sent you back to England and told you to wait for her, to watch out for her. I think perhaps you are merely an instrument, Mr Lodge. An instrument for a woman's plan. A woman with a very particular ability. To get inside men's minds.'

Then the constable tells him of Thorpe Lee House and the murders of the Sybarites, and Henry Lodge wonders if it would not have been better to have drowned beneath those ice mountains, and not feel full of Wapping ale and secrets.

And still he does not mention Maria Cranfield, even though he devoutly wants to.

Maggie Broad will not let him.

WAPPING

It is time, Horton supposes, to go back to Covent Garden and report what he has learned back to Aaron Graham. Though how he should do this – what precisely he should say – is as obscure to him as the far side of the Moon is to the Royal Society's starry gazers.

Between here and Covent Garden, though, sits Lower Gun Alley, and the home he shares with Abigail.

But is that any longer true? Is Abigail still Abigail? Or has he destroyed her? Is that part of his life coming to a close? And if it does, what comes afterwards?

Unbearable thoughts.

He needs a change of clothes, but more than that, he needs to re-establish himself. There has been too much wandering and wondering. He feels unidentified and uprooted. The case shouts to him for attention and clarity. Patterns are beginning to emerge and, with them, his old sense of himself. Damaged, deliberate, despairing Charles Horton, yes. But Charles Horton, nonetheless.

The sharp tang of the ale reminds him of that strangely

terrible night in Thorpe, when witches flew along hedgerows and bonfires sprouted in fields. But his first sip had been as cleansing as taking the waters in Bath. He wonders if the pitchery is still in his system, a malignant manipulator of dreams.

The story has begun to emerge, but an incomplete and odd one. Once again he is in that dark room of his imagination, holding a candle and trying to perceive the full outline of the enormous thing in the middle of the room, assembling its structures from the fragments which the candle illuminates.

A woman, returning from Australia, for reasons unknown but with some deliberate purpose. A woman who, it is said, has the capacity to project her will onto men.

All the Sybarites but two: dead, impossibly so, the only possible killers within the men's own houses, their faithful servants. The only survivors are Tempest and, Horton assumes, Cameron, the one who took Graham's advice to leave London.

The man who procured young women for these men: dead by his own hand, a sword in his stomach.

One of the other women in Sir Henry's dirty little book: also dead, apparently by her own hand.

The *Indefatigable*, returning to Deal in April. Watched for by Henry Lodge, a man who does not seem to comprehend why he is acting as he does. But there was something of Thorpe Lee House about Lodge's haunted and half-absent eyes. Something hidden there, placed deliberately by a woman with an unspeakable capacity.

Did Maggie Broad bring pitchery with her, perhaps? Grown somewhere on her very successful New South Wales farm? Perhaps with advice from those strange natives, with their spears and the bones in their noses, so very different to the natives of Otaheite which the sailors of the *Solander* spoke of, so dark and afraid and resistant to the queries of the North? Did they not eat people? Or is that somewhere else entirely?

Sir Henry, bleeding on his chaise longue. Speared by his own daughter, the daughter who danced in the woods, who seemed half-witch herself. Who told him to leave the woods without speaking the words, and who then removed the memory of it.

The gypsy's wagon, pulling away from the forest.

The story unfolding within his head, impervious to his own desires. The implacability of it, the certainty of it, the clarity of it.

But something is still missing, the essential question. Why is Maggie Broad here? What is her motivation? Simple malevolence would be a bleak answer, and Horton does not believe it.

He leaves the tavern, and walks home. It is dark and there is rain and perhaps thunder in the air. The streets are alive with meaning. He sees two young boys he knows well, part of that little network of boys whose eyes watch the houses and the people on his behalf. They wave as they disappear down some mischievous dark sideway, full of intrigue and curiosity, the world an adventure of thousands of levels to be clambered up. He misses Wapping. He has been away too long.

He misses Abigail.

Lower Gun Alley is almost silent. His windows have the same neglected, purposeless air he noticed earlier today. He goes into the building and up the stairs, and unlocks the door to the apartment with his key. Instantly, he notices a letter which has been shoved beneath the door. He picks it up, recognising immediately the well-formed handwriting on the front, picturing despite himself the small careful hand. The letter is from Abigail.

Charles
I pray this letter reaches you for I dare not leave this place.
Know this, first of all – I am well, and though the visions
which pursued me here and chased me away from thyself are

still much in my mind, they have been greatly displaced by other concerns.

There is something very strange taking place here within the madhouse. There is a girl here, named Maria, who seems to be possessed of abilities which I cannot describe nor quite believe. She seems to have the power to possess men's minds – to force them to do things against their will. More than this, there is an effulgence from this capacity which seems to have spread through the whole house, causing men to scream and shriek and fear. This has happened on at least three occasions.

I do not believe I am imagining this. Also, I fear that the physician in attendance herein – a weak man named Bryson – has no conception of Maria's abilities, and does not know how to deal with her. I have concluded that the only brake on her power – and on her misuse of it – is my attendance with her. She grows calmer when I am with her. I read to her, and I talk to her, and she seems to hear or understand me. But I fear her. Oh, Charles, I fear her terribly.

I shall give this letter to an attendant here who is kind to us but is sadly feeble-minded. I fear it may never reach you. I will not know if it has until you appear, and I pray you do, my husband. We have seen things, you and I, these past three years, and you have told me of other things which pass all my understanding, for all of my books and lectures. I do not understand what is happening in this place, Charles. And I beg you to come and help me.

With all my love
Abigail

WESTMINSTER

William Jealous isn't supposed to be looking for Rose Dawkins. He is supposed to be looking for Charles Horton.

He has tried. Earlier that afternoon Graham had called him into the office at Bow Street and charged him with finding Horton 'immediately'. The magistrate had looked angry and, Jealous nervously noted, he had looked anxious. Anyone with a nose to smell can sense the panic in the air, can see the emissaries from Whitehall carrying notes and warnings, can hear the raised voices and anxious questions of the scribblers in the parlour. But Aaron Graham is normally the calmest of the Bow Street magistrates. It is disturbing to see that calm fractured.

He had travelled to the Wapping River Police Office directly, and had learned that Horton had been there some hours before, but it is now early evening, and no one knows where he is. Jealous waits for a little while outside Horton's lodgings, which look shut up and abandoned to his practised London eyes, but he cannot settle. There is an itch he has to scratch. The itch is called Rose Dawkins.

Rose has, to all intents and purposes, disappeared from view following her release. Ugly, violent, foul-mouthed Rose. Why is he worried about such a one as her? A vicious street-whore. And yet he is hopping from one foot to another on a dirty side-street in Wapping, and for the first time in his young life contemplating insubordination. Horton can look after himself. When he has something to report to Graham he will do so. Standing around is a waste of time.

The dead bodies of the Sybarites are still in their locked-up houses. Surgeons have investigated them and will report to separate coroner's inquests on the morrow; but none of these inquests will unpick the central mysteries of the case. How do five men meet their deaths in their own homes, under lock and key, and under the eyes and noses and ears of constables and watchmen?

The key was the servants, Horton had said. But they have been spoken to, and they remember nothing. Glassy-eyed confusion greets every enquiry. Graham has no answer to this, and nor do any of his fellow magistrates, or anyone working for him, Jealous least of all. But Rose Dawkins has been forgotten since her release, and Jealous is unable to fathom this. He is, after all, a young man, and he finds himself remembering the shape of Rose's hand as he dragged her through St Giles. If he cared to think about it more deeply, he might recognise how much Rose's air of desperate rage is redolent of his sister Joan, who shares the streetwalker's sense of aggrieved amusement at her lot.

His hand remembers the sting of Rose's slapped face, a rebuke and a reminiscence. Why is it only he that can see the woman might be in danger? Is not her friend Elizabeth dead already?

When arrested, Rose had given her address as the building in which they had found Elizabeth Carrington: 27 Brownlow

Street. He'd raised her eyebrows at that and she'd glared at him defiantly, daring him to question it or even slap him again, so she could 'kick his prick off'. He'd said nothing. It hadn't seemed to matter and, in any case, it might be true.

He comes to a decision: to leave Wapping. He takes a carriage to Covent Garden, where he arrives as the streets begin to fill up for the evening to come. Doors are opening all along Brownlow Street, and women of various ages and sizes are stepping out into the street, some individually, others in little chattering groups. When they spot him, they either go quiet or shout obscenities – he is already well recognised by the streetwalkers. He goes to Number 27, and lets himself in.

With a start, he realises the body of Elizabeth Carrington is almost certainly still upstairs. All available men are either guarding the houses of the dead Sybarites, or running errands for Graham, or out on the pavements seeking something, anything, on which to hang a prosecution. A dead whore warrants no protection, and no intervention. He wonders if Elizabeth will always be up there, her hand hanging down, the blood beneath her staining the boards a permanent scarlet . . .

There is a whore in Elizabeth's room, but it is not a dead one. Rose Dawkins is on her knees, scrubbing the floorboards. The body has gone.

He hasn't knocked, and this does not impress Rose.

'Who the fuck do you think you are, comin' in 'ere?' She remains kneeling on the floor, but the force of her character is undiminished by that. 'Get out of it, now. You're no bloody use to me or to anyone.'

The force of her will is like a hand on his chest, and he remembers that feeling of being tugged on the collar as he held her down in St Giles. He feels something like it now – reluctance to do anything other than step out of the room and walk away. Rose's forceful will is almost physical.

'I came to check on Elizabeth,' he lies. 'Who took her body?'

She looks at him, head slightly cocked on one side, like a smart dog checking on the friendliness of a human.

'The parish. I told them what had happened. They were 'ere just now. You lot weren't going to do nothin' about it, were you?'

'The coroner might object to that.'

'Do me a favour. The coroner don't give a toss. He's too busy looking at the bodies of toffs, ain't he? Couldn't care less about a poor bitch like Lizzie.'

She stands, now. That feeling of wanting to leave subsides, leaving only a spark of sensation in the back of the neck, like the footsteps of an insect crawling across his skin.

'What do you want?'

'I was concerned for . . . your safety.'

'My safety?'

'Yes. If there is a killer stalking whores and their gulls . . .'

She frowns, puzzled.

'Free ride round the houses, is it?' she says, her voice sneering but her face open and confused for the first time since he has met her. 'Hopeful that the poor scared little bitch will spread her legs for the brave Bow Street Runner?'

'No!' He steps further into the room, and is now only three or four steps away from her. They look at each other. She is still holding the wet rag with which she had been mopping up Lizzie Carrington's emptied life. 'And besides. I'm not a Runner.'

She smiles a little at that, and then Jealous hears a soft step from behind him, and he turns to see an older woman with dark hair and a terrible scar down one cheek. These things are only the impressions of an instant, though, because she is looking into his eyes and he is looking into hers and he falls into those green circles and hears the sound of his sister laughing, a child's laugh from somewhere down the years, a garden and rain and the feel of wet grass on his warm bare legs, a summer feeling, and he is turning within the garden, turning towards a figure he dimly recognises, a Rose, a Rose in the garden, and he is putting his hands around the Rose's throat, around its flowers and its thorns, and he is squeezing hard, but his sister is calling to him, down the years, and he looks down at her and she is shouting at him, telling him to stop, and Joan has always been the only one who can tell him to do *anything*, and he squeezes and squeezes and Joan shouts and shouts, though her shouts are getting dimmer and weaker, but then she shouts one last thing, hard and sharp and completely unexpected . . .

I'll kick you in the fucking prick!

. . . and he stops and lets go and the garden disappears and Rose falls to her knees as he drops her, coughing and crying, heaving air back into her body through rattling great sobs of breath.

He is about to turn to look at the woman who has come into the room, to ask what her business might be, but then Rose grabs his hand and, without looking at him while she struggles with her air, manages to whisper: 'Don't . . . *look* at her . . .'

He looks at her hand in his, and some vestigial childhood ripple comes back to him – *snap it, snap it like a twig in the garden* – but it is a whispered thing, emptied of its power.

Eventually, Rose looks up at him again, and struggles to stand. He feels sick when he sees the marks of his thumbs on the front of her neck, as livid as petals. Once she's on her feet, she puts a hand on his shoulder, holding him in place, positioning him faced away from the stranger in the room.

'You killed Lizzie. You bitch. You killed Lizzie.'

Jealous hears nothing at first, only the steady breathing of the older woman behind him. This sound, and the sight of Rose's fierce stare, and something else – that disconcerting static prickle – fill the room. He wishes, more than anything, to turn and face down those eyes, but Rose's hand is strong on his arm, holding him in place.

'Have you always been able to do that?' says the woman. The accent is strong; East Anglian, Suffolk or Norfolk, as rural as wheat and hops. The voice is harsh and powerful, almost male in its bearing.

'Do what?' asks Rose, and her fingers tense on his shoulder.

'You know what I am talking of, girl.'

'I'm no girl, bitch. Did you kill Lizzie?'

'Lizzie killed herself.'

'Fuck off. You know what you did.'

'As do you, girl.'

'You made Lizzie kill herself.'

'She was a witness.'

'Witness to what?'

'To the defilement of my daughter. She did nothing to help her. Neither did you.'

'Help her? How could we have helped her?'

'You have some power. You don't have to whore yourself around. You're more than that. You're more than this useless bag of bones that calls itself a patrolman.'

Rose looks at him then, and he sees in her eyes her suspicious hatred, her angry shame, her deliberate viciousness. No one would write poems about those mud-brown eyes – they're warlike and bitter. She turns them back on the stranger behind him.

'He resisted you.'

A laugh, then. A nasty, bullying laugh. The laugh of an overseer with a whip standing over an exhausted negro.

'It was not he who resisted, Rose Dawkins. Now, leave him be and come with me. My work is done. We can leave together, and change your life.'

'I will not leave with you.'

'I am a bad enemy to have, Rose Dawkins.'

'You are an old woman who has no power over me.'

Rose's eyes widen then – he sees them pop into open circles. Her arm stiffens, her fingers bite into his shoulders. The cords in her neck become visible, her brow creases into a dozen folds. She is in pain. Every part of her is in pain. He is about to turn, to throw himself at her attacker, but then Rose goes limp and falls to the floor and behind him he hears the stranger turn and walk briskly out and down the stairs; he even catches a glimpse of her shoulder as she goes, before turning back to the girl on the floor.

She is in a faint. A dribble of blood comes out of one nostril. He raises her head and, sitting down, puts it in his lap. The tough patrolman finds an unexpected tenderness within him. He takes one of her hands and holds it, and with the other strokes her red hair. It is as soft and brittle as new straw. His father would laugh at him if he could see.

After a minute or two she opens her eyes, and breathes in hugely through her nose. She smiles, a fierce little expression which contrives to make her hard ugly face something beautiful.

'What happened?' he asks.

'She gave me a warning,' Rose replies. 'To keep out of what-ever comes next.'

A Treatise on Moral Projection

That final day was calm, and Brooke House was quiet. The shocks and shrieks of the previous night had, God knows, been among the worst things I had heard – particularly that terrible chanting towards the end, as if all the men in the place were shouting from a script written by a lunatic playwright. How could that have been, I asked myself? What consciousness operated upon them, to make them speak with one voice?

A terrible conception had come upon me. My theory of *moral projection* was then barely formed; it has taken these past three decades for me to refine my thoughts upon it. I read my notes from that day and they seem to me to be fractured and somewhat desperate, and I believe I know why – I had become terrified lest Maria Cranfield step into my head once again and extract more memories. I resolved to write every single thing down.

It was a wise course. For soon another would come, who would make Maria's abilities look impoverished indeed. Only my perspicacity and foresight protected my ideas so that I might share them with you, the reader, today.

But I am running ahead of myself. My notes from

that day tell a particular story: how I visited Maria Cranfield's cell. How I found her sleeping, watched over by Abigail Horton. How Mrs Horton begged for someone to be sent to clean Maria's bedding and to accompany the two women so they could clean themselves. I agreed, and went to find John Burroway.

John went up to the women and was gone for perhaps an hour, during which time I wrote more notes and consulted with a few additional inmates. But my heart was not in it. I could not focus on the prattling concerns of these lunatics when, upstairs, almost above my head, there was a female whose abilities, I had already begun to tell myself, would make my name and my reputation.

I consulted my notes again. As I have said, I was becoming concerned that Maria might try to remove memories from me once again, and that these memories might include my own observations of her. Suddenly these observations seemed to me to be of enormous value; to be the means to my own professional rise.

Was it possible, that she might wipe away all recall of these events? I thought it probably impossible; I had, after all, remembered most of the events in the cell two days before. However, the crucial fact of this matter was that the remembrance I had come to had depended, had it not, on the reminders provided by John Burroway. He seemed impervious to Maria's ability to remove memories, perhaps because his own capacities were so damaged.

And so I concocted a plan of self-protection. One which defended me from what was to come, though in ways I could not then imagine. I called for John

Burroway, but was told he was not then in the building, having been sent on an errand. I barely thought about what this errand might consist of, so determined was I on thinking about this new path. I ordered that he be sent to my consulting rooms immediately upon his return, and I went back to collect my notes into some order. I was, it now seemed to me, recording matters for Posterity.

BROOKE HOUSE

John Burroway has had the most extraordinary day. He sits near the doorway of Brooke House as evening falls, and ponders on all that has taken place. It is a long, slow pondering, with many distractions and diversions, but John is careful in his thinking. Far more careful than many give him credit for. He knows his conception is a damaged instrument, and so he takes care when using it, like a man who must climb stairs with a lame leg.

But however careful his thinking, and however rambling, it curls and snakes around one awful concern: *Am I in trouble?*

John is a large man, but also a perpetually anxious one. He had told his sister just this morning that he was going to get into trouble again today, but this was something he said most mornings and his sister had paid it no mind. He seemed to be getting into trouble a lot, recently. The house had once been a charmed place, and John had liked nothing better than looking after it. He thought of it as a grand old aunt with her own peculiar ways. He swept her corridors and cleaned her windows and spoke to all the people who lived in her. These people had one thing or another wrong with them in much the same way he had something wrong with him. Some of them were very sad. Some of them couldn't calm down properly. Some of them said things which couldn't be true, like the man who thought there were flying machines hanging over Brooke House which were forcing him to do bad things to himself and to other people. That man had badly scared John Burroway, but he was the exception. Most of the people in the house were either kind to John or did not notice him.

It has been a sunny day, but it is becoming a stormy night. Rain has begun to pour down outside the little room in which he sits, next to the front door of Brooke House, watching the gate. It's his duty, tonight, to let people in and out. It's not one of his favourite tasks, because people arriving can do unexpected things. They don't stay in one place like a floor that needs sweeping. They ask him to do things, and they act unexpectedly. It is people, more than anything, that make John anxious. And this is why today has been so worryingly peculiar.

First had come the two women. Dr Bryson had told him to go up there and clean the room of the silent woman in the strait waistcoat, the one who had done that thing inside his head, the thing that Dr Bryson kept wanting to talk to him about. John was scared of that woman, but the other who was with her, the sad-eyed one with the beautiful blonde hair that John wanted to stroke but never, ever would, she was nice, and her presence eased him. At least, it did until she told him she wanted him to do something for her.

'I need paper and ink and a quill, John. Will you get them for me? And will you deliver something for me when I've finished? Can you do that?'

He knew what she meant by *can you do that*. She didn't mean *would you do that for me*. She meant *is your poor feeble brain up to doing what I need you to do.* And because she asked it kindly and because John could do things better than most people thought, he agreed he would.

It took a long time though. And Mrs Horton made him lie, which made him think perhaps she wasn't as nice as he'd thought. But she *was* nice. She *was*. John felt it in his bones, and his bones were often better judges of situations than his mind. She made him lie to a nurse about the quill and ink and paper; he told her he wanted to practise his writing, and she'd been so pleased she hadn't asked anything else. And Abigail made him lie to the man who watched the gate during the day, saying he was on an errand for Dr Bryson. And Abigail said he couldn't tell anyone what she was doing, including Dr Bryson and including his sister. John agreed, but added his own silent lie – he would tell his sister, of course. He told his sister everything.

He found a carriage as she said, he told the driver to take him to the address on the first envelope as she said, and when they got to the house he knocked on the door like she said, but there was no answer, so he left the letter like she said and went to another address on another piece of paper with the second letter, the one he was to use only if there was no one at the first house, and a kindly lady opened the door at this second address and read the letter he gave her, and went back inside and came out with money to pay the carriage driver and made a special point of telling John how extremely clever he'd been to pull off this complicated mission so successfully. And the carriage drove him back to Brooke House.

He was tired when he came back, tired but happy (though a little anxious) at having done something which most people would have thought him incapable of. But then Dr Bryson called him into his office, and started giving him *another* task, which while not as complicated as that of Mrs Horton's was nonetheless very *peculiar*. Dr Bryson said he wanted John to hide some notes he had taken, to put them somewhere only John knew about, and then not to tell the doctor about them. Not unless the doctor forgot something that had happened. John had wanted to ask how this could be, but the doctor rushed him out, and said they would talk of this later. John took the notes, and hid them somewhere only he knew about; a certain cavity in the wall in the dark depths of Brooke House, a place in which John sometimes goes to hide, where the bricks seem to remember prayers and songs and where the exposed painting of a priest in full raiment pokes down through the ceiling from the floor above, only the priest's feet and calves visible. It's a big cavity, big enough for a person to hide in for a long time. John hides the notes in there.

A flash of lightning pierces the deepening dark and John cowers like a terrified animal, all thoughts of his peculiar day banished. He is terrified of the gap between the lightning and the thunder, terrified of the coming crash which always feels like the sky is falling down.

But his fear, this day, is deepened by the figure silhouetted by the lightning flash. There is a woman standing at the gate to Brooke House, and behind her John can see the shape of a tall wagon.

When the crash of thunder finally comes it sounds to John like a giant speaking.

'I need to pray,' Maria says. 'I need somewhere to pray. Is there somewhere I can do so?'

Abigail leaves Maria's cell and goes to find Miss Delilah. The woman is reluctant to go anywhere near Maria's cell, but Abigail begs her, and she finally agrees.

Abigail tries to persuade Delilah that Maria should be released from the strait waistcoat, for she wishes to pray, to pray as a human being, not a caged animal. She has had no chance for religious observance in nigh on a month, says Abigail, and the time has come to allow her to speak to God. She tries and she tries, but Delilah just stands in the door staring at Maria, her face stony and her mouth disgusted, saying she can do nothing without Dr Bryson's say-so, and that he is *exceedingly unlikely* to countenance Maria being released.

And then Maria turns her face to Delilah's and moments later Delilah has gone to fetch the keys which unlock the chain. Abigail sees what has happened, and though it makes her feel unsettled and afraid she says nothing, lest those blue eyes turn upon her.

So Maria is released, and Abigail asks the glassy-eyed Miss Delilah if there is a chapel anywhere in Brooke House. She has not seen such a place on her own wanderings, and Delilah shakes her head, but then says:

'The old chapel's just down the corridor. I'll show you.'

She walks out of the cell, and Abigail follows, holding Maria by the hand.

At this corner of Brooke House there is a confusion of staircases and doors between the older parts of the building, where Abigail and Maria are locked, and the newer part at the front. It is as if the eighteenth-century developers scratched their heads at the strange geometries of their fifteenth-century predecessors, and surrendered any effort to integrate the two places. A floor has been thrown across what must have once been a deep room, a staircase navigates this space vertically, and on one wall Abigail sees the exposed image of a priest. It is an old image, painted directly upon the wall, but the priest's rich robes still hold some of their former magnificence. The priest's legs are cut off at the calves by the new floor, and must stretch down into the space below the floor. Despite the clumsy adaptations, the space still has a vaguely sepulchral air.

373

It must indeed once have been a chapel, though it has lost its purpose. There is the picture on the wall, and a pair of low benches which have been placed to one side of it, and there is the memory of religious ritual. Other than these things, the room has been stripped of function.

Delilah unlocks a door and shows them inside, and Maria tells her to leave.

Abigail does not care for the room within. It seems to her to have something poisonous about it, as if it were a malignant historical tumour inside the modern fabric of Brooke House. It is a place where the house remembers its old self, its walls echoing back Tudor plots and Stuart schemes, the air clustered with Catholic ghosts, and old Thomas Cromwell hunched down in front of that priestly picture, seeking expiation for his manifest sins.

But Maria has kneeled, and as she does so a flash of lightning illuminates the secret corners of the chapel, followed seconds later by a boom of thunder, as if God were complaining that an abomination was trying to converse with Him.

John can hear it is raining very hard now, and the lightning is frequent and fierce. Five or six bolts of light repeat that original silhouette: the woman at the gate, the tall wagon behind her. Her face is invisible, which makes it even odder that she has appeared in his head, just like Maria had been, in his head and telling him to do things.

The first thing she tells him to do – silently, across the space between his little sheltered room and the iron gate – is to walk out to her. So out John goes, out into the rain which drenches him immediately, walking closer and closer to her, until he is only feet away, her on one side of the gate, he on the other, and another lightning strike shows him the woman's face for the first time. He has seen her before.

Dr Bryson had once asked John about his dreams, and John had said he didn't dream, at all. The doctor said perhaps he dreamed, but couldn't remember them in the morning, and John said this was possible. He had thought about it a lot after their conversation. It scared him a good deal, this idea that you might think things at night, think them in such a strong way that you dreamed them, but couldn't remember them in the morning.

However, in the years after that terrible thunderstruck night, John will always be able to remember one dream. In that dream, there is a woman standing at a gate, and her face is in darkness, until a lightning strike comes and shows the woman's face to him. Her scar wriggles blackly in the shadows along her cheek. Her teeth are bared, like an angry dog. And her eyes look into him as if his poor empty head were filled with images of her mad daughter.

Let me in. Let me in. Let me in.

John whimpers a little. But he lets her in.

By the time Horton reaches Brooke House the weather has turned the calm warm day into something snarling and soaking. The hackney carriage he has taken from Wapping stops outside the gate. He tell himself to calm down, suppressing the still-desperate panic in his chest which had sent him hurtling out of the apartment in Lower Gun Alley and down into the bustling twilight of Wapping.

The sharp corners of Abigail's letter dig into his chest from the inner pocket of his coat. A slap of rain hits his cheek as he steps down from the carriage and turns to watch it pull away. The wind is howling. A terrible storm has come to Hackney.

The madhouse – *Abigail's* madhouse – squats behind a wall, its silhouette a disturbing combination of order and irregularity. He has been here so many times these past weeks, but always during the day; he has sat under the trees on the opposite side of the road, gazing up into the windows of the place in the hope of seeing her walking down a corridor or glancing outside.

The dark gives the place a new personality, as the dark always does. In the daylight, Brooke House is eccentric and impervious, its bricks occupied with the history of England. In the night-time, it is bleak and desolate, its silhouette resonant with the fearful disturbances that occupy those within.

Somewhere within the raging terror and guilt which has ridden with him from Wapping there has been a space for consideration. The picture which had been forming in his mind over an ale in the Prospect of Whitby is now gaining shape, definition, shadow and colour.

She seems to have the power to possess men's minds – to force them to do things against their will.

This has been the void at the centre of the thing. The deaths of the men in London, and the weird events at Thorpe Lee House, had this in common: that the only *opportunity* to commit them seemed to come from within the house. He realised (as the carriage rattled through Whitechapel and headed north) that opportunity is as important as motive in the hierarchy of explanation for unseen, unexplained events. Without opportunity, motive is meaningless; and without motive, opportunity is doubly so. But in this case, the motive has been separated from the opportunity. This woman – this Mrs Broad, if such be her real name – has had no seeming opportunity.

So where has she found it? That has been the dark question, the imponderable. He thinks back to a conversation with his magistrate, John Harriott, in the old man's office above the river, soon after the *Solander* affair had reached its conclusion. Abigail's dreams had worsened recently, and he had said something to Harriott about it, about his concerns and his inability to understand how these dreams could remain after such a time.

Harriott had looked out at the river from his chair, as he did whenever he wished to remain calm. And he had said this:

'Horton, you are a man of exceptional capability. Your approach to investigation has changed my views on the matter entirely, and Mr Graham's too. You are, it is my belief, a template for the way in which these matters will be treated in the future. But know this: your approach cannot explain everything. I have learned, these past two years, that there are secrets within this world. Some men see these secrets as holding power; we have witnessed, it is my belief, the covering-up of some of these secrets, as those men seek to manipulate unseen capacities for purposes we cannot perceive. But I have been told things, and you have witnessed things, that bear no rational explanation. There are still white spaces on our maps, Horton, and some of those white spaces are metaphorical.'

Harriott had said no more. But Horton thinks of him as he walks up to Brooke House, through the driving rain.

A tall wagon is pulled up in front of the gate. Its shape is familiar, and the coincidence is almost too acute for a moment. But there it is. The wagon he'd seen from the woods in Thorpe Lee House, on the day he'd encountered poor Ellen Tempest Graham, now standing empty outside the building which contains his wife.

All thoughts of calm dispelled, he runs up to the gate and rings upon the bell.

John feels the force of the woman's will like the blast of a gale on his face. It pushes him, he can feel its fingers in his cheeks and in his hair, holding his head while she gazes at him.

They are standing just inside the front door of Brooke

House, the rain a wall of water beside them. The thunder sounds to John like it comes from a distant land; all he can see is the woman's eyes, all he can hear is her voice.

Tell me, John Burroway. Tell me where I will find Dr Bryson.

In the Cottage. At the end of the corridor.

Take me there.

He turns and walks into the house, and she follows him. He is no longer looking into her eyes, but he can still feel her voice in his head.

John has a sudden fear that his sister might appear in the corridor, from somewhere deep within the house, and seek to challenge this woman. He knows how that might turn out, and the thought of it terrifies him. They reach the door to Dr Bryson's apartment, and then he feels the woman's hand on his shoulder, and it exerts a gentle pressure to turn him around. He is so much taller than her that her hand is held straight above her head to reach him, but as he turns she seems to grow taller, and he smaller, such that when he looks back into her eyes they are staring down at him, and he up.

John, go back to the front door. Let nobody in. And forget I was here.

She turns away from him, and goes in. John walks back to the door, his little room, and the rain.

Horton rings the bell at the gate, but as he does so he sees something odd: the front door closing. It must have been open when he arrived, but now someone inside is shutting it up. The movement has something deliberate about it, as if whoever is behind it wants to prevent prying eyes, as if something were going on inside which is dark and terrible. Rain pours down his body, and panic begins to flood down his brain, a strange feeling to one such as he.

He rings the bell, again and again and again. Lightning and

thunder rattle and gleam incessantly, every half-a-minute, an impossible cacophony. His old pea-coat is drenched and the wet air muffles whatever noises may be coming from inside the asylum.

A dark shape appears from the front door and approaches the gate.

'No one can come in after hours,' the voice says, a deep man's voice.

'I am a constable of the River Police.'

'There's no river here, constable.'

The giant shape doesn't chuckle or sneer. It's a simple matter of fact that there is no river here.

'I am investigating a matter which relates to the deaths of several gentlemen in Covent Garden.'

The silhouette moves forward and its face takes shape in the dim moonlight. It is a large face, with the puzzled expression of a child who has been told something mystifying, its mouth open.

'Why were they killed in the garden?'

The giant's confused face waits for an answer. Horton sees the kind of conversation he must have.

'That is what I am trying to find out. Now, you're a powerful fellow, are you not? I need your help, you see. I think there might be someone in here who can help me understand why they were killed in the garden.'

'Do you mean Dr Bryson?'

'Yes. That's who I mean. Dr Bryson. He's an expert in these matters. I need to speak to him quickly.'

'He's not been himself. Dr Bryson. He's been worried about the woman upstairs. The one in the strait waistcoat. The one who gets into your head.'

The rain seems to drop several degrees in temperature. The giant turns his head up to the top of the building, up and away to the left.

'She's up there now?' asks Horton, trying to keep the panic out of his voice.

'Yes.'

The giant turns back to him.

'She can make people do things she wants them to do. She did it to me. I remember. She makes people forget things. But I remember. Why do I remember?'

'I don't know. But perhaps I could ask Dr Bryson.'

'Yes. Dr Bryson.'

'What's your name, fellow?'

'It's Burroway. John Burroway.'

'Well, John Burroway. I think Dr Bryson will want to speak to me. I think I can help him with this woman you speak of.'

'Did she kill the men in the garden? But no! That's stupid! She's in here. How could she kill them if she's in here? Unless,' and the giant leans in towards the gate, and whispers, 'unless she got *someone else* to do it for her.'

'Let me in, John. You must let me in now.'

And with that, the giant pulls out a key and unlocks the chain around the gate, and lets Horton inside. As they walk to the house, Horton asks him.

'Do you stand at the gate a lot, John?'

'Yes, constable, I do. Most days and most nights, when I'm not doing things inside for Dr Bryson.'

'Have you ever seen a woman with long black hair outside? On a cart? On her own?'

'Oh yes. I see her all the time. She scares me.'

'Does she?'

'Yes. She's got an angry face.'

'Have you seen her tonight?'

A long pause as the giant considers.

'She's inside. But she doesn't want me to remember that.'

*

Horton has visualised the interior of the madhouse which contains his wife many times over the past month. It has become a Gothic extremity in his lonely imagination, as massive as Bethlem, as dirty as Newgate, filled with the chatter of lunatics and the rattling of chains.

The reality is quieter and yet more suffocating, as if he were walking into the interior of a doll's house owned by a stupid yet pedantic child. The layout is confused, as if different houses were contained within the exterior. There is a sense of imprisonment here, but it is a distant one, out of sight. The vestibule and drawing room are tidy but nondescript.

The place reminds him strongly of the River Police Office. It has the same air of municipal domesticity, the same sense of a dwelling adapted for other purposes. And both have the unavoidable discomfort that comes from random shouts and screams from within.

He hears them straightaway: the distant clamour of upset minds. They are almost all male, these random howls, and they are emphasised by the worsening storm.

'Who is in charge?' he asks Burroway, who has followed him inside. In the light, Horton can see the man's enormous face, which while clearly that of an idiot also betrays its own calm.

'They shout again,' Burroway says in reply.

'Who shouts, John?'

'The men. They're shouting like before. Dr Bryson.'

'Dr Bryson is in charge?'

'Yes.' Burroway frowns.

'Would you take me to him, John?'

'Yes. Follow me.'

They walk along a corridor that seems to run the full width of the place, which ends in a door that stands ajar. From inside Horton can hear a man muttering and the sound of tearing paper.

He goes inside.

Dr Bryson does not look round when Horton enters. He is standing at the fireplace, throwing papers onto the flames, muttering to himself as he does so as if performing some kind of inventory.

'That's almost all of them, oh the matron's report, mustn't forget the matron's report, and the letter the fellow who brought her in gave me, where is that, oh here it is, is that it all then? Is that it all?'

'Dr Bryson?'

He speaks sharply to draw the man's attention away from the fire. He is so impatient by now that he imagines being able to *smell* Abigail, to detect her somewhere in this building by a sense other than sight or sound.

Bryson is unshaven, his hair is wildly disordered, and his eyes have a look of such frenzy that Horton thinks the mad-doctor may stand up and rush at him. But then he is distracted, almost as if someone had tapped him on the shoulder, and he looks down at a disarrayed pile of papers on the corner of his desk, which stands next to the fireplace. An ink pot has fallen over and is staining papers and wood indiscriminately. A half-empty bottle of what looks like whisky stands beside the overturned ink pot.

'Yes, yes, nearly there, nearly there.'

And he takes the pile and, pausing a moment, throws the whole thing onto the flames. The fire is almost extinguished by the weight of the paper, but then it reasserts itself and billows out from the hearth in its hunger to consume whatever Bryson is throwing upon it.

Horton can hear the sound of men screaming. John Burroway has disappeared from beside him, to who knows where? His only guide to the interior of Brooke House is this deranged man.

'Bryson, I must speak to my wife, immediately.'

Bryson looks around him, desperately, and grabs something off the desk. It is a small, old letter-knife, and he points it at Horton, and opens his mouth in a grin that displays his yellow teeth.

'You're in it together. All of you. You're in it together.'

'Bryson, calm yourself.'

'I am CALM. You will LEAVE. All is WELL here.'

'Bryson, you must listen to me. Look me in the eye. Remain calm.'

'Look you in the *eye?* Ah, you think to control me, do you, constable? You think to assert the strength of your will over mine? Well, look into *my* eyes, man. Do what *I* say!'

He is not a tall man, the mad-doctor, but he straightens his back and raises his chin now, as if he were holding an épée to his chin in readiness for a duel. His eyebrows beetle down over his eyes, his brow furrows, and he fixes Horton with a ludicrous theatrical stare.

Horton turns, and leaves the office. Rushing into the corridor, he almost runs into John Burroway, who is standing against the wall with his hands in his ears. His massive face is strung with unhappiness.

'John!'

The big man just shakes his head and looks at the floor, his hands still covering his ears. Horton grabs one of his thick arms and tries to pull it away from the man's face.

'John – I need you to take me somewhere. To the women's quarters.'

The man can hear, he thinks – he just chooses not to reply.

'John, do you remember what I said to you? When I said I was a constable? Well, you could be in trouble if you don't help me.'

It is the wrong approach. John's shoulders slump even

further, his hands pushing towards each other as if he were trying to lift his head from his shoulders.

'My wife, John. My wife is inside. Her name is Abigail.'

John lifts his head, and looks at Horton. He takes his hands from his ears.

'Mrs Horton? Your wife is Mrs Horton?'

'Yes! Can you take me to her?'

John looks down the corridor, both ways, as if an answer, or at least someone carrying an answer, might appear. He looks at the floor again, and shivers as another massive burst of thunder seems to shake the roof.

Then he turns, and walks around a bend in the corridor, leaving Dr Bryson's apartment behind. Inside, Horton hears the sound of furniture toppling, as if someone were pulling out drawers.

Round the corner, they reach a door. John puts out his hand, saying, 'It's probably locked,' but it opens. Security has become soft at Brooke House, it would seem.

On the other side of the door is a flight of stairs, and John points up them.

'Up there. At the top of the stairs.'

Horton rushes up. At the top of the stairs are two empty cells, their doors open. On the bed of one of these he spies a book, and goes in to pick it up. It is *A Vindication of the Rights of Women*, by Mary Wollstonecraft.

That smell again, clear and present – though not quite a smell, more like a memory floating on the air. This is Abigail's room.

But where is she?

Horton walks out of the empty cell. The noise in Brooke House is rising behind him, a chattering sound of women which has for its bass note the irregular rattling boom of thunder.

The corridor stretches to his right down the side of the building, but to his left a little staircase runs down to another section. From down there, in the gloom, he hears the sound of women arguing.

From somewhere within the building, he hears a door slam and a man shout.

He walks down the staircase, the sound of the women's voices growing louder and louder. A flash of lightning illuminates the corridor. He enters the little room and, in the candlelight, sees the shape of a gigantic footless priest gazing down at him from the wall. Then he sees his wife sitting on a bench, turning to him, and he shouts her name and runs to her. She stands and he embraces her, and as he does so he sees the two tall black-haired women standing before the picture of the priest, and they both look at him.

And then he remembers no more.

Abigail can do nothing. Maria's prayers are relentless and incomprehensible, a monotonous chant in a tense whisper like a strangled shout. She kneels in front of the old painting with her back to Abigail, her dark hair flowing down between her shoulders.

It occurs to Abigail that this is the first day she has seen Maria's arms and hands, the first time they have been freed from the strait waistcoat.

Lightning opens up the shadows in the corners of the chapel, and she pretends she cannot see goblins and gargoyles dancing in there. She says her own silent prayer, but not to God. To Charles.

I am in need of rescue, she thinks.

She wonders what she would do if Satan himself walked into the room, smiled at her with a nod and a wink, and took Maria's hand, the two of them to be married with her as a witness. She hears someone step into the chapel, and for a moment she dare not look, lest what she imagined become true.

She does look, then, and sees a tall woman silhouetted in the door to the corridor outside. A woman as tall as Maria, and with the same long loose hair.

'Maria, it is time for us to leave,' says the figure, and Abigail recognises the voice instantly. The voice in the wall, the one that had read to Maria during those hot August nights. The figure steps into the chapel, and turns its eyes onto Abigail.

Her fear buzzes around her head and thunders through Brooke House, with nothing to settle down on or adhere to, and it grows and grows and grows. The woman's eyes are gleaming obsidian, and a pernicious scar wriggles up her face. Abigail feels naked before her gaze. More than naked: it is as if her skin were suddenly as transparent as glass, her bones and muscles and sinews exposed for this woman's inspection.

'Mother,' says Maria. 'Leave her.'

The dark-haired woman turns her gaze away, leaving Abigail to gasp as if her head had been held in water and then released, that word *mother* unavoidably mesmerising. She watches the woman walk up to Maria, with that painting of the priest behind them. The priest is not looking into the room, but at a point somewhere in the middle distance. Perhaps he is praying to the lightning.

The two women face each other in front of the painting. They look like two queens, discussing an offering from a poor subject.

'What is this, Maria?' says the woman from outside. 'What is going on?'

'God has spoken to me,' says Maria. She looks away from her mother to the picture of the priest. 'He speaks to me again.'

'And what did he say?'

'He said I am unclean. That there is a demon within me

which can only be got rid of by my own destruction. He said I deserve what has happened to me.'

'God is a man, Maria. And men speak lies.'

'That is blasphemy, Mother. Even though you may say it, it is a wrong thing to say.'

'Where did it come from, this truck with God? Not from me.'

'From those who raised me.'

'Ah, indeed? The good Suffolk farmer and his wife. They did what they promised.'

'Until the illness took them.'

'Indeed. The precious gift of disease from your so-called God. Beware men bearing gifts, Maria. And know this – to take thine own life is a sin, if such a God does exist. And this male God will punish you for that sin.'

'I shall not take my own life.'

'Ah. I begin to understand. You are to make a sacrifice of *another's* soul.'

Maria sinks her head. A noise from the door, and a man comes into the room, and Abigail hears her name from her husband's throat for the first time in more than a month.

'Abigail!'

He rushes up to her, and she rises into his embrace, breathing his name and crying into his neck, but then his arms go limp and he sits on the bench beside her, looking up at Maria and her mother with the empty expression of an idiot.

'Maria! No!' she shouts, but Maria shakes her head.

''Tis not my doing, Abigail.'

'Your husband?' says Maria's mother, and she looks at Abigail with those obsidian eyes, and Abigail silently prays that she never looks at her again. 'Last time I saw this man he was lying senseless in a country field. He must be a bloodhound, to have followed me here.'

'Leave him be, whoever you are,' says Abigail, unable to look away from her. 'He is a good man.'

'There is no such creature as a *good man*,' says the woman, and looks back at Maria. 'Just ask my daughter.'

'My papers,' says a voice from the door, and all three women turn to see Dr Bryson standing on the threshold of the room, his little letter-knife held in front of him, his face pale and wet. 'You made me destroy all my papers.' He is, momentarily, framed by lightning.

'Yes, doctor,' says Maria's mother. 'All records relating to my daughter have been destroyed. She was never in this place. I should never have brought her here, but she seems calm now. You have had more success than I did. Than she permitted.'

Bryson steps forward.

'Stay out of my head, bitch,' he says. Another step into the room. 'Evil, it is. The devil's work. I must cut out the evil. It is an infection, and I am a doctor.'

He steps forward, one single shuddering step, and both women turn to face him head-on from the altar. He stops. But then he walks again – directly towards Maria.

'Evil! Evil!' he shouts. He walks like a man being pulled back and pulled forward at the same time, as if he has a piece of rope tied around him and someone outside the room is pulling him away from the women, but the other force is so much the stronger, the force pulling him towards them.

'Maria, would you condemn his soul?' says the older woman.

'Evil!' shouts Bryson again, stepping with stiff legs towards the altar. He has almost reached them.

'I saw those men, Mother,' says Maria. 'I saw what happened to them. What you caused to happen to them. Even in these walls, I saw it. It was a great sin, and I am the cause of it.'

'Is it a sin to rid the world of sinners, Maria?'

'It is God's work, Mother. It is not ours. We are abomina-tions, you and I. It is not right that we should have such capacities.'

'EVIL!'

Bryson is standing directly in front of the two women. Both of them stare at him as they talk, and Abigail feels the fine hairs on her arms and on her neck tingle and stand.

'If it were a sin to dispose of these men, the sin is mine,' says Maria's mother, and Abigail sees a ripple of grey exhaustion pass over her disfigured face, which must have once been as beautiful as Maria's. 'I take the sin upon me, and only me. You are free, Maria. Free at last.'

Then the mother steps forward and grabs Bryson's face between the fingers of her left hand and holds it before her, staring into his eyes.

'Mother!'

As Maria says this, the woman from outside looks away from the doctor and around the room, and Abigail feels some-thing terrible pushing at her head. She holds her hands to her ears, but it makes no difference. She feels like her head is being squeezed by gigantic fingers. She can feel worms burrowing away inside her skull, little creatures of intent, searching for something in her poor deranged brain.

The doctor's body seems to momentarily loosen, as if the invisible rope around him had been dropped. Then his legs become less wooden and his arm comes round, and with a great cry . . .

'*EVIL!*'

. . . he plunges the letter-knife into the older woman's throat. Once, twice, three times. And when he is done, he steps away, and drops the knife to the floor, where it rings a metallic trill on the old stone.

There is a great confusion then. Maria *screams*, and this

scream is accompanied by an even greater sense of *pressure* on Abigail's head. Maria kneels down beside her mother, and Bryson shouts once more, spins and falls to the floor, and lies still.

Maria weeps, kneeling by her mother, who splutters a single sentence.

'Free, Maria, and none shall remember you.'

Then she falls silent. Maria speaks some soft female words which Abigail cannot hear. She finds she cannot move, and next to her she feels her husband pinned by the same invisible chains.

Finally Maria stands, and looks down at her mother. She shakes her head – once, twice, three times – as if to dislodge something within, and then raises her head to the ceiling of the chapel and lets out another scream, one which seems to shake the wicked old fabric of Brooke House just as the thunderclaps had done. Abigail feels that pressure again, even stronger than before, and the noise is everywhere inside her as well as everywhere outside, like a cannonball thundering down from her brain to her body.

Then it stops. Maria steps away from her mother's body and walks towards the door. She stops beside the hunched figure of Charles Horton, and places one hand on his head. She looks at Abigail.

'He will recover soon. But he will forget me. It was my mother's scheme. I see it now. All this sin will collect upon her; all these terrible events and stories must be hers alone. She made the doctor kill her. She has cursed her own soul, in order to save mine. God will know whose hand drove the knife.'

She takes the hand from Horton's head, and places it on Abigail's cheek.

'I suppose I will live a life, after all,' she says.

Abigail senses a crackle of something like electricity beneath the fingers which stroke her face, and a pressure behind her eyes.

'She is gone from your mind, Abigail. The princess who haunts you is no more.'

She takes back her hand, and smiles at Abigail. A beautiful smile, but a sad one.

'And now, you will forget me.'

And she leaves.

PART FIVE

The Forgotten Woman

Persons who have children are more difficult to cure than those who are childless.

Benjamin Rush, *Medical Inquiries and Observations upon the Diseases of the Mind* (1812)

Madness is a distemper of such a nature, that very little of real use can be said concerning it.

John Monro, *Remarks on Dr Battie's Treatise on Madness* (1758)

A Treatise on Moral Projection

Within the finer classes, it may only be military officers who can be said to have seen unspeakable things. I have read of numerous cases where such men lose their sanity, temporarily or permanently, as a result of the awful scenes which play out inside their minds night after night.

Just such an awful scene awaited me on that long-ago morning in Brooke House. I awoke to witness the most terrible of mutilations. I lay on the floor of the madhouse chapel, with no recollection of how I came to be there. Beside me, laid out at the feet of the priest on the wall, was a strange woman, dead from a terrible wound in her throat.

It is impossible to describe the sense of panicked shock I felt at that moment. Try, if you will, to put yourself in my position. Try to imagine waking on a cold floor, with no conception as to how you arrived there, next to the body of a dead woman whom you do not recognise. It is the stuff of the very worst of nightmares.

But then, the nightmare darkened even further. Because by my side, lying on the floor next to me, was my letter-knife. The way it lay on the ground told an obvious tale: I had dropped it as I had fallen. The dark red stain on its blade told another tale, and I glanced from it to the poor woman's open throat, and I struggled not to run from that place, screaming.

Squatting on his knees above the dead woman, inspecting her injuries with an awful calm was a man, dark and quiet and pale, who looked up from the body and looked at me intently. It was Constable Horton – a flash of memory, disconnected from anything I was then experiencing, came to me then, of him visiting me in my study while I burned papers in the fire. But which papers? And why did I burn them?

Sitting on one of the benches to the side of the room, quiet and eyes downcast and moving her lips in prayer, was Horton's wife.

I stood, and saw another figure, a shadow in the back of the chapel, his head down. It was John Burroway.

I forced my mind to travel backwards in time. I tried to make sense of dozens of images and sensations, but none of them would adhere to an Idea. They were as useless as the gibberish of idiots. There were flashes of memory – such as that rendering Constable Horton and I in my study – but they did not serve to enlighten me. I knew where I was – the former chapel at Brooke House. I knew the people who were there with me, the ones who were living, at least. But I did not know this dead woman. And I did not know why she was there.

I stood, slowly, and at the same time Constable Horton rose from his position by the body. He walked over to me and put a hand under my arm, helping me to stand on two feet. I thanked him, but then he looked into my face and said:

'Dr Bryson, I am arresting you for the murder of this woman. Please stay calm while I secure us a carriage to convey us to Wapping.'

Such was the madness of the scene that I did not at once debate this with him. It was a mistake, of course, but it was an understandable one. The woman was killed with my own knife. Anyone with eyes to see would know that.

But why would I have killed her? This was a question which much vexed Constable Horton over the following hours and days; one word he used, over and over, was *motive*, and as I insisted on telling him, I had no such motive.

As we walked from the chapel, John Burroway looked at me, and I spoke to him.

'What happened here, John? Did you witness it?'

He said nothing, and his eyes were murky and feeble. It occurred to me that whatever had happened might have deepened his own idiocy; that he may have been shocked into a kind of silence. This turned out not to be the case, but I did not question it further at that time.

I was taken to the police office in Wapping and was interrogated there by Horton. He was joined, soon after my arrival, by Aaron Graham, the man who had paid for the treatment of Horton's wife. They seemed as perplexed as I by the story, such as it was. In any case, it soon became clear that my involvement in the matter was a secondary consideration. Of more paramount concern was the identity of the dead woman in the chapel. Her body was also taken to Wapping by Horton, and there she was identified as Maggie Broad.

To write of this now is to tell a tale which the whole nation recognises: how Mrs Broad made her fortune in New South Wales, having been sent there as a lowly

Suffolk thief, and how she had returned to this country with, so it seemed, the single purpose of exterminating a group of men who called themselves the Sybarites.

The story has persisted down the decades, not least because it has never been established *why* or *how* Mrs Broad killed these men. She had no apparent relation with them. The men were locked up in their houses, and many of them were under the watchful eye of constables and watchmen (those days, of course, preceded the establishment of our modern Metropolitan Police). The magistrates responsible for investigating these matters were particularly close-mouthed, saying only that Mrs Broad had been the killer, and that this was the end of it.

There were unanswered questions littered throughout this tale. So confused were the magistrates that I was quickly released, for despite the apparently obvious nature of that scene in the chapel, it was not at all clear that I *had* killed Mrs Broad. It was certainly impossible to state *why* I should do such a thing.

And sitting behind that was the most telling confusion of all: I could not remember how I had come to be in the chapel, but *neither could Constable Horton or his wife*. What on earth can have happened? This strange emptiness at the heart of the story infected everyone's thinking.

I had no memory of Mrs Broad arriving at Brooke House the night she died in our chapel. Why had this woman with this extraordinary history made her way to Brooke House? Which only led me to the most important question of all, to my own personal view: why had I killed her?

For it soon transpired that I had, indeed, killed her. It

is something I have never before admitted. But there was a witness to it.

Constable Horton did try and speak to poor John Burroway after that terrible night, but he abandoned the effort after a short time. John was almost completely silent, unable or unwilling to recall anything that had happened, anxious and miserable. Those who knew him, such as I, could clearly understand his trouble, but those who did not, such as Horton, ascribed it simply to his idiocy, and discarded him as a source of information. As it turned out, this was a great mistake indeed.

I did not return to Brooke House. Dr Monro decided this was for the best, and the magistrates agreed. I was given a new position, with immediate effect, at St Luke's Hospital, an institution founded on more progressive principles than Monro's. I had my own rooms, and was given the opportunity to work on more theoretical matters, undisturbed by the needs of individual patients.

About a fortnight after my arrest and release, John Burroway came to visit me at St Luke's with his sister – one of the nurses in Brooke House and, as far as I was aware, a reliable woman. She said John had told her that he knew something important about the night in the chapel, and that he didn't know whether to tell me. She had told him he must tell me the truth.

John looked profoundly unhappy with the circumstance. I asked him what the matter was, and he said he would only tell me in secret – that is, without his sister there. After a good deal of debate, she finally agreed to leave us alone. And then, after even more debate and prodding, he blurted out that I had, in fact, been the one to kill Mrs Broad with the letter-knife. He had seen me do so.

I had, of course, suspected this might have been the case. But it was what John said next which changed everything, and which set me on the course I have been navigating these past three decades.

'She made you do it,' he said.

I was astonished by this answer. It was so unexpected.

'How can that possibly be?' I asked him.

'She can reach inside your head, and make you do things,' John said. 'She made you kill her, and then she made you forget.'

'But why? Why would anyone do such a thing?'

'She was protecting her daughter.'

'Her daughter? Who was her daughter?'

John frowned, then, as if trying to work something out. And then his face cleared.

'Doctor, you told me if this happened, I was to tell you where I'd hidden your secret notes.'

And then he told me about the notes I had made, about Maria Cranfield and her mother, about the strange powers I have described to you within these pages. He had brought the notes with him from their hiding place in Brooke House, and I read them with growing fear and amazement.

The course of my life's work was set. And herewith I present its fruits, with this treatise.

Note from Dr Marchand: Bryson's delusions persist and have not lessened with the years. Indeed, they grow stronger and have achieved a kind of perfection. He is in good health physically, and in person he is a coherent interlocutor, though somewhat prickly as to criticism.

It may be this, indeed, that prevents his recovery. He is unwilling to countenance that the main elements of his story are fantasies. He still believes that events at Brooke House took place in the manner in which he describes, and that he has spent the intervening thirty years researching this strange theory of his while working alongside London's new police as an expert on mental illness.

It need not be added here that there continues to be no evidence for the material found within. There are no records of a patient at Brooke House named Maria Cranfield. The only mention is within Dr Bryson's own notes, clearly fabricated at some point or other. So perfect is Dr Bryson's fantasy that he claims he himself destroyed the official Brooke House records, under the so-called 'influence' of Mrs Broad.

He is convinced that his theories are pertinent and reasonable, and is genuinely outraged that Dr Braid has outlined a similar idea, though with none of Dr Bryson's crazed histories. His rooms at St Luke's are tidy and, in many ways, could be the consulting rooms of a physician at any of England's new asylums. While the costs of his treatment continue to be met by whatever benefactor is supporting him, I recommend his continued confinement.

DR JEREMIAH MARCHAND, St Luke's Hospital, May 1846

WAPPING

The smart carriage, horses and driver outside the River Police Office clearly indicate who is inside. Horton sees them blocking the street, and decides to go straight home instead of visiting the office. He has no wish to see Aaron Graham.

So he turns into Lower Gun Alley, and sees a rather more welcome sight – an open window on the first floor with steam or smoke drifting out of it in an unhurried way. Inside Abigail must be cooking something. His supper may be waiting for him.

He has been careful to be home for supper, on time and every day, this past month. Since her return from Brooke House, Abigail has been her old self – curious, amused, occasionally severe. The woman who had pursued her through her dreams has gone, though Abigail cannot describe why. The treatment at Brooke House, which had ended so bizarrely in that little chapel, had apparently worked.

He has wanted to spend every moment he can with her, and for the first week this is how he behaved, until she shoved him out of the door of their rooms one morning and insisted he not return until the end of the working day. 'Arrest felons!' she'd shouted. 'And leave me alone!'

So he'd returned to work – at much the same time as his magistrate, John Harriott. The old bulldog is somewhat quieter than had been his wont before his illness, but his mind was just as quick and his bark just as loud. He'd grabbed hold of the tail-end of the Sybarites investigation and shaken it until Sidmouth himself had told him to stop.

Graham has been an irregular visitor to Wapping, and while Harriott is much his old self, Graham is not. His clothes are just as fine and bright as they ever were, but his exposure to the fierce winds of journalism have buffeted him severely. He has been made the scapegoat for what the newspapers are calling a Conspiracy of Silence regarding the deaths of the Sybarites. Sidmouth has made him a scapegoat, but one of a very particular kind. The deaths have been pinned on Maggie Broad, but when the obvious question is asked as to how a single woman had managed to eviscerate a half-dozen gentlemen under the very noses of the constabulary, the Bow Street Runners and the magistracy, answer comes there none. It is to Graham that the question has been put, repeatedly and with growing volume.

Horton feels some sympathy for the man – not least because of his glimpse into Graham's tortured domestic arrangements. But this sympathy is gossamer-thin, is veined with distrust, and is dissolved completely when Horton steps into his rooms and realises that Graham is in fact not visiting John Harriott at the River Police Office, but is visiting him.

The Bow Street magistrate rises with a tired smile and Abigail appears behind him, also smiling, as if the presence of this man is some kind of shared joke. Horton supposes that, in a different light, it could be taken as such. Graham had sat here three years before, had he not, making threats about revelations of Horton's personal history, and issuing demands that Horton clean up a mess of establishment making over in Sheerness?

'Constable! You will forgive my impertinence.'

'I will?'

Horton turns his back on his guest, and removes his coat and hat. Abigail takes them from him, and places a warning arm on his. She then steps away into the parlour, leaving them alone in the little sitting room. Not a word or a kiss, wife? He scowls at her back. He is surprised to find himself angry at Abigail. She had, after all, let the magistrate in.

'Does Mr Harriott know you are here?' He asks Graham this without looking at him. Indeed, he sits himself down in front of the fire without once looking at the magistrate's face. There is a fire going; October has turned chilly.

Graham says nothing. His waiting silence is, in its own way, an assertion of authority. Eventually, Horton relents and looks at him. Graham's eyebrow is raised, and he indicates the chair he rose from. Horton nods, and the magistrate sits down.

'Of course Harriott knows I am here,' Graham says. 'I never visit his cherished Investigator without permission. And in any case, it is not you I am here to see.'

Graham smiles at his own impertinence.

'Your wife, Horton. I wanted to speak to your wife. To enquire after her recovery. I am, after all, an interested party.'

He is deliberately baiting Horton, this is obvious. But his charm is also much on display. *See, we mean each other no ill-will*, it says. *We are intelligent men.*

'And what did you learn of my wife?'

Graham sits back, and brushes some unseen piece of time-saving lint off his turquoise silk breeches.

'That she is much recovered. Completely so.'

'Perhaps, then, I may enquire after your own wife. How does Mrs Graham?'

Graham's face is cold.

'She does well.'

'And Ellen? Is she fully recovered?'

'All is well at Thorpe Lee House.'

'Well, I shall not ask after Sir Henry, for the obvious reasons. And with that, our business is done, and you are able to be on your way.'

'Oh come now, Horton. Do not be so dull.'

Such a direct riposte is rare from Aaron Graham, and it has a good deal of irritation within it. And it goes on.

'Your dislike for me is long-standing and well-grounded, that I know. But this surly display is childish and dispiriting. I bring news of the Sybarites case which I thought might interest you. Though if you persist in this thuggish insolence I shall take my leave of you and your charming wife, without thanks for my intervention in her own good health, and we shall continue to avoid each other for the sake of your own pride.'

This little speech is spoken with none of Graham's typical delighted-with-the-world sang-froid. It is deliberate and serious, and Horton remembers that first meeting here so many weeks before, with Abigail incarcerated in Hackney and he loose from his moorings.

'My apologies,' he says at last, though it sticks in his throat. Graham sees this and shrugs.

'Your apologies are unimportant, and are in any case insincere. But I am grateful to you, Horton, for your work on the Sybarites case, and on the extraordinary matters at Thorpe Lee House. I am only here to inform you that Dr Bryson is to be treated at St Luke's for his delusions. There is no one else under suspicion.'

'No one . . .'

Graham raises a warning hand.

'Remain calm, Horton. I wish to explain.'

He waits a second before continuing.

'Horton, you have explained your theory of the matter to me. Mrs Broad, you contend, had discovered how to manipulate the actions of others. The evidence you have uncovered of her life in New South Wales – in particular, of her dalliance with the strange natives of that place – suggests she learned these things over there, rather than it being any kind of latent ability. In any case, she is now dead. I have alerted Sir Joseph Banks to your theories about the pitchery leaf, which you had already introduced to his librarian Robert Brown. The Royal Society will investigate the natural causes of all this further. But it is vital – both for the national interest, and for the good name of the Bow Street constabulary and magistrates – that no whiff of this reaches public ears. It would expose us to ridicule. If there is something to be discovered here, we will discover it – but not in the full view of the public realm. Am I understood?'

'You mean to keep all this secret.'

'I mean nothing of the sort. More powerful men than I believe this matter worthy of investigation, and wish this investigation to remain, yes, secret. Think about it, Horton – the ability to force men to act against their will. To cause servants to slaughter their masters, and then have no memory of it. A drug that can cause hallucinations. These things are potentially significant.'

'Significant?'

'Do not be naive, Horton.'

'Are we talking of a new type of artillery? A cannon of the mind?'

'Do not be ridiculous.'

'This is why you are being forced to absorb these attacks from the newspapers. They are hiding this thing behind you.'

'*They?* Who on earth do you mean, Horton? There is no *they*. There is the Royal Society and there is the government. Both bodies believe these matters to be worthy of investigation and consideration. Why dramatise this so?'

'Because, if I were to say to you now that I will tell the newspapers what I know, you will in turn tell me that should such a matter arise then certain *secrets* relating to my naval career and my involvement in the Nore mutiny would be made public, and that certain of my previous shipmates would be interested to hear such secrets.'

Graham says nothing to that.

'Is that not the case, Graham?'

'Do not be impertinent, Horton. You are still just a constable.'

'I appear to be a constable whose head is now full of things I am not supposed to know.'

'Horton, your own magistrate has told you that we have, in recent years, touched upon matters which should have remained hidden. He knows, as do I, and as do you, that our investigations have revealed aspects of the secret world that, were they to be made public, would at best weaken social morality, and would at worst unpick the beliefs on which our stable society is based. That cannot be allowed to happen. Only a fool would disagree.'

'And only a liar would go along with it.'

'Horton, we are all liars. Some of us are just better at it than others.'

'Your daughter, Graham.'

A warning hand from the magistrate, which is ignored by Horton.

'Your own daughter was subject to whatever capacities Maggie Broad possessed. You would do well to investigate these things further, for her sake if not your own. Did she kill Sir

407

Henry's dogs, Graham? Did Maggie Broad turn your daughter into something like her own self?'

Graham stands, and places his hat on his head. He suddenly looks old and, to Horton's eyes, rather unwell.

'Horton, your wife is well. You are well paid for what you do. You are interested in your work. You are, in this grubby and complicated metropolis, a lucky man. Do not endanger that.'

He walks to the door with the angry threat still reverberating in the room. Horton does not rise to see him off. He instead asks a question.

'Dr Bryson spoke of another woman in his testimony – a daughter.'

'He did.'

'I spoke to the idiot. Burroway. He confirmed Bryson's story. Others say similar things. Rose Dawkins, for instance.'

Graham sighs.

'So, what do you suggest, Horton? That we begin a new line of inquiry, based upon the testimony of a madman, an idiot and a whore? We looked into it. We checked the records of Brooke House, and interviewed all the staff. None could recall this "Maria Cranfield". She only appears in Bryson's case notes. Which indicate, incidentally, that this so-called patient was befriended by your own wife. Does she remember her?'

'She does not.'

'Then accept the truth. There was no Maria Cranfield. Bryson invented her as part of his own delusion, and somehow forced his ideas onto the idiot. Maria is just a figment of his mind.'

And with that, Graham leaves. Horton, with a sigh, falls down into his armchair, and collects himself as his wife cooks his dinner. The fire is warm; October is well on the way outside, but here within all is warmth and health and recovery. He thinks back to those terrible weeks when Abigail was in Brooke House, and they seem to have happened to a different person, one whose mind was full of different things.

While he is thinking, he takes out the little black notebook Sir Henry had given him at Thorpe Lee House. The one that Aaron Graham seems to have forgotten about, or at least to have chosen not to remember. He thinks back to what the hop-farmer had told him, the man who'd identified Mrs Broad's body at Wapping, and had said those strange words to Horton as he'd departed.

A question for you, constable. If I committed a crime on your behalf but I was unaware of it, how guilty would I be of the crime?

He turns to the last page of the little black book. He reads the name *Maria Cranfield* but does not read the black words used to describe her. And he throws the little book onto the fire.

CROSS BONES BURIAL GROUND, SOUTHWARK

The old gravedigger is not quite blind, but over the years he has learned not to see. His spade has turned over too many tragedies to allow his eyes to record the stories which settle into the mud of the burial ground. From daylight to dusk he digs and turns the soil, a dozen bodies a day or more, their flesh piling up beneath the Southwark earth.

So it would be wrong to say the gravedigger sees the woman with the long body and the young-old face who stands beside him, her back against the Cross Bones wall. He is aware of her, as he is aware of many other things: the cold sharp air; the sounds of the city waking up; the pastel smudge of the buildings in the morning fog. He looks at her just once, takes in an impression of long black hair, loose and dishevelled, and a dress which might have once been pretty and almost fashionable but which is now ragged and indistinct in both colour and cut. She looks somewhat familiar, but – as has been said – the old gravedigger is not quite blind.

She makes no sound, this woman. There have been a great

many other women sitting where she now sits. Most of them weep, some of them moan to themselves, and some of them – like this one – stand in silence, never announcing themselves, their exhausted eyes following every slice and turn of the gravedigger's spade.

Thus, in the absence of the woman's tears, the only sounds are the flat and heavy movements of the gravedigger's shovel and the wet thuds as he piles earth onto the tops of five plain wooden coffins, each of them barely two feet long. These coffins are laid out in a row in front of him. To the grave-digger they are just boxes; they contain nothing, not even stories.

The five coffins are the top row in a stack of the dead which reaches down twenty feet into the earth. The gravediggers always put the babies at the top of the burial stacks, closest to the surface. They can squeeze more bodies in, that way. Like all London's burial grounds, Cross Bones is full to bursting, a pit of the squeezed-in dead, men, women and their babies clustering in the darkness. Perhaps they haunt this place; if so, they are well-practised in it. All of them had been ghosts before they died, invisible to the well-off, a flicker at the edge of what people of means were prepared to see. The fact that their final caskets are so clearly visible beneath the crowded earth is the last irony of their existence.

The woman by the wall begins crying, suddenly. Her sobs are bitter and abandoned, and provide the melody for the per-cussive clunks of the shovel. The gravedigger looks up from his task as if compelled, seeing her properly now, and every now and again he takes another glance at the crying woman, shaking his head and making a thick *tsk* sound under his breath before turning back to his work. It is a comfortable rou-tine, this. When he shakes his head, he might be expressing impatience, sorrow, amusement or an old unspoken wisdom. It is the privilege of gravediggers that ordinary folk will never know which it is.

It is obvious to *him* why the girl is crying. Five little boxes of death, being packed into the earth. Anyone with eyes to see would recognise this old and mournful tale.

'*Joshua* . . .'

He looks up again, and sees the girl pointing to the little coffins, now disappeared but still agonisingly close to the surface.

And then he remembers her. Remembers her here. In the spring, wasn't it? She came with another woman, an older woman, her dress fine but muddy as if she had walked through the Lambeth marshes, her arms bare and lined with flint-cuts, nettle-stings and briar-scratches. He remembers those arms, and the way the older woman had put them round the shoulders of the younger, and the way they had watched the gravedigger inter a different set of small plain wooden boxes. He even remembers a name, whispered in sobs over the April air: *Joshua.*

There were five coffins then, too.

He is wonderstruck with remembering. How can this be? It is as if he looks through another's eyes and remembers another's thoughts.

For herself, Maria looks down into the stack which, earlier this year, was being freshly dug. It is now more than half full. Soon, little Joshua will have company, as the bodies of children are squeezed in at the top, alongside those five coffins she'd watched being interred the previous spring.

No headstone marks the spot where her son is buried; only this half-full hole in the ground can be used to identify exactly where he lies. Maria kneels into the mud of the earth and prays to her Father in Heaven. The gravedigger stops his shovelling. Maria prays for the soul of Joshua, that little brittle thing which was here on earth for so little time. She prays for the soul of her mother, believing it to be endangered beyond all expectation of salvation. She prays for the Suffolk farmer and his wife who raised her and did not mean to die so suddenly, leaving her to fend for herself. She prays for Lizzie Carrington – sweet, kind Lizzie, who'd met her begging in the street and who'd suggested another way to earn her crust. Poor Lizzie.

It was she who had told her mother where Lizzie could be found. She tried shutting the location up in a corner of her memory, but her mother had found it.

A young woman walking down the side of the burial ground feels a sudden swell of sadness and sees a picture of a baby boy in her mind's eye, an inconsequential but perplexing image, as if plucked from the recollections of another. She walks on.

She does not pray for the men who took her, one after another, hidden behind their leering awful masks, their bodies stinking of wine and tobacco and of something old and disgusting. Joshua's fathers, united in this poor dead baby who sleeps beneath her knees.

A panderer, standing in a doorway behind the burial ground watching one of his girls negotiating with a gentleman, sees a red image of her lying dead across a bed and rushes out to see off the potential cully. The gentleman is confused and angry. So is the girl.

Maria weeps, and the tears feel oddly wholesome, a sane reaction after so many weeks of empty, frantic grieving. She thinks of Abigail, the kind woman who read to her. She hopes her final kindness towards her – the erasing, from her poor disturbed mind, of those terrible Pacific images – has made her happy. She thinks of poor John Burroway, the idiot, and worries about him.

She thinks of her mother, dead on a chapel floor. She knows what her mother wanted her to do. She knows she could leave this place and continue her mother's work. Dead men would litter the ground along which she walked. Vengeance would sit on her shoulder. Vindication would be her birthright.

Joshua's eyes look up at her from her memory, their dark circles full of understanding, the light in them already fading.

She will not stay hidden for long, she thinks, in the forgetfulness of others. Her name must reappear, so she must take on another.

A carriage waits for her out in Red Cross Street, its horses breathing over the dead of Cross Bones. Inside the carriage is a man of means who has pledged to help her for reasons he cannot seem to explain. She can begin a new life.

But there is business to be completed first. In the village of Thorpe.

She stands up and leaves that place behind, to find kinder memories to live within.

AUTHOR'S NOTE

Like the two books which precede it – *The English Monster* and *The Poisoned Island* – this novel deals primarily with fictional events and invented characters, but in some cases the events are not entirely imagined, and some of the characters are based on real biographies.

Where the events are real, they may have been warped to fit fictional purposes, though I have tried to do justice to them. For example, the *Indefatigable* really was a convict transport and did return to England in 1814, though in September, not April. Aaron Graham really was a magistrate at Bow Street, though by 1814 he was almost certainly semi-retired, and I have no documentary evidence for his impeccable taste in clothes.

Since these kinds of liberties have been taken, the careful reader should note the following.

The madhouse called Brooke House did exist in Hackney at the time of these events, and indeed continued to operate well into the twentieth century. The building itself was finally demolished after the Second World War; its depiction here is based on monographs written by council surveyors at the beginning of the last century. In 1814, it continued to be owned and operated by the Monro family, and the philosophy of treatment ascribed to Dr Thomas Monro in the book is based on the writings of mad-doctors from the period. However, the character of Dr Bryson is invented, as is his theory of *moral projection*, though I know a good many people whose powers of persuasion are sufficiently mysterious to warrant investigation.

The most tangled fictional-factual thicket has grown up around the personal life of Aaron Graham, his wife Sarah and her relationship with her cousin, the baronet Sir Henry Tempest. It is true that Sarah Graham did leave her husband to live with her cousin Sir Henry, though there is no date recorded for when this occurred. The daughter she had with Aaron Graham – Ellen was born in 1799 – was given Tempest's name in addition to Graham's; the other children of Aaron and Sarah Graham were not renamed. Both Ellen and Sarah were beneficiaries of Aaron Graham's will.

It is also true that a good deal of scandal attaches to the name of Sir Henry, though he may not have earned the sobriquet 'worst man in England' I have awarded him within. The tale of how he made his fortune by marrying and then abandoning an heiress is recounted in Caroline Alexander's book *The Bounty*. Sir Henry squandered his own fortune, so set his eyes on another: that of the heiress Ellen Pritchard Lambert, the only daughter of Henry Lambert of Hope End in Herefordshire, whose fortune came down to her from her grandfather. Note the coincidence of her name.

The story goes that Sir Henry disguised himself as a gypsy woman and told the impressionable Ellen that she would meet her future husband at a given hour at Colwall Church. Along she went, and there met Sir Henry, divested of his gypsy disguise. The two were married and as was the legal custom Ellen's fortune became the property of Sir Henry, as did Ellen herself. Sir Henry then threw both his wife and his father-in-law out of the family home; Ellen was also later disowned by the father. Destitute, she was said to wander up and down the Holloway Road on the edge of London. She died penniless, probably in 1817, and probably in Worcester.

Hers is a bitter story but doubtless not an uncommon one. Such behaviour would not have been particularly outrageous among gentlemen of Sir Henry's stripe in the Georgian era.

Sir Henry and Mrs Graham did indeed live in a house in the village of Thorpe in Surrey. My particular thanks to Jill Williams of Egham Museum and the staff of the Surrey History Centre for tracking the house down.

The Sybarites – both the group, and its individual members – are all invented, in some cases by inserting fictional sons into actual families, in others by inventing families from scratch.

Maggie Broad and her friend Henry Lodge are invented, but their shared history is at least plausible. The facts around the *Lady Juliana* are real, as are the experiences of those aboard the *Guardian*. Much less likely is any kind of interaction between a convict woman and the natives of what we now call *Australia*. Whether this is more or less likely than any of the other unlikely things that happen in *Savage Magic* will be for the reader to say.

The final unlikely thing is the use of *pitchery*, or *pituri* as it is more commonly known these days, by anyone European in the early nineteenth century. Joseph Banks first recorded Aboriginal Australians chewing plants 'as a European does tobacco' in 1770. Seventy years later, the diary of the deceased explorer William Wills was preserved by one of his companions, and made reference to 'stuff they call *bedgery* or *pedgery*;

it has a highly intoxicating effect when chewed even in small quantities. It appears to be the dried stems and leaves of some shrub.' This sparked a century of searching and inventing, and all sorts of strange effects were ascribed to what came to be known as *pituri*. Europeans confused different plants, with different effects, used by different Aboriginal groups in different ways. They concatenated different stories and different traditions. It's a classic case of an attempt to *categorise* leading directly to a project to *mythologise*. In effect, pituri is like nicotine – a form of chewing tobacco. The only mass psychosis it has caused was among the explorers and botanists of the nineteenth century.

For wise words, encouragement and skilful editing I would like to thank Jessica Leeke and Mike Jones at Simon and Schuster, and all their amazing colleagues. Thanks as ever to my kind readers, Josie Johns and Dan Dickens. Thanks also to my agent, Sam Copeland. For putting up with sulks and selfishness, I am as always in devoted debt to Louise.